GATES OF GREED

KEEPERS OF THE GRAIL 3

TAMAR SLOAN

JESS CONNORS PUBLISHING

Cover by Laercio Messias
https://laerciomessias.com.br

PROLOGUE

Xeven's forgotten something. He's not sure what it is, but the incessant way it claws at his consciousness tells him it's important. But, no matter how hard he tries, it won't rise beyond the dark veil it's hidden behind.

Even though there's nothing more he wants than to know what it is.

It's days like this that he turns to Cain for help. Somehow, he makes the itchy, uncomfortable sensation go away.

But Cain has been missing for days.

Which leaves Xeven endlessly pacing his mansion, scratching at his skin even though the itch is so much deeper than that. He has to do something. Anything.

He strides to the large ornate mirror hanging above the fireplace. "Azazel," he barks.

All that stares back at Xeven is his reflection. It's a man he barely recognizes anymore. He looks away in disgust. It's a man he can't bring himself to like.

"Ah, Xeven," says a serene, soothing voice.

Xeven turns back, finding the angel now staring back at him.

Azazel's hard eyes glint from his pale, beautiful face. "I was just about to contact you."

"You've noticed Cain hasn't returned."

But the angel simply swats his hand. "That's very inconvenient."

Xeven frowns. "We must find him." Two Gates of Hell have been opened. The third now waits.

"We have more important issues to address."

"But—"

"I can feel the power of the obsidian," Azazel snaps. "It's been freed."

Xeven stills. He knows of the obsidian. He's been warned of what it's capable of. Azazel leans forward and Xeven almost takes a step back as if the angel can step through the mirror. "Its power can best angels. The obsidian is what we must find."

Xeven nods, calmer now that he has instructions. The itchy, restless feeling abates and he lets out a relieved breath. He's a soldier, nothing more.

And he has his orders.

"Very well," he says, his voice emotionless. "I will find the obsidian."

Azazel's image dissolves as Xeven spins on his heel.

Even Cain can't match the obsidian.

CHAPTER 1

REIGN

The streets have become Reign's friends.

Actually, if you define friends by how much time you spend with them, then they've probably reached bestie status.

He jams his hands in his pockets and hunches his shoulders as he takes a right, not knowing where he's going, but not really caring. Right now, the cracked, gray pavements are all the company he wants.

He barely spends any time at the cottage now. Not since Shell's funeral a week ago. It's just too empty without Mac. He still can't believe she upped and left with Sierra. She'd tried to hide her excitement as she told him, but it's like she was trying to contain a packed popcorn machine. She kept hopping from foot to foot, bursting with little jolts of anticipation. When she asked how everything went with Arielle, she accepted his non-committal answer. For the first time in their friendship, she didn't pry and poke and prod. She was off to find answers for something else.

She's off to find the Grail.

Good luck with that.

Reign jams his hands even further into his pockets, tightening them into fists. Mac texts, but not often. Wherever they are, there's not great reception. He misses her. She's the one person he could have spoken to about the other reason he's avoiding the cottage.

Arielle.

And all the could-have-beens that are now associated with her.

Could he have done something different and saved the Innocent?

Could she have kissed him like that, even without Lust hanging around?

Could their attraction have been real?

He kicks the curb, then apologizes under his breath. That's no way to treat a bestie, and right now, he could use all the friends he can get.

Of course, Gabby's called. Even Colt rang. But Reign kept the conversations short. The weight of losing Rachel's father, Paul, so soon after Shell had been a major blow to everyone's confidence. There was little to say.

"Reign, my man!" calls a voice as a BMW pulls up to the curb. "You look like you need a joyride!"

He looks up, seeing Rico in the driver's seat, his arm hanging out the window. Darnell's upper half is poking through the sunroof. "Come on, Reign. It'll be just like old times!"

A few people turn to look, but Reign ignores them, just like Rico and Darnell do. If they were influenced by people's disapproval, they would've stopped attending elementary school.

He walks over, grinning. "Nice ride."

Rico grins right back. "It's my uncle's."

"That Uncle Stan of yours sure is a nice guy," says Reign, shaking his head.

Darnell thumps the roof of the car, no doubt in a way the fictional Uncle Stan wouldn't approve of. "Let's do this, bro!"

"We've got a full tank of gas and we've already been to Chook Nook." Rico jerks his thumb over his shoulder to the backseat. The tinted window winds down and Reign's eyes widen at the stacks of bulging paper bags.

"Were you thinking of feeding a developing country?"

Rico laughs, the sound almost a cackle. "We were hungry, okay?"

"You won't be able to get out of the car if you eat all that," Reign warns.

They'll be trapped by their own bulk in a stolen vehicle.

Rico laughs again. "Keep that up and we won't share."

"Who said anything about sharing?" demands Darnell. He shoots back down through the sunroof and scoops up as many of the bags as he can into his arms. Like they're his children.

Reign chuckles, although he's not too sure that Darnell's joking. "I'd forgotten how crazy you two are."

"That's because you ain't been around much," Rico shoots back. "Time to realize the errors of your way, my friend."

Memories of their wild times rise in Reign's mind. There was no care for the consequences of their actions. For the future. For what others thought of them.

They were hazy days defined by freedom and a total lack of care factor.

He kinda likes the sound of that.

Stepping around the front of the BMW, he clasps the door handle on the passenger side. Rico whoops with excitement. "Reign is in da house!"

Darnell juggles his bags of food, grinning. "I'll give you a small fries just cause it's good to have you back."

Except Reign hesitates.

All the possible consequences of his actions are already tapping on his shoulder.

He's conscious of what this could mean if he gets caught.

Dammit. He cares what Mac or Gabby or Colt or Rachel or Sierra or Blaise or Nim would think of him if he did this.

Or Arielle.

Even though her feelings for him don't extend beyond friendship, he...doesn't want to let her down.

Oh, and apparently he's the Keeper of the Grail.

He steps back. "Actually, I've got somewhere to be."

"Where?" Rico asks, his eyes narrowing. "You gonna go hang with your new friends?" he sneers.

"Ah, no," says Reign, glad he doesn't have to lie. "I might go check out Chook Nook myself and get more than a small fries" he adds, promptly following up with a lie. "Hopefully you haven't cleaned them out."

"They'd better not be," exclaims Darnell. "We said we'd be back for dinner."

Rico guns the engine. "You chickening out?"

In the past, that line always worked. Reign's fearlessness, no matter how misplaced, was his one badge of honor. Something he could actually be proud of.

Even he's surprised when he releases the door and steps back. "I just really want Chook Nook, okay?"

Darnell nods. "I get ya, man. Order the nuggets. You'll be amazed how many you can put away."

"Let's get out of here," Rico growls. "He's decided he's too good for the likes of us."

With a squeal of tires and a puff of blue-black smoke, they roar away.

Reign stands on the side of the street, watching them fishtail around the corner, wondering if he did the right thing. Adrenaline is a rush. It helps you forget.

He could use both right now.

Instead, he heads back the way he came, tired and actually a little bit hungry. Must be the sight of all that takeaway.

The walk back to the cottage isn't far. Although he's been hitting the pavement every day, it's like there's some invisible boundary around Sierra's house that he won't go beyond. Some foolish part of him thinks he should stay close enough if someone needs him.

So far, no one's called.

Walking past the house, he notes that Arielle's car is there before he means to. She's home. He wonders how she's faring considering Sierra's also gone. Those two have a close mother-daughter bond. Sierra leaving would've been hard on Ari just after Paul and Shell's deaths.

Jamming his hands back in his pockets, he hunches back down like a turtle as he strides past. He needs a little more time before he faces her again. He may have been the one to say there's nothing more than friendship between them, but that doesn't mean his heart has listened. It's going to take a little while to get that rebellious organ with a mind of its own under control.

Back in the cottage, the fridge is empty, but Reign knew it would be. It's what's in the freezer that has become his primary form of sustenance.

Double dark chocolate ice cream.

Flopping down on the couch, Reign jams his spoon into the rich, cocoa bliss. He puts it in his mouth and sighs. Damn, it's delicious. He scoops up a larger spoonful and puts the whole lot in his mouth. In fact, he doesn't think he's ever tasted anything so good!

Suddenly, the door flies open, and Arielle strides in, her gaze scanning the room until it falls on him.

The decadent ice cream on his tongue evaporates right

there and then, one word his only thought. Arielle. Hair spun of gold, face molded from beauty. The body that's invaded his dreams.

And she's wearing those sexy, quirky boots of hers.

His heart crashes against his ribs in its need to go to her. He sits up slowly, pulling the ice cream tub a little closer. It's melting, but he'll take any armor he can get right now.

She frowns as she notices the movement. "How much of that have you eaten?"

He glances down at the half empty tub, surprised that more is missing than he expected. "Why? Was I supposed to share?"

Seeming to reach a decision, she walks over and picks up the remote, turning the TV on. "You haven't seen the news, have you?"

"The rise in alcohol-fueled violence is alarming," says a news reporter, a burning building behind him. "This pub was the site of a ten person brawl resulting in the destruction you see behind me. Along with the three deaths at liquor stores across the city, police have been stretched to capacity."

Arielle presses mute as the scene zooms in on the flames gorging on overturned tables and chairs in front of the building. "They haven't linked all this to the increase of armed robberies at supermarkets," she says somberly. "People are killing for food."

Reign shoves away the ice cream tub, already missing the bitter yet sweet party on his tongue. But the memory of Darnell coveting that Chook Nook is turning his stomach. The knowledge that his own hunger was driven by something far more sinister, just like Arielle's feelings for him, is dragging at his heart. "It's the next Sin, isn't it?"

She nods. "That's why I'm here. We have to stop it."

He pushes to his feet. "And the Innocent?"

"We need to find him or her." Arielle's gaze flickers. "Gabby's called a team meeting in ten."

Which means they're going to be working together again.

As friends.

Fucking great.

He walks past Arielle and opens the door, waving for her to exit. "If that bitch Gluttony has ruined double dark choc ice cream for me, I'm going to be pissed."

He's researched the Sins and the Gates of Hell to know what they're dealing with.

The time for avoiding Arielle is over.

The time for avoiding his destiny as the Grail Keeper is over.

Gluttony is in da house.

CHAPTER 2

ARIELLE

As Arielle walks back to the house, she's super conscious of Reign right behind her. Seeing him again was more of a jolt than she was hoping it would be. She told herself that some time apart was all she needed. That his impact on her would fade.

Except her pulse had already been tripping over itself before she even opened the door. Her eyes couldn't seek him out fast enough.

And when they found him, her heart danced. Leaped. Did a pirouette or two. And settled as if everything was right in the world, all at once.

You don't need him. Arielle's foot catches on a brick in the path and she stumbles. *Any feelings he had for you were driven by Lust.*

Reign's arm snaps out and grasps hers. "You okay?"

She jerks herself away too fast, drawing an instant frown from Reign. She resists the need to rub the place where his touch burned her, unsure how she can explain her reaction.

The obsidian is back.

"Yeah, fine. I wasn't watching where I was going."

Reign's hand falls to his side. "You went real pale there for a second."

Dammit. Does he have to be so observant? "Just thinking."

"What about?"

You.

And me.

And where the truth lies.

He will only use you and spit you out.

Arielle frowns. The obsidian has been quiet over the past several days. She'd almost started hoping it failed to take root in her mind. This is a complication she doesn't need right now.

You're stronger alone. That's how you killed Lust.

But not in time. The second Innocent was killed.

"Ari?" Reign asks, sounding concerned.

She looks up at him, her heart kick starting again as she connects with jungle green eyes. So many layers. So many tangles. Each one as fascinating as the last.

He steps a little closer. "Are you sure you're okay?"

The concern narrowing his eyes is unmistakable. Reign cares. It may not be the deep emotion she wants, but he cares.

Take that, she mutters internally. Reign doesn't use people. He doesn't want to see her hurt.

He takes another step forward, his hand rising as if to touch her arm again, only to hesitate. "If you could answer a question, I'd really appreciate it."

She tries to smile. She really does, but suddenly the world's dimming. She gasps and this time, Reign does grab her.

And she grips him back.

The world is disappearing. Another vision is descending, and she's terrified that it's the obsidian's dark hold on her.

An obelisk appears, powerful and tall. And whole.

Arielle holds her breath, waiting for it to crack and crumble. They always crack and crumble.

But it remains as is, punching into the sky, a stone monolith that's withstood the ages. Strangely, her stomach starts to ache, the hollow feeling growing exponentially. In a breath, she's hungry. Starving. So ravenous she almost doubles over, trying to alleviate the pain.

Gluttony.

Before she can move, a bright figure appears beyond the obelisk. White robed and white winged, it runs toward her, hands outstretched. Although she can't make out any features, whether the figure is male or female, she knows it's an Innocent. And that they're scared.

"Save me," the Innocent cries. "Please. The consequences—"

The obelisk cracks, the thunderous sound almost making Arielle cry out, and a whip of golden fire snaps out and wraps around the Innocent. Trapped, the Innocent struggles, back arched as flames devour them. Claws appear in the crevices of the monolith, fracturing it even further. Crimson eyes flash and the sound of hungry growling fills the air.

"No!" Arielle cries.

Not again.

Not another one.

"Ari!"

Reign's voice has the vision vanishing. Arielle blinks, seeing him before her. Feeling his hands gripping her arms like an anchor.

She sags, still holding his forearms. "I saw the Innocent. They were begging me to help them."

"You didn't see any features? Any way we can recognize them?"

She shakes her head. "I tried, but they were glowing too bright. I don't even know if it was a male or female."

"So it was more of a 'get your ass into gear' kind of vision?"

14

Her mouth twists. "Essentially. It's just that..."

Reign waits, watching her closely.

"It's just that every other vision has been a foretelling of what's to come," she finishes.

A deep sense of foreboding is worming its way into her marrow.

"Don't think like that, Ari. These visions are a warning, nothing more."

She nods, not quite sure she believes him. "I suppose so."

They are a prophecy, the obsidian hisses excitedly.

"If you were an evil angel or a dark demon, I'd agree with you. They'd be spelling out how they want this to end. But there's just too much good in you," Reign says, eyes twinkling with mischief. "You're a Pisces, remember?"

This time when Arielle nods, it's with more conviction. "You're right. There's no point in seeing this if we can't change it."

"Exactly. You're being shown these for a reason."

She pulls her shoulders back. "To stop them."

To rejoice in them.

Arielle ignores the insidious voice. She should never have touched the inky stone. She's going to have to do something about it.

Once they have a plan.

Reign grins, the sight dazzling enough to make her blink. "Damn ducking straight we will." He releases her, taking a couple of steps down the path. "In fact you can tell your visions we were already on it. Let's get to this meeting, shall we?"

A new resolve unfurls through Arielle. She has to believe they'll stop this next Sin. That they'll save the next Innocent.

The alternative isn't an option.

Spine straight, she walks past a still-grinning Reign, past the house and toward the car.

"Weren't we meeting Gabby and Colt?" he asks behind her.

Arielle pulls out the car keys and presses the button, making the indicator lights flash. "Yep. But she's given us a location a little out of town. Some sort of farm house. Said it's safer."

"Right." For some reason a ten-minute car trip has him looking far more resolute than the thought of finding the next Innocent and killing Gluttony.

She pauses. "Thanks, by the way."

His foot seems to land a second later than it should have as he makes his way to the car. "Ah, sure."

"Sometimes the visions can be...overwhelming." And now that the obsidian is back, it feels like the darkness is multiplying.

Reign looks away, then glances back. "You've got this, Ari. I don't know how many times I have to tell you that."

She smiles, feeling hopeful for the first time since Paul died. She climbs into the car, stilling as another thought strikes it.

And it's all because of Reign.

Trying not to frown, she starts the car as he hops in, too. Her feelings for him are already running too deep and it's happened far too fast. She entered the cottage less than half an hour ago.

She needs to get a hold of herself.

You don't need him. You're strong.

Her hands tighten on the steering wheel, wanting the voice gone.

In fact, now you're unstoppable.

GABBY

Gabby watches as Arielle's car comes down the gravel drive, glad to see Reign's with her. "A small part of me was worried he wouldn't come," she says to Colt.

He raises an eyebrow. "Just a small part?"

"Okay," she admits with a wry twist of her lips. "Maybe a medium sized part."

"The Reign we met not long ago would've run," Colt observes. "And yet, here he comes."

"I suspect if either of us went and asked him to come, we would've had far more opposition than Arielle."

Colt shakes his head. "We fought it as much as they are, I suppose."

"Well, you did," Gabby points out, raising her own eyebrow.

His delicious lips thin in a way that tells her he's suppressing a smile. To think she used to find this hunk of awesomeness intimidating and hard to read. "Hundreds of years of being hunted meant I had trust issues, okay?"

She slips an arm around his waist. "But now you know I'll keep you safe," she says with a cheeky grin.

"Only because I keep you safe," he quickly retorts.

She squeezes his muscled torso. "It's like we make a good team or something."

"The best," he says huskily, making something melt inside of her.

The car comes to a stop, and Arielle and Reign climb out, eyes scanning the building behind Gabby and Colt.

"When you said farmhouse, this isn't exactly what I pictured," says Arielle.

Reign angles his head. "It's...cute."

Arielle snorts. "That thing is not the definition of cute."

Before Gabby can say anything, another car appears on the

drive, this one driving much faster. It brakes, wheels sliding through the gravel, and comes to a stop on an angle.

"Rachel's arrived," Reign says dryly.

The driver's side door opens and Rachel's ruby-colored bob pops up. "Whoa," she says, shading her eyes as she takes in the farmhouse. "Who put the farmhouse on steroids?"

Gabby rolls her eyes. "Yes, it's impressive, okay?"

They all turn to take in the three-story building stretched out over the gentle, grassy rise a few yards away. Topped with high, gray roofs arched in multiple gables, white-framed windows gaze out over the deep porch stretched around the front. Manicured shrubs, artful symmetry and strategic aesthetics make for a breathtaking home.

"So, why here?" asks Arielle.

"Well," says Gabby, injecting a note of excitement into her voice. "Welcome home, you three."

"Huh?" Rachel asks. Arielle looks confused. Reign looks suspicious.

"Actually, this place is Blaise's," says Gabby. She waggles her eyebrows. "Let's just say she comes from money."

"That explains all the dresses in every color," mutters Reign.

"And while she's gone, she wants you three to stay here."

Stunned silence meets Gabby's statement.

"Why?" Arielle asks, the look of confusion back.

Gabby turns and walks up the paved path bordered by pansies, Colt by her side. "It's probably better if I show you."

The three follow as she steps up to the porch.

"Wow. Middle step doesn't have white ants," Reign says under his breath.

The front door is large and ornate and Gabby pushes it open, having already left it unlocked. They all step into a large, open-plan living area. The timber roof soars high above, while a wooden floor stretches out, colorful rugs spread around. A large fireplace is to the left, leather lounges in a semi-circle around it. A billiard table is to the right, glass cabinets lined behind it. All the wood glows with honeyed warmth, the whole place holds its chin up high with understated opulence.

"I thought Blaise lived with Nim," says Reign.

"She does. This is her family's place, although no one stays here. They all live abroad."

"Of course, they do," he mutters.

"But she wants you three to live here while she's off with Sierra and Mac. She's warded this place to the rafters."

Rachel is doing a slow spin around. "Impressive."

"And then I added a few of my own protection spells," says Gabby. "Just to make this place supernatural-proof."

Reign crosses his arms. "You want us"—he glances at Arielle and Rachel—"to live together?"

There's an edge in his voice that Gabby thought she might hear. She can sense his tension at the prospect, and she doubts Rachel has anything to do with it. This is all about sharing breathing space with Arielle.

But avoiding each other hasn't helped. Gabby's not sure what Reign's been up to seeing as he cuts any phone call short, but Arielle has been a listless ghost floating around her house. Missing her mother. Missing Reign. And not sure what to do about it.

Them, living here together, does something about it.

Gabby smiles brightly at him. "Yep. Let me give you a tour."

Not waiting for an answer, she walks ahead. "Kitchen is down there." She waves a hand at the double door to the right. "Games room is beyond, as is the library." She turns left, heading for the wide staircase. "But the bedrooms are up here."

Their footsteps are cushioned by the deep red carpet as they reach the second floor. A hallway stretches out either side.

"Guys rooms are to the right, ladies to the left," Gabby says jokingly.

She opens the nearest door, revealing a large bedroom, complete with a four poster bed, an antique dresser, and French doors that lead to a small balcony. "Each one has its own bathroom."

"Who cleans this place?" asks Rachel in awe.

"There's a cleaner who comes twice a week. She'll take care of the rest of the house while you're expected to keep the spaces you use neat and tidy."

"And Blaise wants us living here?" Reign asks cautiously.

Gabby understands his guardedness. This is a lot to take in, even Arielle and Rachel are gobsmacked. But Reign grew up poor. She suspects he doesn't feel he deserves to be somewhere like this.

All the more reason for him to be here.

She nods decisively. "This was her idea. And it's a freaking great one."

"It most certainly is," says Colt beside her. "Blaise has moved all of the books from Sinclair Mansion into the basement. You have everything you need here."

Arielle chews her lip. Reign shifts his weight. Rachel crosses her arms. "This has to do with the murders happening all over the city, doesn't it?"

"Yes," Gabby says heavily. "We expected it, seeing as another Sin's been released." She glances at Colt. "And it turns out we're dealing with Gluttony."

"Gluttony will be harder to kill," Colt warns. "She's amassing power much easier than Lust."

Gabby resists the urge to rub her arms. "Food is far more accessible, doesn't need to happen behind closed doors, and has people congregating in groups."

"So, you're saying there will be more murders this time

around," Reign says tensely.

She nods again, wishing it were otherwise. "That's why it's even more important we find Gluttony quickly." She looks around the lush hallway they're standing in. "And you three moving in means you'll be safer while we try to do that. You can look out for each other."

Gabby gets to keep Arielle safe.

Reign, the last Keeper of the Grail, will be safe.

And Rachel's lost her father to this supernatural war. She's never known her mother. She'll not only be safe, but with friends.

Rachel nods thoughtfully, as if she can see the logic in Gabby's words. Arielle's frowning, her eyes unfocused as if she's gazing inward. Reign is a little pale.

Gabby waits with her breath held. She doesn't want to consider what it will look like if the fissures that Lust created within their shrinking team only grow.

"Well, I'm in," Rachel announces. "It was the individual bathrooms that sold me."

Gabby looks to her cousin. Arielle's face is conflicted in a way she didn't expect. She thought that after some initial hesitation, Arielle would see this was a good idea, even with things so uncertain between her and Reign.

The fact Reign is also watching her so closely only reinforces Gabby's view.

Arielle straightens her shoulders. "You're right, Gabby. We're stronger together," she says firmly. Almost as if she's trying to convince herself.

Reign blinks, then nods. "Looks like we're doing it."

Gabby lets out a breath. "Great. I'd suggest moving in ASAP."

"Like, today," adds Colt.

Reign rolls his eyes. "I don't know if I can pack all my

belongings in such a short space of time."

Rachel nudges him. "Great. Because I have a collection of Disney princess dolls I won't go anywhere without."

Reign raises an eyebrow. "Me, too."

"I knew I liked you for a reason." The humor fades from Rachel's face. "Actually, I'm glad we'll be roomies. Or is it housies?"

He slips an arm around her shoulders. "Me, too."

Gabby almost smiles. Rachel's lost her father. Reign would be feeling Mac's absence. Their friendship is going to be a good thing for both of them.

Arielle spins on her heel. "Well, let's get going then. We should be able to have it all done by this evening."

Rachel follows her. "You haven't seen my collection," she mutters under her breath.

They trudge down the stairs and back outside, climbing into their cars and driving away.

"This is the right thing to do, isn't it?" Gabby asks.

Colt's shoulder brushes hers. "They need to learn to work together. It was the only thing to do."

Except Gabby saw Arielle's hesitation. She saw her face when Reign and Rachel were joking together. She sensed the turmoil within her.

It's all worrying.

But before she can say anything, her name floats through the air. "Gabrielle."

Colt is instantly on alert as they both recognize who it is. Her father.

She looks around, wondering why he's calling to her here.

His image flickers before her, but it's not his appearance that makes her gasp. It's the blood covering most of his face and torso. "We need to talk," he wheezes. "I'm at your demon's place of abode."

He disappears, leaving behind shock and disbelief. "What just happened?" Gabby breathes. Her father is an Archangel. He's practically untouchable.

"Things must be bad for him to be waiting in my basement," Colt says in a low voice.

Gabby grips his hand, knowing they need to limit how much magic they use so they don't make themselves targets, but this is an emergency.

They have to get to her father.

Now.

CHAPTER 3

REIGN

R eign stands in his plush, pretty room, his handful of belongings unpacked into the way-too-big dresser, and wonders what he's supposed to do now. There are more pillows on the bed than he's owned in his entire life.

His life has always involved sudden changes. He's become used to it. Actually, he expects it. It means he's not surprised when his world takes an about turn. Home. Homeless. Food. Foodless. Hope. Hopeless.

But this change has unsettled him.

He's gone from avoiding Arielle to living with her.

Feeling edgy, he opens the French doors and steps onto the balcony. The rear of the farmhouse, as this chalet is loosely called, overlooks a plush, pretty garden with a way-too-big pool.

"At least they were consistent," he mutters.

The luxury he'll make the most of. The comfort he'll appreciate while it's here.

But being in such close proximity with Arielle is going to take some serious adjustment. There will be barefoot Arielle.

Morning Arielle. Pajama Arielle. Reign groans. The last thing he needs to wonder is what she wears to bed, let alone find out.

How the fuck is he going to pretend his feelings don't extend beyond friendship? Because he sure as hell doesn't care what Rachel wears to bed, although he suspects it's some Disney princess nightgown. And he's shared beds with Mac countless times. It was comforting. Nice.

He didn't burn with need.

He didn't just about explode with the desire to touch, taste, tangle.

Maybe this wasn't such a good idea...

Grabbing his cell phone, he decides to make a call. It rings twice before the person on the other end picks up.

"Reign, is everything okay?" asks Sierra, trying not to sound concerned over the crackly line.

He glances at the screen. "I thought I just rang Blaise."

"She's busy working on a spell. Is everything okay?"

"I'm not sure. I'm standing on a balcony that adjoins my bedroom."

There's a sharp intake of breath. "You're going to stay there? All of you?"

"Is that what Blaise wants?"

Although that's what Gabby said, Reign needs to hear it for himself. Surely Blaise realizes he doesn't belong here.

"She suggested it—of course that's what she wants. And I wholeheartedly agreed. Surely you know how dangerous this will be."

"Well, yeah..." Gabby and Colt's warnings of how Gluttony is going to be able to easily tap into the universal need to eat really hit that home.

"And that every one of you is important." Sierra pauses, static filling his ear. "Including you."

Reign grips the phone a little tighter. He sighs. "You're going to mention that whole Grail keeping thing, aren't you?"

"There's nothing stopping you now," she says. "It's time to claim your heritage."

He's not sure what to say to that. Before all this started, his past went back as far as he was willing to remember—two, three days, tops.

Now he has a heritage?

One that has people looking at him expectantly. Or waiting on the other end of the phone...

"Look, Sierra," he starts. She needs to realize it's best all round if she doesn't raise her hopes above ground level. "I think—"

"Reign," she says softly, but with a firm edge. "I have total faith you can do this."

He blinks. Has anyone ever said that to him? Mac probably has, but she's his best friend so it doesn't count. She's downright biased.

Clearing his throat, he rubs his forehead. "Thanks," he says, conscious of how awkward he sounds.

"Just stating the truth," she says simply. "Now, there's a great pizza place not far away and a credit card in the top drawer in the kitchen. Enjoy."

Before Reign can ask Sierra to thank Blaise for her generosity, she hangs up. He stares at the phone, knowing that call just cemented everything.

He's staying.

And not just because of the unlimited pizza. Sierra's right. Shit's getting dangerous and this is the best place for all of them.

What's more, everyone's expecting him to start acting like a Grail Keeper. Whatever that looks like...

He heads to the bedroom door, registering voices on the

26

other side. He opens it to find Arielle and Rachel outside their adjoining rooms on the other side of the staircase.

"You can never have too much pepperoni," says Rachel.

"I'm a vegetarian," Arielle points out.

"Okay, then. That might be too much pepperoni for you."

Reigns shuts his door, getting their attention. "You're thinking pizza for dinner?"

Arielle nods. "My mom just texted, saying there's a credit card in one of the kitchen drawers."

"You wanna come for a drive?" asks Rachel. "We can take my car."

Reign keeps his gaze on her, even though he's acutely conscious of Arielle watching him. Moving into a house with her is the definition of adjustment. He's not sure he's ready to share a car with her while trying desperately not to think of the word *pajamas*.

So, he shakes his head. "You two go. I'm going to check this place out a little more."

Arielle loops her arm through Rachel's. "Good idea. We shouldn't be long."

She tugs her away, looking as relieved as Reign's feeling. Rachel's brow contracts as she glances between them, so Reign gives her a jaunty wave. They have to get over this awkwardness. It's the last thing Rachel needs to be around.

The two girls make their way down the stairs and into the kitchen, leaving Reign in the hallway. He's about to let out the breath that's unhappily trapped in his lungs when he discovers he's still not alone.

Joseph of Arimathea appears at the head of the stairs. He looks around, an excited glint in his eye. "You've been reunited with our lore."

Reign glances around, as if whatever this lore is has appeared along with Joseph. "Well, no one mentioned it to me."

TAMAR SLOAN

Joseph practically floats down the stairs. "Follow me."

Against his better judgment, Reign does just that. He's not sure he should be taking orders from a guy who's been dead for two centuries, but Joseph is his only link to anything Grail Keepers right now.

Joseph walks straight past the kitchen, his footsteps not making an impression on the carpet or any noise on the tiles. Not far beyond is a laundry and beside it a door. Joseph stands next to it. "In here."

Reign wonders where it could go. Don't places like this have something called a butler's pantry? Although Blaise is a witch. Is that some kind of storeroom for bottled chicken's feet and frogs' eyes?

He jolts when Joseph doesn't bother to wait and sails straight through the door.

"Easy to be confident when you're already dead," mutters Reign, grabbing the handle and yanking it open with one quick pull.

A set of stairs leads down into darkness.

Great. It's a basement.

He's just stepped through when soft lighting flickers on, illuminating each of the steps. At least it's a considerate basement.

Reign makes his way down, finding himself in a basement that's nicer than a lot of the houses he's lived in. Full of light, one wall is an entire wine rack, while a bar makes up the other side. Beside it is a flat screen TV with leather lounges facing it. A large table sits in the center, complete with plush-looking chairs.

And on the table are several stacks of books.

Joseph is hovering beside them. "These books once belonged to the Grail Keepers," he says excitedly.

Gabby said they'd brought everything from Sinclair

28

Mansion here. These books must be from there.

Reign finds himself moving toward the table and sitting down. He pulls one of the books toward him. "Will these have information on how to stop Gluttony?"

Joseph appears beside him, looking over his shoulder. "These books hold our history," he says with reverence.

Which didn't exactly answer Reign's question.

He opens it, the ancient print almost starting to look familiar. "Where's Mac when I need her?" he mutters to himself. She loves to research.

He'd rather hang out with Rachel's Disney princess collection than be doing this.

But he turns the pages, nonetheless. He's not expecting to find anything that could suggest where the Grail is considering no one's ever seen it, but if he can find any information on how to stop Gluttony, then this is time well spent.

"Any suggestions where I should start?" There's no answer, so Reign looks around. "Joseph?"

But Joseph's gone and disappeared again.

"Of course, he has."

Reign turns back to the book to see the first chapter outlines the story of Joseph's life. Reign remembers the first vision he had, the one where he thought the inevitable had happened and he'd lost his mind. It had been of Joseph, trapped in a cave, screaming at him. *They're coming! You need to stop them!* Man, that feels like a lifetime ago.

The next chapter is dedicated to the theory that the Grail was a chalice or platter used in the Last Supper. Reign keeps flicking, looking for more than a history lesson. He grabs another book, discovering it focuses on the even more ancient references to the Grail, including that of King Arthur.

Most of it is little more than legend.

Wiping his hand down his face, Reign takes the next book on the stack.

"Reign? Where are you?"

His heart jolts at the sound of Arielle's voice. He quickly moves to the base of the stairs. "Down in the basement. I'll be up in a sec."

"Okay. But don't take too long, you don't want the pizza to go cold."

He doesn't point out that he's eaten worse things than cold pizza.

"How optimistic that she thinks it will be hanging around long enough to get cold," Rachel calls out.

Shaking his head, Reign turns back to the table. About a dozen books sit there, waiting to be read.

This is going to take days. Maybe weeks. And they don't have that sort of time.

He picks up the book he just grabbed, quickly flicking through the pages. This one is dedicated to theories of links to the Grail.

"Talk about clutching at straws," he huffs.

"I hope you don't like pepperoni!" calls Rachel.

Reign's shutting the book when something catches his eye. He quickly opens it, brow furrowed, as he scans the picture that caught his attention. Thick and black, it's a horizontal line with two lines transecting the top half, the upper one slightly shorter than the other. He peers more closely. Kind of like a crucifix, but with an extra, longer line below the one crossing it.

Maybe it's just the bold way it's been drawn.

Maybe it's because the crucifix is such a universally recognized symbol.

But strangely, it looks familiar.

RACHEL

Rachel's I'm-coping-fine-after-the-loss-of-my-father facade cracks a little more when Reign appears in the kitchen, trying to pretend he's not frowning. It shouldn't make a difference seeing as Reign's looked unsettled since he got here, but it does.

The fracture between him and Arielle is further proof of Lust's devastating impact.

He climbs onto a barstool beside Rachel. "This looks good."

Arielle doesn't meet his gaze. "I got us all a medium, just because..."

Gluttony is as much a bitch as Lust was.

He nods, picking up a slice of the nearest one. "Good thinking."

He chomps down on it, grimacing when he discovers it's Arielle's vegetarian pizza, but still gazing at it in fascination as he chews. Because looking at the pizza means he doesn't have to look at Ari.

Silence, awkward and uncomfortable, settles in the kitchen.

Rachel shoots to her feet, her eyes stinging. She can play chirpy when she's busy. When there's direction and purpose. But not when she's sitting in a room with two unhappy souls who don't seem to realize they should be together.

The veneer thinner than an eggshell cracks if there's the slightest shard of unhappiness.

"I'm just going to grab something out of my room," she says with false brightness.

She's glad when neither Arielle nor Reign call her back as she shoots out of the kitchen. In fact, maybe some time alone might help them come to their senses.

Rachel saw the way they kissed in the hospital—it practically melted the entire building. And she's noticed the way they see the best in the other. Arielle sees Reign's goodness. Reign sees her strength.

If only they could put as much faith in what they feel as they do each other.

Not wanting to go to her room, Rachel deviates and heads to the porch, drawn to the comfort of darkness. Outside, she finds a wicker setting to the left, and she curls up in one of the chairs.

Tucking her knees up, she rests her chin on them. Crickets chirp, a mosquito whines past. The world seems calm and normal and peaceful.

Except it's none of those.

Gluttony is already killing.

Another desperate search for the next Innocent is looming.

And her father is dead.

Rachel bites her lip as tears sting her eyes. She's cried a bottomless ocean of those suckers already and all it made her was dehydrated.

"I miss you, Dad," she whispers. An owl lets out a mournful hoot somewhere in the distance and she releases a long sigh. "You were my rock."

Especially after her mother left them when she was six years old.

Rachel remembers that's when her father bought the dojo and followed his dream of being an instructor for the sport he always loved so much. It had kept them busy. Given them purpose and direction, just like she's desperately seeking now.

She even remembers the first potential client who walked through the door. It had been a woman named Michelle, and her eight year old daughter, Gabrielle.

While her father and Michelle spoke, Rachel and Gabrielle had run around the dojo, pretending the floor was lava and the mats were the only place they wouldn't be burned alive.

In fact, now that she thinks about it, Michelle and her father spoke for quite a while.

Long enough for Rachel and Gabrielle to pause on their mats to chat and introduce themselves.

"I WANT TO LEARN TO FIGHT," Gabrielle had said resolutely. "So I can punch bad guys in the nose." She'd frowned. "My mom doesn't think it's a good idea."

"My dad will show her it is."

Rachel had looked over to see Michelle brushing Paul's arm. "I'm so sorry to hear that, Paul," she'd said, her voice full of warmth and understanding. Rachel had wondered if Gabrielle had lost a parent, too.

Michelle and Gabrielle had left not long later, and Rachel had been surprised, and a little disappointed, when they hadn't come back.

Rachel sits up with a gasp. The woman, Michelle, had been Shell. The little girl had been Gabby.

She's met them before.

Pressing her fingers to her temples, she tries to understand what that could mean. Does this mean the Innocents were in contact? Do they know each other?

Great Walt, maybe they can find the next Innocent this way!

Rachel leaps to her feet, rushing back to the kitchen. "Ari! Reign!"

Finally, she has a purpose and a direction.

CHAPTER 4

ARIELLE

rielle watches Rachel rush out of the room, guilt tugging at her chest. "I feel awful for her." She jolts, realizing she spoke out loud.

But Reign only nods, his brooding gaze focused on his third slice of pizza. "Me, too. We should've saved her father."

Her gaze snaps to him. "But I was too late."

His own rises to meet hers, connecting and not letting go. "It sounds like you're taking sole responsibility for it," he points out.

She smiles a little at his insight. "Sounds like something you'd do."

That has his own lips twitching. "Although I think we've proven we work better as a team."

They're the ones who slowed you down. Arielle stiffens, trying to ignore the voice hissing through her mind. *That won't happen again.*

She shakes her head. "You're right. That's why staying here is a good idea."

Reign nods slowly, something shifting in the jungle green of his eyes. Something that invites her to explore it. Get tangled among it.

It's Lust's lingering effects. You're stronger than this.

And yet, Lust is dead. And the connection between her and Reign is rising like a phoenix from the ashes.

In fact, she's not sure it was ever really dead.

"Ari! Reign!"

Rachel's excited voice has them both jerking back far enough that Arielle realizes they'd been slowly, inexorably leaning into each other. She spins to face the doorway, willing away the heat that creeps up her cheek.

"I just remembered something!" Rachel says, skidding to halt beside the bench. "My dad met Shell when I was a kid!"

Reign straightens. "They what?"

"I know," she says, a faint tinge of pink apparent in her cheeks that hasn't been there since before the funeral. "Gabby and her mom came to check out the dojo."

Arielle chews her lip. "So Paul and Shell knew each other?"

"Yes," Rachel says excitedly. "And what if the Innocents are connected somehow? Even know each other?"

"That would mean we might have a way to find the next Innocent," says Reign, the excitement sparking in his own features.

"Exactly."

"That's just the lead we were looking for," says Arielle, standing up. "What do we need to do?"

This may give them the advantage they need. The chance to find the Innocent before Gluttony does.

The Innocent will die, like all the others before it, and all the others after it.

Horror jolts through Arielle. The obsidian's words are only becoming darker...

Rachel spins so fast her hair flares out. "I'm going to get my computer and go through all of Dad's files."

Reign turns to Arielle. "Why don't you call Gabby and see if we can go through some of Shell's old photos?"

"Good idea." She pats her pocket to find her phone's not there. "I must've left my cell in my room."

His eyebrows shoot up. "It's probably something you want to keep on you at all times."

You don't need them!

Arielle draws in a sharp breath. The obsidian was an angry shout this time.

Reign's eyes narrow with concern. "Are you okay, Ari?"

Rachel shoots back into the kitchen and places her laptop on the bench. "Let's see what we can find."

But Arielle takes a step back. "I'm just going to get my phone so I can call Gabby."

Before either Reign or Rachel can answer, she ducks out of the room and up the stairs. She slips into her bedroom and closes the door behind her and leans against it.

Yes. We're alone. It is time to—

"Stop!" she cries, slamming her palms over her ears. "No more!"

A few strides and she's at the French doors. Throwing them open, she steps onto her balcony. Cool night air envelops her and she realizes how hot she's feeling. Like she has a fever.

Arielle takes the obsidian out of her pocket. The black stone sits in her palm, the uneven lines and angles seeming to glint, even in the low light. She should never have picked it up. She's not even sure why she did. Something in her compelled her to grab it before leaving the small stone room Gabby had built to hide all those deadly weapons.

Which makes Arielle wonder about the obsidian resting in

her palm. It must be dangerous. And powerful. Otherwise it wouldn't have been hidden away in that tomb.

I will give you all the power you want, it hisses. *I helped you fight Lust. I made you strong.*

Which is true. She's never fought so well, or with such strength. She'll probably need that again to fight Gluttony.

I can make you unstoppable.

Nim's words as they'd stood in Veritas float through Arielle's mind. *It's a very powerful magical object. And magic always has a price. Something it wants in return.*

She doesn't want the dark voice in her mind anymore.

She misses Trinity and her comforting company.

And she doesn't want to find out what the obsidian wants.

Or what it will cost her.

Winding her arm back, Arielle throws the obsidian into the night as hard as she can. The jagged lines intersecting the stone flash, almost in fury, before it goes as black as the night.

There's no sound to show it landed. No sign of where it's ended up.

But Arielle doesn't care. She lets out a breath, feeling relieved.

Now, she'll be able to think straight.

GABBY

Gabby rushes into Colt's apartment, finding her father splayed on the couch, one wing sprawled limply over the back, the other stretched across the floor. And just like the image he projected to her, he's covered in blood.

"Dad?" she asks, falling to her knees beside him. The blood

is scary, but the undignified way her proud archangel father is sprawled is terrifying.

She glances up at Colt, who's stayed by the door, to find him frowning. He knows this is serious, too.

Her father's eyes flutter open. "Gabrielle."

"I'm here, Dad. What can I do?"

"The healing..." he pants. "Is slow... Ensure...no one enters."

"He wants us to protect him," says Colt, crossing his arms.

"Not you," gasps her father. "Gabrielle."

Even in so much pain, her father is unwilling to receive help from a demon.

"Then you shouldn't have come to my place of abode," sneers Colt.

"It's okay, Dad. We'll make sure this place is safe."

Her father nods, some of the strain dissolving from his face as his eyes close again. His body unwinds, sinking further into the couch as he turns inward.

Gabby pushes to her feet. "He'll be healing himself."

Colt comes to stand beside her. "He mustn't have been able to do that while protecting the basement."

In case whoever started this came to finish it.

"Who did this to him?"

"That's a valid question." Colt's lips thin. "Someone powerful."

To have hurt someone as mighty as her father so badly.

As they watch, her father's wings slowly contract and tuck in. Color progressively returns to his face.

The blood fades and vanishes.

Gabriel's eyes flicker once more, but this time they snap open, bright and alert. He sits up, glancing at the couch as if he's surprised to find himself there. Possibly a little disgusted.

Her father, the archangel, is once more before her.

He glances at Gabby. "Thank you, daughter." Gabby's about

38

to point out that Colt came, too, but he continues. "Without my full attention, the healing was taking too long. Making me vulnerable to another attack."

"What? Someone attacked you?"

"Yes. Another angel faction," he spits.

Colt snorts. "This is all making sense now. The angels are fighting amongst themselves."

Gabby's father glares at him. "Raphael is amassing an army. He wants Michael freed from his prison and returned to the Throne of Heaven."

That has Gabby frowning. "His prison is unbreakable." She went to great lengths, almost died, to make sure it was.

Shaking his head, her father stands. He seems to hold himself there for a split second, as if to steady himself. "Nothing is absolute, daughter. You know that."

"Then what does this mean?"

Her father pulls his shoulders back. "Very little. I won't allow it to happen."

Colt raises a brow. "Except you can't say that with absolute certainty."

Her father scowls at him, before turning to Gabby. "Dumah escaped."

"You only just captured him."

"Yes. There was not enough time to interrogate him."

Gabby suppresses a shudder at her father's cold tone. Sometimes there's a fine line between Heaven and Hell.

"I thought you should know," her father continues. "In case he reappears looking for that demon girl."

If the angel Dumah is still determined to kill Mac, it's a good thing she left.

Gabby nods. "Thank you for the warning."

"I didn't do it for her," her father mutters. "Make sure you remain alert, daughter."

"Well, I wasn't exactly napping when you came to me," she points out.

Ignoring her sarcasm, he steps away from the couch, dusting his sleeves. "It's time for me to return. This insurgency needs to stop." He turns away only to hesitate. "Stay safe, Gabrielle," he says, his voice losing its hard edge.

And then he's gone, the air he was occupying barely disturbed. Gabby sighs. Despite his aloofness, okay, his arrogance, her father cares for her. It makes their bond a tenuous one, but a deep connection, nonetheless.

"Do you believe him?" asks Colt. "That this angel war isn't going to be an issue."

"I hope it won't, but like you said, there's no way my father can guarantee it, archangel or not." Humans—mortal and unequipped to deal with the power of the supernatural—are always collateral damage in these situations.

"But we need to focus on finding the Innocent and ending Gluttony."

"Exactly," Gabby agrees. "That's our priority right now."

Colt looks at her questioningly, his chocolate eyes calm pools of faith. "So? What's our next move?"

She walks over to him, slipping her arms around his waist and resting her forehead on his chest. "I can't stop thinking that Sierra's right. We need to find the Grail and finish this, once and for all."

"That would certainly save future Innocents. At the same time, angels and demons have been searching for the Grail since its creation."

Her brow puckers. "That symbol, the septagram with the crosses inside, has something to do with all this, I know it does."

"And someone tried to wipe its existence from your memory," says Colt thoughtfully.

"Which means it's important." She looks up at him. "All we were able to retrieve with Blaise was where I first saw it, nothing else."

"You believe there's more you know about it?"

"I don't know, but what if I do? What if someone hid that from me, too?"

And what if it's the link that's always been missing. The one piece of the puzzle that will lead them to the Grail.

Colt's handsome features turn thoughtful. "You'd need a witch to help you with that, and Blaise left with Sierra and Mac. She's the most powerful witch we know."

"We could go to New Orleans," Gabby offers, even as she knows going to the home of witchcraft and finding someone will take time they don't have.

"Or..." Colt's eyebrows hike into his wine-colored hair. "There's another witch we know. One just as powerful as Blaise."

At first Gabby frowns in confusion, but the expression quickly clears when she realizes who he means. "Dinah."

He nods. "I could feel her power. You would have, too."

She did. Dinah is practically bursting with magic.

"Can we trust her?" she asks, knowing it's a rhetorical question. Dinah works for the Mayor, another supernatural with motivations and a plan they've yet to figure out.

Colt's hands tighten around her waist. "I highly doubt it, but I trust us."

That they'll be stronger than whatever curve ball Dinah tries to throw at them.

He shrugs. "Nor do we have many other options."

There never are, Gabby thinks wryly. It's always a hard, uncertain road that stretches before them.

Her hands snake around his shoulders. "I love you, you know that?"

Colt's eyes soften. "Yes, I do." He smiles. "Although I don't tire of hearing it."

Pushing up on her toes, Gabby brings herself until her lips are hovering millimeters away from his. "You, Colt Grayson, are my Heaven on Earth."

"My soul is yours, Gabrielle Hartley."

They kiss, their mouths sealing the vows they've made countless times before, and will continue to make as long as their lungs draw breath.

Gabby pulls back, hoping Arielle realizes she may have found her own promise of forever in Reign. Facing the intimidating odds they are is always more doable when you have love on your side.

Wishing she could devour this demon of hers, rather than just kiss him, Gabby steps away.

Find the Grail.

End this.

Then kiss as much as she damn well likes.

She straightens her shoulders. "Let's go find Dinah."

CHAPTER 5
REIGN

I t's the early hours of the morning when Arielle comes to Reign.

When he's awake enough to remember.

But not conscious enough to fight it.

She's always smiling as she climbs into bed beside him. They lie there on their sides, facing each other as their breathing slowly falls into rhythm. It's only then that he remembers to ask. To put up a token effort of resistance.

"Why are you here, Ari?"

She slides a little closer, repeating the words she said to him in hospital. "I was tired of fighting how I feel for you, Reign. Friends was never going to be enough."

He reaches out, fingers caressing her cheek as he brushes a strand of pale gold hair out of her face. It's during these barely-awake moments that he speaks the truth. "This has always been more than that."

And then they're kissing. Moving until skin is touching skin. Exploring with hungry tongues and hot hands.

Reign sits up, drawing in a sharp breath. He rakes his fingers through his hair, conscious he's panting like he just ran here.

Lust is gone, and yet, why are the dreams still here? Why do they still steal his breath?

He pulls back the covers and shuffles to the edge of the bed before his brain can get a chance to answer those questions. It's a pointless, useless exercise.

It doesn't matter how he feels about Arielle. It's never been about that. The most Lust could've done is amplify the attraction he's felt from the moment he saw her.

This is about Arielle deserving more than...him.

Pushing to his feet, Reign throws off the sheets, welcoming the cool air on his bare chest. He paces the length of his bedroom, glaring at the dresser as he strides past it. The sheet hanging over the window-sized mirror is proof that he's right. He also had to cover the one in his adjoining bathroom. Who needs two mirrors in two rooms?

He's known it all his life—there's a darkness in him, waiting, staring back at him.

That darkness is why he's jumped from foster home to foster home. Why he could map out his future along an inevitable trajectory.

It will always taint anything he touches.

And he's learned—the more he wants it, the more the darkness will erode it.

It's why there's no point finding the Grail. Because he'll fuck that up like he's fucked everything else up.

It's inevitable.

And Arielle is good. It shines from her in the same way the blackness slithers through him.

The best he can hope for is helping the others find the next Innocent. And to protect Arielle along the way.

Which means he needs to think of where he saw that damned symbol. Reign leans against the dresser, staring at the pale sheet in front of him.

Where? Where has he seen it?

Why does it feel so familiar?

A memory rises through the layers of his consciousness, and when Reign realizes what it is, he initially shies away. There are certain parts of his life that he avoids thinking about more than others. Those passages of time were the ones that had him turning to the oblivion of drugs far more than the petty crime or destitute surroundings ever had.

But the possibility that it's decided to rear its ugly head for a reason has him drawing a deep breath, bracing himself, and letting it play through his mind.

It was his second last foster home and he was thirteen, maybe fourteen years old. The one he'd lasted the longest at. This home had been nicer than the past two, but not quite as nice as the one before those. The couch hadn't been too saggy, there was a games console that actually worked, and there had been another foster kid the same age as Reign. In fact, Lance had the same lean build and black hair as Reign. Sometimes, people mistook them for brothers.

It had been pretty cool at the start.

Until he learned how different he and Lance really were.

He'd left the games room after Lance had killed his character a few too many times, even though they were on the same team, and wandered into the living room. He'd flopped onto the couch and picked up the remote, looking for something mindless to watch.

Lance had followed. He always did.

He'd snatched the remote off Reign. "I want to watch the history channel," he'd snapped as if Reign was dominating it.

Lance loved the history channel. Mostly the shows that focused on wars and battles.

Reign had let him, slouching into the couch without saying a word. Arguing with Lance only got him in trouble. And then

Lance would apologize over and over until Reign said it was fine.

Even though it wasn't.

A shudder ripples through Reign as he's struck once more by the dysfunctional relationship they'd had. He'd been too young to know the difference. Too lonely to cut all ties. And too trapped because leaving meant finding another foster home all over again.

A documentary had appeared on the screen that day, the usual monotone voice associated with anything to do with history filling the room.

Reign shakes his head, wondering why he's putting himself through this torturous walk down memory lane. With no happy weed nearby to mute its effect on him...

The voice on the TV had started droning on about the rise of the Crusades and Reign had slouched even further into the couch. He knew if he moved away, Lance would just follow, and he'd no longer be distracted. He had little choice but to pay attention.

Words like Jerusalem and Knights Templar and Cross of Lorraine had filtered into his head, whether he liked it or not.

Then a symbol appeared on the screen.

One vertical bar. Two horizontal bars, the bottom longer than the top.

"The Cross of Lorraine!" he gasps.

Once found on the coat of arms of the Knights Templar!

Reign sprints out of his room and back to the basement, his bare feet padding down the lighted steps. He opens the book he was looking at yesterday and there it is—the Cross of Lorraine.

But apart from a mention of the Knights Templar, there's little else to tell him why it's significant.

He flips through the next book and then another. It's the third that has him whispering one word. "Jackpot."

He takes a seat on the nearest chair, his eyes devouring the text as he reads aloud.

"The Knights Templar and the Grail Keepers have had a long association. They joined forces centuries ago to fight a common enemy."

Reign's brow scrunches down. A common enemy?

"This organization is believed to be responsible for inciting wars and other violent events throughout the world with the aid of supernatural species brought back from the dead." His eyes widen. "Necromancy."

He hunches over, conscious of his shirtless state as cold prickles his skin. "The species most often employed are blood sucking demons."

Great. Vampires are real?

But it's the alliance, and this shadowy organization they've been fighting that really interests Reign. He needs to find out whether the Knights Templar still exists.

He turns the page, seeing a long list of wars and other awful times in history. Lance would've loved it, he thinks bitterly. But it's what's at the bottom that catches Reign's attention.

A phone number has been scribbled in small, tight scrawl.

There's no name and no indication of what or who it's for, and future pages go on to describe the ongoing quest for the Grail they've never found.

Reign returns to the page with the phone number. He needs to decide what to do with it.

He shrugs. "Only one way to find out," he tells the empty room.

Moving over to the lounges surrounding the large TV, he picks up the phone sitting on a side table. He suspects with all the warding Blaise and Gabby set up that the number he's about to use isn't easily traceable. It probably goes through another dimension or something before it connects.

He quickly dials the number, a little surprised when it starts to ring. It might actually be a legit one...

"Yes?" answers a female voice, terse and businesslike.

Reign hangs up, suddenly spooked. He was expecting someone like Joseph to be on the other end. A wise old man with all the answers ready to go.

Not a female who wanted to bite his head off.

Plus, what was he going to say? "Hey, I'm the last Keeper of the Grail. Is that the Knights Templar? Cause I'm thinking we should talk about the latest Sin escaping Hell."

Snorting, Reign places the phone back down with a firm *click*. He needs to think this through a little more.

"Reign?" Rachel's voice reaches him from upstairs. "You down there?"

"Hey, Rach," he calls back. "Yeah, I was just researching."

She skips down the stairs and appears in the doorway, her eyebrows instantly hiking up into her messy morning hair. "Do you normally do your research shirtless?" She leans against the doorjamb. "Because if that's the case, I might bring the Disney princesses down to watch the show."

Reign picks up the cushion on the dining chair beside him and throws it at her. Rachel grins as she blocks it and it *thumps* softly against the wall. She turns to call over her shoulder. "I found him, Ari."

He freezes. They were both looking for him?

Arielle appears a moment later and Rachel steps out of the way so she can enter the basement. Then stop.

Her eyes instantly rake over his bare skin, sliding down to his low slung track pants, to his bare feet and back up again, lingering over his chest before returning to his face.

Reign swallows. He feels like he just had a once-over with a flamethrower.

"Arielle wasn't sure where you were," says Rachel, strangely sounding like she's far away. "So she checked if I knew."

The delicious pink that had blossomed across Arielle's cheeks deepens.

"Anywho," Rachel says cheerily. "I'm off to make breakfast. Everyone ready to go in an hour?"

"Go?" Reign asks, confused.

"I couldn't find anything on my laptop. Seems Dad hadn't caught up with the digital revolution. So we need to go to the dojo—he kept boxes and boxes of paperwork."

He nods. "Good idea. Sure, I'll be ready."

"Once you get dressed." With a cheeky grin she skips back up the stairs, leaving him alone with Arielle.

Wearing nothing but a pair of pants.

He clears his throat. "I saw a symbol last night that looked familiar. I remembered where I saw it this morning." He doesn't mention Lance. Even Mac barely knows about him. "So I came down here to have another look."

Arielle clasps her hands in front of her. "Oh?"

"It was the Cross of Lorraine. It belongs to the Knights Templar, who have had an alliance with the Grail Keepers."

"Oh." She steps further into the room. "You've found another lead?"

"I'm not sure. Hopefully."

She huffs out a laugh. "And I thought you'd run."

Reign stills. "You'd thought I hightailed it?"

"It's just that...things have been strained between us. I wasn't sure you'd want to hang around."

He suppresses a frown. "I suppose I have a history of being flaky," he admits, as much as he wishes Arielle had a little more faith in him.

Her eyes widen. "That's not what I meant." She shakes her

head. "Sorry, my thoughts have been all over the place at the moment."

"I'm not going anywhere," Reign says quietly. He takes a small step forward. "Is everything okay?"

"It is now," she says with a smile. "I think I just needed to sort some stuff out." Reign's about to ask what she means by that, but Arielle continues. "I'm glad we're here."

His breath disintegrates. Arielle's voice is...warm. Almost as warm as her gaze.

Her flame-blue eyes feel like they're swallowing him. "I miss our banter," she says quietly.

"Me, too."

His answer triggers an instant smile. "I miss *you*, Reign."

He opens his arms wide. "I'm here, Ari. For as long as you need me."

The moment he makes the motion, he knows it's a mistake. Her gaze drops to his exposed chest. Her eyes feel like they scorch every valley and rise of his biceps, then his torso, then his stomach. His body temperature spikes along with his pulse.

With a sharp movement, she spins around and heads to the stairs. "I'll go help Rachel with breakfast," she says huskily.

Reign watches her leave, conscious something has subtly shifted although he's not really sure why or how.

Lust is gone. Arielle shouldn't be looking at him like that.

And yet...she is.

And he has zero, zip, zilch desire to pretend this isn't happening.

The time for fighting it has ended.

CHAPTER 6

ARIELLE

Arielle doesn't get much chance to think over the moment with Reign in the basement.

Shirtless Reign.

Hot Reign.

The Reign who wasn't moving away. In fact, his eyes said the exact opposite.

Not when Rachel's driving.

They squeal around a corner, and Arielle wonders if Rachel took her foot off the gas at all as she clings to the dashboard. Surely she didn't get rid of the obsidian, meaning she can finally think clearly, only to be crushed in an overgrown soda can.

"Is someone pregnant and about to give birth and no one told me?" Reign asks in a strained voice.

Rachel laughs. "Not that I know of." She looks over her shoulder at him. "Although have you seen those documentaries? The I-didn't-know-I-was pregnant ones? Not until I was on the toilet and—"

"Eyes on the road, please!" he calls in alarm.

Rachel faces forward, jerking the wheel so they slot back

into their lane as the car passing them blares its horn. "Go suck a duck!" she shouts at the windscreen.

Arielle sees the turn for the dojo ahead and braces herself. She would have liked to have lived long enough to see if the promise in Reign's eyes was going to be everything her stuttering heart decided it would be.

The car squeals around that corner, too, and Arielle's pretty sure she feels the back tires lose traction for a second. Rachel must notice the white-knuckled grip because she grins sheepishly at her. "Sorry. I drive as hard as I fight."

"What did the road do to you?" Arielle asks weakly.

Rachel giggles, then slams on the brakes. Her small car skids to a halt, stopping perfectly inside a parking space out the front of the dojo. She pulls on the handbrake and looks at Arielle and Reign. "See, I can pull it up as well as a punch."

Reign rolls his eyes. "Let's hope you don't have to sneeze at the wrong moment."

They climb out and Arielle tests her legs, unsurprised to find them a little wobbly. Reign comes to stand beside her and she leans in, speaking under her breath. "Next time, you drive, license or no license."

"Agreed," he mutters.

Rachel rolls her eyes as she walks past them. "I need to find me a nice Scorpio. They know how to live."

Reaching the door, she pulls a set of keys out of her pocket and unlocks it. The moment she steps through, her shoulders tense. Arielle glances at Reign and his face has lost all traces of humor, too. This is going to be hard for their friend.

Inside, the dojo is a cavern of silence. The place looks identical to when Arielle came here to train—the training mats, the punching bags, the weapons on the wall. But it feels completely different. Without Paul, it's empty.

Rachel shuffles past, her head down, and up a set of stairs.

Arielle follows with Reign, her heart aching. She lost Aunt Shell, but Rachel lost her only parent. She can't imagine how that feels.

They reach a mezzanine that overlooks the floor below, and Rachel uses her keys to open the single door they're now standing before. Inside, they find themselves in an office.

"This is where Dad kept all his paperwork," says Rachel. She indicates toward a stack of six or seven boxes. "He was old school when it came to filing and bookkeeping."

"Gabby said Shell was the same. She's dropping off her stuff later today." Arielle walks over and opens one of them, seeing a jumble of papers and receipts inside. "Are they all like this?"

Rachel smiles, her face pale. "I didn't say he was good at it."

Reign shifts a little. "Let's take it back to the farmhouse. We can take our time going through them."

Feeling uneasy herself, Arielle looks around. "You're worried we might get attacked?"

He shrugs, staying close to the door. "Lust took Paul from here. And I suspect we won't be receiving a friend request from Gluttony any time soon."

Rachel nods. "I agree." She blinks rapidly. "Plus, it hurts to be here more than I thought."

Arielle reaches out and grasps her hand, squeezing it. Rachel draws in a shuddering breath before turning to her. "We need to stop Gluttony. We can't let it happen again."

Once more relieved she no longer has the obsidian hissing doubts through her mind, Arielle nods. "That's why we're here."

Darkness won't win. She'll fight it with everything she has.

They quickly move the boxes from the office to the back of Rachel's car, eyes and ears alert for signs of anything unusual. They've just packed the last box in when Reign stiffens. He spins around, on high alert.

Arielle moves to his side, noting the way Rachel instinctively straightens her shoulders and clenches her fists. She's ready to fight.

And Arielle no longer has the obsidian to make her strong. A frisson of nervousness tingles down her spine. She doesn't want to be a liability again.

Except the person who walks around the corner is familiar. Although not exactly a friend.

Dressed as usual in all black, her midnight bangs flicked over her face, Dinah walks toward them, her kohl-rimmed eyes assessing. "I thought you might come back here eventually."

Arielle's muscles tighten. "What are you doing here, Dinah?"

"Waiting for you," she states matter of factly. "I was hoping we could talk."

Reign shifts a little closer to Arielle. "You looking to do another deal?" His words drip with disdain.

"No," says Dinah. "I—"

"Good," snaps Rachel. "Because we want nothing to do with you."

Dinah nods, looking unsurprised, but something shifts in her dark eyes. Almost like she's hurt. "I want to help. Just like I helped you find Cain and gave you the dagger that killed Lust."

"The dagger didn't work without being dipped in Cupid's ashes," says Arielle, anger making her throat tight. "And you told me Cain was in Syria as he wanted the Grail."

But he was there to raise someone from the dead.

Dinah shakes her head, her gaze becoming intense. "Cain most definitely wants the Grail."

"Tell him to get in line," growls Reign.

"But none of that is relevant now," dismisses Dinah. "I—"

Rachel takes a small step forward. "And the tattoo on your

wrist, what organization does it belong to? And what does the Mayor have to do with all of this?"

"You're not listening," Dinah grinds out. "All of that is nothing but a distraction. There are more important things to focus on. Like saving an Innocent and stopping another Gate of Hell from opening."

For once, Arielle knows Dinah's speaking the truth. It means some of the anger dissolves and she says the next sentence almost gently. As if she's letting Dinah down. "We don't need help from someone we can't trust."

Dinah nods even as she hunches her shoulders. "Fair call." She angles her chin, flicking her bangs back from her eyes. "But I'll be here if you need any help."

Rachel snorts. "We're not that desperate."

Arielle turns away, a silent Reign close to her side. "I don't know what you want Dinah, but I've had enough of secrets and hidden agendas. Goodbye."

She nods sagely. "When you realize exactly what you're up against, you'll need every ally you can find." She shrugs. "I'm willing to wait."

Arielle frowns as she returns to the car. She decided that she's not willing to align herself with dark magic in the name of winning when she threw away the obsidian. And they don't know whether Dinah's aligned with good or evil. She climbs in, this time sitting in the back so Reign can ride shotgun. Dinah doesn't call out or stop them, just stands in the parking lot as they drive away. But as Rachel stops to pull out on the street, Arielle glances over her shoulder. She's not surprised to see the mysterious witch has disappeared.

She turns back to find Reign watching her. "Why do I get the feeling that girl isn't the patient type?" he asks.

Rachel yanks the steering wheel down as she takes a corner much too fast. "We don't need the likes of her."

Reign turns to stare forward, bracing one arm on the console and the other on the door. "Because we won't be alive long enough to fight the good fight?"

Rachel flashes him a smile. "I thought you liked a bit of an adrenaline shot?"

"I also like being alive."

Rachel thumps his arm, then returns her hand so she can swerve around a car that had slowed to park. She blares the horn. "Go jam a clam!" she shouts.

Arielle decides she won't point out that doesn't quite make sense. She'd prefer Rachel to keep her easily distracted mind on not crashing.

They reach the farmhouse with a little less rubber on their tires, but still intact. Rachel leaps out of the car and goes to the boot to grab one of the boxes. "The sooner we get sorting through this stuff, the sooner we find a lead on the Innocent."

She carries it up the front porch and balances it on her raised knee as she unlocks the door. She's gone before Arielle or Reign can point out there's no guarantee the piles of paper will tell them anything about the Innocent.

They walk around to the back of the car and reach in simultaneously, their hands crashing. The flare of awareness has Arielle drawing her hand back in a hurry, and she notes Reign does the same.

"Sorry," he mutters.

Arielle watches as he rubs his hand down his leg, as if the touch scorched him, too.

Even though Lust is dead.

Arielle moves in a little closer, her heart thudding. "Reign, I think we should talk."

Now that there's nothing clouding her judgment, no Sin, no obsidian, she knows what she wants.

Reign.

GATES OF GREED

He stills, studying her intensely. Every sweep of his gaze is like a brush of heat over her skin. "I think you could be right."

His words feel like sweet joy and hot promise, all at the same time. Arielle finds herself smiling, and she relishes how good it feels.

What's more amazing, is that Reign smiles right back. The need to touch him becomes overwhelming.

"Hey, you two!" snaps Rachel from the porch. "Are those boxes too heavy for you or something? I could send Cinderella out to help if you need it?"

Grinning ruefully, Reign quickly grabs one of the boxes and tucks it under his arm. He hoists another under the other. With a quick grin, he heads to the door.

Arielle watches him walk away, enjoying the view. His t-shirt barely hides the ripples of muscle down his back. His jeans are snug in a way that has her mouth watering. She jams her hands in her pockets, conscious her palms are beginning to itch with the desire to explore every valley and ridge her gaze is caressing.

Arielle freezes as her fingers brush something.

She didn't drive so it's not the car keys. And her cell phone is in her back pocket. Nor did she take her purse.

Plus, the object is too small to be any of those.

Gingerly, she pushes down a little further, biting her lip so hard it makes her eyes sting when she registers what it is.

Small, smooth, but full of uneven angles.

The obsidian is back.

Its voice slides through her mind as if it never left.

You don't need him.

You have me.

GABBY

Colt studies the front of the small cafe they're standing outside of before turning to Gabby. "You know she allowed us to find her."

Gabby nods, wondering how easy it is to access the rear exit of the building. "It's the only way we were able to locate her so quickly using the demonic spell."

His lips thin. "The question is, why?"

Exactly. Why is Dinah okay with them detecting her magical signature so easily? Like she wanted them to find her.

Gabby grips Colt's hand and walks toward the door. "There's only one way to find out."

The interior of the cafe is small, feeling almost claustrophobic thanks to the charcoal walls, black tiled floor and dark furniture. It's like they just walked into a den or a cave.

And Dinah's sitting in the back corner, her own black clothing and hair camouflaged in the oppressive decor.

Gabby and Colt make their way over. Dinah looks up, taking a sip of her coffee—black, of course—looking unsurprised to see them. "This is my lucky day."

Gabby sits down and Colt does the same, moving his chair closer to hers. She rears back a little when she realizes there's a lizard sitting on Dinah's shoulder. A chameleon, in fact, one cone-like eye trained on them, the other pointing to the ceiling somewhere.

"You have a pet lizard?" Gabby asks, her original question forgotten.

Dinah smiles. "I do now."

"The reptile is new?" asks Colt.

She reaches up to scratch the chameleon under the chin and the lizard arches its neck. "I've always moved around too much to have a pet."

"But now you're staying," he observes, the words more of a statement than a question.

Dinah shrugs. "Godzilla needs stability."

Gabby has to work to keep her eyebrows in place. The lizard's name is Godzilla? She shakes her head, trying to refocus. "We're here because we need a...service."

Dinah raises a thin, black brow. "I didn't think you were here for the ambiance." It twitches a little higher. "Or the company."

"We need a memory retrieval spell," says Gabby, trying not to let the words rush out. "For me."

Dinah's gaze is unwavering as she studies her. "How do you know I can do it?"

"You were powerful enough to extract Cain's demonic essence," growls Colt.

She acknowledges his statement with a brief nod. "You're right. I can. It will take me a couple of days to gather the ingredients, and then we can go ahead."

Gabby's eyes narrow and she feels Colt tense beside her. He's wondering the same thing she is. "What's the price?"

"There is none," Dinah says simply, her hands tightening around her coffee cup.

Colt shakes his head. "There's always a price."

Her gaze flickers away, then returns to Gabby. "Maybe you could put a good word in for me with Arielle?"

Protectiveness shoots through Gabby. "What do you want with Arielle?"

"To help," says Dinah. The chameleon—Godzilla—twitches, its eyes moving in independent directions. Dinah reaches up to pat it. "The remaining Gates of Hell need to stay closed. I don't want to see Lucifer out of his cage."

Gabby can sense Dinah's telling the truth, although why she wants Lucifer contained is a mystery.

Colt leans forward an inch. "Arielle is capable of making up her own mind about who she should trust."

"Although if you help us," adds Gabby, trying to soften the hard edges of her protective demon. "I'll tell Ari what you've done."

Dinah nods, her shoulders dropping a little as she exhales. "I agree to your terms."

Gabby grabs a napkin and scribbles down her cell number, then pushes it toward Dinah. "Call me when you're ready."

"Once I have the ingredients, we can go ahead," says Dinah, taking the napkin and tucking it into her pocket.

Gabby pushes to her feet and Colt joins her. "The sooner, the better," he says.

They need to know what that symbol means.

They leave the cafe, the sunlight a sharp contrast to the somber cafe. They walk away, neither speaking as they clasp hands, deep in thought.

Dinah is going to help Gabby retrieve the remaining information that's been hidden from her. What's more, they could find out who did it. And why.

They've just reached Colt's car when he speaks up. "Are you sure you want to do this?" His dark gaze is steady as it holds the weight of what they just agreed to.

"I'm sure," Gabby says firmly. But then her mouth twists. "I'm just not sure how much we can trust Dinah."

He nods curtly. "Good. We need to be wary of this witch. I could sense her power."

Gabby could, too. Dinah was able to extract Cain's demonic essence because she's a walking powder keg of magic. "But we don't have any other option."

Colt frowns, not liking that she's right. "We need to be careful."

She smiles at him over the roof of his car. "Careful is my middle name."

He snorts as he shakes his head. "And my middle name is Impetuous."

Gabby's smile grows to a grin. Her centuries-old, over-protective, ever-vigilant demon could never be called impetuous.

They slide into their seats and her smile dies as she acknowledges the point he was making. She does need to be careful, even though it's not really in her nature to be.

Dinah has the same symbol on her wrist.

Which means she has her own agenda here. And they have no idea what it is.

CHAPTER 7

REIGN

R eign's just closing the fridge door when he hears someone entering the kitchen. He lowers the soda can he just pulled out, his pulse tripping up a notch.

Reign, I think we should talk.

There had been a world of promise in Arielle's eyes when she said those words. A hint of vulnerability. A daring dash of hope.

It was obvious she wants to discuss what's happening between them. The prospect is terrifying and thrilling.

And he has to admit, he can't wait.

Except it's not Arielle walking up to the bench, but Rachel. She slides onto one of the barstools and takes the soda. "Thanks. I need a sugar hit."

Reign notes the sag in her shoulders. "This morning was tough."

She stares at the top of the soda can as she picks at it. "Going through the boxes will be harder."

He walks around the island bench and sits on the stool beside her. "Is there anything I can do to help?"

Her eyes come up to meet his, moisture pooling along her lashes. "Give Arielle a chance?"

He jolts back. "What does that have to do with any of this?"

"I saw you two kiss, Reign. It was the most scorchingly beautiful thing I've ever seen."

He blinks at the incredibly accurate description. And he got to live it.

Rachel sighs. "It would be nice to know there might be the hint of a happily ever after, despite everything that's happened."

"This isn't one of your fairytales, Rach." And he ain't no prince.

"Believe me, I know." Her hand tightens around the soda can enough that there's a crackle of aluminum. "But I'd like to believe that their message still rings true, that love can conquer all."

He's not sure what to say to that. That's not a world he lives in.

He huffs a short laugh. "Of all the things to ask for," he says wryly.

She may as well have wished for Lucifer to be a good guy.

Giving him a soggy smile, her shoulders sag. "Sorry. I'm a romantic at heart." Her lower lip trembles. "And with Dad gone..."

At the first hiccuping sob, Reign jumps to his feet and wraps his arms around her. Rachel clings to him like an anchor as she tries to keep herself together. "It's okay to miss him," he murmurs.

She pulls in a shuddering sigh. "But much more productive to even the score," she mutters against his shirt.

Reign pulls back, studying her face. "Don't let this eat at you. Believe me, it doesn't end well."

She narrows her eyes, looking at him just as intensely. "So you're saying I should still believe in happily ever afters?"

Reign doesn't miss a beat. "You'll have one. I know it." He squeezes her shoulders. "You deserve to find love."

Quirky, smart, a fighter and a lover, all wrapped up in one. Rachel deserves a hero in her very own love story.

"Oh, sorry." Arielle's startled voice has them both leaping apart.

Reign frowns. Even though they weren't doing anything wrong.

"Hey, Ari," Rachel says brightly. "I was just getting some supplies before we got started on the boxes."

Arielle hasn't moved from the entrance to the kitchen. "Good idea. Gabby just texted to say Shell's boxes will be arriving tomorrow."

"Awesome." Rachel makes her way to the door and Arielle steps out of the way, her movements a little jerky. "Did you want a soda?"

"No, thanks."

Rachel hesitates and Reign doesn't like the tension that's climbing through the room. "Anyway, I got my sugar fix." She glances over her shoulder at Reign. "And dispensed some sage advice, so I'll see you two in the den."

She darts out of the kitchen, leaving Reign and Arielle alone.

"Hey—" starts Arielle.

"I—" says Reign.

They both stop, and although Reign smiles ruefully, Arielle doesn't.

"Going through those boxes is going to be tough for Rachel," he says, pretending to himself that he's saying this for Rachel's benefit. So her two friends can support her through it.

Not because he feels like he just got caught with another

girl. Especially considering Rachel's a friend, and he and Arielle aren't an item.

Arielle nods. "You're a good friend to her. Just like you are with Mac."

Reign doesn't answer, mostly because he's not sure what that means.

Her shoulders rise on a breath. "I was looking for you." The breath whooshes out. "So we could talk."

"I see."

He hasn't let himself think of what this conversation would look like, but if he did, it wouldn't have started like this. There's something different about Arielle. He can't put his finger on it, but it has him on edge. His defenses are ready to roll.

She hunches her shoulders. "Whatever is happening between us," she clears her throat, "whatever has passed, isn't...helpful."

Helpful?

"It's distracting us at a time when we need to be focused. Lives depend on it." She straightens. "I need to be strong."

And he's not someone who makes her stronger.

"I see." Reign knows he's repeating himself like a hollow echo, but he can't think of what else to say. He's far too...angry.

Pissed.

Furious with himself.

Arielle's lashes flutter as her hands clench and unclench. "I'm sorry, Reign. I wish—"

"It's fine," he says, conscious his jaw is barely moving because it's wound so tight. "You're right. You don't need me."

She frowns, her gaze falling away. "I need to show I'm strong."

Once again, he doesn't answer because he's not too sure what she's talking about. He thought Arielle was past needing to prove herself. She seemed to be looking forward to working as a team.

Unless, it's just him she's putting at arm's length.

He looks away, the thought cutting deeper than he expected. He catches a glimpse of his reflection in the window on the other side of the kitchen. His image is sheer and translucent, the gardens beyond sharper and more real. In fact, all that's visible is half his face.

But it's enough.

He takes a step back. "You're right. We need to focus on finding this next Innocent."

Inexplicably, Arielle's frown deepens. Her lashes flicker again, as if a thought just struck her. "Yes. That's what we need to do."

She spins on her heel, her usual grace missing from her tense limbs as she leaves the kitchen.

The moment she's gone, Reign leans against the bench, his head dropping between his shoulders.

Happily ever after, his ass.

He's no knight in shining armor. There is no beauty in his beast. He *is* the big bad wolf.

His fingers slide over the marble countertop as his hands clench into fists so tight his nails dig painfully into his palms.

Why the fuck does he keep forgetting that?

RACHEL

Rachel looks up from where she's sitting cross legged on the floor in the den, one of the boxes in front of her. She'd been trying to work herself up to opening it...

Which means the distraction is more than welcome.

Except, as she watches Arielle flop on a nearby couch, she realizes she hadn't been expecting either her or Reign so quickly. She'd been hoping they'd make out for a good while before joining her. Maybe even got hot and heavy right there on the kitchen counter.

But Arielle doesn't look like she's had some reality-disintegrating lovin'.

She looks...resolute and uncertain all at once. And deep in thought.

"Everything okay?" asks Rachel.

Arielle's gaze snaps to hers, almost like she'd forgotten she's not the only one in the den. "Ah, yeah, sure."

Rachel glances in the direction of the kitchen. "Where's Reign?"

Arielle twitches at the mention of his name. "In the kitchen. He should be here shortly."

"Ari?" Rachel leans forward, not sure what's going on, but certain something's happened. "Are you sure everything's okay?"

"As well as things can be," she hedges.

Rachel's mouth tightens. She's never been one to dance around an issue. "Are you in love with Reign?"

Arielle sits up straight so fast, she almost shoots off the couch. "I beg your pardon?"

"You heard me." One of these two stubborn mules needs to admit their feelings for the other. "Are you in love with Reign?"

"Reign is a great guy," says Arielle, pressing her fingertips to her temples. "I care for him a lot."

"You didn't answer my question," Rachel points out. "Why is it so hard for you to admit your feelings for him, Ari?"

To Rachel's surprise, Arielle flashes a glare in her direction. "I don't need that sort of complication in my life right now."

"Someone who will support you, no matter what?" Rachel

asks incredulously. "A *hot guy* who will support you, no matter what?"

Arielle frowns. "Because I can't do this on my own? Is that what you're saying? That I'm not strong enough?"

Confused, Rachel shakes her head. "That's not what I'm talking about at all. I'm talking about being stronger together than you are alone."

"Then why don't you date him?" snaps Arielle. Before Rachel can assure her that's the last thing she wants, Arielle drops to her knees to pull the nearest box closer. "I don't want to talk about this right now."

"Don't want to talk about what?" asks Reign as he enters the den.

"Whether Pocohontas or Princess Merida from *Brave* has better hair," says Rachel with a bright smile. "A waterfall of black or a riot of red curls. It's a tough call."

Reign shakes his head. "Great to see you're talking about the important stuff."

Rachel studies him, noting the casual way he's holding a can of soda, his other hand tucked into his pocket. Whatever was said in the kitchen doesn't seem to have bothered him.

Except his gaze wanders to Arielle, only to jolt away again. There's the slightest tightening around the edges of his mouth. The appearance of a faint line on his brow. His hand digs a little deeper into his pocket.

Reign looks like a guy who's bracing himself.

As the silence stretches out, Arielle keeps her focus on the box she just opened. She's either ignoring it, or is unaware of it. And the Arielle Rachel knows would definitely be aware of it. She's a Pisces, after all.

Reign comes to sit beside Rachel, which is telling in itself, lifting the lid Rachel couldn't bring herself to do. "So, we're looking for anything that might connect your dad to Shell?"

Rachel suppresses a sigh. It's obvious these two want to pretend nothing's happened or changed. Even though it's obvious it has. "Essentially. Maybe they crossed paths more than just that once."

Arielle reaches into her box and pulls out a sheaf of papers. "Let's see what we can find, then."

Reign does the same, passing Rachel her own handful. She takes it, now the one bracing herself. She can feel her father's presence clinging to these boxes. It's there in the disorganized mess because he always hated bookkeeping, in the dust particles wafting up showing how often he opened them, and in the first receipt she sees—for a Fourth of July barbecue they held in the parking lot for the local kids. Mostly the ones whose families couldn't afford to celebrate Independence Day.

Rachel swallows, not surprised to find the process painful. Her whole body is a tight mass of tears waiting to burst.

Arielle has a ledger book open on her lap. She looks up, her eyes troubled. "I think your dad was in financial trouble, Rachel."

Rachel's about to object when Reign holds up a letter. "This is from some debt collectors. They were planning on visiting the day after your dad died."

She blinks. Her father never mentioned anything like that. Then again, he was very generous with his time and money. And he never worked on expanding the dojo beyond the classes he and Rachel ran.

She nods. "Just put anything like that aside. I'll deal with it later."

When it doesn't hurt so much.

Reign reaches into his box, looking as if he's bringing something up from the bottom. "There's a photo album in this one."

That has Rachel straightening. "There is?" She never knew her dad kept one of those.

Reign passes it to her, and she sees it's one of the older, emerald green ones with gold embossed edges. Her father has probably had this for a long time.

She opens it carefully with trembling fingers, the knowledge she's going to see him again tightening around her chest. The first photo is her father outside the dojo, her six-year old self on his shoulders. They both have their arms out wide, and their grins almost stretch from fingertip to fingertip.

The day they bought the dojo.

Rachel bites her lip so hard it hurts, although it's nothing compared to the loss slicing at her heart. The next page has her father at one of his Fourth of July barbecues, wearing his apron that said *Don't be afraid to take whisks*. A single tear tracks down Rachel's cheek although she barely feels it. She's lost in a world of bittersweet memories.

The next page has her father posing with kids who'd graded through the years—yellow belts, red belts, those who stuck it out and made it to black belt. Her dad had been so proud of each and every one of them. Now she's starting to wonder how many he taught without charging, just so they could experience that feeling of pride.

Conscious that Arielle and Reign haven't spoken, Rachel turns to the next page. She knows they're probably watching and waiting, no doubt seeing how painful this is for her. Except she doesn't look up. The pain isn't optional—her father is gone. But the chance to spend time with what she has, memories, is still here.

She gasps when she sees the three photos tacked onto the stiff sheet. The first has Shell smiling right at the camera. The second has her father and Shell sitting at a cafe, each holding up half a giant choc-chip cookie in salute. The third is a selfie with a third guy Rachel's never seen before.

She looks up to see Arielle and Reign doing exactly as she

thought—watching and waiting. Rachel passes Reign the photo album. "They definitely knew each other."

In each image, the clothes are different. Her father and Shell are a little bit older. They must have stayed in contact from the day Shell and Gabby visited the dojo.

"Wow," Reign says quietly before passing the album to Arielle.

She takes it, the same expression of astonishment lighting across her face. She flicks forward a few pages before returning to the one with the photos that have changed everything. "There aren't any others, but this is irrefutable proof your dad and Shell were friends."

Not just acquaintances. Two Innocents who crossed paths in a single point in time.

Friends.

Reign rubs his brow. "You think they knew they were Innocents?"

Rachel's about to say her father never mentioned anything like that, but he never told her the dojo was in financial strife. Or that he had maintained a friendship with the mother who came past the dojo, even though her daughter never enrolled in classes.

"There's a lot we don't know," she admits.

Arielle taps a finger on the album page. "We need to find out everything we can about Innocents."

"Your mom, Blaise and Nim would've scoured Veritas for any mention of them," Rachel points out.

Reign straightens a little. "The Grail Keepers books may have something. I don't think anyone's had a chance to go through them in detail since they were found in Sinclair Mansion."

It's Rachel's turn to be surprised. Reign actively avoids mentioning anything to do with the Grail Keepers, despite being the only one. Actually, probably *because* he is the only one.

But he has a point. Maybe there's something in those books that could give them some understanding of whether the Innocents are all linked somehow.

She pushes to her feet, a fresh burst of purpose propelling her. "I say we have a look."

Reign does the same, dusting off his jeans as if he's just been digging through dirt rather than documents. Arielle stands, too, but the process is much slower. Almost as if she's carrying far more weight than her slim frame.

"Good idea," she says, although her voice sounds distracted. "I'll be there in a sec. I've just got to get something out of my room."

She's gone before either Rachel or Reign can ask what.

"What was that about?" asks Rachel.

Reign turns away, already heading to the basement. "Whatever it is, I'm sure she has it under control," he says tersely.

Rachel hurries to catch up, glancing over her shoulder to where Arielle's disappeared up the stairs. Arielle isn't acting like someone who has everything figured out. She's distracted. She's pushing people away.

Something is wrong. Very wrong.

But Rachel has no idea what.

CHAPTER 8
ARIELLE

Arielle tucks herself behind the corner of the wall on the second floor as she watches Reign and Rachel disappear down to the basement.

Idiots. They think it's that easy to find an Innocent?

That they can stop this?

The Gates of Hell will fall one by one.

"Stop it," Arielle whispers desperately.

But the obsidian doesn't care. *And then Lucifer will rise.* The sense of victory hissing through her mind is unmistakable.

Along with her pulse rate accelerating as the excitement infects her.

The obsidian is getting stronger. The line between it and her is blurring.

Once Reign and Rachel are gone, Arielle quickly skips down the stairs and out the front door. She doesn't stop until she's past the porch and on the path that leads through the gardens. Bending down, she pries a brick from the border, hefting its weight in her palm.

Please let it be strong enough.

Moving to a nearby stone bench, Arielle glances over her

shoulder as she sits down, relieved to see no one has followed her.

She needs to do this. She has no idea if pushing Reign away was the right choice, but is sure as hell didn't feel like it. Despite that, the words came out, anyway. And the whole time the obsidian had been seething, at times almost screaming.

Of course you're drawn to him. Isn't every girl?

Look at you. Chasing the one who doesn't want to be caught.

Have some pride. Do you want to be a heartbroken fool or a woman others can respect?

Arielle withdraws the obsidian from her pocket, already knowing it's there even though she didn't put it there this morning. She places it on the stone bench where it glints softly in the sunlight.

"I should never have taken you."

There was little choice. Your power is drawn to mine.

She shakes her head, having no idea what it's talking about. She has no power. More like it was drawn to her weakness.

The very reason she picked it up.

Her hand grips the brick so hard the rough edge digs into her palm. "Why me?" There's nothing special about her.

You can feel it, the obsidian says with conviction. And it's right. Even as the prospect makes her nauseous, she can sense the dark energy thrumming through her. It's what helped her defeat Lust. *Together, our power will be unstoppable.*

"What do you want from me?" she whispers, more to herself than the dark voice in her mind.

"Yield to me."

Never.

Arielle's response is swift and forceful. Just as swift and forceful as her swing as she brings the brick down on the stone.

There's a muted *crack*, the power of the blow jolting up her arm. Then silence.

She raises the brick slowly, for some reason scared of what she might find. She wants the obsidian gone.

And yet, a sick part of her yearns for it. For the strength and power it promises.

The brick slips out of her hand when she sees the outcome. Her breath leaves her body in a whoosh, rolling her shoulders in. The obsidian has been crushed into black dust.

Just for good measure, she sweeps the glittering particles onto the ground, then grinds her shoe on any spec she can see.

She's finally, actually free.

Turning, Arielle rushes back to the house. She's been acting odd enough as it is, let alone having to explain an extended absence. And now, she can finally get back to some semblance of normality.

The thought has a smile hovering over her lips as she enters the house. In the kitchen, she pauses. This is where she spoke to Reign.

Had she made the right decision? Is it better they keep things simple between them, no matter how strong these emotions feel?

Especially considering Reign hasn't fought for her once. Never asked for anything more.

Wiping the frown she finds contracting her brow, Arielle descends the stairs to the basement. At least without the obsidian, she can be more confident the decisions she'll make from now on are her own.

Rachel looks up as Arielle appears. "Hey, where did you go?"

"Sorry. Ah, last night's pizza didn't agree with me." Arielle flushes, hoping the hesitation and blush are taken as embarrassment.

"Oh," says Rachel, as if that just explained a whole lot. "Cheese can do that."

Reign looks up, too, although his gaze never quite reaches

her before returning to the book he was focused on. He hunches his shoulders. "We've found out a little bit more on the Innocents."

Arielle walks over to the table, taking the seat across from him. "Oh?"

"There's not much," adds Rachel. "But it does say that they were angels once upon a time who refused to take sides during Lucifer's rebellion."

"So they were sent to Earth as punishment?"

"It appears so," says Reign, still not looking at her. "But there isn't anything to say whether they remember each other."

"It makes sense that they're drawn to one another, though," Rachel points out. "They were kin once."

Arielle nods thoughtfully. "Yeah, it does. And the fact that Shell and your dad were friends reinforces that."

She stares at Reign, wanting him to look at her. Is he hurt after what she said? Angry with her?

Or has she been wrong all along, like she has with so many other things, and it was just a minor rejection he's already recovered from?

The edges of his profile seem to tense as he turns the page and she wonders if he knows she's watching him.

He frowns, leaning closer to the book. "Hey, this sounds familiar."

Rachel pushes up from her chair. "Ooh, more about the Innocents?"

Except Reign shakes his head. He finally looks up at Arielle, but his tight expression tells he's read something that's unsettled him. "It's the Seeker."

Arielle jolts, remembering the object she read about at Veritas. She'd even brought Reign there, hoping to use it to find Cain. But then Nim told them how dangerous it is. That such powerful magic will extract a price. She hasn't thought about it since.

Rachel leans in. "There's a drawing of it." She angles her head. "Doesn't look very impressive."

Arielle finds herself moving around the table, curious to look at it even though she's not sure why. The Seeker is something they should stay away from.

"Well, it's pretty freaking powerful according to what we were told," says Reign, eyes scanning the page. "And not in a good way."

Arielle comes to stand beside Reign as her gaze falls to the drawing they're both studying.

Her breath freezes.

Her heart jolts painfully.

Her eyes wish she could unsee what she's seeing.

A small black stone has been etched into the paper. Its sides angled and uneven, yet smooth and shiny.

Reign reads aloud. "It says here the Seeker can take many forms, but is currently trapped within a piece of obsidian."

The obsidian.

Reflexively, Arielle digs her hand into her pocket. She needs to make sure it's gone. That she's destroyed it.

Shock ricochets through her a second time.

Her fingers brush smooth, angled edges.

The obsidian—the Seeker—is back.

I am immortal. Indestructible.

It's only a matter of time before you yield to me.

"Wow," says Rachel. "Its power is linked to the Grail."

"Not that it says how," says Reign, sounding frustrated.

Arielle lets out a sound that is far too close to a whimper for her liking. It escapes her numb lips, no matter how hard her jaw is clamped. Reign and Rachel's concerned gazes snap to her.

She shoots to her feet. "Ah, I need a minute."

She rushes up the stairs, continuing onto the second floor and not stopping until she's in her room. She slams the door shut and leans against it, although it's all useless.

The danger is in the room with her. It's *within* her.

She has the Seeker. And it's as dark and evil as she suspected it was.

She slowly slides down until she's on the floor, holding her knees. Somehow, she has to find a way to get rid of it.

Before she does exactly what it wants—succumbs.

GABBY

Gabby raps on the apartment door she's standing in front of, her heart tripping at about the same pace.

Colt clears his throat and she looks over her shoulder to give him a warning glare. "Don't you dare ask me again."

His burgundy eyebrows twitch. "I was hoping you'd change your mind." He glances at the door. "Especially now that Dinah's called to say she was able to assemble the ingredients earlier than anticipated."

Actually, Gabby's kind of glad. Less time to do exactly that —change her mind. They need to find out what information was so important it had to be wiped. It just sucks that Dinah's the one to do it. They have no idea whether she's an ally or an enemy.

The door opens before Gabby can answer, revealing Dinah on the other side. She's wearing black, as usual, with Godzilla perched on her shoulder. She steps back, opening the door wider. "Welcome."

Gabby enters, Colt like her shadow beside her. "Why do

witches have to be so dramatic?" he mutters, looking around the lounge room they find themselves in.

The overhead light is dim, leaving the thick candles scattered around to throw their flickering, golden fingers over the room. They dance over skulls on shelves, jars containing indefinable masses, and swathes of midnight cloth covering the windows and much of the furniture.

"It's probably best if you lie down," says Dinah, indicating to a large leather couch in the center of the room. Also black.

Gabby walks over with a confidence she doesn't feel. She's planning on letting this goth chick into her mind. Of all the crazy things she's done...

She sits on the couch, finding it firm and cool, Colt hovering nearby as he's unsure whether he should sit, too. "So, you're certain you can do this?"

Dinah's dark, cool gaze settles on her. "Of course. The strength of the magic will dictate how long it will take, though."

Colt frowns. "How much time do you anticipate this will require?"

"It could take only a few minutes." Dinah shrugs. "Or it might take hours."

Gabby can tell Colt likes the idea of that as much as she does. There's no way she's lying here for hours on end, allowing Dinah to probe her mind.

"You have ten minutes," says Colt, sounding every bit the centuries-old demon he is.

"Then you don't want this information very much, do you?" Dinah snaps back.

Gabby lies back, her head on the arm rest. "We need to know what the symbol I saw means."

If it takes too long, then they can decide what to do then.

"Very well," says Dinah, once more unruffled and calm. She

walks to the coffee table beside the couch where a metal bowl sits with several jars. "I've prepared most of the herbs already."

"What's that?" Colt asks suspiciously.

"A capsule I obtained at the drug store. I've already ground the rosemary and lemon balm, both important for memory. But this table contains Brahmi and ginkgo, clinically proven to enhance memory recall. I thought they would be a useful addition."

Colt shifts a little closer to Gabby. "But you're not sure?"

"They haven't been included in the ancient texts." Dinah arches an eyebrow. "They didn't have clinical trials then. I'm actually relying less on trial and error than my ancestors did."

Freaking great. Dinah's a progressive witch. Gabby isn't sure how she feels about that. Or the mention of the words *trial* and *error* when discussing what they're about to do.

Dinah lights a match and drops it into the bowl. The contents flare, sending manic shadows flitting on the walls and shelves and creepy-looking decor. Smoke quickly follows, curling into the air and tinging it with the pungent scent of herbs.

"Now, just relax," says Dinah, and Gabby wonders if she realizes she's asking for the impossible. "Let what you know of this symbol come to mind."

With a last look at Colt, Gabby closes her eyes. Drawing in a deep breath, then letting it out slowly, she pulls the image of the symbol to the forefront of her mind. A septagram, three crosses within. The one she saw at City Hall.

Dinah starts murmuring, the words too quiet and guttural to be deciphered. Always secretive, Gabby finds herself thinking. Unlike Blaise, who openly spoke her spells.

"Focus," Dinah orders.

Sighing, Gabby pushes away the tension and suspicion and concentrates on the symbol again. If she's going to do this, she needs to give it her all. This is too important to do a half-assed effort.

Consciously unwinding every muscle, she breathes deeply and evenly. The scent of the herbs make her head swim as Dinah's murmuring almost becomes hypnotic. Within her mind, the symbol starts to pulse, glowing like it did the first time she saw it on the tree in the cemetery.

And yet the moment she tries to move closer to it, her consciousness hits an invisible barrier.

"Huh," says Dinah in a low voice. "Angelic magic."

"Angelic?" Gabby hears Colt ask.

"Some of the most powerful I've seen."

Dinah's murmuring intensifies and there's a flash of light beyond Gabby's eyelids, as if she just added something else to the herbs. The symbol flares again and Gabby tries to reach for it.

Once more, she's met by an invisible barrier.

This really is some strong magic.

Letting herself fall deeper under the spell, no matter how risky it is, Gabby focuses harder. She doesn't care who hid her memories, she's going to get them back.

Dinah's chanting increases in volume, and Gabby realizes she's speaking Demoniac. She's tapping into the power of Hell to do this.

"You're using dark magic," Colt gasps. "Stop, stop right this instant!"

But the symbol is almost blazing now, as if the shield around it is thinning. Gabby raises her hand, instinctively finding Colt's arm even though she's deep within her consciousness—proof the threads of her soul are woven with his. "It's okay," she whispers.

It's working.

"I've done as much as I can," Dinah says tightly. "It's up to you, Gabby."

This is her chance. Gabby runs at the barrier, becoming a psychological battering ram. She feels it shatter as she passes through it, traces of the person's magic who did this tingling through her mind.

Suddenly, the memories are assailing her as if they're being fired from a machine gun. Freed from the walls containing them, they pepper her consciousness, one after the other. A sense of familiarity floods Gabby as they fill the void they'd left as if they'd never been gone.

But then she processes what had been hidden from her. And why.

She sits up in a rush. "I remember," she breathes.

Colt quickly sits beside her. "Are you okay?"

"Yes, I'm fine," says Gabby, blinking in disbelief. "I know what the symbol is associated with."

Colt waits, the question burning in his chocolate gaze. Dinah's arms drop by her side and she clasps her hands before her. She would've seen what Gabby did.

"The obsidian," she says, the one word feeling like it stains her tongue. "The symbol is connected with the Seeker."

Colt's eyes widen. "The object you used to power the Spear of Destiny."

She swallows. "The seven pieces I fused together so we could access its power."

"There was little choice," Colt says firmly. "It was the only way."

He's right. Joining the seven pieces of the obsidian was the only way they could be strong enough to trap Michael and stop the apocalyptic war he was planning.

"And I know who wiped it from my memory." She rubs her

temples. It's the last person she would've expected to do it. "It was me."

He recoils in surprise, only for understanding to quickly dawn across his handsome face. "You hid it so well you even shielded it even from yourself."

Knowing how dangerous the obsidian is, she buried it, then tried to remove any trace of its existence, which includes her own memories of it.

"Organizations have been searching for the obsidian for as long as it's existed," says Dinah. She glances at Colt. "Demons want it as badly as angels."

"Exactly why we tried to ensure it couldn't be found," he growls.

She nods in understanding. "The power of the Seeker can turn the tide of battle. The side which holds it has always won."

Gabby grips Colt's hand. "I read the Grail Keeper books before we left them behind in Blaise's basement. The obsidian's power rivals that of the Holy Grail."

Dinah's face turns thoughtful. "That makes sense. One is pure good, the other pure evil." She straightens as something else strikes her. "They must be connected somehow."

Surprise shoots through Gabby as she realizes Dinah is probably right. Her gaze connects with Colt's and she sees the next realization hit.

Maybe the obsidian could be used to find the Grail.

They shoot to their feet simultaneously, making Dinah blink.

"Thank you," Colt says. "You've been immensely helpful."

"You're welcome," says Dinah simply. Gabby waits to see if she's going to say anything else, whether her assurance that she doesn't want payment still holds, but Dinah simply gazes back at them. "Don't you have somewhere you need to be right now?"

Colt's gaze sharpens as he glances around. "This apartment is warded?"

"Of course," Dinah scoffs, sounding a little affronted.

"Excellent. Then my magic cannot be traced."

Gabby tightens her hold on his hand, already knowing what he's going to do next. "Thanks, Dinah, we appre—"

The apartment disappears.

"Ciate your help," Gabby finishes, now standing in the ruins of Mercy Academy.

"Sorry," says Colt. "That place was perturbing me."

Gabby's lips twitch. "Me, too." Colt's old-man's language always makes her smile. "Although Dinah came through for us."

"That, she did." He glances around the soot-covered destruction they're standing amongst. "And it led us here."

To retrieve the obsidian.

Subdued again, Gabby squats down and finds a shard of glass. She murmurs a few words and the ashen piece glitters like new again. "Ready?" she says to Colt.

She suspects when he put the extra protection needing both their blood to open it again, he didn't think they'd be accessing it so soon.

He was probably hoping they'd never have to come here again.

He nods, holding his palm out. She moves in close, slicing across her own first. A thin line of blood appears as she passes it to Colt. Unflinchingly, he does the same and they clasp hands.

Their blended blood trickles down, a crimson globule forming and glittering in the afternoon light. It falls and lands on the stone they're standing on, splaying and splattering over the symbol covered by a layer of ash.

In a blink, they're in the room below ground.

The room is just as she remembers it, although without the

books Colt said he'd removed. The weapons are here, the jars containing ingredients that are best off not seeing the light of day.

Although there's only one thing they're here for.

Turning, Gabby walks to the shelf, blinking a few times. Maybe it's her eyes adjusting to the gloom.

It takes two steps and she's in front of the shelf, but what she's seeing hasn't changed, no matter how much she wishes otherwise.

"Colt," she gasps through her tight throat.

"Son of a donkey," curses Colt.

The obsidian is gone.

CHAPTER 9
REIGN

Reign watches Arielle rush out of the room, her pale, frightened face still branded in his mind.

"So, are you going after her, or am I?" asks Rachel.

His brow slams down. He just got friend-zoned. For the second time.

He's the last person who should be going after her.

But even as he thinks it, he finds himself pushing to his feet. Surely he's not considering going after Arielle. Only a chump would do that.

"You're a good guy, Reign," says Rachel as his foot plants the first step.

No. He's a chump.

But he's also worried about Arielle. There was no color in her face as she'd rushed out of the basement. And the whimper she made before she left...it had a powerful surge of protectiveness rushing through him.

Yep. He's a chump.

He drags himself up to the first floor and knocks on her door. There's no answer, although there's a shuffle on the other side, telling him Arielle's in there. He knocks again.

There's a pause. "Yes?"

Unsure of what he's going to find, Reign opens the door cautiously. He finds Arielle sitting on her bed, clutching a pillow to her stomach.

"Hey," he says, clearing his throat when it comes out huskier than intended. "We just wanted to make sure you're okay."

Arielle smiles, and he wonders if she realizes how wobbly the motion is. "Sure. It's just the pizza..." She shrugs. "Maybe it was the vegetarian curry I had the night before."

Reign enters the bedroom. "This wouldn't have happened with a good lamb korma."

Her smile gains a little more substance. "The sheep will thank me."

He stops a few feet in, hating the awkwardness tangling through his muscles. "I thought it might have been reading about the Seeker."

"What?" Arielle squeaks, alarmed eyes shooting to his.

"Well, you were looking for it a few weeks ago. I thought you were freaking out about what could've happened if you actually found it."

"Oh, yes. That makes sense." Her shoulders drop as if she's relieved.

Concerned, Reign covers the remaining steps to the bed. He sits down across from Arielle.

Is she feeling guilty that she was looking for it? He jolts. Is she *still* looking for it?

"The Seeker is dangerous," he says. "Downright freaking evil."

Arielle pales, making him even more concerned. "I know."

"That bastard piece of black rock needs to stay hidden in whatever bowel it's in, Arielle. We can do this without inviting that sort of darkness into our lives."

He doesn't know much about the Seeker apart from what Nim told them and they just read, but he can feel the truth in his words. The obsidian could destroy everything they're working toward.

Blue fire flashes in Arielle's eyes. "I wouldn't—I don't—want it," she says in a harsh whisper.

Letting out a breath, he nods. That's more like the Arielle he knows. Fierce. Passionate. Fighting for what's right.

"Good. We're making progress as it is."

She nods, pulling the pillow in tighter. "The poor Innocent."

He blinks, not sure what to make of that. He realizes he's been thinking that a lot lately in response to things Arielle's said. He leans forward a little. "Are you sure you're okay?"

"Like I said, something I've eaten hasn't agreed with me, okay?" She angles back a little, frowning.

Her need to put more space between them is like a knife slicing through his chest. Reign stands, wondering why the hell he sat down in the first place.

He's not just a chump. He's a stupid one.

"Well...ah, keep up the fluids."

To his relief, Rachel appears in the doorway. She holds up a glass of water. "I brought you something to drink. I'm lactose intolerant, so I know hydration is important at times like this."

Arielle smiles wanly. "Thanks."

Rachel places it on the bedside table. "I couldn't find anything else in the books," she says, not giving silence a chance to weave its awkwardness through the room. "Just a lot of stuff about the Grail, really."

And the fact it's never been seen, let alone found.

"I figured we're better off going through the boxes," she adds.

"Great." Reign walks to the doorway, suddenly keen to be out of the room. "The boxes it is."

"But first, I'm going to need more than just a liquid sugar fix."

Reign stops at the door. "I've had a look in the pantry. I don't like your chances."

"Me, too," grimaces Rachel. "Blaise has a thing for canned beans and dried herbs."

His mouth twists. "So healthy."

"Exactly. Who takes that into consideration when stocking their pantry?" She pulls her car keys out of her pocket. "That's why we're going to the store."

"I'm going to stay here," says Arielle. Impossibly, she tucks the pillow in closer. "Until I feel better."

Rachel pouts. "Are you sure? Three people means three push carts to fill up."

Reign waits, his breath held. Being around Arielle is a roller-coaster of confusion and wishing. He could use a break.

"I'm sure," says Arielle, shooing Rachel away with her hands. "Grab me something for when I feel better."

"Sure will," assures Rachel with a smile. She sweeps past Reign. "Let's go get some lactose-free sugar-laden goodness."

Hunching his shoulders, Reign follows her without looking over his shoulder at Arielle. He shouldn't have come up here. He should've let Rachel do it.

Arielle doesn't want him around.

Yep. Fucking chump.

THE SUPERMARKET PARKING lot is full, meaning they have to circle a few times before Rachel screeches into a space, then brakes so hard Reign thinks he has whiplash.

He climbs out, enjoying the feeling of solid ground beneath his shoes. Maybe he should walk back to the farmhouse. Not only is he more likely to get there alive, he'll have a chance to work off some of the edginess that's taken residence in his muscles.

Rachel comes around to join him. "Do you get the sense that something's up with Ari?"

He jams his hands into his pockets. "She has an upset stomach."

And a guy she has to keep at arm's length because he won't take a hint.

She purses her lips in thought. "I think it may be more than that. She's not acting like herself."

"She's probably just dealing with everything that's happened." Reign strides toward the supermarket, ending the conversation and giving Rachel little chance but try to keep up.

He hunches his shoulders when he sees a cop car parked a few bays away. Police always assume people like him are up to no good.

In all fairness, in the past he usually wasn't.

Outside the entrance, there are no push carts in the bay so Rachel grabs a basket and loops it over her arm, then grabs one and passes it to Reign. "There's no way this is a one-basket shop."

"Surely there are not that many lactose free candies in existence."

Rachel rolls her eyes. "Rookie."

She walks straight past the produce, scanning the aisles for the candy section. She finds it and is about to head down when a large man wearing a trenchcoat comes barreling out with a loaded cart.

She leaps back. "Sorry," she says with a polite smile, even though she wasn't at fault.

The man scowls at her. "Get out of my way."

He hurries past, glaring at Reign as though he's thinking of jumping him.

"Rude," mutters Rachel.

Reign shrugs, having dealt with bigger and less savory people. "Come on. Let's get this truckload of junk food and get back."

But as they turn into the aisle, they find every shelf is empty. Bare. Looking as if they wouldn't know what to do if a packet of marshmallows were to sit on them.

"They've even taken the licorice?" Rachel asks, astounded.

Reign takes a few steps further in. "What's going on?"

"Some sort of truck driver's strike?" offers Rachel. "A supply issue?"

But for *everything* to be sold out?

A shout and the sounds of a scuffle cuts off anything Reign was about to say. They spin around and run to the front of the supermarket. There, the man who shoved past them is shouting at people to get out of the way as he breaks into a run. People scatter, screaming when he doesn't bother to wait.

He plows through the checkouts and out the sliding doors, which open just in time. A packet of biscuits flies off the top of the mountain of food in his cart, but he keeps going.

"Not again!" shouts the teller.

Reign breaks into a run, not surprised to find Rachel beside him. They chase the man outside, finding him already part way across the parking lot.

"Stop!" shouts Reign.

The man glances over his shoulder. The sight of Reign and Arielle has him hunching down and running faster. "Get your own," he shouts.

He rounds a car, darting down the next row. Reign pushes himself to run faster, taking the corner only a few seconds later.

It means he sees the woman step from between a truck and

a van, her gun already raised. Reign reacts instantly. He grabs Rachel and pulls her behind a car, drawing her down so they're both squatting.

"She has a gun!" Rachel whispers in shock.

"Give me the cart!" the woman screams.

"Fuck off, bitch," the man hollers back.

Reign peeks over the bonnet. His eyes widen as Rachel gasps beside him.

The man has a sawn-off rifle pointing at the woman. He's standing in front of the cart as if he intends on protecting it with his life.

When Reign hears the sound of running, he spins around to warn whoever's approaching to stay back, but he sees it's the two cops they passed when they went in.

"Police!" shouts the man. "Put your weapons down!"

The man in the trenchcoat, the one that would've been hiding his shotgun, looks over his shoulder. "This bitch is trying to steal my groceries."

The groceries he stole.

"It's people like you, keeping everything to yourself, that's causing the problem," snarls the woman.

The man lifts the shotgun. "Get the fuck out of my way."

"No," breathes Rachel.

Before she's finished the word, the woman fires the revolver. The man jolts as the bullet slams into his stomach. As he staggers backward, he pulls the trigger on his shotgun.

The woman's chest explodes with red and she collapses instantly.

"Shit!" shouts the female police officer. "Not again!"

Not again. That's exactly what the teller said. How could something like this be happening *again*?

"What the actual..." breathes Rachel.

Reign grips her arm. "Come on. We need to get out of here."

She nods mutely, understanding.

There's nothing else they can do here.

And they can't be witnesses to a crime that they know far too much about, despite never knowing the victims.

Silently, they climb back into her car. For the first time, Rachel drives almost sensibly as they exit the parking lot, eyes averted from the crowd accumulating around the crime scene.

Two people just died as they tried to steal food.

As they drive away, they see one policeman loading the contents of the cart into the boot of their patrol car, the other standing guard with her hand on her pistol.

Gluttony is wreaking her havoc.

DINAH

Dinah rubs Godzilla along the ridge between her eyes, then down the scales of her rounded spine as she clings to the cloth of her top. "We did good today," she murmurs.

Gabrielle and Colt are starting to trust her, she could sense it. Dinah adjusts herself where she's laying on the couch, enjoying the weight of the lizard on her chest. It makes the warm feeling of triumph ballooning in there all the more noticeable for some reason. Gabby and Colt are still unsure, which is to be expected, but she's making progress with them.

Her finger pauses its rhythmic stroking and both of Godzilla's eyes twitch around to focus on her. "Sorry," she says with a small smile, resuming. "It's just that they're not the ones I need to trust me."

Arielle Hartely.

She's the key to it all. Dinah can feel it deep in her witch marrow. She's the one Dinah needs to befriend.

And although helping Gabby and Colt brings her one step closer to her goal, it's a slow one. And an indirect one.

There's no guarantee it'll achieve what she's seeking to.

Her cell rings and she picks it up off the coffee table beside her, her heart jolting when she sees who's calling.

"Yes?" she asks tersely.

"I have what you ordered," says the muffled, male voice.

Dinah sits up, cradling Godzilla so she doesn't slip off. She hadn't expected them to find it so quickly.

"I'll meet you," she states, then hangs up.

Dinah lays back down, allowing herself a rare smile. It feels as alien as it does good.

It's only a matter of time before she's inside Arielle's circle of trusted friends.

CHAPTER 10

ARIELLE

Arielle glances over her shoulder as she slips through the doors of Veritas Library. Although she'd watched Reign and Rachel drive away and waited a full ten minutes before leaving the farmhouse herself, she's still worried someone has followed her.

Enemies are everywhere.

They will try to stop you.

You cannot let them get in the way.

Realizing the paranoia is a product of the obsidian, Arielle grits her teeth. The Seeker is messing with her emotions as much as it's messing with her thoughts.

She needs to find out what she can about the evil that resides in her. She needs to find out how she can be free of it.

Which is why she's creeping into Veritas.

Surely there's some information somewhere in the countless books within these walls.

Although she has to get past Nim, first.

The library is silent and still, as if it's holding its breath. A quick scan reveals Nim isn't at the desk or among the nearest shelves. Arielle tiptoes further in, her heart thudding.

If she asks too many questions, kill her.

Horror roots Arielle to the spot. The need for blood and chaos is thrumming through her veins, no matter how much she tries to deny it. She shakes her head vehemently, her hands clenched.

"Never."

The low chuckle in her mind sends shivers skittering over her skin. *You will yield to me. It's only a matter of time.*

And then no one will be safe.

Clamping her hand over her mouth, Arielle rushes to the shelf she brought Reign to when showing him what she'd found on a magical object that could help find Cain.

Little did she know it was the Seeker.

Or that she'd find it, even after deciding it was far too dangerous.

She kneels down and pulls the book out, glancing around hurriedly. Veritas is still quiet and still, as if she's the only one here. Maybe Nim's out somewhere, running an errand.

That will certainly be lucky for her.

Arielle ignores the ominous threat, opening the tome, and quickly flitting to the page she first saw. She runs her finger down the handwritten words, noting that it's trembling. But all she reads is what she already knew. There's an object powerful enough to locate demons.

I can do far more than that, scoffs the obsidian.

Nim's words from that day quickly follow. *Magic always has a price. Something it wants in return.*

Yes, the obsidian hisses. *Yield to me and untold power is yours.*

Arielle's stomach clenches as nausea shoots up her throat. Telling Reign and Rachel she was unwell is almost true. She's infected with evil.

She flips the page, scanning the next one, then the next. But all she finds is what they've already learned in the Grail Keeper books. The obsidian is powerful. Dangerous. And somehow connected to the Grail.

Her spine sags with frustration. She has to fix this. Make it right.

Before someone gets hurt...by her own hands.

She continues to skim until she reaches the end of the book. "No," she moans.

A quick glance around her confirms she's surrounded by books. More than she'll be able to count in her lifetime. There could be more information on the obsidian somewhere among those endless pages.

Or there could be nothing.

You're starting to understand the inevitability of your fate.

The triumph laced through the obsidian's words have Arielle's back straightening.

"No. I don't."

She opens the book one more time, just to make sure her anxious mind didn't miss anything. She's going to fight the obsidian with everything she has.

She reads a little slower this time, absorbing every word. She thinks an hour passes, maybe more, but it's certainly enough time to confirm there's no new information to be gleaned.

The obsidian is as mysterious as it is dangerous.

Refusing to feel dejected, Arielle lifts the book to close it. She stops when she sees a sliver of paper jutting just above the bound pages. Frowning, she slides her finger over it, feeling the slight bump.

Opening the book once more, she flips through until she finds it, discovering a small note tucked close to the spine almost at the end. Using her nail, she carefully pries it out.

And gasps as she recognizes the writing.

"Mom?" she asks in surprise.

Why would her mother have left something in this book?

Little known about the Seeker. Maybe more to be found in Ryder's books?

Arielle reads the note several times, trying to process it. Her mother knows of the Seeker. Was possibly looking for it herself.

And she thinks some guy called Ryder might have more information about it.

Tucking the note in her pocket, she quickly slips the book back into place on the shelf. Running to the door, she exits Veritas library, heart thudding again, but this time with something far preferable to fear.

Hope.

She has a lead.

Maybe if she finds this Ryder guy, she'll learn how to free herself of the obsidian.

GABBY

"How the hell can it be gone?" Gabby almost shouts.

She scans the shelf. Runs her hand over it just in case the magical bastard has turned invisible. Then she scours every shelf in the small room, Colt doing the same.

Neither of them find it.

"It's most certainly gone," Colt says heavily.

Gabby shakes her head. "But how?" It doesn't make sense. She did everything she could to ensure it would remain hidden here.

"I've only been here once," says Colt, frowning. "That time

with Arielle and Rachel when we dipped the dagger in cupid's ashes."

"It couldn't have been them. I rendered it invisible to anyone not supernatural."

"Yes, I remember," rumbles Colt, frowning fiercely. "Arielle and Rachel wouldn't have seen it."

Not when they're human.

"So it must've been someone—something—else." Gabby starts to pace, chafing at the size of the room. "Maybe an angel. Or a demon."

"Many a supernatural would want to get their hands on the obsidian."

Gabby's fingers spear through her curls. "And I put a cloaking spell on it. There's no location spell that will find it."

They won't see the obsidian until they're standing right in front of it.

"This is bad, Colt. Real bad."

She can't help but feel a sense of responsibility. She's the one who united the seven pieces of the obsidian. She thought this dungeon would be enough to keep it hidden.

He engulfs her in a hug, tucking her head into his shoulder. "This is not your fault, Gabby," he says fiercely, knowing exactly what she's thinking. "If you didn't merge the obsidian, there would be no world to fight for right now."

Michael would be sitting in the Throne of Heaven. She sags into him, knowing he's right, but still feeling awful.

There's a flash of space and time and she finds herself once more within the ruins of Mercy Academy.

"This is what Earth would look like," Colt says softly.

A world of ash and devastation.

Gabby sighs as she squeezes his hand, thanking him for the reminder.

But as they return to his car, neither of them speak. They both walk a little heavier.

The obsidian is out there, somewhere.

Intending to wreak the very same destruction they thought the world was finally safe from.

CHAPTER 11
REIGN

Reign's head snaps around the moment Rachel enters the den, telling him he was waiting for her to return from upstairs more tensely than he would've liked. "Well?"

"She's asleep," Rachel says in a hushed voice, even though there's no way Arielle could hear them from here. "All tucked up under the blankets."

He nods, unsure why those words don't temper the uneasiness. Arielle resting in bed is a good thing.

Maybe it's the shooting they witnessed at the supermarket, but he definitely feels unsettled. In the past, it's about now he'd start prowling, looking for something to take the edge off. Alcohol. Weed. A cruise down the wrong side of the law to kick some adrenaline through the system.

But he can't, which means he has to put up with it.

And that sucks.

Rachel sits down beside him on the leather couch, eyeing the three boxes stacked on the coffee table. "This is Shell's stuff?"

"Some of it," he says. "Gabby said Shell kept *everything*. There's fifteen more to be delivered."

"Yowsers." She lifts the lid off one of the boxes. "And with no sugar fix."

Reign pulls out a packet of kale chips he'd tucked behind him. "It's the best I could find."

She pulls a face. "Yay." She looks inside the box, her eyebrows hiking up. "I think this one is full of cookbooks."

Reign opens the one beside it. "This one is full of sheets of wrapping paper." He holds up a blue sheet with yellow ducks on it.

Rachel grabs the packet of kale chips. "We're going to need these."

Reign moves to the last box, wondering what they'll find. Knitting patterns? "Huh," he says as he registers what he's looking at. He reaches in and pulls one out.

Photo albums.

"Jackpot," says Rachel excitedly. She grabs the one he's holding and sits back down. Opening it, her eyebrows shoot up into her bangs. "Seems Shell was into scrapbooking."

He glances over, seeing a couple of photos of what looks like Shell and Sierra when they were young. Balloon stickers and bright pieces of ribbon have been pasted around them. Two words have been spelled out in gold lettering in the center —*friends forever*.

Taking the next photo album out, he sits beside Rachel, reflecting that Shell was well loved. Maybe Arielle's withdrawal has just as much to do with her grief as it does the vegetable curry.

He opens the album, breath catching when two blonde girls smile up at him from a large photo. One has a riot of curls, Gabby, the other has two cute pigtails. Arielle. They have their arms around each other, their smiles almost as bright as the sun behind them.

Slowly, almost as if it aches, he turns to the next page. Arielle and Gabby are a little older in this one. Still smiling as they sit at a table, a brightly iced, if a little lopsided, cake sits in front of them.

This is the life he could've been part of.

If Sierra hadn't given him up.

Clenching his teeth, he turns to the next page. Sierra's in this photo, as is Shell, and they're all packed into a car, pulling silly faces at the camera. No doubt off on some family outing.

They're happy. Having fun. Both of those were only sporadic moments in his childhood. And yet, he's no longer angry with Sierra. With a bit of time and distance, he can see the pain that was weaving through her as she told the story.

His fractured, failure of an upbringing is never what she would have wanted.

She wanted that outcome as much as he did.

In fact, if there's anyone at fault, it's Mikki. She's the one who tossed him to the welfare system the moment David died. Discovering the anger hasn't diminished, just diverted, Reign turns the page. Like most of the injustices in his life, there's nothing he can do about this one.

The rage and resentment will just have to fester. There are bigger things to focus on right now.

"Whoa," says Rachel beside him. "Scored."

Glad to push the photo album away, Reign leans over. "What?"

She brings it closer to him. "Check this out."

The same photo of Shell and Paul sitting at the cafe is in Shell's scrapbook, each holding half of a giant choc-chip cookie. The caption underneath reads: *In the cookie of life, friends are the chocolate chips.*

Rachel turns the page, her hand stilling. This time Shell is with a red-haired woman, arms around each other as they smile at the camera. This caption says: *True friends are never apart, maybe in distance, but never in heart.* Reign realizes there's something familiar about the woman. Is it the angle of her smile? Has he seen her before?

It's Rachel's suspended animation that has him realizing. "That's your mom."

She nods, swallowing hard. "Yeah."

"I thought she was dead."

"She could be. I have no idea." She shrugs, blinking rapidly. "She left when I was six and we never heard from her again."

"I'm sorry," says Reign, knowing how deep the pain of abandonment can go.

She shrugs again. "Whatever." She turns the page almost dismissively, then pauses again. On the next page is another photo of Shell and Paul. With a third man. "I've seen him before," she murmurs, frowning.

Leaning over, she grabs her dad's photo album, opening it to the images that first had them realizing Paul and Shell knew each other. Reign sees what had her going back to it. Paul is at what looks to be a soup kitchen. With the same guy Shell and Paul are with in Shell's album.

"I think we're looking at the next Innocent," Rachel breathes.

Could their theory be right? Could the Innocents all be connected somehow?

Reign blinks. "We need to find out who he is."

"Yes, we do." Grabbing her cell, Rachel zooms in and snaps a photo of the guy. She presses a few buttons, her brow puckered in focus. "Time to do a little research."

Reaching for her laptop beside her, she flips it open and

starts tapping. "I've sent the photo to myself. Let's see if our mystery guy is on the net somewhere."

Reign holds his breath as he watches Rachel type, scroll, then type some more. The screen fills with images, but none of them are similar enough to the guy from the photo.

"Of course it's not going to be that easy," sighs Rachel. "Or legal."

To his surprise, Rachel heads over to the DMV's web browser. "You're going to hack the Department of Motor Vehicles?"

She shrugs. "I'm willing to bet our dude has a driver's license."

Reign watches in fascination as Rachel sets about typing, tapping, and scrolling all over again. Her brow puckers and her gaze is laser focused on the screen. Periodically she mutters something like, "Challenge accepted," or "Firewall, my ass." At one stage, she almost smiles with relish. "Nice cryptographic algorithm."

As he watches, Reign marvels at what he could do if he had Rachel's talent. Namely, make his criminal record disappear. He suspects Cain has added a few extra misdemeanors on there, just for the heck of it. The next time Reign's pulled over by the cops, their computers are going to light up like the Fourth of July.

Although, he'd never ask Rachel to do that for him. What she's doing in the name of finding the next Innocent is risky enough.

"Boom," says Rachel triumphantly as she throws her hands in hair.

Shaking himself from his thoughts, Reign finds an image on the screen. The photo of the guy they're looking for.

"Jeremy Williams," she reads aloud. "A fellow resident of Mercy City."

Reign scans the address. "Only a few suburbs over, in fact."

Rachel grins. "We have an Innocent to save."

He shoots to his feet, the possibility that they'll get there in time for once making his heart do a little dance. "We need to get Ari up. She'll want to come with us."

Nodding, Rachel quickly taps a few buttons. She puts her laptop aside and skips to the staircase. "Well? Are you coming?"

Reign quickly overtakes her, taking the stairs two at a time. This is the news Arielle needs to help her feel better. They have the chance to stop another Innocent being killed. Jeremy's loved ones won't have to go through the pain she and Rachel are.

They reach her door and Reign knocks, trying to keep it soft. He and Rachel may be excited, but Arielle doesn't realize they've just had a massive breakthrough. When there's no answer, he knocks a little harder.

Still no response.

Rachel chews her lip. "Maybe she's a deep sleeper?"

Reign opens the door, peeking around it. The curtains are pulled closed, leaving the room dark, and Arielle's little more than a lump under the blankets. He hesitates. He's not terribly keen on going in and getting in her personal space again.

Rachel pushes past him. "Ari? We have news!"

The lump doesn't move.

Rachel walks past the bed and throws open the curtain. "Wakey wakey, who wants some gravy?"

Reign shakes his head. "Gravy?"

Rachel shrugs. "It kinda rhymes and, in all honesty, it would get me up in a hurry."

But Arielle still hasn't moved, not even to hunker further under the blankets. Or point out she's vegetarian.

Reign and Rachel exchange a glance and the uneasiness from earlier trickles down his spine. She quickly walks to the bed and gently grabs the top of the lump, right where Arielle's shoulder should be.

The blanket collapses as if there's nothing there.

With a quick jerk, Rachel yanks back the covers, revealing there's definitely something underneath.

A pillow.

Fuck. Arielle's run off.

RACHEL

"What the flock?" Rachel exclaims. "She tricked us!"

Reign pulls his cell out of his pocket, his face tight with worry. Or maybe that's anger. Probably both. He holds it to his ear before cursing. "It went straight to her message bank."

He tries again, but Rachel already knows Ari won't be answering. She went to some effort to hide the fact she left. Which means Arielle didn't want them to know where she was going.

Arielle's keeping secrets.

"Still not answering," growls Reign. "She could be anywhere!"

And Gluttony is out there, sparking shootings in parking lots.

Rachel withdraws her own cell from her pocket. "Let's have a look, shall we?"

"You can track her?" Reign asks incredulously.

She feels her skin flush and she hopes it's not noticeable. The need to know where the people she cares about started when her mom left her. Losing her father has only intensified it. "I only stalk people I care about, okay?"

Reign angles his head as he holds up his phone. "Are you tracking me?"

Rachel considers lying for a split second, but quickly changes her mind. She prides herself on her honesty. So she decides to own it. "Sure am!"

To her astonishment, Reign grins. "For the most part, no one's given a crap where I was." He winks at her, and she doubts he has any idea what a heart-fluttering gesture it is. "It's nice to know someone cares."

Flushing a little deeper, she rolls her eyes. "Lots of people care about you."

His grin dims. "Yeah, I know."

Reign puts his phone back in his pocket, seeming to concentrate on the simple task with great focus. Rachel realizes Arielle must have said something to Reign. Something that has him believing she doesn't care as much as he'd like her to.

Except Arielle cares. A lot. Rachel knows she does.

Then why isn't she showing it?

"So," he says, sounding determined. "Where are we stalking to?"

Knowing there's no way to resolve the Reign-Arielle conundrum right now, Rachel glances at her screen. She taps a few times, then pulls the phone closer as she registers where the dot is. "She's at Veritas."

Reign blanches. "If this has to do with the obsidian..."

Surely not... But Rachel doesn't say it out loud. Arielle's been acting strangely lately, and although she can be impulsive, disappearing without telling them where she's going is definitely outside the norm.

Wordlessly, they leave the farmhouse and climb into her car. Reign is so preoccupied on the way there, he doesn't even make a comment about her driving. And Rachel drives extra fast, too. She always drives faster when she's worried. Or angry. Or happy.

But right now, she's worried. Something's happened to Arielle. She can feel it.

They arrive at Veritas Library and she's not surprised to see Reign rush out before the car's engine has stopped. They run in, for once, the expansive peace of the place having little effect on Rachel.

She'll breathe again when she knows Arielle's safe.

"Arielle?" Reign calls out, walking further in. "Arielle."

But there's no answer.

Looking at her phone, Rachel curses. "She's not here anymore." It didn't occur to her that they were going on a chase. She zooms in to the new location on the map, double checking what she's seeing is right. "She's at some apartment block a few miles from here."

They exchange a glance, the same question in both their gazes.

What the Walt is she doing there?

"Come on," she says. "We can't afford to miss her again."

"Hang on a sec." Reign spins on his heel and strides toward a nearby stack of shelves.

He squats down, running his fingers over the spines of the leatherbound books stacked along it. He pauses, hitting one that's about an inch further out than the others.

Rachel joins him, sensing this is significant. "Reign?"

He opens the books, his shoulders sagging when he reaches a particular page. He holds it up to show her. "This is the book Arielle showed me when she first learned about the Seeker."

"Oh." A shiver of worry dances down her spine. "But maybe—"

Reign shakes his head. "Nim is obsessive about keeping the books all pretty and aligned." He indicates to the shelves around them and she sees he's right. Every spine sits perfectly next to each other, creating a corrugated wall of leather.

But the book Reign's holding wasn't.

Crapsticks. Arielle is interested in the Seeker.

He replaces the book, ensuring it's lined up with the others, and they exit.

Outside, Reign stops. "I'm just going to tell Gabby and Colt where we're going."

"Good thinking."

Someone else needs to know what's going on.

But a moment later, Reign lets out a frustrated breath. "They're not answering either." He jams his cell in his pocket. "Come on, we can't wait."

As they walk to the car, Rachel's glad they're not wasting any time. Gluttony or no Gluttony, they need to find Arielle. And soon.

It's the only way to get rid of the dread coiling through her gut like a restless serpent.

CHAPTER 12
ARIELLE

There are about half a dozen Ryders living in Mercy City.

And as Arielle pulls up outside a soaring apartment block, she's determined to speak to every one of them.

Whatever it takes to be free of the evil residing within her.

She checks the address she scribbled down in her hasty research, confirming she's in the right place. The tall building with its modern architecture is exactly what she expected from the more upmarket area of the city.

It's what's inside that's unknown.

You're wasting time. You can't stop the inevitable.

The hiss in her mind has Arielle jumping out and resolutely walking to the entrance. In the foyer she finds that Ryder Grant lives on the fifth floor. A quick ride up the lift and she's standing outside his door.

Pulling in a steadying breath, she hopes to heck she'll think of what to say if someone opens the door.

Arielle knocks and waits. To her relief, she hears shuffling movements on the other side. The door opens a moment later, revealing an elderly man with rounded glasses. "Yes?" he snaps.

Smiling despite the gruff reception, Arielle wonders if maybe she's come across the cranky, mage type. Those shrewd, distrustful eyes might be concealing a deep understanding of the supernatural. "Hello, my name's Arielle Hartley. I'm looking for a Ryder my mother used to know."

The man's hand tightens around the doorknob. "How did you find me?"

"An internet search of the name," she says warmly. "Luckily there aren't many Ryders in Mercy City."

"That's because it's a stupid name," he snaps. "My mother was high on petrol fumes when she gave me that name."

"Oh," says Arielle. She dials up her smile even brighter. "I really like it."

"Of course you do. You ever sniffed petrol yourself?"

She blinks. "Ah, no." This man isn't just cranky. He's kind of rude. "Well, my mother knew a Ryder. Her name's Sierra. Did you ever know a Sierra?"

Arielle holds her breath, trying not to get her hopes up. She'll put up with rude if it means getting the obsidian out.

"Sierra," says the man, as if he's testing the name. "Sounds as stupid as my name. Does she know an Ajax? Maybe a Wolfe?"

"So you don't know her?" Arielle tries to keep the disappointment out of her voice, but she fails miserably.

"Of course I don't know a Sierra," snaps Ryder. "I have standards."

Without waiting for a response, he slams the door shut.

Arielle blinks, staring at the smooth, cream surface. It's fine, she tells herself. There are more Ryders on the list.

You should kill him, seethes the obsidian. *You should not be disrespected like that.*

Her hand twitches, unwanted fury sparking along her fingertips, and she quickly turns away and dashes to the lift.

She presses the button over and over, trying to channel the anger that's progressively building within her.

"Come on, come on," she mutters.

Turn back.

End him.

He will never talk to anyone like that again.

Arielle focuses on digging her feet into the thick carpet, as if she's growing roots. The obsidian will not dictate her actions.

It can't.

A soft *ding* punctures the air and the lift doors open. Relieved, she enters, repeatedly pressing the button to close the doors until they're shut. Once she's cocooned in stainless steel, she allows her muscles to unlock, leaning against the cool metal wall behind her. She almost expects it to sizzle, her skin feels so hot.

The lift doors open as she reaches the ground floor, and Arielle hurries out. The more distance between her and that man, the better. Outside, sunlight pierces her eyes, making her squint. She hesitates, wondering what she should do now.

Track down the other Ryders on her list?

Or go back to the farmhouse? Maybe it's time to admit she needs help... She withdraws her cell phone, staring at the screen in thought.

Yes, go back. Tell them everything.

Because you're weak. You know you can't fight me alone.

Pressing her fingers to her temples so hard it hurts, Arielle shakes her head. "Shut up."

They'll learn you stole the obsidian. That you were drawn to my dark power.

What will Rachel think of you then?

What will Reign...

Arielle almost doubles over. What would it do to her to have Reign look at her in disappointment? Disdain?

TAMAR SLOAN

Disgust, adds the obsidian. *He would hate you.*

"No," she moans.

"Arielle?" says a voice beside her. "Are you okay?"

She looks up, not recognizing the voice straight away, but conscious of the fission of alarm that just streaked down her spine.

"Dumah," she breathes in shock.

The angel smiles at her from his dark face, his muscled chest shirtless. His wings are nowhere to be seen. "Hello." He cocks his head, staring at her cooly. "I'd like to have a word."

"No," she says, already spinning on her heel and about to break into a run.

But Dumah's hand shoots out, gripping her arm painfully. "I thought you might not be agreeable."

She tries to yank her arm away, only to find his grip is like steel. "Let go of me," she snarls, surprised to find her voice lower than she expected.

He will die for this, roars the obsidian.

Dumah smiles. "Oh, the human is angry," he sneers. "I'd be happy to release you...once you answer some questions for me."

"Please," begs Arielle, knowing she's sounding desperate, but not caring. What if she can't contain the obsidian's fury? "Let me go."

Dumah yanks her closer. "Tell me where Mac is."

Arielle's eyes widen as his words register. Even if she knew where Mac was, she wouldn't tell him. Meaning she can't give Dumah what he wants.

She needs to get away before something really bad happens.

Twisting, she throws a punch at Dumah's jaw. The unexpected move almost makes contact, except his head snaps left at the last moment. Arielle's fist skims past his jaw, puncturing the air behind.

Yes. Hurt him.

"Violent humans," Dumah spits, grabbing her other arm and yanking her against him.

No one can contain us.

Ignoring the obsidian, Arielle struggles to be free. She doesn't want to hurt Dumah. She doesn't need to prove anything. She just wants to get away. She whips her knee up, trying to find soft flesh, but Dumah spins her around so her back is to his front.

Undaunted, Arielle snaps her head back, colliding with his jaw. He grunts as he discovers she's stronger than he expected, his arms tightening like clamps.

Arielle twists and fights, desperate to get away. "Help—"

Her stomach bottoms out as they shoot into the air, two alabaster wings moving in her peripheral vision.

"No," she cries. There's no way to know where Dumah could take her.

Wind rushes at her face as they power higher and higher, stealing her denial and instantly dissolving her scream. No one can hear her now.

There will be no way to find her.

Wait. Revenge will be ours.

Although she has no intention of listening to the obsidian, Arielle has no choice but cling to Dumah's arms until she learns where he's taking her.

It's only a few seconds later that she has her answer as they land on the roof of the high-rise building, the ground several floors below. Arielle's feet have just touched cement when she's roughly turned and shoved against a wall. Her hands are yanked behind her back and bound around a pipe of some sort.

Dumah steps back, dark eyes glinting with satisfaction. "Now, we can talk."

Arielle jerks her hands. Dumah wasn't carrying rope, so

there's no way to know what has her tied, but it's tight. And strong.

Dumah's wings expand, blocking out the sun and leaving Arielle in shade as he towers over her. "Tell me. Where is the demon Mackenzie?"

Yield to me.

When we combine our powers, no binds will contain us.

"No," snaps Arielle, answering both beings simultaneously. "Never."

Dumah's black gaze flares. "I have my orders. Find Mac. Kill her." He shoves his face close. "I'd suggest you save yourself the pain and just tell me now."

Pain will make you weak.

Or pain can make us stronger.

"I don't care what you do or say," she shouts. "You won't get what you want."

Dumah curls his lip. "Very well. I will find out for myself."

Cold, sharp fear stabs through Arielle. She has no idea what that means, but she doesn't want to find out. Tugging on her arms so hard it hurts, she fights. Tries to get her hands free. Kicks out with her legs.

Dumah simply steps back, his penetrating gaze never leaving hers.

And then she feels it.

A prickling in her mind. A clawing at her consciousness.

Dumah's trying to probe her memories!

Arielle turns her face away as if breaking their gazes will make a difference. She squeezes her eyes shut, trying to expel the invasion.

She refuses to betray Mac. She won't be responsible for her death.

But Dumah probes further. Deeper. As if she doesn't get a say.

"I will learn what I need," he growls determinedly.

Nausea crawls up her throat as she feels him enter fully and she realizes she has no way of stopping him. Her mind is his to ransack.

Except suddenly, her mind is surrounded by a wall of night. It pulses, contracting then expanding like a black lung, and Dumah gasps. Arielle opens her eyes to see him reeling as if he was just physically expelled.

His chin drops, his head angled to glare at her with animosity. "I will kill whoever is protecting you." He bares his teeth. "No doubt an angel."

Angels, scoffs the obsidian. *Never willing to admit there is something more powerful than them.*

Arielle watches Dumah with unblinking eyes, realizing the obsidian just protected her. But now Dumah is pissed.

"It was that bitch, Gabrielle, wasn't it?" he snarls, practically spitting her cousin's name. "She will die for this."

"No!" she screams. "You leave her alone."

He doesn't even blink in acknowledgement. "But first, I'll kill you."

Arielle's blood turns to ice. Her breath freezes in her lungs. Dumah's words are far more than a threat.

They're a promise.

Yield to me, hisses the obsidian urgently. *You will be strong enough to fight this.*

"No," says Arielle through gritted teeth.

The price would be too high.

Dumah's nostrils flare as he advances. "It's humorous how humans assume there's a choice."

You die, so does Mac. So does Gabby.

That is the price you want to pay?

Arielle strains to pull away as Dumah reaches out a hand and wraps it around her throat.

"A single snap is all that's necessary," he purrs. "So vulnerable. So easy."

Arielle's pulse is a panicked flutter and judging by the triumph in Dumah's gaze, he can feel it.

Yield to me and these bonds will be unable to hold you.

Yield to me and you live.

Her knees go weak at the choice she has to make. Save herself and those she loves?

By melding with evil...

A sob escapes her throat just as Dumah tightens his grip, cutting off any chance of screaming. "Goodbye, Arielle."

A gray light, so bright and powerful it has her squeezing her eyes shut, explodes around them. Dumah curses as his hand is wrenched away from her throat. Arielle gasps as her hands are freed. Her knees crumple and she lands on all fours, breathing hard.

The world swims and her head buzzes as she lifts it, trying to understand what just happened.

As blackness swallows her, the last thing Arielle sees is Dinah walking toward her.

GABBY

"You don't have to be here for this if you don't want to," Gabby says to Colt, brushing away the curls the sea breeze just wafted into her face.

They spring right back, tangling in her lashes and he gently tucks the unruly strand behind her ear. This time it stays, and she suspects he may have used a little magic to do it. "I would like to hear what he says."

Gabby's lips twitch. More like he wants to watch her father

as he talks because he doesn't trust a word he says. "Okay, but be nice, alright?"

He inclines his head. "Always."

She rolls her eyes. Colt and her father are mortal enemies.

She laces her fingers through his as she turns to face the waves. Maybe a few moments just listening to the rhythmic crash will help calm her. It feels like her stress levels peaked when they discovered the obsidian gone, and they haven't come down.

Colt tenses and Gabby knows her father just arrived. Time to get some answers.

They turn simultaneously to find Gabriel standing a few feet away, his hair and clothes unmoving as if the sea breeze doesn't dare touch him. He glances at Colt then looks away, dismissing him. "Daughter? You called me?"

Gabby decides to get straight to the point. "The obsidian's been stolen."

Her father's stoic clam fractures for a second as a deep frown embeds itself. "You said you'd—"

"I did," she says. "I used every precaution there was."

His eyes narrow. "Raphael," he growls.

"You think it was an angel?" asks Colt.

Gabby's father slides him a glare. "He's the only one strong enough to break a spell so powerful." He inclines his head. "Apart from Michael."

"Or Lucifer," adds Colt, no doubt noticing the way the name of the fallen angel creates tight lines around her father's mouth.

"But both of them are trapped," Gabby points out, trying to focus the conversation.

"Which means it must have been Raphael," her father spits. "And we both know what he wants the obsidian for."

Gabby nods. The knowledge came back to her along with the memories. "The obsidian originates from Hell. Thrown out by Lucifer to corrupt human faith in angels. Except Uriel broke it up into seven pieces so that couldn't happen."

Her father crosses his arms. "Until you fused the pieces so that you could power the Spear of Destiny."

He says the words matter of factly. Like a history lesson.

But they still sting.

Angels don't seem to mind making hard decisions in the name of the greater good, but she grew up human. She's not detached like her father is.

Which means being part of what's brought them here weighs heavily on her shoulders. Her heart. Her very soul.

Colt's fingers twitch, a barely-there motion, but one nonetheless. He's telling her he's here. Like he always is.

Lightening the load.

It means she raises her gaze to meet her father's. "And I used the Spear to trap Michael in an alternate dimension."

Colt curses, uncaring of her father's frown. "Raphael wants to free Michael."

"Which is as I suspected all along," says Gabby's father. "He will try to use the same spell to free Michael from his prison and restore him to Heaven's Throne. The obsidian will give him the power to do so."

Bringing on the apocalypse they worked so hard to avoid.

Gabby's stomach is a mass of knots as she wonders how they can stop that again. They barely succeeded last time.

They almost didn't survive.

Her gaze shoots to Colt. There was something else she remembered. "The obsidian is connected to the Grail. In the same way the obsidian brings death and destruction, the Grail brings life and light."

Understanding dawns in his mahogany eyes. "The Grail is the only thing that will be able to triumph over the obsidian."

That's how they'll stop Raphael. Michael. The apocalypse they're so eager to unleash.

"The Grail has been sought after as much as the obsidian," says her father, pointing out the elusiveness of the Grail.

"And the obsidian was found," she responds, hope once again kindling.

Her father draws in a deep breath, expanding his massive chest and throwing his shoulders back. "I'm going to find out what I can about Raphael and the obsidian."

In a blink, he's gone, his prints in the sand quickly blown away by the breeze.

Colt raises a brow. "Look out Raphael."

"Well, while they have their pissing contest, we're going to be focusing on the bigger picture."

That human lives count just as much as angels'.

Colt's face falls serious. "We need to find the Grail."

CHAPTER 13
REIGN

Reign launches out of Rachel's car the moment it pulls up to the curb, almost glad for her crazy-fast driving.

Arielle's in trouble. He can feel it.

The high-rise apartment building they've traced her to looms over them as Rachel joins him. She holds up her phone. "She should be right here."

Reign scans the apartment block, squinting as he cranes to see the top floor. "You mean inside?" He'll knock on every door in the place if he has to.

"No. This tracing technology is pretty accurate. It's saying she's out here."

Except the pavement is practically empty. Apart from a guy sitting on a park bench reading a newspaper, there's no one.

Rachel lifts her cell a little higher, waving it one way, then the next. "It's definitely saying she's here." She angles it one way, stops, then takes a few steps, frowning. "It's saying she's over there."

And the cell is angled in the direction of the guy on the park bench.

Reign strides over, encouraging the anger that rises through him like hot lava. He jerks down the newspaper. "What have you done with her?"

The man instantly curls up, wrapping his arms around his head. "Please don't hurt me!" Several packets of veggie chips float to the ground.

Reign steps back, frowning. "I'm not going to hurt you," he says in a quieter voice, conscious that the man's probably feeling the influence of Gluttony.

Rachel appears beside him. "You sure were acting like it," she huffs.

He glares at her. He didn't mean to scare the crap out of the guy. It's just that the need to find Ari has him feeling like a wound coil. He glances back at the man, finding he hasn't unwrapped from his protective stance.

And watches as a cell phone slips from his contorted lap and lands on the bench seat.

Ari's phone.

Reign grabs the guy by his shirt and hauls him up. "Where is she?" he roars.

The guy pales. "Please, I was just reading my paper. Please don't take me away, too!"

Reign shakes him. "I'll take you to Hell and back if I have to."

"No, please! All I was doing was reading the paper," he wails.

Rachel presses her hand on Reign's straining arm. "Reign. He'll talk better if he's not choking on his own testicles."

He loosens his grip a little, the man's panicked expression filtering through his rage. "Why do you have Arielle's phone?"

The man's gaze flickers between the two of them. "That's her name? Arielle?" Reign's muscles coil again. Patience is something he doesn't have right now. The guy must notice because he starts to speak rapidly. "She exited the building over there. Some guy came up and talked to her." He swallows. "Then he...took her."

Reign's stomach bottoms out. He has to consciously stop himself from gripping the guy tighter again. "What did he look like?"

"Dark skin, dark hair. No shirt."

"And you didn't try to stop him?" Reign demands.

The man's gaze slides away. "I couldn't."

Rachel leaps in, possibly sensing that Reign's almost at snapping point. "We understand." She throws Reign a glare. "We all get overwhelmed by emotion sometimes."

"It wasn't that," says the man defensively. But then his gaze slips away. "It wasn't that," he says again, once more shaken and pale.

"Why?" Rachel asks. "What's got you so scared?"

He pulls his head into his shoulders. "I couldn't because he took her up there," he whispers hoarsely, pointing at the sky.

Reign releases him, realizing the guy not only witnessed an abduction, but a supernatural one.

His gut clenches painfully. That Arielle was possibly taken by one of Gluttony's henchmen.

"What color were his wings?" asks Rachel softly.

The man's gaze darts to hers, shocked that she believes his story. "White," he almost whimpers.

Reign steps back and turns to Rachel. One name hangs between them.

Dumah.

There's a scuffle and they turn to find the man running away, leaving behind a flurry of foil packets. Rachel pushes up to her tiptoes and cups her mouth. "I'd lay off the crisps if I were you! It's well known that they can have hallucinogenic properties!"

The man doesn't turn around, but he ducks like she just

hurled the words at him. Rachel turns back to Reign, dusting her hands off. "Well that takes care of seeing an angel *and* any overeating tendencies that may have been settling in."

Reign picks up Arielle's phone from the bench. "We have to find her, Rach."

She sobers. "Yeah, we really do. But tracking Ari when we have her phone is about as easy as tracking Dumah."

The prick they released trying to help Mac when she was in a coma.

Rachel crosses her arms. "Maybe we should call Gabby and Colt?"

He hesitates. Gabby and Colt would've contacted them by now if they weren't doing something important.

Plus, would Arielle want Gabby to know something's happened the moment she ran off without telling anyone where she's going? She worked so hard to prove she's not impulsive or reckless after everything that happened, like letting Dumah out in the first place.

If Gabby hears of this, she'll be disappointed. And will probably abandon whatever she's doing.

Reign shakes his head. "I think there's one more thing we can try before we call the big guns."

"There is?"

"While the Archivists have been busy, well, archiving, and the Grail Keepers have been unsuccessfully searching for the Grail, another organization has been fighting supernaturals."

Rachel straightens in surprise. "There has?"

"I only just learned of them. Descendants of the Knights Templar. They call themselves the Order of the Knightly Rose."

"Now that's cool," she breathes. "And totally worth a shot."

Reign waggles his phone. "And I have their number."

Rachel grins. "You Grail Keepers sure know people in high places."

"Let's hope so," he mutters.

Otherwise Gabby and Colt will be the next one they're calling.

"Oh, I have an idea." Rachel indicates for him to follow her to the bench seat where she pulls out her laptop. "I'll try to triangulate the location of the number as you're calling." She wrinkles her nose at him. "In case they hang up or something."

Impressed, Reign sits beside her, kicking aside the crisps packets. "You worried I'll chase them away like the last guy?"

She pauses, her fingers hovering over the keyboard. "I get it, Reign. You're freaking out about Arielle." Her eyes narrow a bit. "Because you have feelings for her."

Tired of denial, he holds her perceptive, intelligent gaze. "Yeah, I do," he says on a sigh, almost relieved to have the truth out.

Rachel grins again. "I knew it." She returns her focus to her screen with renewed determination. "Let's find Arielle."

Reign doesn't point out what she's conveniently forgetting. Those feelings aren't reciprocated.

Or that they're feelings that he'll never voice beyond this moment.

"Okay," Rachel says with a flourish. "I'm connected. Call away."

With a few taps of the cell phone screen, Reign's dialed the same number he did when he first came across the Order of the Knightly Rose. It rings. Then rings again. Rachel barely blinks as she watches him.

"How did you get this number?" answers the same female voice as last time, already sounding pissed.

Reign's jaw tightens. This has got to be a record, even for him.

He's already got her off side.

RACHEL

Rachel watches as Reign's brows knit down and her stomach clenches. The phone call doesn't seem to be off to a good start.

She holds her breath. Although she's only just learned these descendants of the Knights Templar exist, she can sense the puzzle they're in the midst of just grew, and that these people just became another piece.

Possibly an important one.

"I found this number in a book," he says. "My name's Reign. I'm the, ah, Keeper of the Grail."

He ducks his head as he says the words and Rachel stays where she is, even though she wants to hug him. High five him. Then hug him again.

Reign is slowly accepting his destiny.

There seems to be silence on the other end, then a female voice. Although Rachel can't make out the words, the woman sounds...suspicious. It has Rachel gripping her laptop tightly.

Please don't let Reign's questionable people skills sabotage this...

His eyebrows more firmly entrench themselves in a frown. "No, I can't prove it. Can you prove you're from the Order of the Knightly Rose?"

Rachel almost facepalms. But there's a bark of laughter, followed by more words, these ones sounding more assured.

"An hour?" asks Reign. "Can we make it sooner? This is urgent."

A second later his frown is practically touching his nose as he stares at his phone. "Whoever she is, she's not big on negotiating." He turns to Rachel.

"But she agreed to meet?" she asks, her feet bouncing enough that her computer jiggles on her lap

Reign nods, his own sense of victory flickering in his gaze. "At a place in the city called The Idle Deli." But then the frown hovers again. "She said in an hour."

That cools her own excitement. Time isn't a luxury they have.

He indicates toward her laptop. "Did you get anything?"

Returning her focus to her screen, she taps a few keys. "The phone call was pretty short..." She taps a few more, triumph almost making her shoot to her feet. "But yes, we have a location!"

"Where?"

The high is short-lived as Rachel registers where the phone call was traced to. "It's impossible."

Reign leans over, scanning the screen himself. "The 9/11 memorial," he asks incredulously. "That's not even near Mercy City."

In another tab, Rachel searches for the geological surveys of the area. "And it couldn't even be below ground. There's nothing showing up." She sighs. "At least we know they have some good technology to scramble the location so effectively."

Reign's face shows exactly how great a consolation prize that is. He pushes to his feet. "Come on. We'll wait at the deli."

Rachel tucks her laptop back into her messenger bag. "Hopefully they do a mean BLT."

An hour is a long time to wonder and worry what's happened to Arielle.

CHAPTER 14

ARIELLE

Arielle's eyes fly open as she sits up. She glances around frantically, finding herself in a room of some sort. A bedroom, but not one she recognizes.

She stumbles to her feet, her fingers at her temples, conscious that she was lying in the corner of the floor. She escaped Dumah, somehow.

Someone saved her.

She's taken a step when she registers a bed in the middle of the room. And that there's someone on it. Trying to stop her forward momentum she reaches out for an armchair nearby, gasping when her hand sails straight through it as if she has no substance. She rights herself, gasping again when she recognizes the person lying still on the bed.

Herself.

"What is going on?" she whispers, panicked.

The door opens and to her relief, Reign enters.

She rushes toward him. "Reign, thank goodness."

"Arielle," he says softly.

Her heart soars at the sound of her name, but then she registers he's not looking at her. He's looking at the bed.

And his voice is drenched in pain.

He sits heavily on the chair beside the bed. "Are you going to make me beg again?"

"What are you talking about?" she says, her voice becoming strident. "Reign, look at me."

"Please, wake up, Ari," he whispers hoarsely. His gaze on her sleeping form, he picks up a hand, entwining their fingers. "You can fight this. I know you can."

"Fight what?" she asks, almost shouting. "Reign! I'm right here!"

He bows his head as if she hasn't spoken. As if she's not even in the room.

And yet, she is. And he's holding her lifeless hand.

She shuffles backward, her breaths coming in hard, sharp gasps. She wants to close her eyes in the hope this is all a dream, but she can't drag her gaze away from the sight of her comatose body, of Reign holding her hand so tenderly. It's achingly beautiful and devastatingly terrifying.

Suddenly, the sleeping girl's eyes pop open. Arielle covers her mouth in terror.

Black, sightless orbs stare at the ceiling.

She stumbles, her feet as numb as the rest of her body, and begins to fall. She quickly reaches out to a nearby bookcase to steady herself, only to be reminded she doesn't really exist.

There's nothing to grasp.

No wall to stop her.

Arielle screams as she topples backward into nothingness, squeezing her eyes closed. The sensation of falling only lasts a second but she keeps her eyes closed for a little longer.

She wants this nightmare over and done with.

"Gabby, this is too far, even for you."

Colt's voice has Arielle's eyes springing open, and she finds she's in a bare-looking basement, Gabby striding in through the door, Colt right behind her.

"Gabby?" says Arielle, finding her voice weak and trembling.

But Gabby doesn't hear her. She spins around to face Colt, her hands on her hips. "Do you have a better idea?"

Colt frowns ferociously, even glancing around the room in frustration, his gaze sweeping straight past Arielle. "But summoning...that?"

Gabby turns back to face the open room consisting of little more than cement floor and walls. She waves her hand and several symbols flare to life on each of the walls. "Everything is ready."

"Even for you, this is dangerous," warns Colt. "The price could be too high." A visible shudder ripples through his body.

Gabby drops her shoulders. "We're out of options," she says heavily.

She moves to the center of the room and Arielle instinctively steps back, heart thudding. The nightmare isn't finished.

Her cousin starts to mouth words Arielle doesn't under-stand. The sigils on the walls flare with silver light, and Colt's scowl deepens.

Suddenly, a copper lamp appears in front of Gabby's feet. Before Arielle can try and comprehend what's happening, a wisp of smoke curls out of the spout, quickly condensing and thickening as it expands.

She watches in fascinated horror as a...genie gains form.

"Djinn," Gabby intones. "I have a favor to ask."

The genie—djinn—crosses his arms as he smiles. "Of course. That's what we do best."

There's a note of anticipation in his voice. He's looking forward to whatever Gabby's about to ask of him.

Colt moves to stand behind Gabby, his hands fists by his side. "Name your price, first."

The djinn throws back his head and laughs. But as his gaze falls back down, he doesn't look at Gabby or Colt.

His eyes fall on Arielle and they flare with fire. "It may be more than you're willing to pay," he purrs.

The words spark a fresh blaze of terror through her.

It will be worth it, hisses a voice through her mind.

"No!" she cries.

But before the word has finished, the scene has changed again. Arielle takes an instinctive step forward. "Mom?"

Her mother stares at the wooden floor she's squatting above, a dagger in her hand.

"Mom!" Arielle screams, even though she knows it's useless.

Her mother can't hear her. Can't see her. Arielle's cursed with watching whatever this is, whether she likes it or not.

Her mom begins to carve a shape into the floor, the sound of scraping and scratching digging down Arielle's spine. The lines flicker and glow as fire sparks along them.

The symbol complete, her mother steps back, the burning sigil reflected in her eyes. The sound of a howl pierces the room and the charred floor crumbles away. A beast appears before her.

Large and black, with crimson eyes, it bares fang-like teeth as it snarls. Arielle's frozen to the spot, terrified she's about to witness her mother's gruesome death.

"Hellhound," her mother commands. "Go find the girl named Shanaya."

The beast lets out another blood-curdling howl, then launches past her mother and out the door.

Her mother's shoulders sag. "It's the only thing that could find her," she whispers to herself. "Shanaya is the only one who can break the demon's compulsion."

A hand lands on Arielle's shoulder. She screams and spins around, now scared that this is all real. Suddenly, the prospect that this is nothing but a nightmare isn't so chilling.

A woman with ageless skin and hair piled up in ornate braids smiles at her. "The Dreamscape isn't the place for you right now."

"I'm dreaming?" Arielles asks, relieved. She glances around. The room is empty. Her mother's gone.

"The Dreamscape shows what can be, the future that is currently mapped." The woman inclines her head. "But it is not absolute."

Once again tense, Arielle rubs her arms as if she's cold. "So they could happen."

Her lifeless body. Reign's grief.

Gabby and Colt making a deal with djinn.

And her mother calling on a hellhound to track someone down.

The woman smiles peacefully. "They are just manifestations of what might be, a figment of imagination that could turn out to be true, but not necessarily."

"You're not answering the question," says Arielle, shaking her head.

"The future is not for you to know," the woman replies calmly. "Only to be discovered."

Arielle leans in a little closer. "Who are you?" How is this woman here, telling her all this?

But the woman just smiles her enigmatic smile. She reaches out and presses her fingers to Arielle's forehead.

The world goes black.

And then Arielle's eyes fly open and she sits up. She glances around frantically, finding herself in a room she doesn't recognize.

Please, no.

Not again.

GABBY

Gabby and Colt have just reached the parking lot beside the beach when she stops. "Maybe I could track the obsidian!" she says, eyes widening.

Colt's brow furrows in thought. "Well, you've used it before, so you'd be familiar with its magical signature."

"Exactly. I might not be able to locate it exactly, but the obsidian is dark energy. I should be able to trace it. Maybe find its last known location."

He nods, determination setting his handsome features in stone. "It's worth a try."

Gabby looks around, seeing a set of change rooms nearby. She arches a wicked brow. "We need privacy."

Colt follows her line of sight and lets out a breath. "I could come back and wipe anyone's memory that happens to see this," he offers.

She takes his hand and tugs him toward the brick building. "We're supposed to be protecting humans, remember?"

"So you keep saying," he grumbles.

Gabby wraps herself around his arm, allowing herself a smile despite the difficult circumstance. Colt makes a show of griping about helping humans, but he does it. In fact, he's put his life on the line several times.

Her demon has the most beautiful heart she's ever seen.

As they approach the toilet block, Gabby decides to walk into the men's section. She angles a cheeky grin at Colt. "So you're not uncomfortable if we go into the ladies."

He scowls at her, but she sees the glint of humor in the

depths of his mahogany eyes. Too bad they can't make this a bit of a rendezvous...

Except the moment they step in she wrinkles her nose at the smell. "Guys are gross."

"They most certainly are," Colt agrees with fervor.

Tugging him into the nearest stall, Gabby decides it's time to get this over and done with. The need to trace the obsidian.

They crowd in and lock the door. Colt pulls her against him. "It's best if we don't touch the walls." He frowns. "Maybe I should do a sanitizing spell."

"Shh," she admonishes, pressing her hands to his chest. "Let me focus."

She closes her eyes, bringing the image of the obsidian to mind. The memory of its insidious power returns, impossibly contained within a small stone. It had been almost impossible to curb, let alone control. It had seethed with the need to hurt. Kill. Devastate.

A breeze brushes Gabby's face, smelling a whole lot fresher than it did a moment ago, and she opens her eyes. She tightens her hold on Colt when she realizes where they are.

They're on a rooftop somewhere in Mercy City.

And the obsidian had definitely been here.

Colt stiffens. "An angel was here."

She realizes he's right. Along with the dark signature of the obsidian is the essence of an angel. "What would an angel be doing here?"

Colt walks around, studying the ground and the brick wall nearby. He runs his hand over a pipe beside it. "There was a struggle."

Joining him, Gabby sees the scuff marks in the white paint. They scour wider for any sign of what may have happened, only to find nothing. She sighs, frustrated that they've hit a dead end again so soon.

Closing her eyes again, she concentrates. Maybe there's something they've missed. She senses it almost immediately. Little more than a trace, but there nonetheless. A third magical signature.

Her eyes fly open. "The angel was banished," she says, surprised. "I can feel it."

"That would mean someone was tracking the angel, or the obsidian."

"The question is who."

Colt's lips thin. "The other angel faction?"

Gabby sighs. Just what they need. "Unfortunately, that would make the most sense." They already deduced that Raphael's faction wants the obsidian.

Colt's eyebrows twitch up. "Although, we now have a lead. Track the angel, close in on the obsidian." They rise a little more. "We find the Grail, we save Earth from both Heaven and Hell."

"And Raphael's faction is going to be a whole lot easier to find," Gabby adds, feeling her hope surging.

There could be more than one way to find the obsidian.

She takes Colt's hand. "Come on. We need to find out everything we can about this angel faction."

They've just turned toward the door that will take them to the stairs—the more magic they use, the more likely they, themselves, could be traced—when there's a soft thud behind them.

They spin around, instantly ready to fight when they discover they're no longer alone.

A demon, her large onyx wings folding into her back, grins at them. "I have a message for you."

CHAPTER 15
REIGN

The Idle Deli is swarming with people. A quick glance tells Reign all the tables are full, with more people standing around, sipping coffees and eating paper-wrapped sandwiches.

"They're not looking idle," Rachel comments dryly.

"And how the hell are we supposed to know which one is the woman from the phone call?" growls Reign.

He scans the seated patrons again. If it were him, he would've arrived early to scope out the people he'd agreed to meet. Although he has no idea who or what he's looking for, no one jumps out as the contact for the Knights Templar.

Rachel arches a brow. "You thinking of using your super-effective interrogation skills on each and every one of them?"

"If I have to," he snaps. He glances at her, his chest tight. "Arielle's in danger. I can't stand here and do nothing."

Rachel brushes his arm, her face softening. "If Dumah wanted her dead, he would've done it there and then. He took Ari because she has something he wants. We need to play the game and meet this woman, then go from there."

"You're really annoying when you're right, you know that?"

She grins. "So I'm, like, annoying *all* the time?"

He shakes his head, a rueful smile playing at the edges of his lips. At least he's got Rachel's sharp mind to keep him busy while they wait.

"We've still got twenty minutes," she points out. "Why don't we get something to eat while we're waiting?"

Reign shifts a little. "I don't know if we should."

He's permanently hungry in a way he's never been before, and he knows exactly why. Gluttony's infecting the city, one person at a time. His lips twist. Lust messed with his emotions enough as it is.

And look how that turned out.

Rachel frowns. "Yeah, I feel it, too. But we need to eat. Do you think Princess Jasmine beat Jaffar on an empty stomach?"

"She could just wish the calories away," he mutters.

If he had three wishes right now, he knows what he'd use them for.

Have Arielle safe and sound.

Gluttony would be dead.

And he could eat as much double dark chocolate ice cream as he damn well likes.

There's a snuffling noise to their left and they turn to see a red-haired woman sitting alone at a table, cutting into a large stack of what looks like pancakes. It's hard to tell under the bacon, sausages, ham, corned beef and salami. Oh, and the steak.

Rachel looks away. "Maybe we should be each other's portion control."

Reign nods, no longer feeling like ice cream, but hating that he's still hungry. How long before he's ordering something like that woman has?

And yet, Rachel's right. They need to eat.

"Okay," he says. "We'll get a BLT each."

They join the line, and Reign scans the patrons again, avoiding looking at the woman gorging on her meat-pancake mountain. The sounds of her eating can't be missed though. The frequent clanging of cutlery on porcelain, the non-stop chewing, the barely muffled grunts.

It makes Reign a little nauseous.

But he has no idea who he's looking for, and therefore no idea if the woman is here.

If she even turns up...

They reach the front of the line quicker than he expected and Rachel smiles at the exhausted-looking server. "Hi, could we order two BLTs, please?"

"Sorry. We're out of bacon." He glances at his notepad. "And tomato."

"For some reason, a lettuce sandwich doesn't sound as appetizing." Rachel scans the menu taped to the bar in front of her. "What about the corned beef hash and eggs?"

"Sorry. Also sold out."

"Ah, the cheese blintzes?"

"Also gone."

Rachel's brows pinch. "What do you have in stock?"

The guy checks his notepad again. "Decaf coffee and grape-fruit juice."

Reign glances over his shoulder. No wonder the line moved so fast. Everything's been eaten.

"I'm glad to say, I'm not that hungry," Rachel announces. She turns to Reign. "You?"

He shakes his head. "I have a biological need for caffeine. Oh, and taste buds." A grapefruit and a juicer should never have been put in the same room together.

The guy shrugs, looking too tired to care.

They turn and move to the side, and the man behind them moves up, no doubt about to find out the same thing they did.

Rachel sighs. "We have five minutes. We'll just have to wait."

Reign returns to scanning the tables scattered around, wishing he could pace. It's hard to tell how much of the edginess comes from the knowledge Arielle's out there, in danger, or the growing hunger clawing at his gut. He skips over anyone male, which at least halves the number of people he needs to focus on. There's a mother spoon feeding her toddler, unsuccessfully keeping up with the tearful demands for more. An insanely thin girl wolfing down a double-decker BLT. A woman with a super-sized milkshake, her focus on her cell as her thumb flips over the screen repeatedly. She glances up, casually looks around, her gaze barely brushing over Reign, before she returns to scrolling.

"That's her," he says under his breath.

But Rachel hears him, no doubt as wired as he is. Her gaze follows his line of sight. "How can you tell?"

The woman doesn't look up again, but her brief glance was all Reign needed. It wasn't a casual return to reality. It was a calculated look that assessed her surroundings in a split-second. He knows. He's spent his life doing them.

What's more, there's a glint in her eye that said "I've seen more shit than you know exists."

Reign takes a step forward, only to be stopped by the man who was in line behind them. He rushes past, carrying a cup of coffee—no doubt decaf—and a glass of juice the color of bitter citrus.

If he needed proof people are getting desperate, that was it.

"Come on," he says to Rachel. They need to find out if this woman can help them find Arielle.

He weaves through the tables, Rachel behind them, and he notices the way the woman's hand tightens ever so slightly around her cell. She hasn't looked up, but she knows they're coming.

It's her.

Dark blonde hair pulled into a tight ponytail, she's wearing a figure-hugging black tank top and jeans over her lean, muscled frame.

She even looks like a vampire hunter.

A strangled sound behind him has the woman's head snapping up. Her gaze flies to him, then to whoever made the noise. Her eyebrow arches up and she shakes her head in disgust before returning to her cell.

Reign spins around to see that the red-haired woman with the meat-pancake mountain's hand is at her throat, her eyes bulging above.

He jolts into motion, leaping over and hauling her up to her feet. Three hard, sharp thumps to her back and half a sausage flies out of her mouth, bouncing over the table and onto the ground. The handful of people who had stood up, about to render assistance, sit back down again.

Rachel is on the woman's other side. "Are you okay?"

The woman's eyes fill with tears. "Yes." She looks up at Reign. "Thank you so much, young man."

He nods, stepping back. "No big deal," he says, suddenly feeling awkward. "As long as you're okay."

The woman shakes her head so hard her red hair wobbles. "It is a big deal." Her lower lip trembles. "I could've died. Killed by a sausage!"

"But you didn't," he points out, his arm crossing to rub his other elbow. He pulls up a smile. "Isn't that great?"

Rachel shakes her head at his awkwardness before leaning over again. "I'd suggest being a little more careful. Maybe slow down a bit?"

The woman's shoulders sag. "I'm just so hungry," she says tearfully.

Rachel straightens. "I know it's hard. But it's really important to not let the hunger take over."

She nods, staring balefully at her half-mountain of food.

With a glance at each other, Reign and Rachel move away. By the time they've taken two steps, the woman is eating again.

Frustration bubbles through Reign's gut, searing away at his own hunger. People aren't only killing each other, they're killing themselves.

He stalks to the woman with the milkshake, planting his hands on the table. "Is that how people in the Order of the Nightly Rose act?" he hisses. "They just sit by while a woman chokes?"

The edge of the woman's mouth tips up. "It's not what a Grail Keeper would do."

He blinks as he realizes that the woman choking became some sort of test. This woman waited to see what he'd do. "It's what anyone should do," he snaps back.

She glances around the tables. "Apparently not."

Only a handful of people stood up. And none of them got to the woman before him, even though they were closer.

They probably didn't want to leave their food unattended, Reign thinks sourly.

The woman stands, extending her hand. "The name's Kenna. Kenna DeVoe. Nice to meet you, Reign."

She knows his name. He narrows his eyes as he shakes her hand. "How long have you been watching us?"

Rachel pushes in, extending her own hand. "Hi, I'm Rachel. Lovely to meet you." She glances at Reign pointedly.

He's getting in trouble for lack of social graces again.

Well, maybe when he's seen Arielle is fine the scowl will be tucked away.

Kenna shakes Rachel's hand. "Yes, I know. Rachel Donovan."

"Nice to meet a kindred stalker," says Rachel with a grin.

Kenna inclines her head. "I'm glad you appreciate the value of information."

Reign slides into the chair across from Kenna. "We need your help," he says, getting straight to the point. "We're looking for a friend."

Rachel takes the seat beside him. "Please." She smiles again. "Pretty please."

Seeming unaffected by either Reign's curtness or Rachel's friendliness, Kenna angles a sharp gaze their way. "You want to know where Arielle is."

For the first time since they discovered her missing, Reign's heart jolts, as if it had been in suspended animation the whole time. Holding its breath. Waiting to see if there's any point beating again. "Yes! Do you know where she is?"

Kenna arches an eyebrow. "Is that really the priority right now?"

CHAPTER 16

ARIELLE

Heart thundering up a storm in her chest, Arielle frantically looks around. She's in a living room this time, a couch beneath her. She gasps when she sees skulls on the shelves, glass jars containing who-knows-what, and far too much black.

Where has she dreamed herself into now?

Something moves in her periphery and she yelps when she discovers a lizard in a large terrarium beside her, watching her through impassive, beady eyes.

"That's Godzilla," says a voice from her left. "She's quite friendly."

Arielle spins around. "Dinah?"

She nods solemnly. "Hey."

"You can hear me?" Arielle's so surprised, she shoots to her feet.

A wave of dizziness engulfs her and she sits back down on the couch, clutching her temples.

"I'd take it easy if I were you. Blasts powerful enough to get rid of an angel can really pack a punch."

"I've noticed," Arielle says dryly. At least she's back in reality. Whatever that psychedelic trip was, she's glad it's over.

"How are you feeling?"

Arielle looks up at Dinah, starting to process that it was her who saved her. She wouldn't be alive without her. "Why are you helping me?"

Dinah walks over to the terrarium and removes the lizard. She clasps it gently, stroking the unusual looking reptile. "Let's just say, your quest is one I believe in. Like I told you, I want to help."

Arielle's head is too heavy and sluggish to try and decode what that could mean. All she knows is that Dinah's helped her more than once, and now saved her life, but she's still not sure if she can trust her.

"Well, thanks. I appreciate everything you've done for me."

Dinah focuses on stroking her lizard. "That's what friends do."

Friends? That's what Dinah thinks they are?

Arielle shoots to her feet for the second time. Her friends! "I need to get back. Reign and Rachel will be looking for me."

Dinah angles her head, still stroking the lizard. "That didn't seem to cross your mind when you left them. I suspect you didn't tell them where you were going, either."

Of course not, stupid witch.

We don't need her or anyone else.

Arielle stills as the obsidian's voice returns. It was because of it that she left alone, desperate to find answers. She sits back down, the heaviness in her head spreading to the rest of her body. "I can't go back," she says. "Not until I have answers."

"And how's that working out for you?" Dinah asks dryly.

Arielle's gaze snaps to hers. "You don't understand."

"Dumah sure appreciated you going out alone," she continues, not backing down. "And next time you might really be alone."

There won't even be Dinah to help her.

We don't need her or anyone else. We were about to end that angel.

If Arielle had yielded to the obsidian. If she'd let it consume her.

It was the only way she could've survived without Dinah arriving.

Arielle wraps her arms around herself, suddenly cold. What is she supposed to do now?

"What did Dumah want?" asks Dinah, sitting on the coffee table across from her.

Glad that Dinah's jumped to the wrong conclusion about why she's so rattled, Arielle rubs her brow. "He wanted to know where Mac was. So he could kill her." She straightens a little. "But I didn't tell him."

"Which is why he tried to kill you," says Dinah flatly. "You need to stay with the others from now on. Even if Dumah doesn't come back, there's still Gluttony and her minions wanting you out of the way."

"Didn't you hear me?" Arielle snaps, then instantly frowns. She's never been short tempered. "I can't go back," she says more softly.

Dinah simply watches her, those kohl-rimmed eyes dark and assessing.

"I have something personal to deal with, okay? Something...important."

The confession slips past Arielle's lips, and she feels dirty even alluding to the mess her choices have found her in.

To her surprise, Dinah's lips soften. It's not quite a smile, but it's the closest Arielle's ever seen. "I can help you with that. If you'll let me."

Nothing can stop the inevitable merging of our powers.

No, Arielle almost screams in her mind. There has to be a way to stop this. She just has to find it.

Dinah's eyes narrow. "What you need to focus on is finding the next Innocent and stopping the next Gate of Hell opening. No matter what's going on."

"I want to," Arielle whispers.

She's the one who has the visions of the obelisks. Her aunt was the first Innocent they failed to save. There's nothing more she wants than to stop it from happening again.

"Then you need to trust those who want to help you," Dinah says firmly. "Your team, like Gabby, Colt, Rachel. And Reign."

Arielle flinches. "I trust Reign with my life. But things are... complicated with him."

"It seems straightforward to me."

"Not after what Lust did to us. How can I trust what I'm feeling?"

Dinah's face turns thoughtful. "Are you hungry right now?"

Arielle shakes her head. "No." The last thing she feels like doing right now is eating.

"That's what I thought. You're not hungry, while the rest of the city is gripped by Gluttony's sick power. That suggests that maybe Lust wasn't a factor in your attraction to Reign at all."

Arielle's mind swirls with the words Dinah just spoke. Is it possible? Could everything she's tasted with Reign be real?

Except Lust is why he was drawn to you, hisses the obsidian. *You'd be an idiot all over again to believe anything else.*

Aren't you tired of looking like an impulsive, emotion-driven fool?

Arielle's back on her feet, her arms wrap back around her middle. "Could I use your bathroom, please?"

Dinah frowns. "Sure. Just down the hall and to the left." She stands, too. "While you're in there, I'll call Reign."

Nodding, Arielle rushes out, ignoring the way her head swims and the nausea it triggers. She stumbles into the bathroom, shuts the door, and sits on the edge of the bath, breathing deeply.

Dinah's right about one thing. She needs to focus on finding the Innocent. On stopping another Sin from wreaking havoc on Earth. And she needs to do that as part of a team.

With Gabby and Colt and Rachel.

And Reign.

Pushing to her feet, Arielle leans over the sink and splashes water on her face. The coolness is refreshing, and it clears some of the cobwebs from her mind. She looks up at her reflection.

Can she fight Gluttony?

At the same time as fighting the obsidian?

Her pale face stares back at her, blinking slowly. She looks vulnerable and strong, all at once.

Can she trust what she feels for Reign?

There is only one you can trust.

She gasps, her hands tightening on the sink until her knuckles turn white as her reflection changes.

Black orbs for eyes stare back at her.

GABBY

The demon arches her neck as she angles her head from side to side. Short, platinum blonde hair frames her face in a pixie cut. The vicious smile spreads wider across her face.

"I have a message from Gluttony."

Gabby subtly straightens, aligning each vertebrae above the

other as she prepares to fight. Her senses are highly aware of Colt beside her, the open space around them that's free of witnesses.

Of the threat in front of them.

"And she was too scared to deliver it herself?" says Gabby.

The demon's eyes flash fire. "Gluttony's busy. If you haven't noticed," she goads.

The fighting. The insatiable hunger. People willing to kill for food.

Gabby's noticed.

"Get to the point," snaps Colt.

He's never had much patience for his kind.

The demon curls her lip at him. "Traitor," she hisses. She turns her crimson gaze back to Gabby. "Gluttony wants you to back off. She doesn't like angels interfering with her business."

Gabby plants her hands on her hips. "I don't like Gluttony trying to tell me what to do. So tell her to go shove it."

Colt takes a menacing step forward. "Now, go back to whatever cesspool of Hell you crawled out of."

The demon's wings snap out as her face twists. Just as Gabby suspected, her message isn't complete.

The demon runs at them, pumping her wings for speed. But Gabby and Colt were expecting this.

And they're two halves of a whole.

They launch forward simultaneously, both leaping into a kick. The demon's eyes widen as she sees the two bullets of power coming at her. She tries to block, even jumping back, but she's nothing against their combined strength. Their feet plow into her midsection, drawing out an "oomph" as she folds in half.

Gabby and Colt push off each other, spinning midair before landing. Fists raised in mirror stances, they watch as the demon rights herself, her arm cradled across her midsection.

"Time wasted for you is more time for us to find the Innocent," she snarls before running to the edge of the building and leaping. Her wings snap as they catch the wind. With a few powerful pumps, she disappears into the cloudless sky.

Gabby drops her fists and shakes her hands out. "I hate that she got the last word," she mutters.

"We got the last, in fact, the only strike in, though," says Colt, also coming out of his fighting stance.

"That's true," she says, grinning. "Did you see the look on her smug face?"

"Right before she ran like a coward?" asks Colt, his own lips twitching. "Yes, I did."

Gabby's grin dies as quickly as it grew. "Lust didn't do this. She hid in the shadows." She frowns. "Gluttony isn't afraid to show her hand."

"Very true," agrees Colt. "Gluttony is threatening to bring the fight to us."

Gabby slips into his arms, drawing strength from his warm, muscled body. "We need to stop this."

"And fast," rumbles Colt, wrapping strong arms around her.

They don't voice the other words they're both thinking. They don't need to.

They know the other is thinking by the way their hold tightens.

If they don't, the next Innocent will meet the same fate as the first two.

CHAPTER 17

REIGN

Reign considers shouting his denial of Kenna's suggestion that finding Arielle isn't a priority. No, screaming it. Roaring it.

There's nothing more important than finding Arielle.

"Of course it's a priority," he grinds through clenched teeth. Arielle is a vital part of their team. How can no one else see that?

Kenna rests her arms on the table as she leans forward. "When another Gate of Hell is about to be opened? When demons are now working with vampires?"

"Vampires?" Rachel squeaks.

"Yep. Evil, blood sucking bastards," Kenna spits. "Just as dangerous as those Hell spawn."

"My best friend is a demon," says Reign.

"Well, vampires are more dangerous, then," Kenna shoots right back. "They're not something you want to befriend. They'll suck you dry the moment you turn your back on them."

Great. Another thing to deal with. Reign's hands clench into fists and he doesn't bother to hide it as they rest on the table. "All the more reason to—"

"If another Gate is opened, more demons will be released," Kenna hisses. "Making their numbers stronger, and the vampires stronger. If we want to end this, we need to work together."

"What do you propose?" asks Reign, realizing Kenna wants something from them. That puts him at an advantage.

"You take care of the Innocent and keep the Gate of Hell closed, we'll deal with the vampires."

"Great idea. To do that, we need Arielle."

Kenna's eyes glint. "Our technology can help you find the next Innocent."

"Ooh, technology!" gasps Rachel. "What sort of technology?"

"A lot of technology," says Kenna, a slow smile spreading across her face.

"Why don't you use it to find Arielle then?" snaps Reign.

Kenna shakes her head in disgust. "You have no idea what we're up against. It's possible demons and vampires are only the beginning." She leans forward again, her face tight with intensity. "We need to work together. The Knights, the Archivists, and the Grail Keepers."

Reign doesn't point out that Grail Keeper is singular, not plural. There's only one left—him.

He leans forward, too. "I'll agree if you help find Arielle."

"Deal," Kenna says instantly. "We have a large network of informants throughout the city. It's how we've been able to watch your movements until now. We would've helped fight for the last Innocent if we weren't dealing with a vampire Master."

"They have Masters?" Rachel asks, sounding horrified and fascinated.

"Every city has one," says Kenna with a nod. "It means they're more coordinated than we'd like." Her lip curls. "Unless we kill him, just like I did the King."

"Good for you," says Reign, not willing to be sidetracked, even by blood-sucking supernatural beings. "So, you'll let me know if you hear anything about Arielle?"

Kenna sighs, her face now molded in frustration. "Yes. It won't take me long to find her whereabouts."

"Excellent. Then we can get onto dealing with not making this shitfight worse."

Kenna pushes to her feet, nodding. "I'll be in contact."

She strides away in powerful, self-assured steps. Reign watches her leave, not sure if they've actually made any progress in finding Arielle.

"I think I just met your female alter ego," says Rachel.

"What?" he asks, frowning.

"Gruff, straight to the point, and gets shit done." Rachel grins. "I bet she's a Taurus, too."

"That's probably why I like her, then," he says, rolling his eyes. He sobers. "This alliance is a good thing."

The Keepers of the Grail and the Order of the Knightly Rose have worked together throughout history. It seems it's time for that to happen again.

"So, vampires, huh?" says Rachel. "Just what we needed."

Reign sighs. "And they've formed their own alliance."

With the hordes of demons that escaped when the last Gate of Hell was destroyed.

"Maybe there are some nice vampires," Rachel offers. "Just like there are nice demons."

"Who knows," says Reign. "Let's hope we don't spend enough time with vamps to find out."

She chews her lip. "So, what now?"

He wipes his hand down his face. "I suppose the mature, smart thing to do is go back to the farmhouse and wait for news."

Rachel lifts a single eyebrow. "So, we'll hit the streets?"

Reign grins as he stands. "Damn freaking straight."

Just as Rachel's stood, too, his cell phone rings. His heart jolts. Could Kenna have news of Arielle already? A quick glance at the screen reveals a silent number.

Or it could be a telemarketer.

"Yes?" Reign answers, knowing he's being curt, but unable to stop himself. He's trying not to let himself hope.

And failing.

"Reign, it's Dinah. I have Arielle at my place."

His hand tightens around his cell as heat injects through his muscles. "You bitc—"

"She's fine," Dinah snaps. "And safe. I won't hurt her."

"No, you won't. Because I'll make sure you regret it."

"I'll text you my address."

"Put her on, Dinah. I want to talk to her."

"I can't. She's in the bathroom."

"That's the best excuse you can come up with?" he demands. "If you don't—"

Dinah hangs up, and Reign curses. He can't call her back, either. He looks up and finds Rachel watching him with wide eyes. "Well?"

"That was Dinah," he says, his mind working in overdrive. "She has Arielle and she's texting me the address."

"Wow! That's great news." She hesitates. "Isn't it?"

Reign's cell dings and an address a few suburbs over appears on this screen. "That's definitely something we're going to find out. Let's roll."

They leave the deli, heading toward the parking lot that has Rachel's car. She pauses as they reach it. "Maybe Dinah genuinely does want to help."

Reign slides an unimpressed glance her way. "Less Disney, more reality, please."

She pokes her tongue out. "Was Maleficent really a villain?

Or just a woman trying to deal with a crappy card?"

"I can't believe I'm having this conversation," he mutters. "Not when Dinah's probably working with Dumah."

Rachel chews her lip. "So, do you have a plan then? If we're going into a trap."

"I'm working on it."

"That would be a no."

Reign glances around the parking lot, not liking that Rachel's right. Walking in unarmed or unprepared isn't smart.

But then again, when has that ever stopped him?

He's about to turn back to Rachel when a store across the black top catches his attention. A hand painted sign sits above it. *The Witching Hour.*

He grins at Rachel. "Of course I have a plan."

He walks away, Rachel quickly catching up. "Hey, where are we going?"

Reign lets their feet do the talking as they approach the witchcraft store. Two large windows are framed by dark timber, a dark red awning over the top. Reign's eyebrows twitch up when he sees the windows have been blacked out.

"That's not creepy," mutters Rachel.

"We'll be quick," he assures her. "All I need is one thing."

He pushes the timber door open and a bell jingles above him, putting him even more on edge. Inside, the store is poorly lit and smells of dust and incense. Reign makes sure Rachel stays close to him. If he didn't need what he's here for, he'd walk straight back out.

"Hello?" says an elderly female voice.

A white-haired woman appears behind the counter that extends along the entirety of the left wall. Rows of glass jars sit on wooden shelves behind her, containing every shade of murky green and several of unusual browns.

Reign walks up to the counter. "Hi. I'm after some jimson

weed."

The woman angles her head, studying him. "Hmm, not the type to smoke it for its hallucinogenic properties," she murmurs, almost as if she's talking to herself.

Reign arches a brow. She has no idea what she's talking about.

She looks him up and down. "You don't have swine flu."

"Not as far as I know," he says dryly. "Could I have a jarful, or however it comes packaged?"

She purses her lips. "It's a very potent herb. I usually sell it in one ounce lots."

"I'll take a pound then."

She leans forward. "Is this for asthma? Because it works, but it's also highly toxic when taken in the wrong amounts."

"Yeah, it's for asthma," he says, making a point of introducing a slight wheeze to his in-breath. "Can I have it now, please?"

The woman stares at him for long seconds but Reign holds her gaze. He's been lying to himself and the world since he was born. There's no way she'll see through this.

With a huff she turns around and walks to the far end of the counter, running her finger over a row of jars.

Rachel leans in close to him. "What the hell is jimson weed?"

But before Reign can tell her, the old woman's head twitches up as if she heard Rachel. But she doesn't turn around. Instead she looks straight ahead and Reign jolts when her gaze connects with his.

Beneath the dust, barely visible in the poor light, is a mirror. In fact, it runs the entire length of the wall.

The old woman's hand flies to her mouth and Reign freezes.

Surely she can't see what he does.

His true reflection.

She spins around, clutching a small jar to her. Shuffling back to the counter, not quite meeting his gaze. "Jimson is a very specific herb. It has no impact on vampires, angels...or demons."

Reign doesn't blink. "Good thing I'm not planning on taking any of those on in the next hour or so then."

Just a witch.

The woman nods, her hands trembling slightly as she pours the contents of the jar into a piece of brown cloth. She quickly ties it up and passes it to him. "No charge for that today."

Reign's too uncomfortable to object. "Thanks," he mutters and quickly leaves. The musty store was starting to feel oppressive.

Outside he draws in a deep breath, vowing he'll never return to this place. He's about to walk away when Rachel grabs his arm.

"What was that about?"

"Jimson weed," he says, deliberately misunderstanding her. "I read in one of the Grail Keeper books that it nullifies a witch's power." Not giving Rachel a chance to reply, he strides away, wanting as much distance between himself and the store as he can. "Come on. We need to get to that address."

Rachel catches up, but it's slower than he expected. A brief glance shows her features scrunched in thought. He really, really hopes it's because she's focused on what they're about to face.

She unlocks the car and they both climb in. Reign pushes down the scene from the store. Very soon it'll become a memory, one he'll pretend never happened.

He has more important things to focus on. He hefts the small pouch of herbs, deciding it's a small price to pay for obtaining the jimson weed.

If Arielle's hurt, Dinah's going to pay.

CHAPTER 18
ARIELLE

A rielle exits Dinah's bathroom, feeling even more shaken than when she went in.

They have to focus on finding the next Innocent. She can't afford to be weak.

No more running. No more distractions.

Saving the Innocent is all that matters.

And when you fail, I'll be here.

Waiting.

Arielle ignores the obsidian. She'll become deaf to its vicious words. Immune to its effects. Until she can figure out how the hell to get rid of it.

She has to.

Dinah's putting the lizard back in its terrarium as Arielle enters. "There you go, Godzilla," Dinah says with the most warmth Arielle's ever heard. "Don't go throwing any crazy parties, okay?"

Arielle leans against the doorway, wondering at this witch of contrasts. Hard and unemotional, yet saying she wants to fight for good. And she saved Arielle's life. And obviously cares for her strange-looking reptile.

She straightens as Arielle enters, her eyes turning assessing. "You look like shit."

Arielle inclines her head in acknowledgement. "I feel it, to be honest."

Dinah's lips turn down at the edges. "The impact of the blast shouldn't have affected you this much."

Stupid witch. She has no idea what she's talking about.

She'll be one of the first to die.

"That's because it's what's inside me that's taking its toll," Arielle mutters before she can stop herself.

Dinah stills, her frown deepening. "What are you talking about?"

"Nothing," Arielle hurriedly assures. She enters the living room and grips the back of the couch. "I need to get going. Like you said, there's an Innocent to save."

Dinah's dark eyes turn shrewd. "Reign and Rachel are on their way."

For some reason, relief floods Arielle. She needs to see her friends.

She needs to see Reign.

"And I'm going to try a spell to locate Paul's Grace," continues Dinah. "Then we can use that to track them."

"Why, Dinah?" Arielle asks, even though she knows she's repeating herself. Not only is this topic a distraction, but an answer that makes sense would be nice. "Why are you so determined to help?"

Dinah shrugs, her gaze no longer quite meeting Arielle's. "I've spent a long time floating, aimless, serving one organization or the other. It's nice to have a purpose again." Her eyes snap back to Arielle's. "I like what the Keepers of the Grail stand for—saving the world and all that."

Arielle blinks, wondering if this is the most she's ever heard Dinah speak.

She shrugs again, as if it's of no consequence. "And I like the world the way it is."

More questions rise in Arielle's mind, one after the other. What organizations is Dinah talking about? And what did she do for them? What could've happened that she's so willing to keep the status quo?

But there's no chance to ask any of them, because the doorbell buzzes. They both still. Dinah's the first to recover. "That would be your team."

Her team.

You don't need them.

The sooner you realize that, the better.

The doorbell buzzes again, several times, communicating a clear impatience. Dinah inclines her head. "I think they want to see you."

Arielle rushes to the door, understanding how they feel. She should never have left without saying anything.

She almost didn't return.

She yanks open the door, stopping at the sight of Reign in front of her. Sweet heavens, he looks good. Frantic. But downright everything she needs right now.

She's in his arms before she's even conscious either of them moved. She presses her face to his chest, holding onto him tightly, reveling in the way he's holding her just as hard. Almost with an edge of desperation.

Sweet heavens, he smells good. Feels good.

Feels right.

It's these moments, when they're together, touching, nothing but honest emotion flowing between them, she knows the truth.

This is where she belongs.

You're so weak. So needy. Throwing yourself at him.

Has he ever told you he cares?

Arielle tries not to let the obsidian's words get to her, just like she promised herself, but like the others, they hit her where she's most vulnerable. They echo the doubts she'd rather not voice.

She pulls back, hating that the moment was just tainted. And admittedly, wanting some confirmation the insidious words aren't true.

Reign's face is tight with intensity as he studies her, his green eyes full of concern and something else...But before Arielle can name it, his face shutters.

He steps back. "Are you okay?"

Once more feeling cold and alone, she tries to smile. "I'm fine."

"You don't look fine," he says with a frown.

Arielle rolls her eyes, trying to lighten the mood. "That's what Dinah said."

Rachel shuffles in. "She looks amazing as always," she says, admonishing Reign with a glance. "Just a little...peaky."

"Which is essentially what I said," scowls Reign. He looks around the room, stilling when his gaze falls on Dinah. "You lied," he growls.

He strides around Arielle, anger vibrating through his body.

"Reign?" Arielle asks, unsure what's happening. "I said I'm fine."

He glances back at her, eyes blazing in a way she hasn't seen before. "No, you're not. Something's happened. I can feel it."

Arielle freezes. His words are too close to the truth. Does he suspect what's happened? Her knees go weak.

He'll hate her.

He spins back to face Dinah, who's calmly standing in the same spot. "What did you do to her?" he asks quietly. Coldly.

"Nothing," Dinah states flatly. "I'm not the enemy here."

"Anyone who hurts Arielle is no friend of mine," he snaps.

"I'm going to ask one more time. If it wasn't you, who hurt her?"

Dinah lifts her chin. "You need to focus on the bigger picture. The Innocent."

Arielle's hands twist. Dinah's protecting Arielle. She's not sharing what she knows.

"I will," growls Reign. "Once I've made sure this doesn't happen again."

The threat in his words are unmistakable, but Dinah doesn't move. She simply holds his gaze. "I don't want to hurt you."

"That's what they all say," he snaps.

He delves into his pocket and pulls out a small pouch and holds it up. Dinah lifts her hand, energy already crackling along her fingertips when her eyes widen. The energy snuffs out.

"No," she breathes.

She turns to run, only to collapse over the arm of the couch. She grips it, trying to get back up, but crumples again.

"Reign!" shouts Arielle, trying to understand what's going on.

Yes. End the witch. One less to deal with later.

Reign's killing Dinah?

Dinah saved her and this how she repays her?

"Stay back, Arielle!" He steps closer, raising the pouch higher. Dinah throws her head back and screams in agony, a black mist climbing from her mouth. Her body trembles, as if it's disintegrating from the inside out.

Arielle takes a step, only for her body to seize.

Accept your destiny. Watch her die.

She glances over her shoulder at Rachel to find her watching the scene, stricken. But she's also not moving. She thinks Reign's doing the right thing.

Arielle tries to move again, finding her limbs locked. Her body is no longer her own.

"No," she moans.

Yes, it hisses. *This is only the beginning.*

Anguish slices through Arielle, bringing hot tears to her eyes.

The obsidian's winning.

GABBY

"I say we follow our feathered friend," says Gabby, striding to the edge of the building and looking out.

Colt joins her. "I was thinking the same thing. She has information that could be helpful."

She scans the sky. "As much as I'd love to fly..."

There's something special about flying with Colt, no matter the circumstance. There's a freedom in the air they don't often get to experience.

"But too risky," he finishes for her, the same regret she's feeling in his tone.

"Another time," she promises.

He brushes her cheek, the same vow reflected in his eyes. "Another time."

With a sigh, she focuses on the faint threads of energy the demon left behind. Fighting her, no matter how short it was, meant they got to touch her, if you could call their powerhouse kick that. Which means her energy connected with theirs.

It should be easy to track her.

She and Colt clasps hands. "Shall we?"

He nods curtly. "Let's finish what we started."

Gabby closes her eyes, tracing the dark energy through the ether. The demon hasn't gone too far. Maybe they injured her more than they realized.

With a slow breath out, she allows their magic to follow the trail. To go to the same location.

Gabby opens her eyes and finds they're in a house, a living room. A house that's familiar, but not one she can place easily.

She looks around, trying to remember. "I've been here before."

The realization of where she is hits her just as a scream echoes through the living room. They jolt into action, running up the stairs in the direction the terrified sound came from.

"Doris!" Gabby calls, frantically scanning the rows of doors at the top of the stairs. "Doris!"

Another scream pierces the air, coming from an open doorway down the hall. They race in, Colt entering first, Gabby right behind.

She gasps at the sight that greets her.

The demon is at one end of the room, Gabby's mother's elderly friend on the other. Plastered against the wall. Her head almost touching the roof.

The demon ignores Gabby and Colt, her hand extended as she keeps Doris pinned. "Who else?" screeches the demon. "Who else did Shell know?"

Doris's face is as pale as the wall behind her, her mouth working but no sound coming out. She stares at the demon, tears trickling down her soft cheeks.

Because the demon's face is no longer human, but a creature twisted by the bowels of Hell. Sunken eyes, razor sharp teeth, gray skin. And a mouth that's opening wider and wider. Becoming a cavern, ready to devour.

Without a word, Colt and Gabby move. Colt goes to the woman, ready to catch her as Gabby closes in on the demon. She pushes her hands out, calling on the fire within her.

Celestial fire.

The demon balks when it sees the flames shoot out of

Gabby's palms, quickly weaving into a swirling ball. She turns to run, aiming for the window, no doubt intending on smashing through it, trying to escape.

But terrorizing Doris is the last thing she will ever do.

Gabby unleashes the fireball and it streaks over the few feet between them. It engulfs the demon and she drops to the floor, writhing and screeching.

Gabby's stomach clenches and bile burns the back of her throat as she has to watch what will happen next. The demon curls up, flames licking at every inch of its skin, yet not burning anything else around her.

"Even if you stop this," she screams. "What about the next Innocent? And the one after—"

She never finishes her sentence. Her face is too melted. Gabby looks away, unable to stomach the skin bubbling and peeling. Hair now nothing more than a black skullcap. Black smoke pouring out, dissipating into nothingness the moment it touches the fire.

Then, there's silence, and all that remains are a small pile of black ashes.

Gabby spins around to find Colt cradling an unconscious Doris, no doubt thanks to one of his sleeping spells. Hopefully she didn't see the demon's demise. He lays her gently on the bed and pulls the cover over her. "She'll sleep for a while."

Gabby rubs her arms. "The demon was here because Doris knew my mother. They both went to a pilates group and bonded over coffee afterward." She smiles a little. "They kept up the coffee dates, but not the pilates."

Colt nods. "It appears Gluttony has reached the same conclusion Rachel did—the Innocents are all connected somehow."

Which means no one in her mother's circle of friends and acquaintances is safe.

Gabby moves over to stand beside the bed, looking down at Doris. Her face is relaxed and at peace now, her mind blissfully far away from demons and angels and the supernatural fight of good versus evil.

She looks to Colt. "You need to do it."

He nods again. "I already have."

No wonder she looks so peaceful then. Colt wiped her memories of everything that just happened.

"She'll wake up thinking she had an impromptu nap," he says. "I didn't probe too deeply because of her age. She may remember some parts, but assume it was all a terrible nightmare."

"That's good," she says, relieved. Doris shouldn't have to live with what she saw just because she met her mother once a week for coffee.

"There's something else," says Colt, his face is more serious than usual. "I read the demon's mind. There was a reason it didn't run. It wanted information, but it was also a decoy. Demons are planning to attack an angel hideout."

Gabby shakes her head. "But my father wouldn't have his angels all in one location. Not this close." She stops as the realization hits her. "It's not his angels. It's Raphael's faction."

"And I know where it is. On the outskirts of the city."

Frustration simmers in Gabby's gut. "I can't believe we have to deal with angel factions after all." With a sigh, she moves forward to clasp Colt's hands. "Your turn this time."

He'll need to take them to the location.

She grips his hand, the frustration morphing to anger. This is the last thing they need. Not with Gluttony on the rampage.

Colt's lips twitch. "You're angry."

"Damn straight I am. I'm going to banish every one of their asses."

His gaze flares. "I'm looking forward to seeing that."

Gabby presses a quick kiss to his lips. "Nothing like a mass banishment to get a girl in the mood."

Colt grabs her and deepens the kiss. "The sooner we end this..."

The sooner their life can be about the passion that just flared like dry kindling.

Stepping back, she adjusts her shoulders, preparing herself.

They're about to morph into an angel-demon battle.

CHAPTER 19
REIGN

Arielle's denial barely slips through the haze of anger that's exploding through Reign. Dinah is going to lose her magic so she can never hurt anyone again.

But it does. A single word, strangely full of anguish.

"No."

He turns around, still keeping the pouch of jimson weed high and angled at Dinah. "Ari?"

She's a few feet behind him, seeming to be rooted to the spot. Her throat works but nothing comes out. And yet her eyes are pleading with him.

For what?

And why can't she move? Does Dinah have her under some spell?

He turns back to the dark witch, who's now on the floor, her back arched, her face twisted. The black smoke continues to trickle out of her mouth. The Grail Keeper books never mentioned a witch losing her magic was so tortuous. Or slow.

But he'll do what it takes. He's never been one to back down from the tough choices in life.

Another strangled word reaches him and he turns back to

Arielle, finding she still hasn't moved. And yet her eyes are asking him to do something. Begging him.

Dropping the pouch, he quickly covers the distance. "What, Ari? What do you want me to do?"

Her eyelashes flicker, but nothing else moves. She's definitely under the influence of something.

And yet, Dinah's writhing on the floor. She has to be one hell of a powerful witch to still be controlling Arielle.

Reign grips her shoulders, trying to understand what's going on. "What do you want me to do?" he says again, blocking everything out as he watches her intently.

Her lips tremble. A tear tracks down her cheek. But Ari doesn't talk.

"Tell me," he urges.

Something's going on. Something bad.

"Reign..." Relief seems to wash over her face. "Stop."

She wants him to stop? When Dinah's doing this to her?

But the anguish vibrating through Arielle has him doing as she asked. He runs back, picks up the pouch and throws it across the other side of the room. It lands and skids into the kitchen.

Dinah instantly unwinds. Her mouth clamps closed and the smoke is cut off, trapping it inside her. She closes her eyes, breathing hard.

She's been through the wringer, but she's fine.

Reign turns back to Arielle, finding she's moving, too. She's bent over, her hands on her knees, her cornsilk hair obscuring her face.

He takes a cautious step forward. "Ari?"

Her head angles up and her flame-blue eyes connect with his. They're a startling mix of relief...and gratitude. She straightens. "Thank you. Dinah was the one who saved me from Dumah."

"I don't believe you."

"It's true," she says. "Dumah kidnapped me and said if I didn't tell him where Mac was, he'd kill me."

Ice streaks through Reign's veins. "Dumah's still after Mac," he says, feeling sick. And he threatened Arielle.

"I didn't tell him," assures Arielle. "Which is why he was going to kill me." Her face pales. "Dinah arrived just in time."

There's a sound behind him, no doubt Dinah getting to her feet, but Reign doesn't turn around. As hard as he finds it to believe that Dinah's the hero in this story, there's something else that isn't adding up.

"What's going on?" he asks, his voice strained. "Why couldn't you move or talk?"

Arielle tenses. "I...ah..."

Rachel moves in a little closer, her own brow furrowed in confusion. "Something was going on with you. What?"

And suddenly, Arielle looks scared. No, terrified. Her gaze flickers around the room as if the answer's hiding behind a skull or under a length of black velvet. "I was..." Her eyes trail away along with her words. Neither rise again.

Arielle at a loss for words isn't something he's really seen. Coupled with the fear and the evasiveness, it has Reign on edge.

And determined to get an answer.

"Ari, you need to tell me—"

Suddenly, Dinah appears between them. She throws her arms out in frustration. "Why did you stop him?" she practically shouts at Arielle.

She blinks in shock. "I..."

"I could've stopped it whenever I wanted to."

Arielle's mouth snaps shut. "That's not—"

"I was testing him!" Dinah says, her voice still elevated.

"Testing me?" Reign asks. What the hell?

Dinah turns to him. "I wanted to see if you had what it

takes, Grail Keeper," she sneers. "Whether you'd kill to protect Arielle. That's why I had her frozen in place."

His gaze snaps to Arielle to find she looks dazed and confused. He waits for long seconds, but she doesn't deny it.

Furious, he spins back to Dinah. "That. Is. Fucked. Up."

"I never claimed I wasn't," she retorts. She straightens. "Now that we've got that out of the way, you have an Innocent to save."

Reign presses the palms of his hands to his temples, trying to understand how this mindscrew just unfolded. Who the hell does Dinah think she is? And how much of her agony was show, and how much is a willingness to go to some pretty extreme lengths?

One last question ravages him from the inside out. Hasn't he shown how far he'll go for Arielle? Nothing would stop him from making sure she's safe.

Nothing.

Rachel steps forward. "Have I missed something?"

She looks as confused as Reign feels. Probably because none of this makes sense.

Dinah glares at her. "We don't have time for you to catch up. I'm going to try to locate the Grace so you can track the Innocent."

Rachel frowns, even her clever brain struggling to keep up with the sudden change of topic.

"Dinah's right about the Innocent," Arielle says quietly. "That has to be our focus right now."

Reign doesn't point out they had to put that on hold to go searching for her. That's a conversation to have another time. There's an entire mess of shit-that-doesn't-make-sense to untangle.

"Actually, we already know who the Innocent is," he says,

getting a small jolt of satisfaction from the surprise on Dinah's face.

"You do?" asks Arielle.

"Yep. But I'm not having this conversation here." He glances pointedly at Dinah.

She almost looks amused. "Don't trust me, huh?"

"Maybe you'll have to pass a test of mine before I can trust you," he says, trying not to sound bitter and failing.

Dinah inclines her head. "Looking forward to it."

Rachel crosses her arms, shifting her weight toward the door. "I think we should get going."

Reign couldn't agree more, although he waits to see what Arielle will do. Frowning, she turns and walks to the door, her gait slightly stiff and halting. Fighting Dinah's magic must've really done a number on her.

Another reason not to trust the witch.

He follows her to the door and they exit. As they leave, Arielle glances over her shoulder, her gaze connecting with Dinah's. A look passes between them.

A look that confirms Reign's suspicion that more happened here than they're letting on.

His gut clenches. He doesn't know what that look was about or what the hell they just communicated, but it did tell him one thing.

Despite everything that just happened, Arielle's still hiding something from him.

CHAPTER 20

ARIELLE

They've just reached the parking lot, when Rachel spins around and jams her hands on her hips. "Okay, girl-friend. What the hell is going on? Why did you run off like that?"

Arielle suppresses a wince. She's been desperately trying to come up with an explanation since they left. The whole time ignoring the obsidian's ranting.

I had you! For those moments, you were mine!

Next time, there will be no reprieve!

It was saying Reign's name that loosened the choker hold on her throat. That meant she could save Dinah.

So Dinah could go ahead and save her from telling Reign the truth.

Arielle's not sure whether she's scared or elated. She won against the obsidian's grip on her.

But only barely.

"Well?" Rachel demands.

Arielle sees that Reign is watching her closely. He wants this answer as much as Rachel does.

"We know you went to Veritas," he says. "That you were researching the obsidian again."

For the second time today, the truth hovers on Arielle's lips. She wants to tell him. She knows she can't fight this on her own.

Go ahead. Tell them your dark, dirty secret.

That you carry me within you, alongside your stained soul.

Watch him turn away.

She shakes her head. She saw in Dinah's apartment that she can't do this without Reign. She can't risk losing him.

"I...I thought it could help," she stammers, trying to think fast. "And then I discovered my mom also learned it's connected to the Grail. So I followed a lead."

"A lead?" asks Reign.

She shakes her head. "It turned out to be nothing. I'd just realized I should never have gone out alone, without telling you two, when Dumah snatched me." Arielle meets both their gazes, glad to be finally telling the truth. "The rest of the story is the same as I told you in Dinah's apartment. She saved me."

"The obsidian is dangerous, Ari," says Reign, frowning. "I thought we'd agreed on that."

She smiles weakly. "Sometimes a girl's got to find out for herself." She sobers. "But yes, I've realized how dangerous it is. I want nothing more to do with it."

Which is also the truth. If only she could make it a reality.

Rachel raises a brow. "You pinky promise?"

Arielle nods fervently. "I swear with every digit on my body."

Rachel turns to Reign. "That's good enough for me."

He doesn't answer straight away. Instead, Reign looks thoughtful. Pensive. Like he's weighing up everything she didn't say in his mind.

Arielle holds her breath. She needs him now, more than

ever. And all she's done is lie to him, avoid him, and lead him to believe she doesn't care.

It's too much to ask for.

His lips soften. "I'm just glad you're okay. That's what matters."

He smiles and so much light fills Arielle that she discovers exactly how dark her heart and mind had become. It's like she's been trapped in a cave and has had her first taste of the sun. She smiles back, relishing the happiness that's sparking through her veins.

Yes. Make them believe everything is fine.

They'll never see it coming.

"Excellent," announces Rachel. She pushes the button to unlock the car with a flourish. "Let's go meet our next Innocent!"

Glad for the distraction, Arielle quickly climbs in the back. She makes sure she asks questions the whole way there, quickly learning that a mutual friend of Shell and Paul's is a guy called Jeremy Williams.

"And we're pretty sure he's the Innocent?" she asks.

"It totally makes sense," says Rachel, getting more and more excited the more she talks about it. "He knew both Shell and my dad, and from the looks of the photos, has for years."

"But you've never met him?"

Rachel swings them around a corner and the back end of the car shudders. "I know! Weird, huh?"

Arielle doesn't answer as they weave through suburban streets and Rachel actually seems to slow down. She hopes this Jeremy is the Innocent, but how will they tell? Up until now, the Innocents haven't even known themselves.

They reach a modest, blue weatherboard house with an unkept front yard. The grass is long, weeds reach as high as the rose bushes, and ivy is growing rampant over one side of the house. The place barely looks lived in.

"If he's moved house and not informed the DMV, I ain't gonna be happy," mutters Reign.

Rachel strides up to the front door, her shoulders back. "He'll be home," she says assuredly.

Arielle and Reign follow, reaching her as she raps jauntily on the peeling paint.

For long seconds, there's not a sound, and Reign's brow starts to inch down. But then there's shuffling sounds beyond the door. It opens a moment later, revealing a crumpled looking man who looks as unkempt as the yard. His shirt is untucked, the cardigan he's wearing over it is crooked. His thin, brown hair sticks up at odd angles, while thick, bushy brows are sunk low over his eyes.

He doesn't look happy to have visitors.

"Hi, Jeremy," Rachel says jauntily, putting her hand out. "I'm Rachel, Paul Donovan's daughter."

His bushy eyebrows shoot up. "Young Rachel?"

"The one and only!" she beams.

Jeremy's face drops. "I was so sorry to hear of his passing."

Rachel's shoulders constrict. "I really miss him." She summons up her smile again. "When I saw you were friends, I just had to track you down."

Jeremy looks up, seeming to realize Rachel has others with her. To Arielle's surprise, he smiles. "Why don't you all come in? I was just making tea."

"We'd love to," says Rachel.

Jeremy leads them through a narrow, empty hall and into a small kitchen with a round dining table. "Sit down, sit down," he says warmly. "I'll grab the kettle."

"Actually, we're here to talk," says Reign. "About both Paul and Shell."

Jeremy spins around, his bushy brows hiking up to his chaotic hair. "You knew Shell, too?"

Arielle nods. "She was my aunt."

Shaking his head, Jeremy takes a seat at the table, the tea forgotten. "Terrible what happened to them. Both sacrificed at some horrible altar."

Which is what the news has everyone believing.

Rachel pulls out a chair across from Jeremy and also sits. "What do you know about it?"

"Well, the news didn't say it, but..." He glances both ways as if to make sure there's no one else listening. "I worry it has to do with the satanic cult we came across all those years ago."

Arielle and Reign both sit down, too. Rachel leans forward. "A satanic cult?"

Is it possible that Jeremy knows of the supernatural? Maybe he even knows of the Innocents.

"Yes," Jeremy spits out. "Terrible people. I'm a university lecturer and some students started whispering about it. About dark things like sacrifices and black magic." He glances at Arielle. "In fact, it was Shell who convinced me to report them to the police."

Feeling more hopeful by the second, Arielle nods. "Aunt Shell was always trying to do the right thing."

Jeremy's face softens. "She was a very special woman." His gaze clouds over. "Although I did take my concerns to the police. A Detective Kane—I remember his name clearly—said it was nothing but conspiracy theories and sent me home."

Reign's spine stiffens at the mention of Cain and Arielle almost reaches out to touch him. In fact, her hand rises of its own volition.

The closer you get to him, the greater chance he knows the truth about you.

TAMAR SLOAN

She curls her fingers in, creating a tight fist. She can't taint Reign with her darkness. It's not fair.

She has to deal with the obsidian before she considers revealing how she feels about him.

"You think this had something to do with her death?" asks Rachel.

Jeremy adjusts his cardigan as if he's suddenly realized he has guests. "I wondered. I mean, what if they want revenge?"

Rachel leans forward a little more, her hands clasped on the table. "Do you think the supernatural was involved?"

Jeremy barks out a laugh. "I'm a man of knowledge, young lady, not some child who believes in the Tooth Fairy. There is no such thing as the supernatural."

Arielle deflates a little. Jeremy knowing whether he's an Innocent or not would've made things a whole lot easier.

She should've known that would be too much to ask for.

I can make things simple for you.

Yield to me.

"Of course there's no such thing," scoffs Rachel. "I was being silly."

Reign nudges her. "Ease up on the Kool Aid, okay?" he jokes.

Rachel rolls her eyes at him, joining in the charade. She returns her focus to Jeremy. "I have some photo albums of Dad's younger years. It's where I learned about you. Could I bring them over so we could go through them?"

Jeremy's face shifts, looking as if a walk down memory lane would both be nostalgic and painful. Eventually, his brows shift down again. "That would be lovely, Rachel."

Rachel smiles at him as she stands. "Thanks for the tea. I'll come back soon."

As they walk back out, Arielle's struck that things are now even more complicated.

Jeremy's life could be in danger.

But they have no way of knowing.

GABBY

Gabby opens her eyes and finds she and Colt are standing among the ruins of a house. Beyond are green pastures dotted with trees, surrounding them is a horde of demons.

Instantly, she and Colt are back to back, circling slowly as they take stock.

Dozens and dozens of demons. But not one angel. And yet it's obvious there's been a battle here. They're standing amongst broken timber and shattered glass.

Had the demons just won? Were the angels outnumbered?

The demons hunker down, snarling. "Two came back," one growls with excitement.

Gabby doesn't let her surprise show, but it still spears through her. The angels retreated...

Another's crimson eyes flare. "No, only one was stupid enough to return. The other is a traitor."

Jagged teeth flash through the army of demons, and Gabby's not sure if they're more excited at the prospect of killing an angel, or one of their own who turned their back on them.

Too bad they won't get a chance to do either.

"Oh dear, whatever will we do?" she calls out dramatically. "Only two of us and so many of you."

"There were as many angels as there are of us only moments ago, and they all ran like the gutless cowards they are," shouts one.

The other demons sneer as one. Black wings snap out, creating a wall of night dotted with flaming eyes.

"Ready?" Gabby says under her breath.

The barest twitch of Colt's back shows he heard her.

Her own alabaster wings exploding from her back, she drops to one knee. One hand presses to the ground, burning away the debris until she's touching bare soil. Around her, the movement triggers the onslaught of demons.

Many leap high, intending on coming down like black wrath. Others shoot straight forward, planning on overrunning them. Like a swarm of hatred, they try to engulf Gabby and Colt.

But Gabby focuses on the only thing that will save them. They're woefully outnumbered and surrounded. They could blink out of here, no doubt like the angels did, but that would leave behind a horde of demons hungry for blood. Any humans nearby would be collateral damage.

Concentrating, she feels the energy coursing through the earth beneath her hand. She draws on every drop she can find, amplifies it, and combines it with her own celestial magic.

Behind her, Colt's body jerks, screams and groans filling the air as he keeps the demons at bay. For a brief second, his contact with her back breaks, making her heart jolt. But then he presses his leg against her, digging his heel into the ground. He knows they have to remain touching. Otherwise the same fate that's about to befall the demons will be wrought on Colt.

Which means she has to do it now. Left to fend off the demons, he could be wrenched away from her any second.

Digging her fingers into the soil she mutters the spell. Enochian, the language of angels, tumbling from her lips with the same familiarity as English. The dirt trembles, then ripples. The energy now coursing through it has the veil thinning and dimensions tearing.

Suddenly, Colt is standing still. The demons are no longer

attacking. Gabby looks up, her hand still pressing into the ground.

The demons are retreating, walking backward and glancing around as they sense something has changed. Several look down, no doubt feeling the subtle shift occurring beneath their feet.

Panic flickers across faces. Fiery eyes dim as realization dampens their bloodlust.

Then, they're frantically running, pulling at their hair and crying out.

"No!" one screeches.

"I can't go back," screams another.

But it's too late. Their bodies collapse as if gravity just multiplied exponentially. They writhe and claw at their faces as inky smoke pours from their mouth, nose, eyes. It's instantly sucked into the soil, drawn down to the place they should never have left.

The demons are being banished back to Hell.

Many try to flee, taking to the sky, only to be dragged down by an invisible hand. They crumple, the same black smoke pouring out and into the soil.

Gabby presses down harder and harder until her hand is covered in dirt. She sucks every one of them dry, sending their vile hatred back to Hell.

Colt's hand lands on her shoulder. "It is done."

She stands slowly, dusting off her hand, heart already aching at what she'll see. Leaning against Colt, her eyes slowly roam over the consequences of what she just did.

The destruction of the home this once was wasn't her doing. But the bodies littered among the debris are.

With the demons banished unwillingly—she hasn't met many who choose to leave their host—the humans they inhabited lost their lives. They lie at odd angles and in tortured poses for yards, like a field of broken mannequins.

"There was no other way," Colt says quietly.

Gabby nods. She did this to save themselves, along with any other human who would be unlucky enough to be caught up in this war. But that doesn't make it any easier to see so much death strewn around.

Colt wraps his arms around her and gently takes her into the air. They sail over the carnage and land a short distance away.

"And this means dozens less demons doing Gluttony's dirty work," he points out.

Sighing, she nods again. "I don't understand why the angels retreated."

Colt frowns, no doubt digesting the implications. That suggests the demons were winning. Or that the angels were just toying with them, uncaring of the public display of supernatural fighting.

There's no way of telling who might have seen what happened here.

"They didn't retreat."

Gabby and Colt spin around at the extra voice to find her father standing several feet away.

He crosses his arms over his broad chest. "They diverted."

"You were here?" Gabby asks, astounded. "And you didn't do anything?"

"It was Raphael's faction they were fighting. I was hoping the demons would do the dirty work for me."

"But then Colt and I arrived," she points out.

"And you took care of the situation," her father says, pride glinting in his blue eyes.

Nausea coils through Gabby's stomach. What just happened isn't something she'll ever be proud of.

Colt tightens the arm still wrapped around her waist. "You said the angels were diverted?"

Her father's eyes narrow, no doubt unhappy he has to speak directly to Colt. "Yes. I received information they've been ordered to go to Rome."

"What's in Rome?" Gabby asks, already sensing she's not going to like the answer.

"I don't know, but I can certainly guess," her father growls. "They have a lead on the Grail."

Now alert, Gabby narrows her eyes. Raphael's faction getting their hands on the Grail is as bad as demons getting a hold of it. "What sort of lead?"

"Also something I do not know." Her father's arms tighten, forming a thick pretzel. He looks frustrated. "But it was important enough to leave the fight against the demons mid-battle."

And angels are beings of pride. They would never do that lightly.

"They must think they're close," says Gabby.

Her father's lip curls. "It seems so." His arms unwind and he straightens, looking every part the Archangel Gabriel. "I will find out. Raphael cannot get hold of the Grail."

Gabby senses he's about to disappear again. "Dad, wait!"

She needs to know what this will mean for everyone else.

His gaze returns to her, his mind having already moved on. He glances around. "Of course," he says, as if he was remiss to forget.

With a flick of his hand, the massacre of home and humans burst into flames. Gabby winces as she turns her back. The bodies will be incinerated, not even ash left behind. The people unlucky enough to be possessed will probably be listed as missing. Except they'll never be found. Their loved ones will never know why they suddenly disappeared or what happened to them.

The only way they could know the truth is to learn of the supernatural, and that can't happen.

She or Colt would've done the same if her father hadn't. But with less callousness. They would've acknowledged these people's lives matter. Surely that has to count for something...

Her father imperceptibly nods. "Stay safe, daughter."

And then, he's gone.

Gabby sags, pressing her forehead against Colt's chest. He holds her, rubbing her back as he rests his chin on her head. "This kaka just got complicated."

Her lips twitch. Only Colt can have her thinking of smiling in moments like these. It's part of the long list of things she loves about him. "It really did."

"I don't think your father's faction should have the Grail, either," he says gently.

"I know," she assures him. "Angels are just as power hungry as demons."

"But the only way we could stop them is to go to Rome ourselves."

Gabby looks up at him, having thought this herself. "But we can't go. There's Gluttony to deal with and an Innocent to save."

"Hence the kaka."

"Yep," she sighs. "Hence the kaka."

The tinkling sound of her cell phone startles Gabby. Sometimes, it can be weird to live in a world where technology and magic both exist. Removing it from her pocket, she sees that Nim's calling her.

And the last time Nim rang her, was when the symbol first appeared. The information Gabby learned set her on a quest to find the obsidian. "Hi, Nim."

"Hey, are you okay?" says Nim.

"Peachy," sighs Gabby, rubbing her forehead.

"That great, huh? That might explain why the spirits have been whispering again. In fact, they won't shut up."

Colt moves in a little closer, his handsome face intent. He wants to hear what the spirits have to say as much as she does.

Gabby loosens how hard she's pressing the cell against her ear. Colt's exceptional hearing will be able to detect it from there.

"They keep repeating the riddle Sierra discovered just before Arielle was born. In fact there were two riddles, but we solved one and it took us to an old grave." She pauses. "Legend says the other riddle relates to the location of the Grail."

"What riddle?"

"It wanders, it travels, a power to close all doors," says Nim, almost reverently. "Residing in humanity, it transcends immortality. It rests in a river of red."

The last line has a shudder rippling down Gabby's spine. It sounds like a prophecy of blood.

"The next part doesn't really make sense," continues Nim. "They keep saying the word Rome. And something to do with scrolls hidden beneath an ancient church."

Gabby's breath disintegrates. "The spirits aren't big believers in coincidences, are they?"

Nim chuckles. "There's no such thing when Fate exists."

"Thanks, Nim. I think Colt and I have some decisions to make."

"I suspected as much," Nim says warmly. "I'd say that's why the spirits insisted I call you."

They hang up and Gabby's gaze meets Colt's. It's just as somber and heavy as she feels.

She tries to smile. "Plot twist."

"Expect the unexpected is practically a commandment for you and me." He takes her hands. "You know what we need to do."

"We need to go to Rome," she says heavily, not quite believing she just uttered those words.

Rome means leaving Arielle and the others. With a Sin wreaking havoc and an Innocent to be found. And the obsidian lurking in the shadows.

"The Grail can end all this," Colt points out.

She nods, feeling older than she'd like. "I know."

They have to find the Grail before the other angel faction does.

The fire has already burned down, leaving behind little more than a razed patch of dirt, when her cell rings again. And this time, it's Arielle.

Gabby quickly answers it. "Ari, is everything okay?"

"Peachy," her cousin says dryly, making Gabby smile. She forgets that sometimes they share mannerisms. "But I might have good news."

Colt's eyebrows shoot up, seeing as he can hear every word. "Good news?" he mouths.

"That's great," says Gabby, waiting with her breath held.

"We think we may have found the next Innocent."

CHAPTER 21

REIGN

R eign can tell there's something up with Gabby and Colt, but he doesn't say anything as he sits at the kitchen bench of the farmhouse, munching on nachos. Gabby's more...energized than usual, while Colt is even stiller than usual. The guy is practically a statue as he watches the love of his life pace so fast, her curls are blowing back.

"So, you're sure this Jeremy guy is an Innocent?" asks Gabby.

Rachel nods, reaching over and dipping a corn chip in the salsa. "He's connected to both my dad and Shell. He has to be."

"It definitely makes sense," says Reign as he crunches on another nacho. Plus, it sure would be nice to have a win for a change.

Gabby frowns in thought as she spins on her heel and heads to the other end of the bench. "I'm impressed with everything you guys have achieved."

Reign glances over to Arielle, knowing it means a lot for her to hear that. Sitting on the other side of the bench, she's frowning. Not eating. Not saying anything.

And not seeming to be impacted by her cousin's praise.

Reign keeps his face neutral, although he wouldn't mind frowning. Something's definitely up with Arielle, and he has to decide whether he should do something about it. A friend would probably not push too much. Let her talk when she's ready to talk.

But his instinct is to do far more than that. He wants to get her alone and demand she tell him what's going on. To trust him with whatever is bothering her so much.

He wants her to let him in.

In other words, he'd be acting like far more than a friend.

And that's not what Arielle wants. She's told him more than once.

Jamming another corn chip into his mouth so hard it jabs his gum, he stays silent. As Rachel reaches over for one of her own, he realizes how much they've eaten. Far more than he's ever consumed in one sitting.

He looks up at her, eyebrows raised. "I think we might be done."

She glances down, startling to see how much of the take-away tray is bare. She slouches, crossing her arms on the bench. "The annoying thing is I'm still hungry."

Reign pushes it away, disgusted in himself and annoyed that he can understand how Rachel's feeling. The urge to finish every last crumb is overwhelming.

"We need to find a way to keep Jeremy safe until we take care of Gluttony," he mutters.

Gabby nods as she paces. "Especially after what we learned."

Arielle straightens. "About what?"

"We were tracking the obsidian when we came across a demon."

Arielle's hand flies to her throat. "And?"

"We were fine," Gabby assures her. "One demon doesn't stand a chance against Colt and me."

"It doesn't stand a chance against either of us if we were alone," he adds.

Gabby's eyes glint. "Very true." She turns serious again. "We followed the demon and found her terrorizing Doris."

"Oh no, not Doris," gasps Arielle. She glances at Reign and Rachel. "She's a friend of Shell's."

"She won't remember a thing," Gabby assures. "But it means Gluttony has also figured out that the Innocents are connected."

Rachel shoots to her feet. "Jeremy's in danger!"

"I put a warding spell on his house the moment you gave us the address," says Colt. "He's safe."

Reign narrows his eyes. "As long as he stays inside."

Colt acknowledges that. "I also compelled him to stay home. As a short term measure."

Rachel hovers over her barstool. "So Gluttony can't touch him?"

"We have a day or two," says Colts. "While we figure out what to do."

Gabby stops, rubbing her brow. "Having him here, at the farmhouse, is the safest place he can be."

Reign angles his back to the nachos. Their salty, salsa smell keeps creeping up his nose. He crosses his arms, tucking his hands in. "I'm not sure Jeremy will be too open to that."

The man looked like he'd set up a messy cave to disappear his messy person into. If Rachel wasn't Paul's daughter, he would've growled at them and chased them off his property.

"This place is far too neat and organized for him," adds Arielle, her eyes twinkling.

Reign's smiling before he can stop himself. She knew exactly what he was thinking. He quickly looks away before the smile can extend to his heart. A moment with Arielle is the last thing that mushy organ needs.

Rachel flattens her hands on the bench. "I'll convince him," she says confidently. "I have to. His life is at stake."

Reign feels a little more assured that it will be possible. Rachel's a determined, smart girl. Poor Jeremy will be agreeing to it before he even knows what she wants from him.

"Excellent," says Gabby. "You guys really are all over this." Although, for some reason, she sounds more relieved than pleased this time round. She draws in a breath. "Because there's something else we found out."

Reign notices the way Arielle stills, which tells him he didn't read the note in Gabby's tone wrong.

Shit's about to get serious.

And it hasn't exactly been a bucket of laughs so far.

Gabby and Colt glance at each other before she turns back to the others. Her gaze falls on Arielle. "We think we've found a lead on the Grail."

Reign stiffens. He's the Keeper of the Grail. Shouldn't that information be delivered in his direction?

Unless they don't believe he's worthy... Unless they've already figured out he'll just screw it up.

Gabby's gaze doesn't leave Arielle. "There are some scrolls in Rome that have information on its location."

Reign finds himself emulating Colt's statuelike stillness from earlier. That's why Gabby was focused on Arielle. "You're leaving," he breathes.

Gabby subtly flinches. "We have to check this out before anyone else finds it."

"But..." Rachel frowns. "The Innocents..."

"You found this one without any help from either of us," says Gabby. "You guys have totally got this."

"And there are others who can help you," adds Colt. "We'll

make sure of it."

But none of them will be Gabby or Colt. They've been the foundation of this team. The two most powerful weapons in their arsenal.

All so they can go on a wild chase after the nebulous Grail.

But as the shock wears off, Reign quickly adjusts. His life has been defined by instability, whether he liked it or not. People enter his life, then leave. He's coped before. He'll cope again.

He shrugs. "Y'all gotta do what you gotta do."

Rachel tucks her chin into her chest. "I suppose finding the Grail is pretty important," she concedes.

There's a sharp scraping sound as Arielle shoots to her feet. Then a crash as the barstool topples over. Her pale face is tight with anger. "Family is important," she spits. "Being there for those you love is important." Her voice rises with each word. "Not abandoning me is pretty freaking damned important!"

She spins on her heel, her cornsilk hair flaring out, and strides out of the kitchen.

Gabby looks stricken. Colt seems disappointed. Rachel's head sinks into her hands.

Something tears in Reign's chest. Arielle lost her aunt, her mother left, and now Gabby. And unlike him, she's not primed for loss. She hasn't had years to develop defenses.

She's hurting.

And he needs to decide what to do about it.

DINAH

Dinah enters her apartment swiftly, shutting the door and uttering a quick spell to lock it in more ways than one. No one can enter while she does this.

She places the square, brown-wrapped package on her coffee table, stepping back to look at it. When she got the phone call an hour ago saying it had arrived, she'd insisted the handover occur immediately. The contents are too powerful to fall into the wrong hands.

When the cloaked man in the park had passed it to her, walking on as if the exchange never happened, Dinah could feel the magic pulsing within the box. It had a frisson of excitement tingling down her spine.

This will give her what she needs.

Pulling Godzilla out of her terrarium, Dinah sits the chameleon on her shoulder. "Shall we?" she asks, noting the edge of breathlessness in her voice.

She hasn't been this excited in a long time.

Sitting down on the couch, she carefully unwraps the plain, brown paper. Then opens the cardboard box that's been revealed. She reaches in with both hands and reverently pulls out what's inside.

Glossy and clear, the crystal ball is heavy as it sits in her palms. Completely transparent, light passes through it as if it's barely there. Yet Dinah can feel the energy trapped inside, swirling and circling. Waiting for a question to be asked.

Dinah glances at Godzilla. "First, to test it."

Godzilla's eyes snap to the crystal ball, as if she's just as fascinated.

"There's no point asking what you want," Dinah chides. "It'll just show me more crickets."

Focusing back on the crystal ball, Dinah connects with her magic. It took her longer to replenish it after Reign's jimson weed, possibly because she was so weakened from the pain herself. But it was worth it. It had given her another opportunity to prove herself to Arielle.

And annihilating the offensive pouch in her kitchen had been truly satisfying.

As her power swells, Dinah asks the one question the crystal ball can answer. "What is it that I truly want?"

White mist appears within the sphere, swirling and curling just like Dinah could sense. It forms a whirl of smoke, its own miniature milky way, trapped within its own galaxy. And then an outline forms, quickly gaining substance.

A stone. A black one. Smooth, but full of odd angles and unusual facets, the piece of obsidian slowly rotates within the crystal ball.

Two words appear in her mind. *The obsidian.*

"Yes," whispers Dinah.

The mist dissolves, and the crystal ball becomes clear once more. All that's visible is a warped image of her living room on the other side.

She turns to Godzilla. "It works," she says triumphantly.

Adjusting her position on the couch, Dinah connects with her magic again. "What is it that Arielle Hartely truly wants?"

The mist accumulates again. Spins. Creates a universe within a universe.

And a man's face appears. Handsome with dark hair, there's an intensity about him. Something oddly familiar. Dinah gasps. He has Arielle's vivid blue eyes.

A name shifts through her mind.

Ryder.

Dinah rests the crystal ball in her lap, blinking as if she's just come out of a dark room. She already suspects she knows who this man is.

Now, all she has to do is find him.

CHAPTER 22

ARIELLE

Arielle's always suspected there's something deeply wrong with her. As she stands on the porch, gripping the railing, her head drops under the weight of the admission. It's why she picked up the obsidian in the first place.

Why the obsidian is so sure it'll win.

And it's why her father didn't even stick around to see her born.

Now, her mother's left. And Gabby's leaving, too.

Arielle's hands tighten so much it feels like she could snap the solid timber. She finally realizes she can't do this alone, and everyone goes and leaves.

You're not alone.

And soon, we'll be one.

A shudder ripples down her back. "Never," she grinds out, even as she has no idea how she's going to ensure that.

"Ari?"

She spins around at the sound of Reign's voice. He steps through the door, and she's struck by his magnetic good looks. His face is molded from strong angles and dark beauty. His body carved from unconscious strength and supple grace. His eyes are green sanctuaries she wants to lose herself in.

Yes. Tell him. Tell him everything. The obsidian chuckles. *Lose him forever.*

A fresh wave of pain slices through her. Not Reign, too...

Knowing he's waiting for an answer, she tries to smile. "Sorry about that. It was...a bit of a shock."

He moves closer, the twilight clinging to him. "Heck, even I didn't see that one coming."

She leans against the railing, letting out a breath. "I just assumed..."

Then again, she assumed her mother would always be here. What an idiot she is.

"Gabby wouldn't be doing this if she didn't think it's important." He shoves his hands in his pockets, the movement hiking his shoulders up. "Everyone seems to think the Grail will solve all of this."

His defensive action. His words. They have Arielle gasping. "You're the Keeper of the Grail."

His brow slams down. "I've decided that piece of information isn't relevant to this conversation."

Arielle pushes away from the railing, unsure her heart can take this next blow. "You'll want to go with her." There's a painful tearing in her chest. "You *should* go with her."

His lips twist. "I've never been very good at shoulds."

She stills, her mind too full of pain to understand what's going on. "What are you saying?"

Another step, and Reign's only a handful of feet away. If she reached out she could touch him. Feel that skin that makes her own tingle. Discover the magic that's only ever sparked with him.

But, she holds still. Holds her breath.

Despite everything, despite protecting him from her awful truth, Reign could be leaving anyway.

"I'm not going anywhere, Ari," he says softly. Firmly. Like the words are a promise.

"You're staying?"

"It never occurred to me to leave."

Arielle takes an instinctive step forward, drawn to the simple beauty of those words. Drawn to Reign.

"Why, Reign?" she asks, heart thudding.

"My place is here," he says simply, his green eyes no longer a tangled jungle. They're clear with conviction. "It always will be."

Arielle swallows. "With me?"

"I'll always be here for you, Arielle. No matter what."

He has no idea what he's promising.

Do you really want to test his foolish vow?

But the sweet warmth blossoming in every cell drowns out the serpentine hissing. It's like there's no room for it in her body. She's overflowing with her feelings for Reign.

The words hover on her lips.

I have the obsidian. It's inside of me. And it's trying to devour my soul.

The screen door creaks. "Oh, sorry."

Reign spins around. "Hey, great timing," he says jovially. "We've said everything that needed to be said."

Arielle blinks as the moment is shattered. A part of her already wants to desperately pick up the pieces and put it back together. To go back because there were things she wanted to say.

Gabby hesitates in the doorway. "Are you sure? I can come back."

Reign angles his head. "I got the feeling you're leaving...soon."

"We don't have a lot of time," she responds, ducking a little.

Although she doesn't agree that everything that needed to be said has been, Arielle knows it's a conversation that will have to wait for another time. Gabby's leaving, even sooner than she expected.

"We should talk then," she says softly.

With a flash of a smile, Reign's gone, leaving Arielle with Gabby.

Not entirely sure where to start.

Gabby comes to stand beside her and they both turn to gaze out over the gardens. Crickets chirp out a soothing rhythm as a gentle breeze plays with their hair.

"Ari—"

"Gabby—"

"I'm really sorry," they say in unison.

They stop, laughing a little as the tension eases. Arielle tries again. "I'm sorry. I shouldn't have said that when I stormed out."

She'd been shocked and angry, and the obsidian had amplified those emotions. She'd said those words and exited, her blood pumping and her muscles coiled, before she'd realized what was happening.

Gabby shakes her head. "I probably would've done the same thing."

Arielle can't help but smile. It's exactly something her cousin would do. She's just glad Gabby isn't asking too many questions as to why she's now acting like that.

"I don't want to go," Gabby says softly.

"That makes two of us," jokes Arielle as she nudges her cousin with her shoulder.

"But I have to. The Grail can close every Gate of Hell, stop every Sin."

"Unless it's another dead end," Arielle points out, wondering if Reign's starting to rub off on her.

The Grail isn't in Rome.

Arielle stiffens, for once not desperately trying to pretend the voice in her head doesn't exist.

They won't find it there.

Which means Gabby shouldn't leave. She'll be on a wild ghost chase that will leave her empty handed. While the rest of the team try to desperately save the Innocent and battle Gluttony.

Arielle just needs to make her see that.

Gabrielle's eyebrows tug down. "I have to try, Ari. Especially after I lost the trail on the obsidian."

"The obsidian?" Arielle tries to keep the fright out of her voice and fails. The two words are pitched too high. Her throat's too tight.

"Yeah," Gabby says on a sigh. "It's the most dangerous, evil entity I've ever come across. Believe me, I know. I'm the one who united the seven pieces so I could put Michael in his cell."

Glad her cousin misread her fear, Arielle grabs the railing, needing to anchor herself. "You united it?"

"It was desperate times," says Gabby, leaning against a post as she becomes subdued. "And then I thought I'd hidden it from everyone. Including myself."

Until Arielle saw it. Was seduced by that very power. "And now it's out."

"I know," says Gabby heavily. "I did a spell to trace it, but we found ourselves on an apartment rooftop, the obsidian long gone."

Arielle's hands clench around the railing so hard her knuckles are a ghostly white in the dark dusk. How soon after did Gabby arrive? What would she have done when she discovered it was her own flesh and blood there on the rooftop with her?

"That's why I need to go after the Grail directly, Ari," Gabby says earnestly. "It's the source that can end all of this."

"I think you should go," she says past a dry, constricted throat.

Arielle needs Gabby gone before she learns the truth. For foolish moments she thought she could tell Reign. But of course, it wouldn't stop there. She hadn't thought as far as the others knowing. Colt. Rachel. Her mother.

And Gabby.

She'd be sickened. Revolted that her very own cousin harbors the very being she tried to disappear.

Gabby straightens, clearly surprised. "Are you sure?"

"Of course," Arielle says, trying not to move in case she snaps.

"I wouldn't be leaving if I didn't know you could do this, Ari."

Arielle blinks, her stomach clenching at the absolute trust in Gabby's eyes.

Stupid, stupid angel.

They're always over-confident. It's been their undoing over and over.

"You've got Rachel's smarts and fighting skills, and Reign's tenacity aka stubbornness." Gabby winks. "He's not leaving your side any time soon."

Which is exactly what he just promised her.

"And you certainly didn't need me to find the Innocent."

Arielle smiles, hoping the disappearing light is enough to hide how false it is. "We're all over it."

Jeremy's not the Innocent.

"I never doubted it."

Gabby engulfs her in a hug, and Arielle returns it, grateful to be showing some honest emotion for a change. They hold each other for long moments, pulling a little tighter. The only time they've had to say goodbye in any real way is when Gabby went to college.

But that wasn't far away. And they knew when they'd be seeing each other again.

"I'm going to miss you," whispers Gabby.

"Me too."

Pulling back, they smile tearfully. "I'll text whenever I can," Gabby promises.

If it's as often as Arielle's mom and Mac have reception, it won't be very often. "Sounds good."

With another quick hug, they turn to the door. Arielle follows Gabby back inside, deciding she's going to retire to her room. She doesn't want to be there when Gabby leaves, blinking out of her life with Colt by her side.

It'll hurt too much.

Especially knowing Arielle encouraged her to leave.

All because if Gabby stayed, she might discover exactly how close the obsidian is.

XEVEN

Xeven steps off the treadmill, breathing hard. He finds pounding out the miles on the machine is as productive as trying to run from his incessant thoughts. He does it ruthlessly, determinedly, repeatedly. And he gets nowhere.

He wipes his face down with a towel, pacing around the downstairs gym of Cain's mansion. There's still no word from his master.

Nor any sign of the obsidian.

Being at loose ends isn't good for him. It feels like something is crawling under his skin, looking for a way out. And yet he has no idea what.

"Hello, Xeven."

Azazel's pale, cold face appears on every mirror lining the east wall of the gym, duplicated over and over. It has Xeven instantly coming to attention. "Azazel."

"I've detected the obsidian."

Xeven's chest fills with excitement. "Where? How?"

Azazel chuckles. "I do like your enthusiasm, Xeven. An angel used her magic to trace the obsidian. I intercepted it and discovered its unique magical signature."

"Where is it?" Xeven demands.

This time, Azazel's chuckle grates down Xeven's spine. "That will take time. The obsidian knows how to hide. It's not easily found."

Xeven clenches his hands. "Tell me what to do."

Keeping moving is the only way to keep the awful, crawling feeling at bay.

Azazel's pale blue eyes flash, the image duplicated down the length of the wall. "Follow my directions and it's only a matter of time before you find it."

VIRGINIA

The Mayor strides into her secret office, smiling when her visitor rises to meet her. "Lydia, thank you so much for coming."

The white-haired witch nods regally. "What name do you go by now, my dear?"

"Virginia. Mayor Virginia Goodstone."

Lydia arches a pale brow. "Interesting." She rests her hand over her first as it wraps around the top of an ornately carved cane. "Why have you sought me out?"

Virginia smiles, excitement buzzing through her veins. "I need a spell. A powerful spell. One that can break into the mind of one of the oldest souls on this planet."

"I see," says Lydia, her white eyes cool and assessing. "You haven't decided to bury that old grudge, have you?"

"No," spits Virginia. "I will never do that."

"And why would you think I'd agree to do this?"

Virginia's face hardens. Lydia could keep herself young like most other witches. Like Virginia has herself. She could look like a supermodel if she wanted to. But she chooses this wisened, ancient shell instead.

She wants people to know she's old. Shrewd. A force to be reckoned with.

"Because you like a challenge."

If Lydia were to break Cain's mind, she would prove her strength. She'd do what no witch has been able to do.

Lydia's smile is slow and cunning. "You know me too well." She releases her cane to scratch the mole on her chin. Virginia suspects she keeps that out of a twisted sense of humor. And possibly to unsettle people in the same way her white eyes do. "I will need a powerful source to channel such magic."

Virginia tenses. "Like what?"

Lydia's smile grows. "The death of an Innocent would do the trick."

Her own smile mirroring the white witch's, the Mayor can almost taste victory. "That can be arranged."

CAIN

Cain yanks at the clamps around his wrists, rattling the chains that keep him bound to the wall. It's a useless action. One he's done hundreds, thousands of times since he was captured, but that doesn't stop him from doing it again.

He'll never stop trying to escape.

He can't have come this far only to have failed. Only to have his chance at peace ripped away from him.

Not when he was so close.

The door opens, letting in a sliver of light. Cain squints even as he tries to identify who's entering. Maybe his enemy is finally ready to reveal themselves.

But the familiar face that appears has his eyes narrowing even further. "Lydia."

There's no way of knowing whether the powerful witch is friend or foe.

She inclines her head. "Greetings, Cain."

"Release me," he demands.

She enters, walking calmly and gracefully until she's before him. "You are not my prisoner to release."

"Then tell your master—"

"I work for no one," she snaps coldly.

Cain clamps his mouth shut. This is the time he needs to think strategically, no matter what disadvantage he's at. "That's true," he concedes. "In fact we've worked together. We've helped each other. Like friends."

"I helped you find a couple of Grail Keepers. I wouldn't call that a friendship. More of a...mutually advantageous agreement."

So Lydia's placing herself in the enemy camp. Interesting. Whoever's hired her has promised quite the reward.

She steps closer, her milky eyes roving over his face. "Why,

Cain? What do you have to gain from opening the Gates of Hell and releasing all those demons?"

"Isn't that the million soul question?" he sneers.

"Is that what you're willing to sacrifice to do this? Is no price too high?"

Cain's mouth clamps tightly shut. So his captor wants to know why he's doing all this. Interesting...

Lydia's eyes narrow, becoming thin slits of frost. "This would be much easier if you just told me."

The hard promise in her tone tells Cain she intends on using her unique talents to get the job done. The same ones she used to find out what every Grail Keeper he's caught knew. And he suspects Lydia hasn't failed an assignment yet. It would be a point of pride for her.

Well, he's going to ruin her streak, no matter how many hundreds of years old it is.

"I will give you nothing," he vows.

Lydia nods, unsurprised. "Breaking most things isn't easy or straightforward, particularly a mind as old as yours. It will be...painful."

"Isn't anything worth fighting for?"

She inclines her head, acknowledging the truth of his words. "And yet, pain can make even the bravest souls forget why their quest is so important." She turns and gracefully walks toward the door. "Rethink your answer, Cain," she warns. "When the Innocent is about to be sacrificed, I will return."

Because she'll channel the immense power released at such an auspicious death.

She's trying to scare him. To show him she intends to use that power to demolish him.

Cain yanks on the chains with renewed vigor, screaming as the door closes and leaves him in the dark once again.

But it isn't a scream of fear like Lydia wanted.

Fear is a wasted emotion. Panic at the prospect of something that hasn't even happened yet. It was replaced by determination centuries ago.

This is raw, guttural anger.

He will not be broken.

CHAPTER 23

REIGN

They've just stepped through the doors of Rising Phoenix Dojo when Rachels pipes up. "Jeremy and I can sit over there while we look through the albums."

Reign spins around, finding her patting the bag hanging over her shoulder as she smiles at the older man beside her. "But we came here to train."

With the shock loss of Gabby and Colt, it was decided that the three of them needed to hone their fighting skills. Right now, they're the only thing that stands between Gluttony and humanity...and the next Gate of Hell being ripped wide open.

Inviting Jeremy had been Rachel's idea. A way to train but also keep an eye on him. Reign was a little surprised Jeremy agreed so easily, but didn't comment on it. It's nice when things actually work out for a change.

Jeremy straightens his still-crooked cardigan. "Wonderful idea, my dear. I don't need a tour, I've seen the dojo before."

Rachel stops midway through the door. "You have?"

"Why, yes. Your father was very proud when he first bought it."

Her brow puckers. "I've never seen you here."

Reign focuses a little more closely on Jeremy. Rachel says she's never met Jeremy. And yet he's talking like he and Paul were old friends. That seems kinda odd.

Jeremy runs his fingers through his hair, spiking it even further as his gaze slides away. "I preferred not to visit."

"That's okay," croons Rachel. "We don't need to talk about it now." She turns back to Reign. "We'll look at photos while these two train."

Highly conscious of Arielle beside him, Reign realizes he's frowning. "You're the black belt among us," he points out.

He's not ready to go full body contact with Arielle yet. He needs to put on armor or something first.

Rachel rolls her eyes, a cheeky twinkle sparking in their depths. "I'm pretty sure Ari doesn't need to know the difference between a sidekick or a roundhouse." She heads toward the staircase that leads to the second floor, indicating for Jeremy to follow her. "Right now we're focusing on 'don't die.'"

"Goodness, you take this martials arts stuff even more seriously than your father," says Jeremy, trotting along behind her.

Rachel takes two chairs from a nearby stack and places them next to each other. "You never know what's lurking in the shadows, Jeremy." Sitting down, she looks at Reign expectantly. "You could start with some defensive moves?"

Unsure exactly how he got to this moment, he turns to Arielle. "Looks like it's me and you."

She shrugs. "I hope you're okay with being annihilated by a girl."

He rolls his eyes, liking her spunk. "Please. Mac is my best-friend. I call that a day ending in a 'y'."

Grinning, she walks over to the nearest square of mats. "Wathca got, sensei?"

Deciding to get serious, he joins her, standing a few feet

away, face to face. Teaching Ari to protect herself is important. Really important.

He lifts his fists, holding them in front of his face, eyebrows hiking when she mirrors him. "Nice."

"Rachel's been giving me pointers."

"She's learned from the best!" Rachel calls out from her self-appointed front row.

"Good," says Reign. "The basics are the bits that count. A good fist. A solid foundation." He looks down, pointing out the way his feet are shoulder-width apart, his knees loose and slightly bent. "And being ready for any—oomph."

He doubles over in surprise as Arielle's fist connects with his gut. She bounces back, her fist returning to tuck close to her body.

"Atta girl!" calls Rachel.

"Be ready for anything?" Arielle asks teasingly. "Expect the unexpected?"

Rubbing his stomach even though it didn't hurt, Reign looks between the two girls. "I've been set up?" he asks incredulously.

Jeremy chuckles. "This is why I'm glad I had a son."

Rachel turns to him. "You have a son?"

Jeremy's smile instantly falls away, the I-don't-want-to-talk-about-it expression returning. "I did."

Rachel opens the first album she brought, the one they found the photo of Jeremy in. "Let's have a look, shall we?"

Glancing at her gratefully, Jeremy leans in. "Ah yes, there's the lovely Shell."

Reign turns back to Arielle, the mood subdued once again. Talking about dead people will do that.

She loosens up her shoulders, keeping her fists close to her face. "What else you got?"

Pushing away the mystery that is Jeremy, Reign focuses again. "The more damage you can do at a distance, the better," he says, stepping a little to the side and noting the way Arielle mirrors him. "You want to avoid close combat."

She nods as if she just filed the information away.

"Always be aware of your opponent, but also your surroundings. There are weapons to be found if you look hard enough."

Arielle stops and looks around. "Like what?"

Reign does a slow turn. "The chairs, for one. That table if you had to—oomph."

This time, he falls forward as a foot jams into the back of his knees. He instantly bounces to his feet and spins around. "I can't believe I fell for that," he mutters, flushing as Rachel's giggle floats through the air.

"I learned the hard way, too, if that helps," she says, blue eyes twinkling.

"Not so much," he grouches, once more preparing to fight.

"No more Mr. Nice Guy, Reign!" says Rachel, proving she's a supporter of dirty fighting, no matter who's doing it.

Arielle tilts her head, and he tries not to notice the way her ponytail swishes over her shoulder. "I thought there wasn't a Mr. Nice Guy bone in your body."

"That's it," he states flatly. "Now the training really starts." He circles around the mat, once more noting the way Arielle mirrors him. "I'm going to throw a few punches, you need to block them. I'll go easy to start with."

Arielle nods, her blue eyes once more laser focused. Reign assesses her stance, seeing the vulnerabilities. She leaves her left side more open than her right. Leaping forward, he throws out a punch as if he was aiming for her jaw. Nothing too hard. Nothing too fast.

She blocks, the motion almost instinctive, and steps away. "Are you trying to imitate a demon on Valium?"

Grinning, Reign repeats the process, but a little quicker this time. Arielle once more makes the block look easy, then quickly creates more space between them.

Rachel's obviously been giving lessons more frequently than he realized.

Reign starts to move more, bouncing a little as he warms up his muscles. He won't hurt Ari, but she's right. She'll be going up against demons. And they don't play nice.

He executes a double punch, one to the head, one to the solar plexus, intending on stopping short before he actually hits her. But he doesn't need to. She blocks. Then blocks again.

Stepping up the pace, he goes for a triple combo. Punch. Kick. Punch.

Block. Block. Block.

And this time, Ari follows up with a punch and kick combo of her own.

"Whoa," says Rachel. "I knew I was a good teacher, but I didn't know I was *that* good."

Reign maintains their dance around the mat, his pulse picking up a bit. There's a red flush on Arielle's cheeks showing she's getting warm also. And a sparkle in her eye that suggests maybe she's enjoying this, too.

He feints left, then kicks right. She nimbly steps out of the way. He follows her, trying again to connect his foot with her thigh, but she moves so fast his foot slices through air.

Arielle flicks her ponytail back over her shoulder. "You said to avoid close combat," she points out.

"Now you listen to me?" he teases back.

They continue, him the hunter, her the prey. Prey that's far quicker than he'd anticipated.

Suddenly, Arielle goes on the attack, coming at him with her own volley of punches and kicks. Now on the defensive, which to be honest, isn't a position he likes, Reign refuses to back down. He steps forward, dodging and blocking her blows.

Bring on the close combat.

Arielle becomes a flurry of flashing blue eyes, flushed skin, and sweat-dampened hair. And the sight quickly joins the list of one of the sexiest things he's ever seen.

That slight distraction is all it takes. Arielle's fist aims straight for his jaw, a hard glint in her gaze he's never seen before. He turns his head and arches back as it sails past him, brushing the skin of his cheek.

She misses, but there was so much power in the punch, her body follows through on the momentum, tumbling straight into him. And Reign's already off balance.

When he realizes they're falling, he grips Ari's arms, bracing her. A second later, his back hits the not-so-soft mats, drawing a grunt out of him.

"Reign! Oh my gosh, I'm so sorry!"

He blinks, discovering he's flat on his back.

With Arielle flush on top of him.

Oh. Shit.

Her hands flutter over his shoulders. "I didn't mean it. I swear."

He clears his throat, his hands still gripping her upper arms but not ready to let go. "I'm fine."

Her panicked gaze roams over his face, then locks with his.

Stops.

And doesn't let go.

Somehow, her flame blue eyes spark and melt all at once. Her lashes flutter. Her lips part.

Shit.

Shit.

Shit.

His throat too tight and his mouth too dry, he wills Ari to get off. To stop the slightly pinker shade of red from climbing up her throat and blossoming across her cheeks.

But she doesn't move. In fact, her body seems to turn molten along with the heat in her gaze. Soft curves mold to him like they're finding home.

For long seconds they stay where they are, locked in suspended animation. Their breathing quickens. Their hearts pound against their chests, as if they're trying to reach the other.

And then Arielle's gaze slides to his lips. Her own tongue flicks out to moisten hers.

He can feel that the next move either of them makes will be to consummate the desire that's a living, throbbing blaze between them.

Jeremy's chuckle barely registers through the roaring in Reign's ears. "They remind me of your father and mother, Rachel."

Those words, along with Rachel's sharp gasp, have Reign snapping out of his passion-filled trance. Arielle leaps to her feet and he's by her side a second later.

Did Jeremy just say he knew Rachel's mother?

RACHEL

Rachel tears her gaze away from the hot scene that was unfolding before her, turning her shocked gaze to Jeremy. "You knew my mom?"

Jeremy startles, almost as if he only just realized what he said. "Well, yes. She and your father were there to help me through a very difficult time in my life."

Probably when he lost his son.

But there's no way Rachel's focusing on that right now.

Jeremy knew her mother! She closes the photo album. Jeremy's stories will give her far more than faded, two-dimensional images. "How did you know her?"

"We all went to the same college—Mercy College." He smiles fondly. "We spent a lot of time in the library."

"My dad hung out in the library?" Rachel asks skeptically. Maybe Jeremy's memory isn't the best...

He chuckles. "Your father was only there because your mother was. He was infatuated to the point he pretended he liked to read."

Rachel smiles softly. That's exactly something her father would've done. "I remember them laughing a lot together."

Most of her early memories were happy ones. In fact, it was her mom who instilled the love of Disney in Rachel. They'd have popcorn movie nights, where her father would grouch about having to watch chick flicks, but cuddle up with them, and sigh dramatically over the happily ever after endings. It was those nights, when her parents would goo-goo eye each other when they thought Rachel wasn't looking, that had her believing that sort of love existed in the really real world.

Jeremy lets out a breath, his back hunching. "Theirs was an epic love. The forever kind. In fact, your father gave up competing in martial arts for her, and it was never a sacrifice. He used to say he gained a wife and a child, nothing could compare to that."

Which is what she remembers. Her parents so happy. So full of love. "Then why did she leave?" she whispers.

Jeremy shakes his head. "I don't know. One day they were soulmates, the next she was gone." He tries to draw up a smile. "And your father bought the dojo."

"Why didn't you tell me you knew her?"

He looks away. "It hadn't really come up."

Rachel's mouth pops open. Of course it hadn't come up! She didn't know that Jeremy, her dad, and her mom were besties in

213

college! But she quickly snaps it shut, unsure of how to proceed. Jeremy isn't much of a talker, and she suspects him being here is an achievement.

But now that she knows he could have more information on her mom, how can she just sit here and let the topic slide?

"She sounds like she loved you very much," says Arielle, covering the few steps to stand before them.

"Not enough to stay," says Rachel, unsurprised by the bitterness in her tone.

"Your dad did," Reign says softly.

Rachel's eyes flutter closed at the bittersweet pain his words trigger. Her dad really did love her, with everything he had. Reign didn't have that growing up. She was truly lucky to have that in her life.

But her father's dead. Murdered right before her eyes.

How can she reconcile so much love with so much loss?

She opens her startled eyes when a hand wraps around her own clenched one. Jeremy leans forward. "I was told to never tell you." He straightens, tugging on the hem of his cardigan. "But that was when Paul was alive."

Rachel freezes, unsure where the love or loss bucket is about to get a top up. "Tell me what?"

"I know where your mother is. I can take you to her."

CHAPTER 24

ARIELLE

Rachel doesn't move for long moments. So long that Arielle goes to reach out, wanting to offer some support as she tries to assimilate what Jeremy just told her.

But before she gets a chance to move, Rachel snaps to attention. "Wow. She's in Mercy City, isn't she?"

Jeremy nods. "From memory, somewhere in the northern suburbs."

The other end of the city.

"And she never came to see us," Rachel grinds out. "Not once."

Arielle blinks as she realizes what Rachel must be thinking. Her mother was never far away. And she chose to keep her distance.

Rachel pulls up a megawatt smile that never reaches her eyes. "Let's continue with our training, shall we?"

She goes to walk past Reign but he grips her arm. "What are you doing?"

"It's pretty obvious, isn't it?" she says, her false smile still in place. "We need to be ready."

"You just found out you could go see your mom."

"I know," Rachel says through clenched teeth. "I was there for the conversation that happened twenty seconds ago."

Reign's watching her closely. Although his grip on her arm is loose, she hasn't moved or pulled away. "Training can wait," he says.

"That's not what we decided this morning."

"That was before we learned you can go see your mom." He repeats the last words with intensity, as if to make sure Rachel understands what they really mean.

"Go and see the mother who left us? Who never visited? Who wants nothing to do with me?"

His face softens. "Yep. That's what I'm saying."

"No. Thank. You."

Reign moves in a little closer, his voice dipping. "You'll have answers, Rach. I'd sure love to have those about my parents."

Rachel blinks rapidly. "Reign..."

He shakes his head. "This isn't about me. This is about you, getting a chance to know why. To see her again, even if it hurts."

Arielle's heart constricts at the raw honesty in his words. Reign will never be able to see his parents. Rachel has that chance.

Her lower lip trembles. "She might slam the door in my face."

"Then you know she's a bitch and not worth all the 'what ifs' that have hung over your head most of your life. That she's hurt you enough."

A tear trickles down Rachel's cheek as she bites the wobbly lip.

"Or, she's ready to mend bridges. Everyone makes mistakes." Reign's mouth twists, his eyes sparkling with warm humor. "Believe me, I know."

Rachel brushes away the tear. "You think I should go see her."

His lips tip up at the obviousness of her statement. "Yes, that's what I'm saying."

Arielle holds her breath, noting that Jeremy's doing the same. This would be a tough decision for Rachel.

Going from stop to go with a suddenness Arielle's starting to associate with her, Rachel gives Reign a swift, hard hug, barely giving him time to return it before turning to Jeremy. "I'd like to go see her."

Jeremy nods, his eyes shining with moisture. "Excellent." He pats his pockets. "To do that, we'll need to stop by my place." He flushes. "My cell phone's at home and her address is in there."

"That's fine," Arielle assures. "We can go get it."

"I rarely bring it with me," he admits, gaze sliding away. "It's not like there's anyone checking up on my whereabouts."

Compassion wells through Arielle. The loneliness is apparent in Jeremy's voice.

"I rang you today," Rachel points out teasingly. "Inviting you here. What would've happened if I couldn't get hold of you?"

They would've come to the dojo without Jeremy and not found out everything they just did.

Jeremy smiles, his cheeks pinking. "Very true. And you rang at the time I go on my morning walk." He frowns quizzically. "I felt a strong urge to stay home today."

Thanks to Colt's compulsion spell. Which is only going to last another day or so. Those walks are going to make Jeremy vulnerable.

Good. The sooner he's dead the sooner we can focus on more important things.

Although he's not the Innocent.

Arielle heads toward the door, as if she can create distance between herself and the hateful things the obsidian says. "I say no time like the present."

Jeremy strides over to join her, looking the sprightliest she's seen so far. "Excellent idea, my dear."

Rachel glances at Reign. He smiles. "I'll be there with you every step of the way."

"Damn straight you will be," she says, nudging him with her shoulder, clearly appreciating his support.

She pulls her car keys out of her pocket, throws them up and catches them. "It'll probably be quicker if I drive."

Reign chuckles and Arielle grins, while Jeremy wonders what the joke is. Rachel drove like a normal person the moment they picked Jeremy up from his house, proving she's perfectly capable of respecting the speed limit. And braking. And not taking the laws of gravity as a personal challenge.

Rachel locks up the dojo and they climb into her car, Jeremy in the front. In the backseat, Arielle pretends she's not highly conscious of Reign's proximity. The strong body that she inadvertently plastered herself across is only a few inches away. Those ridged muscles and delicious valleys her body had molded to. The heat she's only ever felt with him...

Touch him. Taste him.

Then tell him...

Arielle plants her hands in her laps, weaving her fingers together. That's exactly what she wants to do. But she can't trust the obsidian. She's not sure she can trust herself.

In the front, Jeremy begins to describe the history of much of what they pass. Rachel makes a point of looking fascinated and asking questions. They pass city hall and Jeremy starts to talk about some architect called Sir Jeremy Mercy Davenport who famously designed the building.

Arielle notices Reign doesn't seem to be listening. He's staring out his window, but seems deep in thought. She opens her mouth to speak but quickly stops. She wants to tell him she was touched by what he did for Rachel. Pushing her was just what she needed, and he did it with care and humor. But this isn't the time to talk about it.

Unless they're more than friends...

Once again, Arielle ignores the obsidian. Pretends the flash of jealousy that scorches her veins doesn't happen.

She won't let either rule her actions.

Reign's never looked at Rachel the way he did when Arielle landed on top of him. His green gaze scorched every inch of skin it landed on.

Stupid, naive girl.

You're mistaking physical lust for emotional attachment.

Maybe. That's what she assumed when Lust was alive. But she's dead. Arielle made sure of that. And that assumption means she never got to find out what was truth and what was the lies her mind tells her.

Just like the obsidian does.

"Oh, goodness me," says Jeremy. "Does no one have any self-respect nowadays?"

Arielle looks around, spotting what has Jeremy's attention. A woman is hurrying across the road, her dressing gown flapping in her rush. One of her worn slippers flicks off in her haste, but she barely notices. She glances around frantically as if she's being followed. Her arms are laden with packets of chocolate biscuits.

Jeremy looks away. "It seems not."

Arielle wonders if Jeremy notices the way the atmosphere within Rachel's car sombers. He doesn't know that Gluttony is influencing that woman's actions. Like so many others.

Rachel slows as a delivery truck ahead does the same, its reversing lights flashing on as it pulls into a loading zone. They drive around it as two armed guards exit alongside the driver.

Their hands rest on their holsters, fingertips brushing their guns as their alert gazes comb the area. Arielle realizes the guards are there for the delivery man's protection.

People's safety is no longer guaranteed.

"Ari," Reign says quietly. As she sees what he's looking at, she stills. The two people waving placards to passing motorists are as worrying as everything she's seen so far. She rereads their message just to make sure she got it right.

We are blessed.

Angels are among us.

"People will believe anything," mutters Jeremy. "Self-respect is progressively going extinct in Mercy City."

Arielle turns to Reign. "Surely…"

But the apprehension pulling his features tight tells her he doesn't think this is a coincidence.

Somehow, those people know angels exist. And they're confidently declaring that to the world.

Yes, hisses the obsidian. *It's happening. The end is coming.*

It's only a matter of time now.

Arielle yanks her gaze away from Reign before he sees the impact of those words. The strain it takes to pretend they weren't said. The shame that she's hearing it at all.

The fear that the obsidian is right.

The rest of the drive is silent, even Jeremy no longer giving them the history lesson. Rachel's knuckles are white on the steering wheel as they pull into his driveway, and Arielle wonders how much is seeing the impact of Gluttony and the angel reference, and how much is the fact they're about to get her mother's address.

That she'll be seeing her again after all these years. Possibly today.

Probably all of the above.

They've just come to a stop when Jeremy gasps. "What in tarnation!"

Reign instantly leans forward, alert. "What?"

It's Rachel who sees it first. "You've been broken into?" she asks Jeremy, aghast.

Jeremy's front door is wide open, a window has been smashed, and the overgrown grass is trampled.

Reign leaps out. "Stay here. They could still be in there."

Excellent.

Hopefully the demons will take care of him.

CHAPTER 25
REIGN

Reign finds Arielle and Rachel by his side before he's reached the open front door. "I don't even know why I bother saying that anymore."

Rachel winks at him. "Me neither."

"Because you're a protector, through and through," says Arielle.

Reign looks away before she sees the impact her words have on him. The way they make him feel stronger. Better. Worth the air he breathes.

He pauses at the front door, listening, Arielle and Rachel right behind him. Furniture is overturned and the phone has been yanked out of the wall, but there's no movement. Apart from a gentle breeze blowing down the hallway, everything's silent.

Stealthily, they enter. Glass litters the floor from a smashed mirror and Reign carefully steps around it, avoiding any chance of seeing his reflection. Truth be told, this is how he prefers mirrors.

A quick sweep through the house reveals what Reign suspected. No demons.

"They were looking for Jeremy," says Rachel tensely.

Reign nods. "They must've found a way to break through the warding spell."

"Maybe they were waiting for it to weaken enough to get through," says Arielle, frowning at the mess the demons left.

They wanted them to know they were here.

That they're closing in on the Innocent.

Jeremy enters, his face pale and shell-shocked. "They've really done quite the number." He frowns as he scans the living room they're standing in. The TV's lying on its side, knocked over, but still intact. "I don't think they took anything."

Reign recognizes the opening for what it is. "They weren't after valuables. They were after you."

Arielle nods, her face earnest. "Your life is in danger, Jeremy."

Jeremy startles, looking almost as surprised at that than his house being broken into. "Me? What would someone want with me?"

The angelic essence he doesn't know he carries.

Rachel opens her mouth then quickly shuts in, frowning in consternation. How are they supposed to impress on Jeremy the very real threat to his life when he doesn't believe in the supernatural?

Reign brightens as an idea strikes him. "It's the satanic cult you told us about. They're back."

"Yes," says Arielle. "And they want revenge for ratting on them."

Rachel nods. "They're dangerous. They're the ones who killed my father and Shell."

Jeremy slams his fist into his palm. "I knew it!"

Relieved he's buying it, Reign steps closer. "And you're next on their list."

"Thank you for warning me," says Jeremy, looking serious,

but not particularly concerned. "Forewarned is forearmed." He looks around his home. "I'll need to get this place secure again."

Rachel smiles. "Why don't you come and stay with us for a few days? We have a great big farmhouse with plenty of space."

"That's very generous of you, Rachel, but no thank you. I like my privacy."

"We insist," says Reign, trying to sound gracious and not tense. "I'm sure there are more photo albums to go through."

Jeremy lifts his hand as if to stop the insistence as he shakes his head. "No, really. I have no intention of staying anywhere else tonight or any other night."

Reign, Arielle and Rachel all glance at each other. They have to find a way to convince him.

"You don't have a front door," he points out.

"I'll call a locksmith."

"And they've smashed a window," adds Arielle.

"I'll call a glazier." Jeremy's brow climbs down with each response as he digs his heels in.

"You don't understand what you're up against," says Rachel, urgency creeping into her tone. "This is all related to what's going on out on the streets. People gorging on food, killing each other over it."

"How can this possibly be connected to that?" Jeremy asks incredulously. He narrows his eyes. "Are you going to start talking about magic or angels or any of that mumbo jumbo again? Because I won't hear of it. There's no such thing."

Rachel sighs while Arielle frowns.

Reign decides the time for talk is over. With one swift movement, he steps forward and clocks Jeremy in the jaw.

His head snaps back as his eyes roll up before disappearing behind his eyelids. He crumples and Reign catches him as he loses consciousness.

Reign lowers him to the ground, propping him up against a

buffet hutch lying on the floor. He straightens to find two unimpressed young women looking at him with their hands on their hips.

He shrugs. "He was never going to agree to come."

Rachel's eyebrows almost hit the roof. "So we're going to kidnap him?"

"Who's going to report it? He lives alone, and we'll tell any nosy neighbors that he's staying with us while his house is repaired."

Arielle bites her lip. "Which is technically the truth."

Rachel rolls her eyes. "At least we're honest kidnappers, I suppose."

They make quick work of Rachel driving her car into the garage, carefully placing Jeremy's groaning self onto the backseat, and getting out on the road. Rachel takes the suburban back roads until they leave the city behind and are on the stretch out to the farmhouse.

They only speak again once Jeremy is stretched on the couch beside the large fireplace. They all stand around, looking at the older man, who's now even more disheveled than usual.

"Kidnapping successful," Reign says cheerily.

"I can't wait to put that on my resume," says Rachel dryly.

Arielle bends over, inspecting Jeremy a little closer. "He brought it on himself."

Reign suppresses a frown. He's never heard her talk quite so...callously.

Jeremy groans the loudest so far and Arielle straightens. "I think he's waking up," she whispers.

As if she gave him permission, Jeremy's eyes flutter open. He blinks a few times, trying to bring the world into focus.

Then registers he's most definitely not somewhere familiar.

He sits up, alarmed, looking around frantically. Rachel

quickly steps in his line of sight. "It's okay, Jeremy, you're somewhere safe."

Jeremy frowns. "Rachel?"

He looks beyond her and sees Reign, his eyes widening. "You..."

Reign grins. "You forgot to block."

He shoots to his feet, spluttering. "This is preposterous. You've kidnapped me!"

Rachel holds her hands out in a conciliatory gesture. "Look, what we did was extreme." She glances dryly at Reign. "And could be considered kidnapping, but you're in danger, Jeremy. We need you to listen to us."

Jeremy's face is like watching a ripening tomato on time lapse. It progressively goes redder and redder. "I will not have this. Let me go."

Arielle moves to stand beside Rachel. "This is the safest place for you right now."

"It may be more opulent and organized than my humble little house, but it's no safer," Jeremy snaps.

Reign crosses his arms, his patience fast disappearing. "Is your house warded to the rafters against every magical being in existence?"

Jeremy throws his arms out in frustration. "Are we back to that again?" he practically yells.

"He's telling the truth," Rachel says quietly. "Demons want you dead, Jeremy."

Arielle nods. "We can help you."

He looks at them one by one, before settling wide eyes on Reign. "You're insane." He turns to Rachel and Arielle. "You're all certifiable."

Rachel winces. The hurt that flashes across her face has Reign going from annoyed to angy. Rachel's treated Jeremy with kindness and openness, desperately looking for a living link to her dead father. She looked beyond his cantankerous, unkempt exterior and connected with the fellow human inside.

And he just told her she's crazy.

Jeremy snorts in disgust and pushes between them, striding past. "I will not stay here."

Arielle and Rachel's stricken faces as they watch Jeremy walk away are the final straws. They're terrified another Innocent's blood is about to stain their souls.

"Stop!" roars Reign.

Jeremy stiffens like the word was a blow to his back, but continues on. He's just reached for the doorknob when a shudder ripples through the house.

Everyone stills, looking around in shock.

The second tremor is bigger than the first. Picture frames knock on walls. Glassware rattles in display cabinets. The very floor seems to be churning.

Reign is by Arielle's side in a second, but by then, the shaking has stopped. They look at each other, and she looks as nonplussed as he feels. If he didn't know better, he'd say he caused that. But he's not supernatural. At this stage, he's barely a Grail Keeper seeing as he's not even out looking for it.

But he's never heard of earthquakes in Mercy City or its surrounds, and the chances that one would happen just as Jeremy was about to leave...

Jeremy turns around, his face pale. "What was that?"

Reign strides back, thinking quickly. Although he has no idea what that was, he's going to use it to his advantage. "Gabby said the warding spells will keep nasties out, but also anyone who needs to be contained in."

"What?" Jeremy squeaks.

"If you open that door, it'll set off the booby trap."

He pales. "Booby trap?"

"I'm not exactly sure what limb it will target, but this place is owned by a witch, and they have one hell of a sense of humor."

"I'm...I'm just going to sit down for a moment." Jeremy returns to the couch on wobbly legs and sits down, clasping his trembling hands. He stares at the floor as if he wants to disappear into it.

"Jerem—" says Rachel.

But he snaps his hand up. "I need a moment to think."

Reign indicates for her and Arielle to join him by the door. "He can't leave until we've taken out Gluttony," he says in a low voice. "But someone needs to stay with him."

Arielle frowns. "We'll have to split up again."

Rachel rubs her arm. "I'll stay. Poor guy hasn't had a good day."

"But he's alive," Reign points out. He glances at Arielle. "And you're right. Splitting up isn't ideal. That's why I think we could use a hand."

"From where? My mom and Mac are who-knows-where. Gabby and Colt are in Rome...as far as we know."

Reign grins. "I know who we can call."

"Who?" Arielle asks as Rachel's face fills with realization.

"The Knights Templar."

RACHEL

Rachel gingerly sits on the other end of the couch as the sound of Arielle's car recedes. Jeremy hasn't moved in the short time it took Reign and Arielle to get organized. He hadn't acknowledged Reign making a call to Kenna, explaining they'd found the Innocent and needed help. He hadn't twitched when Reign said they were leaving as Kenna gave him a location to meet.

And now he doesn't even seem to notice that Rachel's the only one with him.

It means she almost startles when he speaks. "You know, this wouldn't be the first breakdown I've ever had."

Rachel's chest constricts. "Jeremy, this was all a shock for me too—"

"The first time was when my wife left me, taking our son with her."

"I'm so sorry," she says, realizing Jeremy needs to talk through this. It seems the painful experience he just went through has triggered the memories of another.

"When I realized they were gone, I tried to find them. With everything I had I tried to find them. But she just…disappeared. She didn't want to be found." His hands knead each other as he stares at them. "And when I realized there was nothing I could do, I sat down and stayed down. I didn't move unless I had to. Didn't shower, barely ate. I'm not sure how long for."

Rachel clasps her own hands, wishing she could offer some sort of solace but knowing she can't. The pain of loss is one that never goes away.

"It was your father and mother who were there for me. They helped me carve out a life again."

No wonder Jeremy didn't care about the state of his house. Or even himself. He was still grieving.

Rachel shuffles forward. "I could help you find your son."

His gaze snaps to hers. "How?"

"No hocus pocus," she promises, her hands up. "I'm as human as you are. But one with a talent for finding any information filed away on the world wide web."

"I could see Julian again?"

"You helped me find my mother." She offers a small smile. "It's only fair I help you find your son."

After everything that Jeremy's been through, by no fault of his own, it's the least she could do.

Something flickers in Jeremy's eyes. Something that looks very much like hope. "He'd be a couple of years older than you. Probably in college." He smiles. "He loved to read."

Rachel shifts closer to him and wraps her hand around his. "I promise we'll find Julian."

Jeremy's lips press tightly together as he tries to contain his tears. "I would like that," he finally says.

Relieved and glad she's finally brought something good into his life, she grins broadly. "We'll start first thing in the morning."

"After we've visited your mother," Jeremy says with a teasing glint.

Her heart trips just like every time anyone's mentioned her name since Jeremy said he knows where she lives. The thought of seeing her, after all this time, is...giving her palpitations. But Reign was right.

She needs answers, no matter how painful they might be.

Jeremy glances at the door. "Can I really not leave?"

Unsure whether she's doing the right thing, but no longer wanting to lie, Rachel shakes her head. "We had a freak earthquake and Reign made the most of it."

Jeremy shakes his head. "You kids were all playing some trick on me, weren't you?" He glares good naturedly. "It wasn't funny."

It almost triggered a breakdown in a man made fragile by loss. And yet, all they told him was the truth.

And his life is still at risk.

"Why don't we make something to eat?" she suggests, pushing to her feet. "We can talk more then."

"That sounds lovely. I've been quite surprised by my appetite lately."

Rachel keeps her smile in place, despite Jeremy's words. Gluttony's effect is even more proof that they need Jeremy to understand what's going on.

Jeremy stands but before they can move, there's a thundering *crash*. The house shakes in the same way that it did when Reign and Arielle were here. Followed by silence.

Jeremy's eyes are once again wide and frightened. "Another earthquake?"

"Maybe," says Rachel, although she's not even sure that's what the first one was.

She rushes to the window by the door and peers through a gap in the curtains. Her own eyes widen when she sees what caused the awful smashing sound.

A car is lying on its side several yards away, engulfed in flames.

"What is going on?" breathes Jeremy beside her.

Rachel jolts to find him there. She's about to say she's not entirely sure when another car appears, blazing them with its bright headlights. It roars as it gains speed.

It's coming straight at them.

Rachel grabs Jeremy's arm, ready to yank him to safety when, with a sudden jerk, the driver's thrown out, landing on the ground in a crumpled heap as the vehicle stops like it just hit an invisible wall. The car bursts into flames, coming to a stand still beside the other burning vehicle.

"What is the world..." gasps Jeremy.

Rachel's not sure what has him more gobsmacked. The fact an invisible force just ejected someone from a car, or the dual burning vehicles that seemed to self combust. She yanks her cell out of her pocket, heart thundering.

Demons have found them.

But both Reign and Arielle's numbers go straight to voicemail. Wherever they are, they don't have reception.

Jeremy jams his fingers through his hair. "There has to be a reasonable explanation."

She turns to him. "If you believe in magic, there is."

He opens his mouth to object, but a voice beyond the house has Rachel's veins icing over.

"I know you're in there," calls a female in a sing-song tone.

Rachel turns back, blinking at the specter now standing beside the burning cars. Tall and voluptuous, the blonde woman is wearing little more than a yellow bikini, exposing rolls of undulating flesh. Expansive ebony wings frame her luminescent flesh.

Gluttony.

Jeremy takes a step back. "No, no, no."

Gluttony's wings arch up. "I know you have the Innocent." She smiles, her red eyes blazing. "And I want him."

"What is going on, Rachel?" asks Jeremy, his voice trembling.

She tears her gaze away from the horrifying sight of the Sin, finding Jeremy rooted to the spot. Just like during the earthquake, his skin is the color of ash and his eyes the size of moons. "Everything we told you is true," Rachel says, trying to be gentle, but knowing there's no time. "My father and Shell were sacrificed by demons. Sins have been wreaking havoc on Mercy City, that's why people are eating so much." She swallows, hating that there's a punchline. "And you're an Innocent, just like my dad and Shell. And Gluttony wants to sacrifice you."

Jeremy doesn't move. Doesn't blink. Seems to have forgotten to breathe.

Rachel's chest aches at the knowledge this has probably broken him all over again.

"Very well," calls Gluttony, taking a step back. "Let's have a little fun."

She extends her hands and glowing balls of yellow energy

burst from her palms. With a twisted smile, she unleashes them. Rachel leaps in front of Jeremy as he doesn't even flinch. But the golden fireballs hit an invisible wall several yards away from the farmhouse and are instantly absorbed.

Just like Gabby promised, there's a shield surrounding the place. It's what prevented the cars and the demons driving them from getting anywhere near it.

And that seems to piss Gluttony off. She squares her shoulder and unleashes a volley of fury, releasing fireball after fireball. Yellow bursts of energy explode against the shield, splatting like the sun against a window, then disappearing. Over and over, Gluttony batters the shield, her eyes glowing brighter with each onslaught, as if the promise of destruction is feeding her.

Despite her hammering heart, Rachel tries to keep her cool. Jeremy's life depends on it. Is each burst weakening the shield? How long will it last?

Does Gluttony have the place surrounded by demons?

The Sin stops as abruptly as she started. "If you do not give me the Innocent," she shouts. "I will do the same to houses, malls, to city hall itself. I will raze Mercy City to the ground."

Rachel gasps. Gluttony wasn't trying to weaken the shield. She was demonstrating her power.

Turning to Jeremy, she grips his arms, finding his muscles locked and hard. "We killed the last Sin, Lust," she assures him. "We'll end this one, too."

She just has to figure out whether they stay and bunker down, hoping for reinforcements, or whether they run.

Considering Jeremy hasn't twitched a hair since Gluttony arrived.

Running to the next window, she finds a demon staring at her with the promise of Hell in its eyes from beyond the backyard. The next window is the same. She reaches the other side of the room, and glances out the side.

"Demons everywhere," she mutters to herself.

"I won't wait long," warns Gluttony. "I'm hungry for Innocent."

"Go eat one of your own," Rachel shouts back, wishing the Sin would shut up. She needs to think.

Jeremy has a son to reunite with.

"I can't do nothing. Not this time."

Rachel jolts at the sounds of Jeremy's voice. Then she realizes he's not only talking, he's moving. He's gripping the door handle. Turning it.

"No," she screams. "Jeremy! Don't do it!"

He opens the door, glancing over his shoulder. "I can't let an entire city be decimated because of me. Because I just sat around, defined by apathy."

"No!" she screams again, breaking into a sprint.

But Jeremy's already out the door. He runs down the path, straight toward Gluttony. The demon opens her arms, like a mother welcoming her child. Never losing momentum, Jeremy propels straight into them.

The Innocent just willingly gave himself to the Sin.

Triumph twists Gluttony's fleshy features as she wraps first her arms around him, then her black-as-death wings. And disappears, taking the other demons with her.

Rachel's left standing just beyond the door, heart crushed and mind shattered.

All that's left behind are two burning cars and hot tears running down her cheeks.

CHAPTER 26

ARIELLE

Arielle stands beside Reign as they survey the burned out hulk of a building before them.

"Kenna said this place was used as an illicit liquor bar during prohibition—a speakeasy," he explains. "When someone realized it had such a colorful history, they turned it into a legit place."

Arielle nudges a charred brick with her toe, still reeling from their conversation in the car. Vampires are real. And there's an organization tasked with exterminating them, descendants of the Knights Templar. And Reign knows their leader, Kenna. "I don't think the place had a happy ending."

"Nope," says Reign. "It burned down and no one has touched it since."

"And this is where she said to meet us?" Arielle looks around. The old bar is along an empty street, a handful of stores dotted around that are just as empty. Whatever commerce was done here is long dead.

"Yeah," says Reign, stepping through the hole where the front door used to be. "She said to look for the symbol."

Following him, Arielle frowns. "The symbol?"

"Uh huh, the symbol." Reign's voice fades as his focus sharpens, looking around the burned out hulk. The far wall is nothing but an expanse of black, charred shelves lining it, shards of mirror dotted between like a half-finished mosaic. What must've been a bar stretches before it. The odd singed chair or table is overturned, while above them hang the ruined remains of twisted light fittings. Arielle doesn't see a symbol, although it's not like she knows what she's looking for.

A doorway to their left catches Reign's attention and he turns, glass and charcoal crunching underfoot as he makes his way over. He peers inside. "Looks like it used to be a storeroom."

Arielle follows. "The Knights Templar are vampire hunters," she says, needing to hear it aloud. "How fascinating."

The storeroom isn't very large, another door showing a stained sink in what's probably a bathroom on the other side. More shelves, these ones less fire damaged than those behind the bar, line the walls, but far more broken and dilapidated cling to the wall in haphazard lines.

"They use a different title now—the Order of the Knightly Rose—but that's who they descended from." Reign steps into the storeroom, looking around. "They've worked closely with the Grail Keepers throughout history."

"And you think they'll help us with finding Gluttony and ending her?"

"From the excitement in Kenna's voice, I don't think it matters what evil supernatural being it is, she's up for it." He pauses, his gaze transfixed on the shelves. "Hello, symbol."

At first Arielle doesn't see it, but once she does, she can't unsee it. A central beam runs up the center of the shelves, most missing down the bottom, but some of the higher ones still intact. The top row almost creates a double crucifix, the one below it slightly wider than the first.

The Cross de Lorraine, whispers the obsidian, never far away. Seeing everything she does.

"The Cross de Lorraine?" Arielle repeats, having never heard of it.

Reign turns to her in surprise. "Wow. You've done better than me. If I hadn't seen it in some documentary when I was a kid, I never would've known what it was."

Arielle flushes. "That must've been where I saw it, too."

"So much for being impressed with my memory," he jokes lightly.

Arielle smiles even as her stomach tightens. She can't tell Reign the truth that he did notice something important as a child and remembered it. Otherwise she'd have to explain how she knew what it was...

He turns back to it. "Now, to figure out what to do with it."

Stepping forward, he runs his hand over the nearest shelf at the edge of one of the perpendicular arms of the cross, but finds nothing. He moves along it to the other side, and still nothing happens. He gets the same outcome from the top shelf, too.

Arielle angles her head as she looks at it. "It's crooked."

Reign joins her, dusting his hands on his jeans. "It is?"

"Look." She points to the longer shelves on the right. "They're longer than the other side."

"Oh yes, they are, too."

"It might be to conceal the symbol, just like the other shelves dotted on the wall..."

Reign grins at her and Arielle's heart compulsively jolts, as if there are threads directly connected from the edges of those lips to her chest. "Or maybe it's not."

He strides over to the long end, presses his hand against the edge of the extra length of shelf and pushes. With a jerk, the entire row shifts to the left, lining up perfectly with the shorter one above.

There's a barely audible *click*. Then a *thud* somewhere deep in the wall. And the whole expanse opens like a door.

"Yep, definitely not," says Reign, his eyebrows hiking up in his hairline.

Almost as soon as the door opens, it begins to swing shut. He holds out his hand. "Quick!"

Arielle rushes forward and takes it. Together they slip through the disappearing gap, finding themselves in an identical room on the other side. The door slides closed, plunging them in darkness.

Reign's hand instantly tightens around hers as he moves closer. "You okay?"

You're a killing machine.

You can face anything that comes at you.

Arielle presses her arm more firmly against Reign's, trying to ground herself in the warm, comforting sensation. "How many spiders do you think are in here?"

"Absolutely none," he quips. "Let me get my phone."

The moment Reign moves to get it, they're bathed in light. Blinking, they look around, seeing light fittings along the wall, which apparently have movement sensors. Stone steps are a few feet away, also lit, but curving into darkness.

Now in a brightly lit room, Arielle realizes exactly how close she's standing to Reign. In fact, she's practically wrapped around his arm. She steps away, but can't bring herself to release his hand.

Reign clears his throat. "I doubt there are any spiders down there, either."

"A dark, creepy, secret basement. Definitely not favored spider hangouts."

"Exactly what I was thinking."

They move simultaneously, and Arielle's glad that Reign's still holding her hand.

Out of pity.

Because you won't accept your destiny. To be the most powerful force on Earth.

They find the stairs light up as they approach them, and their descent is illuminated. This place is obviously well set up. They're almost at the bottom when sounds reach them. Thuds. Grunts. Bodies colliding.

The sound of fighting.

Rounding the curve, the space opens out to reveal what almost looks like Rachel's dojo, but this one is full. About twenty people are sparring in groups of two to five, all sweaty, some sporting a swollen eye or a split lip. The large room is well lit, and largely covered in mats. Punching bags and gym equipment are to the left, while there are two doors to the right.

A woman strides up to them, not particularly tall, but lean and hard, her dark blonde hair in a tight ponytail. Wearing black tights and an army green tank top, she looks both feminine and para-military.

"Arielle, this is Kenna. Kenna, meet Arielle."

"Hey," she says before turning to Reign. "What took you so long?" she practically snarls.

Arielle blinks. They found the cross and how to enter pretty darned quickly.

Insolent bitch.

Kill her.

Stiffening at the virulent words and the unwanted flush of fury, Arielle locks every muscle from her head to her toes. The obsidian's need for blood is growing.

"The directions you gave us were shit," Reign snaps back, shocking her all over again.

Kenna grins. "They really were." She slaps him on the shoulder. "Good to have you here."

"We need to talk," says Reign. "We have the Innocent."

TAMAR SLOAN

For as long as Jeremy believes that bogus explanation Reign gave him for the weird-ass earthquake.

"Let's go to my office."

Kenna leads them around the perimeter of the room, skirting the training Knights. "Felix, stay focused," she shouts. There's an *oomph* as someone gets hit. "See what I mean?"

Opening the first door, she leads them into a small office that's as spartan and austere as Kenna is. A metal desk sits in the center, bare apart from a laptop, three metal chairs around it. "Please, have a seat," she offers.

They sit down, Kenna on the other side of the desk as she clasps her hands on it. "We've been trying to pinpoint Gluttony for days," she says, getting straight down to business. "But she's slipperier than a lard-covered anaconda. Every time we hone in on a location, we walk into a vampire ambush."

"So they are working together," mutters Reign.

Kenna snorts. "Demons are using vampires to do their dirty work for them, and they're too stupid to see it." She grins. "The good news is, we're taking out vampires each time it happens.

"That's good," offers Arielle.

Kenna frowns in response. "Except the demonic attacks are increasing. Gluttony isn't just happy to let humans kill each other, she wants to up the death toll. It's attracting the attention of the Federal Government. We have intel there's a military division on its way to the city."

"That's not helpful," says Reign.

"They'll just get in the way," agrees Kenna. "The good news doesn't end there. There's been reports of angels fighting demons. Even angels fighting angels."

The image of the people holding the placards flashes through Arielle's mind.

Angels are among us.

240

But if they're fighting among themselves, then no one is going to be feeling blessed.

Kenna's hands tighten around each other. "They're going to bring the fucking apocalypse crashing down on our heads."

Reign's jaw is tight and his lips thin. "Releasing another Sin isn't going to be good for the situation."

"Exactly," snarls Kenna. "Which is why we've deployed all our resources to tracking down the bitch."

The knock on the door has them all spinning around. "Yes?" barks Kenna.

It opens to reveal a smiling young man with a mop of blond wavy hair. "We've got another location on Gluttony."

Kenna pushes to her feet. "Where?"

Arielle and Reign glance at each other. A small army is going to go after the demon. This is just what they needed to even the odds.

The young man looks at the tablet in his hand. "Somewhere on the outskirts of town this time." He taps at the screen. "Looks like a farmhouse. Out on Three Stars Lane."

This time, Arielle and Reign launch to their feet. "Rachel," breathes Arielle. "Oh no. Jeremy."

"What?" demands Kenna. "What is it?"

Arielle and Reign move simultaneously, launching for the door so fast the young man leaps out of the way. "The farmhouse is where we're staying," he calls over his shoulder.

"And it's where the Innocent is," adds Arielle.

They've just hit the stairs when Kenna's shout reaches them. "Roll out, Knights!"

Please don't let them be too late.

They can't lose the Innocent. Not when they're so close.

CHAPTER 27
REIGN

They're too late.

The flaming vehicles stacked almost on top of each other pouring black smoke into the sky is the first sign.

Rachel, crumpled and sobbing on the porch, is the second.

The absence of Jeremy is the final one. Like a nail in a coffin.

They've lost the Innocent.

Arielle kneels beside Rachel, wrapping her arms around her. "What happened?"

Rachel looks up, face saturated with her grief. "Gluttony came, but Gabby's warding kept her at bay, no matter what she threw at us. But then she threatened to raze Mercy City to the ground if I didn't give Jeremy up."

"There's no way you would've done that," says Reign. Rachel is more stubborn than him.

Rachel shakes her head, strands of her red hair sticking to her wet cheeks. "Jeremy gave himself up. I tried to stop him, but he ran straight to her. He said he couldn't sit by and let her do that."

Arielle's arms tighten around Rachel. "You did everything you could."

Rachel looks up at her. "He has a son, Ari. I promised him we'd find him. It's the least I could do after everything he's been through."

And is yet to go through, Reign thinks sourly. Especially if they don't get to him in time...

Kenna appears, the young man with blond hair by her side. "It was definitely Gluttony," she says, waving a tablet around. "And she had at least twenty demons with her."

Rachel pushes to her feet, Arielle helping her. "We have to get him back," she says desperately. "We have to."

The young man nods. "That's the plan, and we have the technology to do it."

"In fact, we now have some of the clearest energy signals so far seeing as Gluttony was here so recently," says Kenna, tapping her screen. "We should be able to trace her demonic essence."

Rachel brushes her hair away from her face. "That's some pretty impressive technology."

The young man smiles. "We adapted some infrared scanners with a little extra, ah, juice."

"Interesting," she says, chewing her lip. "And how exact is it?"

"To a four foot radius."

Her eyebrows shoot up. "Nice."

"Marlowe," Kenna snaps. "We're going to need a clean up crew."

"On it," he says, hesitating, then spinning on his heel and striding away.

"We're used to making things disappear," she says, indicating toward the burning cars. "They won't be here by morning."

"Thanks," says Reign, impressed himself. When he decided to call in the Order, he didn't realize how well resourced they are. Not only do they have fighters and technology, they even get rid of evidence!

"Keepers and hunters have always worked together." She turns to Rachel. "Were there any vampires?"

"I...ah...don't think so." She frowns. "How can I tell?"

Kenna's lips twist. "You can't, not until the bloodlust overtakes them and their fangs show." She frowns in a way that has Reign focusing even closer. "There's something else you should know."

Rachel tenses like she's bracing herself, and he can't blame her. He's feeling kinda wary himself.

"Vampires usually report to a King, but the throne has been empty for some time now." She lifts her chin. "The Order took care of him and all his heirs. Since then they've been run by a Council, with each area under the control of a Master. They haven't been as strong, or as organized."

"But something's changed," says Reign.

"Yeah. Someone else, a third organization has been funding them and making sure they keep in line. That's what enabled them to join forces with demons."

"What third organization?" asks Arielle.

"They call themselves the Tenth Legion. An old organization, and a deeply evil one. They've had a hand in every war ever fought by humans."

Reign resists the urge to shift a little closer to Arielle. "I don't like the sound of that."

Kenna's face twists with anger. "We've been keeping track of them as much as we can. And learned they've been working with angels. But I don't think these angels are here to fight demons. They want something else."

Arielle gasps. "The faction Gabby told us about."

"Gabby?" asks Kenna. "Gabby Heartley?"

"You know here?" asks Arielle, surprised.

"We met at Mercy College. She's one kick ass angel."

"She sure is, and she's my cousin. She told us that her father's been fighting a rogue faction of angels. They want to free their overlord, the Archangel Michael, from his prison."

"The one Gabby put him in," snarls Kenna, obviously unhappy to hear this news. "Where's Gabby now?"

"With Colt, searching for the Grail."

Kenna's lips twist. "Good luck with that."

Reign decides he likes Kenna a little more. Finally, someone who realizes it would be nice to have a panacea for all this, but that could be little more than a pipe dream.

"Shit's getting complicated," mutters Reign.

Demons working with vampires.

The Tenth Legion aligning with angels.

And somewhere amongst this all, they need to keep the next Gate of Hell shut.

By saving Jeremy.

Reign glances around, noting the Knights of the Order swarming around the farmhouse, several trekking inside. "How long will this take?" he asks. Right now, each second feels like it's progressively multiplying in weight.

"Hopefully not long. Maybe an hour or two."

His gaze connects with Arielle and he sees the same worry coiling through his ribs reflected in her blue eyes. Rachel crosses her arms and shifts her weight.

They don't know if Jeremy has that long.

Although, the Order is likely to locate him much faster than they could. They just have to hope it's soon enough.

Saving the Innocent is becoming more important than ever.

"Kenna!" Marlowe jogs over, holding a tablet. "We have a location on Gluttony."

"Already?"

He grins, holding the tablet up to show her. "Must be because we got a good quality trace. And so soon after she was here." He glances at Rachel. "It's like tracking. The better and more recent the footprint, the more information we can extract."

Rachel's eyes flick to the tablet, clearly intrigued. "Cool."

Reign wonders if Marlowe's deliberately trying to reel Rachel in. If so, he's definitely found the right bait.

Although that's a question for another time. Reign, Arielle and Rachel glance at each other.

This is their chance.

Kenna waves a finger in the air in a circular motion. "Roll out, Knights. We got us a Sin to kill."

DINAH

Ryder is most definitely Arielle's father. As Dinah drives through the suburbs of Mercy City, she reviews what she's been able to find out.

He was involved with Sierra, nine months before Arielle's birth. He was a cop on Detective Kane's squad—none other than Cain himself.

And he disappeared off the face of the Earth about nineteen years ago, which means Dinah's tracking of him has come to a standstill. He's either dead, or now goes by another name. But she knows what he looks like, so that's a starting point.

And she refuses to believe he's dead.

Not when this information could have Arielle trusting her. Welcoming Dinah into the fold of the team.

Passing Mercy City University, Dinah brings up the fragmented images she was able to conjure with the crystal ball. Once she'd suspected she'd stumbled onto Arielle's father, she'd asked it another question.

What does Sierra want most in the world?

The answer hadn't been one image, but multiple. Snippets of memories. All of Ryder.

Ryder at a party, moving to a beat that can no longer be heard. Ryder laughing, blue eyes glinting with happiness. Ryder's face smoldering with passion.

Sierra wants to find him as much as Arielle does.

But for some reason, Ryder doesn't want to be found. Which doesn't make sense. It was obvious he was as drawn to Sierra as she was to him.

Still following the locator spell she cast, Dinah finds herself pulling up outside an apartment block. Neat gardens surround the tall, pale building, which she'd expect in this up market suburb. This was the last known location she could trace Ryder to, using little more than the images Sierra's memory had provided. Dinah has no idea how long ago that was, but she's hoping it'll lead to more clues.

Some information as to why Ryder abandoned Sierra and their unborn child.

Climbing out of her car, she follows the tug of magic low in her gut to an apartment on the ground floor. There's a knocker on the front door, but no doorbell, but that doesn't matter. Dinah doesn't plan on announcing her arrival.

She grips the doorknob and closes her eyes, murmuring quietly. "Resigno." There's a soft click and the knob turns. Dinah quickly slips through and closes the door behind her.

Being able to slip in and out of locked rooms so easily was certainly helpful during her days as an assassin for the Tenth Legion.

That, and her ability to trace just about anyone.

The apartment is clean and sparse, with an empty feeling suggesting no one's been here for a very long time. Still, Dinah remains cautious. A quick amplification of her senses reveals no other breath or heartbeat apart from her own within the apartment.

Unless there's an undead person or a ghost in here, she's alone.

Staying light on her feet, Dinah moves through the living room she's in, past a round dining table and a small kitchen. Beyond she finds a bedroom, and quickly recognizes it from the brief memory of Ryder with hot, heavy eyes. Sierra's been in here. With him.

Just like the living room and kitchen, everything is neat and orderly. And untouched.

Sensing something, Dinah moves to the wardrobe, using magic to slide open the door. Another advantage of being a witch is not having to leave fingerprints behind. Inside, sitting on a bottom shelf, is what drew her supernatural perception.

Books. Three of them. All large, leatherbound, and old.

Dinah levitates them to the bed, when she puts them down gently. With a wave of her hand, they open. A flicker of her fingers, and the pages turn slowly. There's enough time to see they're largely on demonology. None of it is information she hasn't read before.

It's the scribbled notes that are tucked in a few places that catch her interest. The scrawly, masculine writing reveals Ryder had been searching for the Holy Grail. She wonders if he still is.

She picks up one of the slips of paper, wishing she didn't have to touch it, but knowing she has no choice. Although it will mean leaving a trace that she's been here, it's the only way she can use the note to try and locate Ryder.

Dinah closes her eyes, focusing on the faint energy still clinging to the paper. She conjures Ryder's image and silently recites the ancient demoniac locator spell. With Ryder gone so long, she needs powerful magic for this. Dark magic.

The black power slithers through her veins and coils around her bones, thickening and flourishing. Mentally, she fashions it into a projectile. One designed to seek and discover. She propels it out into space and time. Ryder's current location would be most useful, but she's willing to cast her net wider considering it's been nineteen years since he's been seen.

The onyx energy instantly explodes as if it just hit a wall.

"What the..."

There's a block around Ryder. A shield stopping him from being found.

"Challenge accepted," she mutters.

Dinah tries again. And again. On the fourth attempt, she gives the power more time to amass. To become an atomic bomb of dark magic.

The shield surrounding Ryder absorbs it as if she's little more than a novice witch unable to harness anything greater than a thaum of magic. And she can certainly create more than a darned pigeon. But she can't get past whatever's protecting him.

Ryder's working with someone. Someone powerful. So powerful she's not sure she can break through the barrier surrounding him.

Dinah grinds her teeth. She doesn't like being bested.

With a frustrated swipe of her hand, the books return to the bottom shelf, exactly as they were when she first found them. She's tempted to slam the wardrobe closed, but tempers her anger. She didn't make a name for herself as a cold, calculating assassin with outbursts like that.

Instead, Dinah comes up with a Plan B, just like she always does.

It's time to visit the Tenth Legion.

CHAPTER 28

ARIELLE

The neon sign above the old bar saying *Heaven* is as dark and dead as the bar itself. Arielle stands outside it, Reign on one side and Rachel on the other, as they watch Kenna instruct the Knights to split up and swarm around the sides and back.

"Heaven could be a reference to angels," says Reign. "This could be it."

Arielle's body coils with tension. An Innocent has always been sacrificed somewhere connected with angels.

"And doesn't look like anyone's been here for a while," he adds.

The location of the sacrifice has always been away from prying eyes. Reign's right. This could be it.

Rachel nods. "Been closed for about three years according to a quick spot of research."

"You really want one of those tablets, don't you?" he asks, somehow still able to inject a teasing note into his voice despite the circumstances.

She flashes him a cheeky glance. "Do you reckon Kenna would notice if one went missing?"

He snorts. "I'm not sure losing all your limbs is worth the risk."

Rachel huffs out a laugh, turning back to scope out Heaven, her shoulders not quite so tense.

Arielle finds herself instinctively shifting a little closer to Reign. How could she not be drawn to him? He's the poster boy of unflappable in the face of adversity, possibly because he's seen so much in his life. It lowers the blood pressure of everyone around him, even as they're preparing to fight.

You have nothing to be concerned about.

Violence makes you strong. The thirst for bloodshed powers you.

Arielle stiffens. The obsidian's excited at the prospect of what's coming. The need to hurt is thrumming through her veins.

Reign glances at her. "You've got this," he says in a low voice, misreading her uneasiness. "You're a damn good fighter."

Yes, she is.

Stronger and more powerful than any of you.

She tries to smile, but her stomach is like a cement mixer. "Thanks. Just a little pre-fight jitters, that's all."

But his intense green gaze doesn't leave her. "We need someone on lookout. We can't afford for anyone to walk in on this."

For a brief moment, Arielle considers taking him up on the offer. The promise of dark power when Dumah was about to kill her flashes through her. It had been so tempting. And yet she knew if she gave in, it would swallow her whole. Will it be like that again?

Can she risk that?

She shakes her head. She's strong enough to fight the obsidian. She can't let everyone down now, not when they're so close. "No. I've got this."

Reign's sexy lips nudge up at the edges. "Didn't I just say that?"

Holy heck, she wants to kiss him. Touch him. Tell him everything.

Kenna appears by his side, passing each one of them a wooden stake. "The signal is definitely strong, meaning Gluttony's probably here, but we need to be prepared."

Arielle grips the smooth timber, stomach recoiling at the thought of spearing it into someone's chest.

Yes, hisses the obsidian. *Glorious blood. Exhilarating death.*

Kenna's hand punches the air, indicating toward the bar. They're going in.

The handful of Knights with them jolt into action. Like a SWAT team, they converge on the door, kicking it open. Wood splinters as it slams into the wall. The Knights swarm in, Kenna among them.

With a quick glance at Arielle, Reign follows. She leaps to join him, Rachel by her side.

The entrance leads to a set of stairs, meaning the bar is below ground. They're descending into Hell rather than entering Heaven.

Especially if Paul is here, about to be sacrificed.

Hopefully he already has been.

Then we can focus on more pressing priorities.

Arielle doesn't want to know what those are. They'll inevitably involve the blood the obsidian thirsts for so much.

Pounding footsteps echo down the stairs, bouncing off the dark walls on either side and matching the thundering of Arielle's heart. Reign is before her, Rachel behind. Gloom engulfs them along with the faint scent of stale cigarette smoke.

The obsidian pants one word with each descending step, like a rabid wolf.

Kill. Kill. Kill.

They reach the bottom and Arielle realizes she should've stayed above and been the lookout. The obsidian is seething, making her blood heat and muscles twitchy. She's no longer sure she can control it.

The Knights spread out, others appearing on the other side of the room they find themselves in, having entered through the rear door. With fast movements and alert eyes, they discover what Arielle quickly realizes.

The bar is empty.

Chairs and tables are stacked against the wall on one side, a bar on the other. Between is a wide expanse of vacant floor, a single table and chair sitting in the center.

"Make sure there are no surprises," orders Kenna tersely, sweeping her torch around. Several Knights disappear into the shadows to check any adjoining rooms.

Kenna's beam of light arches over the table and chair and Rachel gasps. A cardigan is hanging over the back of the chair.

Rachel rushes forward, Reign and Arielle by her side. Kenna and Marlowe join them, torches scanning the shadowy corners of the room as they move.

They stop beside the table and Rachel picks up the cardigan. "It's Jeremy's," she whispers.

So Gluttony was here. She's toying with them.

"Reign," Arielle says quietly. A note sits on the undisturbed dust covering the table.

You're going to have to do better than this.

Kenna grabs it and scrunches it in her hand. "Dammit."

Another Knight appears. "All clear. The place is empty."

"Double fucking dammit," she mutters harshly.

Rachel's shoulders sag. "I second that."

As much as Arielle's disappointed they haven't found Jeremy, a small part of her is relieved. If he'd been here with an army of demons, she wouldn't have just been fighting them. She'd have been fighting herself.

When they fought Lust the obsidian gave her the advantage of strength and speed, but it's not like that anymore. It's growing in power, its obsidian claws steadily piercing her soul. It's slowly taking over, from the inside out.

If she fights, she doesn't know who will be the one in control of her body.

"Roll out," snaps Kenna, clearly frustrated. "We'll start tracing that fat bitch again."

Arielle's taken one step when she freezes.

We're not alone.

Her hearing sharpens. Her sense of smell intensifies. The sound of more heartbeats than the sum of the Knights drum over her ears. The scent of...blood teases her nose.

The obsidian's right. There are others here.

Many of them.

Before Arielle can turn to Reign and the others to warn them, a mass of bodies drops from above.

"Vampires!" Marlowe shouts.

They were hiding in the rafters.

Almost silently, the vampires rain down on them, a Knight screaming as one lands on her.

At last.

One lands directly in front of Arielle, opening its mouth to flash glistening fangs. Red hot fury punches through her veins as her hands clamp into fists.

That will be the last thing it does.

The need to kill it, to show it whose blood is about to be spilled, is an overwhelming wave.

It terrifies Arielle. It floods her with power.

Before she can decide whether to defend herself, no matter the cost, Reign leaps between them. A quick thrust of his arm and his wooden stake impales the vampire through the chest.

No! That was our kill!

The vampire stumbles backward, eyes wide with shock, the stake withdrawing with a sickening *slurp*. He arches his back, dissolving into black ash.

"I don't think so, blood sucker," mutters Reign. He turns to Arielle. "You need to get out of here."

For once, she agrees with him. The coppery scent of blood is multiplying, working the obsidian up into a frenzy. No matter how many times she's told Reign she can hold her own, she can't be here.

The need to see every vampire broken. Bleeding. Dead. Is becoming visceral. Primal.

And she can sense the obsidian won't stop there. It's indiscriminate in its drive for chaos and death.

Before she can nod, another vampire runs at Reign from behind, a glinting knife held high. Arielle reacts instinctively. She brandishes her own stake, steps around Reign, and spears it into the vampire's heart.

The woman crumples, dead before she hits the floor.

Finally.

More.

Another vampire screams as he sees one of his comrades down, leaping at Arielle. She blocks the blow swinging for her head, slips under the vampire's arm, and drives the already-bloody stake into his back. Warm, red fluid coats her hands.

Yes.

More.

There's a cry and Arielle recognizes Rachel's voice. She spins to find her friend battling a vampire, the sounds and clash of battle raging around them. The vampire strikes Rachel, his fist powering into her chest. She stumbles back and he quickly recovers the space between them, lashing out again. She blocks that one, even attempts to get a strike of her own in, but the vampire is fast. Inhumanly fast. He grabs Rachel by the throat and pins her against the wall, fangs flashing as he exposes them.

"No!"

Marlowe runs toward them but he'll be too late. As the vampire angles his head toward Rachel's throat, Arielle throws her stake with a sharp flick of her wrist.

It propels through the air like a bullet, lodging between the vampire's shoulder blades. He arches and falls, but doesn't shatter into ash like the last one.

He's not dead.

It's not finished until he's dead.

Her heart a strange mix of hot thudding and icy calm, Arielle runs toward the fallen vampire. She pulls the knife from the sheath attached to his belt. There's no hesitation as she slashes it across his throat. The gush of blood has only just welled up through the gaping gash when he splinters into a million black particles.

Arielle turns, breathing heavily not because of the exertion, but because the scent of blood is so intoxicating.

More.

It's then that she registers Reign's shocked gaze. No, not shocked. Horrified.

And yet, she's never been stronger. More capable of protecting those she cares about. Doesn't he see that?

The cry of a Knight has them both turning to find a woman of the Order, blood pouring down her cheek from a gash as two vampires lunge at her again. Kenna leaps high in the air, spins and plows her foot into one vampire's head. He slams into his comrade, shaking off the blow, but it's the interruption the Knight needed. She impales one vampire with a stake.

Arielle's already by her side to dispatch the second.

In the end, the fight is brutal but short. Arielle isn't sure how many vampires she kills, all she knows is it's not enough. The Knights make short order despite the vampire's strength and speed. The floor is repeatedly sprinkled with their remains like black confetti.

When she sees that Reign is fighting one of the last remaining ones, dodging the man's rapid blows while looking for openings to get a few of his own, she runs toward him. Squatting down she picks up a knife lying on the floor amongst the ashes, barely breaking stride.

She plows into the vampire, pushing him backward. He crashes through the stacks of chairs and tables, the sound of splintering wood giving Arielle an exhilarating rush. He crashes into the wall and she raises the knife to his throat.

Yes.

More.

She's about to slice the exposed skin of his neck when a hand lands on her shoulder. "Stop, Ari."

It's Reign.

She blinks, realizing her vision is both darker, and yet so much more acute.

No! He wants the last kill for himself!

End this bloodsucking demon. Kill him!

Her hand tightens around the hilt of the blade. This one was trying to hurt Reign. It would've killed him if he could.

"We need answers, Ari."

We have all the answers we need! Kill! Kill! Kill!

She hesitates, the words taking longer to filter through than she expected.

"Jeremy," she whispers. She'd forgotten about Jeremy. Reign's right. Maybe this vamp knows where he is.

She slams the vampire so hard against the wall it cracks. "Where's the Innocent?"

The vampire's head lolls and he mumbles incoherently.

He's faking.

Arielle jerks her arm and slams him again. "Where. Is. He?"

The vampire's eyelashes flicker before opening to reveal dark eyes full of arrogance and superiority. "With Gluttony," he sneers.

This time, Arielle presses her face close, doing the same with the blade against his throat. "I will bleed it out of you." She pushes the blade in and a bead of blood trickles down his skin, the scent flooding her nostrils.

The vampire smiles, revealing his fangs. "I look forward to it."

Frustration coils through Arielle. The vampire has no intention of talking. They can't afford to play this cat and mouse game with Gluttony.

Yield to me. I will make him talk.

Blackness begins to cloud her vision. The promise of infinite power thrums through every cell.

You will have everything you want, the obsidian promises. *Nothing will stop you.*

She could find Gluttony. Kill her. End all of this.

The vampire's eyes widen, a flash of fear flaring in their depths. "I don't know where the Innocent is, I swear! Gluttony only tells her most trusted demons."

See! He's talking. He senses your power.

The vampire starts trembling. "But I do know you have until the full moon to find him. That's when she'll sacrifice him."

Suddenly, the terror pouring off the vampire is like dousing of ice water. Vampire or not, this isn't who she is.

Yes, she wants to protect those she cares about. The Innocents. The vulnerable humans who are getting caught in the crossfires.

But not like this.

Not with fear and violence and dark power.

Arielle releases the vampire and steps back, feeling nauseous to her core. For a brief second, she wonders if she's going to throw up.

The vampire darts away the moment he's free. There's a cry, then the fleeting scent of singed skin and Arielle knows one of the others ended him.

She turns slowly, her eyes scanning the crowd that surrounds her. The Knights have varying levels of impressed on their faces. Kenna gives her a short, approving nod.

Rachel looks stunned and...uneasy.

But it's Reign who Arielle's searching for. His expression that she needs to see just as much as she dreads.

He's to her left, closer than she expected, although she shouldn't be surprised. His protective streak would've kept him near. Her stomach clenches painfully as she registers the emotions flashing across his face.

He's shocked.

Troubled.

She's not sure, but she thinks disgust flickers over his handsome features.

She can't blame him. She's disgusted with herself.

He won't accept you.

He will never accept you.

Not now. Not after what you just did.

And this time, Arielle knows the obsidian's right.

Reign's seen the darkness she carries.

She's destroyed whatever was blossoming between them before it ever had a chance to flourish.

CHAPTER 29
REIGN

Arielle clamps her hand over her mouth, her blue eyes large and luminous above. Without saying a word, she spins and runs up the stairs.

Reign is rooted to the spot. What. The. Fuck. Just. Happened.

Rachel appears by his side. "I'll go talk to her."

"No," Reign says through a tight throat. "I will."

She studies him for long seconds, whatever she sees seeming to make her hesitate. But she finally nods. "Okay. We need to find out what's going on."

He nods, flashes of what they just saw still on a loop in his head. Arielle unflinching as she killed. Arielle uncaring of the blood on her hands. Arielle looking like she could've done this for hours. For as long as it took. Forever.

Something's wrong. Very. Very. Very freaking wrong.

Reign jogs up the stairs two at a time, still breathing a little hard from the battle. That's the first time he's faced vampires. Those teeth were chilling. And they were fast. And strong.

And those teeth...

He suppresses a shudder as he reaches the top of the stairs. And yet Arielle was fearless. Tenacious. A fighting machine.

He should be glad. They won, and as far as he can tell, only a couple of the Knights were seriously injured.

Except Arielle's not a killer. It hurts her to hurt others. She only does it when it's necessary. What he just saw isn't the Ari he knows.

Outside the bar, he finds her down the side of the building, washing her hands under a tap. Red-tinted water flows into the drain by her feet as she scrubs frantically.

"Hey," he says quietly.

She stiffens but doesn't stop scrubbing. "I don't want to talk right now, Reign."

He crosses his arms but doesn't respond. He's willing to wait.

Arielle glances up at him through her hair. He angles his head. "What about now?"

With a sigh, she turns the tap off and straightens. "Look—"

"If we had time for you to be stubborn, I'd go along with it, Ari. I'm the king of not wanting to talk about it. But we don't." He steps closer. "What's going on?"

She scowls, something else he's never seen her do. "I thought you'd be happy to see the vampires killed before they could hurt anyone."

"I am. I just didn't expect you to be the one to mow them all down."

Her angry gaze snaps to his. "You killed some, too! So it's okay for you, but not for me?"

Frustration simmers somewhere deep in his bones. "I'm a street rat, Ari. I lost my conscience a very long time ago. I'll be able to sleep tonight even after what just happened. The Arielle I knew, won't be."

She crosses her arms and juts out her chin. "Maybe that's not me anymore."

"I'm kind of hoping it still is," he says quietly.

The Arielle he knew is the one who has him here, now, fighting for this. She had a heart he fell for, no matter how hard he tried not to.

She flinches but quickly straightens again. "If it was Mac you wouldn't be worried. You'd be high fiving her."

As a deflector from way back, Reign recognizes Arielle's trying to sidestep. To make this about something else. He shakes his head, frowning even deeper. "This isn't about—"

"You respect Mac!" Arielle's arms fly out as her voice rises. "You admire her strength!"

The frustration not only rises, but it detonates along his veins, like a series of small, angry explosions. "But I don't have feelings for Mac!" he half-shouts back.

Arielle blinks and his breath disintegrates as Reign registers what he just said. The words hang in the air, waiting to be acknowledged.

He's never felt more vulnerable.

She blinks again. "You don't know what you're saying."

"There are few things I'm more sure of," he says fiercely. No Sin could concoct something so pure and beautiful, especially considering his black heart.

She shakes her head. "You can't," she whispers, her blue eyes almost begging him to take his words back.

Reign's not sure what's going on, but all he knows is Arielle's trying to deny how he feels. Is it because she's denying how she feels, too?

Or is that just wishful thinking?

He takes a step forward and she doesn't move. Another step and there's only an inch between them. Reign lifts his hand, his fingertips brushing over her porcelain cheek.

She doesn't pull away.

In fact, her body sways towards his. He's not even sure she's aware she's doing it.

He cups her face and angles his mouth toward hers, drawn to the promise of her lips. Does she feel this, too? Can she tell that this is far more than a demon's manipulations?

Arielle's hands creep up, her actions mirroring his. Her warm palms clasp his face, sending shivers skittering over his skin.

Her eyes flutter closed. "Reign..."

And then they're kissing, their mouths pressing against each other's with achingly sweet pressure. They cling to each other, mouths barely moving as if they don't want to break the exquisite contact. Reign's breath stutters in his chest. He thinks it might cease to exist. He's not sure.

But he doesn't really care.

This isn't mindless passion. This is tenderness. Connection. Pure emotion.

It not only steals his breath, it strips away anything but the girl he's holding. Who he's kissing like his soul depends on it.

The one who's kissing him right back.

With a startle, he registers the moisture under his finger tips. He pulls back, confirming that tears are trekking down Arielle's cheeks. "Ari?"

Her hands tighten for a brief second before sliding away. "I...I can't do this."

Reign strokes his thumb over her cheek, sensing the war that's playing out within Arielle. "It could be just me, but I'm pretty sure we just did."

Fresh tears follow the path already created by the others. "I'm..." She shakes her head, loosening his gentle grip. "This is wrong."

The final word is like a battering ram through his chest.

Wrong?

The one thing he thought was finally right?

Arielle takes advantage of his stunned pain, because she slips away. "I'm sorry," she whispers.

Reign hears her running across the parking lot. He closes his eyes as she starts the car.

Then slams his fist into the wall as Arielle drives off.

Agony detonates through his knuckles and ricochets up his arm. For a short moment, he considers doing it again. The pain is nothing compared to the cracking feeling in his chest.

He should've run, like he always has. Defenses are there for a reason.

Arielle has feelings for him.

But for some reason, it's not enough.

And that just makes the agony worse.

RACHEL

Rachel stays where she is just outside the doorway of the pub. Watching the achingly beautiful kiss between Reign and Arielle had been the sweet ray of hope she'd been searching for amongst all this death and loss.

She'd clasped her hands to her chest and melted. She'd been about to turn away and give them some privacy when Arielle pulled back, said something, and ran away like demons were hot on her tail.

And Reign was crushed all over again.

Watching him punch the wall had made her wince. Rachel had almost gone to him, but she knew that's the last thing he'd want. No one wants their rejection witnessed.

Sliding down the wall, she lands on her butt. Could she be any more useless?

She clasps her knees and drops her head onto her arms. Today is about to take second place in the worst-day-of-her-life awards. Losing her father will always be the proud winner of first.

"Hey."

Rachel looks up to find Marlowe standing above her, the afternoon sun gilding the blond waves of his hair. He hunkers down, gray eyes almost the color silver soft with compassion. "I'd ask if everything's okay, but that's a rhetorical question."

"I'm failing them all," she says, knowing she sounds forlorn and pitiful, but not really caring. She feels forlorn and pitiful. "Jeremy. Reign and Arielle. Mercy City itself."

He shakes his head as he squats down. "You couldn't have stopped Jeremy. He chose to sacrifice himself rather than let others needlessly die. It was a brave thing to do."

Except Rachel promised him she'd find his son.

"And do you really think with two people who feel as intensely for each other as Reign and Arielle, that their feelings just go away because they've hit a hurdle?"

She picks at some imaginary lint on her knee. "It looked like a pretty big hurdle," she mumbles.

"And Mercy City has a lot of people fighting for her. Just like Jeremy does. And Reign and Arielle." He angles his head, the sunshine caressing his skin. "And they all have you."

Glancing up, Rachel's struck once more by his good looks. Silver-gray eyes, a strong nose above sculpted lips. Sandy hair that brushes his ears and neck, a thick mess of waves on top.

He's super hot, and it turns out he's super nice.

Oh, and he can really fight. She noticed.

"You're not just a pretty face, huh?"

He grins. "I was hoping you'd notice."

TAMAR SLOAN

Her own smile feels like a blossom unfurling under the sunshine that is Marlowe. This super hot, super nice, fantabulous fighter is flirting with her.

The sound of others coming up from the bar, Kenna shouting orders, quickly curbs the sweet feeling. Rachel pushes to her feet, dusting off her backside.

Her father was murdered not long ago. Jeremy is slated to be next. They're facing a ravenous Sin, demons, vampires, and ambitious angels, all hell bent on world domination.

She's not sure if she's grieving or pissed from one minute to the next.

Rachel sighs. "Unfortunately, there's too much going on right now." Too many stories are unraveling, and the chances of a happily ever after keep feeling just out of reach. She can't afford to invest in an uncharted story of her own. "Maybe when this chapter is done."

His silver eyes twinkle, not seeming in the least rebuffed. "Looking forward to it."

CHAPTER 30
ARIELLE

Arielle drives blindly, not really caring where she's going because it doesn't matter.

The obsidian will always be with her.

We are one, it hisses, always in her thoughts. *Accept it.*

A sob climbs up her throat, jagged and anguished. After what she did to all those vampires, after coming the closest she has to giving in to the obsidian, the kiss with Reign was a moment of light. Of beauty.

And oh so undeniably real.

Which is why she couldn't let it continue. Not when he doesn't know. He isn't the one with the dark heart and tainted soul. It's her.

Yes, you are.

The glee, the black joy in the obsidian's voice makes Arielle sick. She pulls over, dropping her head onto the steering wheel as she draws in great gulps of air. She doesn't know what to do. Where to go.

How to make this right.

Leaning back, she gasps in surprise as she realizes where

she is. Climbing out of the car, she almost stumbles in her rush to get to the house she's parked outside of.

She's come home.

Letting herself in, Arielle stumbles through to the living room. Although they haven't been long in the farmhouse, she's still surprised to find everything's the same. The couch, her mom's chair. The faint smell of incense, as if its repeated use has stamped the scent into the walls.

Sitting on the couch in the corner that she used to curl up with a book, Arielle wraps her arms around herself.

She misses her mom. She misses Gabby. And she misses Aunt Shell.

They'd know what to do.

They're not broken and damaged.

I can make you whole.

"Go away!" Arielle screams.

"When we just got here?"

Arielle shoots to her feet at the unknown voice behind her. Her eyes widen when she sees a man with glowing red eyes on the other side of the couch.

Demon.

He grins and lifts a hand, flicking his fingers. More demons pour through the door she mustn't have locked, streaming into the living room. In the space of breath, she's surrounded.

More fighting. More blood.

The obsidian's excitement is unmistakable. It ramps up her heart rate, has adrenaline pumping through her veins.

"What do you want?" she asks tersely.

The demon who spoke leaps over the couch, making her take a hasty step back. "You thought you could fool us?" he hisses.

There's a chorus of more hisses from the demons around her, creating an atmosphere alive with anger. Arielle's pulse thrums even faster. How could they know about the obsidian...

In a split second, she decides to run. She's tired of fighting. Sickened by the bloodshed.

No! screams the obsidian. *They are no match against our power!*

But she doesn't care.

The moment she moves, the demons close in. Arielle leaps and somersaults over the woman running at her, teeth bared. She lands on the other side, never losing momentum. If she can get out of the house, the demons will retreat. They won't want to cause a commotion where humans can see.

She's just reached the hallway when something sails over the top of her head. A demon, wings tucked in close as it spins like a missile. As he crests over her, one wing snaps out, striking Arielle across the cheek.

She cries out as she stumbles, quickly righting herself. She reaches the door and wrenches it open, freedom giving her another burst of speed as she propels herself through.

Straight into the solid body of another demon.

He quickly shoves her back and slams the door, cutting off her link to the safety beyond.

Arielle's back hits another demon and his clawed hands grip her arms painfully.

Fight!

She has no choice. If she doesn't, they'll kill her.

End them!

Arielle bucks, ripping her right arm free. She spins and punches the demon in the throat. He staggers backward, gripping his neck as he coughs and chokes. But before she can reach for the door again, there's a growl somewhere to her right as a boot whips out and connects with her thigh. Pain explodes up her hip and spine as her leg gives out.

Yield to me!

"No," she cries out, powering back up with a wild uppercut that connects with a jaw.

They will kill you!

The demons come at her as one growling, furious mass. Arielle throws punch after punch and block after block, but it's inevitable that she's overpowered. A blow connects with her solar plexus and she doubles over. Another demon grabs her hair and yanks her head back, bringing tears to her eyes. Claws scrape her skin as her arms are trapped, then pulled back and out like they plan on crucifying her.

And then the demons stop, holding her there as she pants with pain.

The door flies open and Gluttony swaggers through, closing it behind her with a flick of her wrist. "Hello, Arielle," she purrs. "I'm so glad I can get this opportunity to thank you personally for releasing me from Hell."

Arielle hides her wince, hating how deep the barb cut. "Shouldn't you be at an all you can eat buffet somewhere?"

Gluttony rubs her hands over her curves. "I have almost the entire population of Mercy City doing that for me. Each time they give in to their greedy impulses, I grow stronger."

Arielle struggles against the tight grip on her arms, even though it's useless. "Where is Jeremy?"

"I'm glad you brought that up," says Gluttony, her face hardening. "You thought you could fool me? A Sin of Hell?" She stalks forward. "Where is the real Innocent?"

"What?"

"Such a good actor," she sneers. "You all had me convinced."

Arielle shakes her head. "I don't know what you're talking about, but you need to let Jeremy go."

"Jeremy is dead unless you tell me who the real Innocent is."

Arielle stills, trying to process that. Surely Gluttony's lying.

And yet, deep down, she knows she's not. Arielle can feel it in her marrow.

Jeremy isn't the Innocent.

Just like the obsidian predicted.

Gluttony reaches out and grips Arielle's face, her nails digging into her cheeks. "The deal is simple. Jeremy in exchange for the real Innocent. If not, he dies, and I take Mercy City down with him."

"I will never make a deal with a demon," Arielle spits. "Especially a Sin of Hell."

Gluttony is too driven by death and destruction. She has no intention of following through on the deal she just offered.

Sick excitement flares in the demon's eyes. "You haven't disappointed me. The easy route is never as much fun. Now, I'm going to have to kill you to show the others I'm serious." She glances at the demons holding Arielle. "Release her. This human is no threat to me."

Stupid, stupid demon.

Arielle staggers forward as her arms are released. She straightens, registering the way the demons form a tight circle around them. Gluttony snaps her onyx wings out, her eyes blazing with the fires of Hell.

The first strike is fast, but Arielle blocks the punch. She ducks the kick that comes flying to her head. She executes a sweep, but Gluttony easily leaps. She uses her wings to hang midair for an extra split-second before propelling forward, feet first. Her boots slam into Arielle's solar plexus, thrusting her backward. The demons divide, cheering and throwing in kicks of their own for good measure.

Yield to me. With my power, you can end her.

End them all.

Arielle lands on the floor, her head cracking against a wall. She blinks through the pain fracturing through her skull as she pushes to her feet.

She can do thi—

The edge of black wing explodes across her cheek, making her head snap to the side. She spins, her body following the powerful strike and smashing into the wall again.

Yield! You are losing!

As she presses her hands to the wall, Arielle's vision begins to darken. Power coils through her muscles, insidious and inklike. She could end Gluttony with one strike.

Isn't that what you want? To kill the Sin?

It's what everyone wants.

But not like this. The price is too high.

Yield to me!

The words are a roar in her head. A ferocious scream that leaves Arielle's ears ringing. She drops to her knees, covering them.

She'd rather die than give in to the obsidian.

"I was expecting more of a fight," growls Gluttony above her. "Pathetic."

Except Arielle is fighting the fight of her life. Against the obsidian.

A part of her wishes Gluttony would hurry up and end this. Maybe death is the only way to end the obsidian.

Gluttony grabs Arielle's head and slams it into her knee. Blood spurts over her face but Arielle keeps her eyes tightly closed.

She's going to take the obsidian down with her.

Yield.

To.

Me!

The next blow is to her chest and pain is like a grenade through her torso. Arielle curls up into a ball, as if that will keep the evil inside of her from escaping. Agony and fury are a hurricane within her.

"I'm going to enjoy seeing you die," seethes Gluttony.

But before the next strike can inflict its damage, the front door comes crashing down. Arielle opens her eyes in shock, watching as a boulder powers into the house. To her amazement, the clay-coloured rock fragments into a million pieces, each one connected to the other in an intricate web. It quickly reforms into a humanoid figure with little more than dark depressions for eyes and mouth in a mud face.

It roars, the sound making the floor beneath Arielle tremble. The demons attack, wings deployed and claws exposed. But each time one tries to strike, the mud-being rearranges itself so the kick or punch connects with nothing but air. As the demon staggers with the foiled blow, the mud-being plows fist after fist into the Hell creatures. It becomes a battering ram of fists, an endless array of arms shooting out from every angle.

Stone crunches against bone. Rock pounds flesh. The demons cry out as they fall one by one.

Arielle pushes to her feet, astounded at the turn of events. A flurry of black from the corner of her eye reveals Gluttony leaping through a nearby window. She bares her teeth over her shoulder. "I'll find the Innocent myself."

With a mighty contraction of her wings, she shoots for the sky. Arielle turns back, seeing the last of the demons fleeing, too. Wisps of black smoke curl through the air, all that's left of the ones who didn't make it.

The hulking mud-being straightens, its head almost touching the roof, and Arielle freezes. She assumed it was her savior, but she has no way of knowing that.

Is she next?

The being starts to fold in on itself, earth sliding and contracting as it shrinks. It compresses until it's shorter than Arielle, face taking shape and gaining the color of skin. Slender arms extend, legs encased in jeans appear. After a breathless second, a young woman stands before her.

Arielle blinks. "Klae?"

It can't be the awkward friend from Gabby's academy. Klae had directed a play Gabby had performed in. A murder mystery called One Murder Please. Klae had been friendly and enthusiastic, if a little unusual, and Arielle remembered liking her. She stands speechless as the random facts pepper her mind.

Klae had braces and pimples. There were no signs she's supernatural.

"Hey, Ari," she says cheerfully, not even out of breath.

"What are you doing here?" She swallows, another far more pressing question hot on the heels of the first. "What are you?"

"Gabby asked me to keep an eye out on you," says Klae with a cheery smile. "And I'm a golem. A creature made of earth and mud, brought to life with some pretty impressive magic." She ducks her head. "Weird, but I try to tell myself, also kinda cool."

"Most definitely cool," Arielle assures her. No wonder Klae's a bit odd. She's a supernatural creature most have never heard of.

Klae looks up, straightening. "You really think so?"

"You just decimated an entire room of demons and saved my life, so it's a resounding yes from me."

Beaming, Klae flushes, once more pulling her head down between her shoulders. "Just trying to help out."

"So, Gabby asked you to look out for me?"

"Yep. She wanted to make sure you'd be okay," says Klae. "She felt awful at having to leave." She takes a step forward. "Are you okay?"

Arielle wipes her sleeve across her nose, knowing she must look a mess, and is quickly surprised to find there's nothing there. Pressing her hands across her face, she finds there's no pain, no bruising. The rest of her body feels the same.

She's healed.

So you can make the right choice next time, seethes the obsidian.

"Ah, yeah, I'm fine."

"That's good," says Klae, looking relieved. "I don't want to let Gabby down."

Arielle nods, knowing how she feels. She doesn't want to disappoint Gabby or her mother, either. Which is why she ignores the fury festering inside of her. There's more important things to think of right now. "I need to get back to the farmhouse. Gluttony is looking for the real Innocent."

Klae's eyes widen. "Yes, you really do." She glances at the door she smashed though. "I'll take care of this. You go warn the others."

Arielle was about to stride to her car when she stops. "You're not coming?"

Klae shakes her head. "I'm more of a behind the scenes kind of gal."

"Are you sure?"

"Positive." Klae ducks her head a third time. "I prefer it that way."

Rushing over, Arielle gives her a quick, fierce hug. "Thanks, Klae."

She pulls back to find the young woman flushing. "Aw, anytime."

Slipping through the shards that is now her front door, Arielle jogs to her car, a sense of urgency building inside of her.

She just proved to herself she can resist the obsidian.

She saw that if she works as a team, they have a chance of winning this.

And she now knows they haven't yet found the true Innocent.

CHAPTER 31

REIGN

Reign's pacing the length of the farmhouse when the door bursts open, revealing an out of breath Arielle.

His first instinct is to rush to her. Ask her where she's been. Make sure she's okay.

But that urge is quickly curbed by the stinging memory of what she said to him.

This is wrong.

So he stays where he is, rooted to the spot as Rachel barrels toward her and engulfs her in a hug. "Where have you been, Ari? Are you okay?"

They pull back and Arielle nods. "I went home." Her gaze rises to meet Reign's. "And Gluttony paid me a visit."

"She what?" he roars, striding forward as if the bitch is here and he can pummel her right now.

"I'm okay," Arielle assures. "A friend of Gabby's arrived and took care of them."

Reign frowns. After her show at the pub, he would've thought Ari could pretty much take care of them herself.

"Gluttony was furious that we'd played her."

"We have?" asks Rachel, clearly baffled.

"She demanded the exchange of Jeremy for the real Innocent."

Rachel gasps. Reign's stunned. Kenna curses, having taken that moment to enter the room along with Marlowe.

"But Jeremy *is* the Innocent!" she snaps.

Arielle shakes her head. "I'm not so sure. Gluttony was pretty angry. She said Mercy City is going to pay unless we hand over the real Innocent."

Rachel turns to Reign, looking stricken. "So Jeremy's life is in danger for no reason?"

"Everyone's life is in danger," says Kenna as she comes to stand beside Reign. "That's why we have to figure out if the Innocent is still out there."

He tears his gaze from Arielle. Whatever he feels for her—feelings that he shouldn't—are going to have to wait. "How are we going to do that?"

It took them days to find Jeremy, and it looks like they closed in on the wrong guy. They no longer have that sort of time.

Marlowe takes a seat on the couch, placing the tablet he always seems to have on his lap. "I've been doing some research." He glances at Rachel. "Based on your theory that the Innocents are all connected somehow."

She walks over and sits beside him, looking intrigued. "And?"

"I created a web of sorts, inputting anyone associated with Shell or your father." He taps on the screen, then swipes. "I've got a total of fifteen names."

Reign joins them, leaning over the back of the couch, watching as Marlowe flicks through photos. "Fifteen people are going to take time to research."

"We'll send a team of Knights to investigate each one," says Marlowe. "Hopefully we can find them all quickly."

"That's assuming they're all in Mercy City," Reign points out. What if the Innocent they need is living in Uzbekistan?

Marlowe throws him a baleful glare. "We'll deal with that if we have to."

Reign shrugs. "Just keeping it real, man." He doesn't believe in false hope.

Arielle comes to stand beside him, also focused on the images flicking across the screen of the tablet. Reign tenses at having her so close. Their kiss feels like a lifetime ago and yet it still burns his lips only a couple of hours later.

He turns away and focuses back on the screen. Whatever he feels for her needs to stop. It's only going to get in the way.

A picture of a woman appears on the tablet and Arielle gasps. "That's her! That's the Innocent!"

Reign looks closer at the image. The woman is beautiful, with a halo of red hair. There's nothing about her that says 'Innocent.' "How can you tell?"

Arielle shrugs. "I don't know, I can just feel it. I was never totally sure Jeremy was the Innocent. It probably has to do with me being able to see the obelisks."

"Rachel?" Marlowe asks, frowning.

Because Rachel hasn't moved. In fact, she looks so frozen that Reign's scared if someone touched her, she'd shatter.

"Rach?" he asks quietly.

"I know that woman," she whispers, even that sounding strained. "It's my mother."

Looking back at the photo, Reign wonders how he didn't see it. The red hair. The angle of the nose. The full lips waiting to smile.

Rachel jolts as if she was just electrocuted. She looks to Marlowe, Arielle, Reign. "We have to stop Gluttony. I can't lose both my parents."

"We'll find her," promises Marlowe.

Reign and Arielle glance at each other. There's no way he can guarantee that.

But it seems to be what Rachel needs to hear, because her taut body unwinds a little. "Damn straight we will." She holds out her hand for the tablet. "May I?"

"Of course," Marlowe says with a smile as he passes it to her.

Her brow pinched low, Rachel rapidly taps away on the screen. "Jeremy was in contact with mom. He said he had her contact details on his phone."

Reign moves around to sit on the coffee table across from the two of them. "We don't have his phone," he points out.

"No, we don't," agrees Rachel, not looking up. "But maybe he's saved some information in the cloud. Phone numbers. Emails. That sort of thing."

Marlowe leans in. "Yes, good thinking."

A faint tinge of pink colors Rachel's cheeks, but she doesn't answer. She continues to tap, processing whatever information she's sifting through with impressive speed. Arielle quietly moves, coming to sit beside Reign. He doesn't shift his gaze from Rachel even though he's highly conscious of her body so close to his.

Is this what it's going to be like? Fighting evil, side by side, as if the moments between them never happened?

Does someone like him really have the right to ask for more?

Reign grits his teeth. He needs to stop asking himself rhetorical questions.

"You're using a packet sniffer?" Marlowe asks, eyebrows raised.

Rachel nods. "I saw him on his phone. If he used the wireless network, I can track the cookie."

Marlowe falls silent, although it's clear he's impressed.

Reign can't blame him. Rachel blows his mind on a regular basis.

"And it's an affirmative," Rachel breathes. "Now, for the cookie cager."

A few more taps and swipes and Marlowe glances at Reign, Arielle and Kenna. "She's in Jeremy's email." He narrows his eyes as he glances back at the screen that Rachel's scrolling through. "He obviously doesn't clean out his inbox. There's a lot to sift through."

"Lots of work related stuff," mutters Rachel, almost as if she's talking to herself. "And he subscribed to several literary magazines."

Marlowe leans in, their heads almost touching. "At least he was meticulous in keeping information. Most contacts have either an address or a phone number." He angles his head. "And he has a folder called Big Pumpkin."

Rachel stills. "Big Pumpkin?"

"Yeah, is that significant in some way?"

She doesn't answer, now tapping even faster. "My mom used to call me Little Pumpkin." She swallows. "I told her that made her Big Pumpkin."

Reign doesn't allow himself the luxury of breathing as he watches Rachel stop and scan whatever information is now on the screen. Beside him, he doesn't think Arielle is either.

Rachel's about to find her mom.

The next Innocent.

It only takes a few seconds before Rachel looks up, blinking as if she just found herself in an alternate universe she didn't think could exist. "I've found it. I have my mother's address."

RACHEL

Knowing her mom's been living on the other side of Mercy City all her life is more painful than comforting. It means she could've visited Rachel, but didn't.

Could the rejection be any more complete?

As she stands outside the top floor apartment door, Reign, Arielle, Kenna and Marlowe behind her, Rachel lifts her hand to knock.

What does she say? The questions clamoring in her mind aren't ones she can voice. Not without sounding pathetic.

How could you? Why did you?

When did you stop loving us?

"Rach?" Reign says softly.

She turns, finding him and Arielle right behind her.

"You got this," says Arielle with a confident smile.

"And you got us," adds Reign, his gaze steady. "Whether you punch her or hug her."

Rachel blinks away the moisture pooling in her eyes. How is it these two can be united against a common foe, but the moment they have to face each other, everything falls apart?

She turns back to the door, feeling a little stronger. She's no longer the little girl crying in her bed as her father tried to comfort her. She's a whole lot taller now.

Her knuckles rap out three sharp knocks and she steps back, breath held.

The door opens quickly, almost too quickly. Rachel isn't sure she's ready.

Not that she's sure she'll ever be ready.

It opens to reveal a woman identical to that in the photo. Long red hair pulled up in a bun—the reason Rachel always keeps her own short. Hazel eyes feathered with laugh lines— laugh lines that have multiplied since Rachel last saw her.

Slender fingers that flutter to her throat—strangely still wearing her wedding band.

Evelyn Donovan.

Her mother.

Her eyes pop open in shock. "Rachel?" she whispers. "My Little Pumpkin?"

She reaches out, slowly, as if her daughter might be a mirage. As if this is too good to be true.

Rachel's heart is struggling to work in her too-tight chest. She should move. Her mother doesn't have a right to look at her like some long lost daughter returning to the fold. As if this reunion is as heart wrenching for her as it is for Rachel.

And yet, she doesn't twitch a muscle.

She hasn't felt her mom's touch in eighteen years.

Her mother's lashes flutter and her gaze sharpens, as if she's just snapped out of a trance. She yanks her hand back, curling her fingers in to make a fist. "You can't be here. It's too dangerous."

She goes to close the door, but Rachel jams her foot in the way. Like hell she's closing the door and acting as if this never happened. She pushes it open and strides it. "Actually, you're the one in danger."

The others file in behind her, quickly filling the neat living room Rachel finds herself in. She looks around, stomach contracting when she notices how few personal touches there are. Apart from the photos, that is. Dozens of them. All of Rachel and her father, many of them of after her mother left.

She crosses her arms. She well and truly has no idea what's going on here. Reign and Arielle come to stand beside her, for which Rachel's grateful. She's also conscious that Marlowe moves in closer.

Her mother enters last, her own arms crossed. "They're coming, aren't they?"

Shock spears through Rachel. "You know?"

"I've known for a long time that I'm an Innocent," says her mother, her hazel eyes pools of sadness. "And that your father was one, too."

Blindly, Rachel sits on the closest chair she finds, discovering it's a couch. She clasps her hands, realizing they're trembling with the emotion coursing through her. "I don't understand."

Her mother spears her fingers into her hair, a movement Rachel instantly finds familiar. She'd forgotten she did that when she was stressed. "It started with small bouts of power. Nothing major. Setting things alight when I hadn't intended to. Moving things with just a thought." She smiles faintly at Rachel. "Healing Middling the goldfish when he was belly up and barely moving."

Middling the goldfish. Rachel had forgotten about him, too. Middling because he was the smallest pumpkin in the family.

"An angel came to me in a dream. He told me everything. That I'm an Innocent. Destined millenia ago to protect a Gate of Hell, but now long forgotten, our powers dormant or suppressed." Her eyes mist with tears. "He showed me how to find other Innocents."

"Evelyn," Reign says carefully. "Did you just say you know how to find other Innocents?"

She nods. "Yes. I can show you."

Rachel's glad she's sitting down. Too much information is coming at her too fast. All too laden with emotion.

Her mom comes to sit beside her, hovering on the edge of the couch. "I found out your dad was one, too. And Shell."

"Why?" Rachel asks, simply. Almost forlornly.

A single tear trickles down her mother's cheek. "The angel told me that once one Innocent becomes aware of the truth and continues to be in close proximity to the other Innocents, they tend to become aware as well." She bites her lower lip as it quivers. "And when they all become aware, they turn into an angelic beacon for anything supernatural."

There's silence in the room as everyone digests that. Rachel finds she's breathing shallowly. Painfully. Either her ribs have shrunk or her heart is swelling, unable to contain the pain exploding within it.

Her mom reaches out hesitantly, and when Rachel doesn't move away, gently clasps her hand. Rachel's eyes flutter closed at the contact. It hurts and heals all at once.

"I had to leave," her mother says, her voice thick with tears. "To protect your father. And to protect you."

Rachel's own tears clog her throat. They feel like hot, jagged shards of ice. So much of what she remembered was true. Her parents loved each other with everything they had. Like Jeremy said, it was a forever kind of love. And yet they were torn apart.

And now her father's dead.

Rachel's eyes fly open. "We have to get you to safety."

She's not losing her mother. Not after she just found her. Not when she finally understands.

Her mom squeezes her hand. "I was already planning on leaving."

"What? No!" Rachel grips her mother back. "You're not going anywhere."

"Rachel, the reasons I left are only more imminent. I can't put you in danger."

For the first time since arriving, Rachel smiles. "Too late. I threw myself into this months ago." She waves her arm to the others in the room. "I'd like you to meet the Reign, Keeper of the Grail, Arielle, an Archivist, and a few representatives of the Order of the Knightly Rose."

There's a round of nods and murmured hellos as it's her mother's turn to be stunned. "Well, I..."

Rachel stands, bringing her mother with her. "Let's talk about this back at the farmhouse. It's warded to the rafters with protection spells."

"I suppose so," says her mom, glancing around the apartment. "I already have my suitcase in the car."

Rachel realizes how close she was to missing her. If they'd arrived an hour later, probably even less, her mother would've been gone. She grips her mother's hand even harder.

She never would've known. Her mother didn't leave because she doesn't care.

She left *because* she loves Rachel.

Kenna strides to the door. "We can finish this reunion back at the farmhouse. This place makes me nervous."

Rachel's mom looks at Rachel with raised eyebrows. Rachel suppresses a smile. "She scared me too, in the beginning. But there's a big heart under that tough armor."

Marlowe leans in. "In fact, she has a nephew who she cares for like her own," he says in a conspiratorial whisper.

Rachel blinks at him in surprise. Kenna plays mom? Although she finds it hard to imagine, Kenna would certainly be a fierce protector of anyone she cares about. Rachel grins at Marlowe. "This is my mom," she mouths.

Another woman who has gone to great lengths to protect those she loves.

Marlowe grins back. "Seems you come from a line of fierce, strong women," he says softly, but loud enough for her mother to hear.

She glances over, something glinting in her eye as she regards him. "I get the sense he's not just a pretty face," she says to Rachel.

Rachel giggles. "Me, too."

She slides a glance at the handsome boy beside her. Maybe

she closed the book too quickly on their story. Maybe happily ever afters aren't quite so impossible...

Without warning, the door to the apartment flies open, crashing into the wall and splintering. Vampires swarm in, baring their fangs. Rachel screams, pushing her mother behind her. The Knights rush forward, Kenna at their helm, but the vampires are too fast.

They're not interested in a fight.

They shove and sidestep the Knights, their hard gazes on one target. Rachel's mom.

Rachel leaps into a fighting stance, but all it takes is one vampire feinting right and going left, while the other feints left and goes right. They criss-cross in front of her, one striking her so hard she's knocked to the ground, the other grabbing her mother.

In a flurry of movement and a high-pitched scream, her mother's gone, along with all the vamps.

"No!" shouts Rachel. "Mom!"

Reign shoots after them, scanning the hallway. "They've taken her to the roof!" He disappears after them, Kenna and Arielle with him.

Marlowe helps Rachel up and together, they follow the others. At the end of the hall they find the door to the fire stairs open, but no sign of the vamps.

"The bastards are fast," mutters Marlowe.

"We can't let them take her," Rachel says desperately.

Not after they'd just reunited.

They race up the stairs, Rachel running the fastest she ever has in her life. She's breathing hard when they burst out onto the roof of the apartment building. Bright sunlight glares off the pale cement, making her squint for precious seconds.

Rachel's pulse is thunderous as she looks around frantically.

A breeze brushes her hair across her face, and she desperately swipes it away.

The rooftop is empty.

Apart from a trail of spotted blood leading to the edge of the building.

She runs, following it, finding Kenna beside her.

"Gluttony has her," Marlowe calls from behind. "And she needs her alive."

The relief is short lived. Gluttony wants her mother alive so she can sacrifice her on the night of the full moon.

Tonight.

Rachel reaches the edge of the building and leans against the chest high cement wall. Wind rushes up, and although she knows Marlowe's right, she still scans the street eight floors below, eyes stinging.

But her mother's body isn't down there, crumpled and crushed.

"We'll find her," promises Kenna, her voice hard with determination. "And we'll get her back."

"We have to," whispers Rachel.

When a vampire leaps out from beneath the ledge they were leaning over, Rachel rears back and screams. He scrabbles up, fingers digging into the mortar, his fangs bared.

With one swift movement, he grabs Kenna by the shirt and hauls her over the side of the building. With impossible strength, he clings to the side of the building as he holds her out over the busy street yards below. Kenna grips his hand, legs kicking, eyes wide with something Rachel hasn't seen on the indomitable woman's face.

Fear.

"No!" screams Marlowe, the desperation in his voice echoing Rachel's denial of only a few minutes ago.

"This is for killing our King," growls the vampire.

Grinning, he opens his hand.

Kenna plummets, arms and legs scrabbling for purchase and finding nothing but air. She cries one word as she drops.

"Caleb."

Marlowe slams into the cement wall a second later, his hand stretching out as if he can reach her.

It means he's there to witness his leader's final seconds. With a sickening thud, Kenna lands on the street below. Within seconds, blood pools, creating a thick red halo around her head.

Rachel blinks, bile scorching her throat and burning her tongue.

Scaling the wall of the apartment building like a spider, the vampire disappears around the side.

No doubt off to boast he just killed Kenna DeVoe, the leader of the Order of the Knightly Rose.

CHAPTER 32

ARIELLE

"How can she just disappear?" Rachel jams her hands through her hair, tugging at it as she paces the farmhouse den. "There has to be something to give us an indication of where Gluttony is."

Marlowe hunches his shoulders as he stares more intently at the screen. "We'll find her," he growls.

Arielle sits in one of the armchairs, legs curled up. She wishes she could comfort them somehow. She's already made Rachel tea. Sat beside her as she frantically typed away at her laptop. Put out sandwiches for everyone.

All while the obsidian relived Kenna's death in her mind. Rejoicing in it. Excited by it. Glorying in the bloodshed.

Barely able to contain its delight at the prospect of more.

"I thought you had the technology to trace this," says Reign, standing beside the fireplace. He hasn't sat down since they arrived. Although he isn't showing the same restless energy Marlowe is, or Rachel's quiet desperation, he's just as upset. It's there in the white-knuckled grip on the mantelpiece, the way his shoulders are hunched as if he's shielding himself, in the banked fire in his green eyes.

He wants what Rachel wants—to save her mother.

And he wants what Marlowe is hungering for—vengeance for Kenna's death.

Marlowe strides back to the coffee table where he left his tablet. "We've always been able to trace a demon once we had their demonic signature. I don't understand."

Rachel tugs at the roots of her hair again, hovering as if she's not sure where to move next. "But nothing's coming up."

"I don't mean to start a fire under this pressure cooker, but tonight is the full moon," says Reign, rubbing at his brow.

"I. Know," Marlowe bites out.

If they don't find Gluttony, they can't save Evelyn. Another Gate will be opened. And another layer of Hell will be peeled back, releasing the next Sin and countless more demons.

Gluttony has warded herself.

You won't find her.

"She's warded herself with spells." Arielle jolts when she realizes she just said that aloud.

Marlowe's lips thin. "I'm thinking she has, too."

"What does that mean?" Rachel asks, suddenly looking so young and vulnerable that Arielle wants to go over and hold her. Just like Reign, she'd do anything to make this better. For her to have her mother back.

You can end this.

Yield to me and you will be powerful enough to kill Gluttony and all her demons.

Anything except that.

Because the death and destruction won't end there. Arielle can feel it. The obsidian will be insatiable in its drive for more. Killing the vampires gave her a taste of what would come.

And just like the vampires, she'll be the one with blood staining her hands, no matter how hard she tries to scrub it off.

Reign pushes away from the mantelpiece. "You can't trace her, can you?"

Marlowe's spine straightens. "We're doing everything we can. And we'll keep doing everything we can."

A single tear tracks down Rachel's pale cheek as the knowledge that the chance of finding her mother is slipping into the realms of impossible hits her.

"Well, I'm not sitting around and hoping that works." Reign strides to the front door and grips the handle. "I'll take the remaining Knights and hit the streets. We'll go door to door if we have to. We'll turn Mercy City upside down. We'll find that bitch."

Arielle leaps to her feet. "I'm coming with you."

Rachel is hovering again, clearly unsure what to do. Stay here and hope technology gives them the answers they need, or actually get out there and hope aimless searching won't be just as much a waste of time.

Marlowe grabs his tablet as he shoots to his feet. "We'll all go, and we'll take this stuff with us."

"For crap's sake, why didn't I think of that?" mutters Rachel, walking over to her laptop and scooping it up.

"Because you're scared for your mom," Arielle says, pushing away the obsidian's glee and focusing on the compassion she feels for her friend. "I was the same when my mom was missing."

Rachel sends her a grateful glance. "Such a Pisces," she says, almost smiling. "And I love you for that."

Warmth flushes through Arielle and she wonders if she's blushing.

And yet, you refuse to help her.

You could save her mother.

The flush quickly turns to one of guilt. The obsidian knew Jeremy wasn't the real Innocent. And it knows Gluttony has warded herself so she can't be found.

Arielle can find and save Evelyn, kill the Sin and keep a Gate of Hell closed...

"Let's get going," says Reign. "The more feet we have on the streets, the better."

Marlowe nods. "We'll divide the city into grid squares. We'll cover as much as we can."

Before the moon becomes a pale orb in the night sky. Watching over another ritual sacrifice.

What a useless endeavor.

They think Gluttony will be so easily found?

Arielle pretends those words didn't just slide through her mind as she walks forward, joining Reign by the door. Even if it's hopeless, they have to do something.

You can do something.

Reign yanks open the door, his face grim with the knowledge they're faced with an impossible task, only to stop. "What the fuck are you doing here?"

Dinah arches a black brow as she stands on the other side. "Delivering your Girl Scout cookies."

"I doubt this city has any left in stock," he snaps, going to slam the door closed again.

But Dinah takes a step forward, jamming her shoulder in the way. "That would explain the riot I just had to bypass. I would've gotten here five minutes earlier if I didn't have to take the back roads."

Just like Arielle and the others did when they drove back from Evelyn's apartment. Without Evelyn. Or Kenna.

"Another two minutes and we would've been gone," says Reign, sounding like he wishes that had been the case. He's not happy to find Dinah blocking their way. "Let's pretend that's the case, shall we? You never saw us."

He goes to move forward, but she lifts her hand and he

stops before they touch. "I have some information."

"We don't trust you," he replies instantly.

Dinah turns to Arielle, her black-rimmed eyes somber. "I know who your father is."

The words seem to suck the floor right out from under Arielle. She floats in a state of shock for precious seconds.

Her father?

The unknown that she's always carried with her.

And Dinah's saying...

Arielle holds her gaze. "What do you know?"

"Ari," Reign mutters. "She's just going to tell you what you want to hear. She knows as much about your dad as she does about my parents."

"He's alive," says Dinah, her intense eyes unblinking. She glances into the farmhouse. "I can tell you everything I've learned."

Arielle steps back. "Come in."

Reign reluctantly does the same, opening the door wider. "Yeah, come on in."

Dinah walks through, her back straight and her gaze sharp. Even though she's the one who turned up here, it's like she's expecting to walk into a trap.

She stops just a few feet in, quickly noting Marlowe and Rachel now watching her just as closely. "I didn't think we'd have an audience."

"These people are my friends," says Arielle, conscious her arms are crossed as she returns to stand beside the lounge chair she was sitting on. "I don't keep secrets from them." She covers her wince as she says the last sentence, but the obsidian pounces on the well-meant words.

Liar!

You carry the biggest secret of all!

Dinah shrugs as if it's of little consequence. "Fine by me."

She flicks her head so her bangs aren't in her eyes. "Your father's name is Ryder."

Ryder. The same name her mother had scribbled in the book. For a brief moment in time, she was looking for him... Arielle tucks the precious piece of information away. Having a name makes him more real somehow. More than just a dirty secret.

"And from what I can tell, he disappeared before you were born."

Arielle blinks. There's a possibility her father doesn't even know she's alive? The rejection she's always felt, even though it's from a man she's never met, and never thought she would, thaws a little. Why didn't her mother tell her all of this?

"What else?" she asks, conscious of how strained her voice is.

Reign frowns, coming to sit on the arm of the chair beside her. "And how did you find all this out?"

Dinah ignores him, keeping her gaze on Arielle. "I found some books. It seems he was searching for the Grail."

No wonder she'd left a note in the book. Her mother has been searching for the Grail as long as Arielle's been alive. Maybe that's how they met? Arielle's always sensed the deep, abiding love her mother feels for her father. For Ryder. Her face would tighten if Arielle ever tried to bring it up. Her mouth would become a thin, pale line. Arielle assumed she couldn't talk about it because the grief was too overwhelming.

"How did he disappear?" she asks. "And why?"

Dinah shakes her head. "I haven't been able to find out. I do know that he was working for Cain, though."

The excited fascination is doused by icy cold reality.

Her father worked for Cain. One of the most evil people she knows.

No wonder her mother didn't tell her anything about him.

She was ashamed.

Reign vaults to his feet, standing beside Arielle. "I think you should leave." He turns to her. "Don't listen to her. Even if she's telling the truth, there's more to this story. There's no way your mom would've fallen for someone who was as bad to the core as Cain is."

Arielle looks at him, wanting to believe him.

This is why you chose me. There's a darkness inside of you.

There always has been.

Dinah frowns. "I thought Arielle would want to know. I wanted to give her something, to show I can be trusted."

Reign strides to the door and yanks it open. "Get out." He arches a sardonic brow. "Unless there's more trouble you want to stir up?"

Dinah remains where she is. She almost looks...lost.

"Well?" demands Reign. He waves his arm to the open doorway. "We have a Sin to find."

That has her spine stiffening. "And *if* you do find her," Dinah spits, her tone suggesting how likely she thinks that will be, "how do you intend on killing her?"

"With my bare hands," Reign snaps back.

"That will end up with your demise, not hers. You needed a blade to kill Lust." She arches a brow. "One I provided you with, I might add."

Reign's jaw works as if he's chewing over this information. "Well, unless you're here with something helpful, like another dagger, then get. Out."

"Last I heard, the Tenth Legion has it."

Rachel gasps, while Marlowe's hands curl into fists.

It's almost impossible to find Gluttony.

And they have as much chance of killing her.

"You're really the bearer of good news, aren't you?" snarls

Reign. He pulls the door open another couple of inches. "We don't need the likes of you."

To Arielle's surprise, Dinah smiles. "You really do." She reaches into her coat and removes a dagger. "Luckily for you, I figured you'd need this."

The light glints along the silver edge of the blade. Just like the first, it has an ornate handle, this time, with a single red gem encased in the hilt. Rachel rushes forward, reaching out as if she needs to make sure it's real.

Dinah passes it to her. "This is the only weapon that can kill Gluttony."

Rachel tests its weight in her hand. With a quick flick of her wrist, she twirls it, the red ruby in it twinkling as if it's enjoying it.

Reign shuts the door and stalks forward. "Is anyone else wondering how Dinah managed to get her hands on this?"

Dinah takes the blade back. "I stole it from the Legion. So I could prove to you that I'm on your side." She narrows her eyes. "You don't have to trust me to use the blade."

Arielle glances at Reign. "We need it."

It's as simple as that. They can't win against Gluttony without it.

Reign sighs, acknowledging she's right. He glares at Dinah. "I don't suppose you know where she is?"

Dinah raises her chin. "I can find her," she says confidently.

Reign looks at her assessingly. "You find her, and you're in."

Arielle waits with her breath held. They now have the dagger. If Dinah finds Gluttony, then there's no reason to consider the obsidian's awful offer.

You will choose me.

It is your fate.

"I'll need a map of Mercy City," says Dinah.

Marlowe jogs out of the room, returning quickly with a folded map. He spreads it out on the nearby dining table and steps back. They all gravitate toward it. Rachel's arms are wrapped around her middle, Reign's arms are also crossed, but over his chest. Marlowe is almost bouncing on the balls of his feet.

Arielle understands their edginess. This is probably their once chance at finding Gluttony.

Dinah stands at the head of the table. She opens her jacket again and withdraws a small pouch. She tips out the contents onto the map, several beige colored objects clatter onto the table.

Bones.

Small ones, probably from fingers or knuckles, but bones nonetheless.

"Of course she carries pieces of dead people around with her," mutters Reign.

Dinah ignores him as she scoops them up and cups them between two hands. She shakes them, the bones rattling inside her palms as her mouth begins to move. Strange, guttural words tumble past her lips, sounding like no language Arielle's ever heard.

"Demoniac," says Marlowe in a low voice. "She's obviously a witch of dark magic."

Dinah frowns, her head dropping closer to her hands as her voice grows in intensity. Reign shifts, his own frown darkening. It seems Dinah's having as much trouble as they did in trying to locate the Sin.

Rachel's face is now papery white. As if she knows they have no idea what they're courting by allowing Dinah to do this for them.

Thank goodness Arielle didn't use the obsidian. It's a million times more unknown and dangerous than Dinah.

With a quick flick, Dinah throws the bones onto the map.

They scatter over the table, tumbling in all directions. Then they sit where they landed, unmoving.

Like the spell didn't work.

Arielle and Reign glance at each other. If Dinah can't get past the warding spells protecting Gluttony...

The bones tremble and shiver, drawing their attention back to the map. They begin to move, forming a circle along the outer edges of Mercy City, spinning faster and faster. In a blink, they're moving so fast they're little more than a sand-colored blur. When Arielle sees the first spark, she assumes she imagined it. But then there's another and another.

Within a few seconds, the bones form a ring of fire, scorching the map and making everyone shift back. Everyone except Dinah.

She throws her head back as she raises her arms. The circle of flames explode and leap into the air. Reign moves in close to Arielle, his body subtly shielding hers as he raises his arm to protect his face.

A second later, it's all gone, as if it never existed.

Arielle steps around Reign, wide eyes registering that the map has been incinerated. All that remains on the table is a small pile of Dinah's bones.

"I almost lose my eyebrows and it didn't work?" Reign demands.

Rachel sits heavily on a nearby chair. "It was nothing but an impressive light show."

Dinah glares at them as she snatches her bones. "You all have so little faith." Arielle gasps as she sees a small portion of the map survived beneath the pile. Dinah picks it up, her eyes triumphant. "This is where Gluttony is."

CHAPTER 33
REIGN

Reign can't believe they're here again. Different location —this time outside an old abandoned mansion on the outskirts of town—but same goal.

Save the Innocent.

Stop a Gate of Hell from opening.

Except this time, they need to be successful.

He glances at the people around him as they scan the tall wrought iron gates before them. At the very top are two cherubic angels facing each other, trumpets held to their chubby cheeks.

Seems Dinah was actually telling the truth. All the other sites for the sacrifices have had some link to angels.

Although it doesn't mean he trusts her.

"No one's lived here for over a decade," says Rachel, scanning the tablet in her hand. "There was a fire in the back kitchen and the owners couldn't afford the repairs." She swipes the screen. "Two main entries left. The front and the back."

Marlowe nods, his face hard. "We'll have to split up."

Reign tenses. He doesn't like the sound of that. They split up last time and everyone knows how that turned out. He stiffens even more when he sees Dinah move closer to Arielle.

Why the frick is the witch so interested in Ari? Even going as far as snooping around her past and learning everything she can about her father.

Marlowe leans closer to Rachel, showing her the screen of his own tablet. "Here are the heat signatures."

She frowns. "There are a lot of them. Like, *a lot* of them."

Of course there are.

And this time, they're facing this without Gabby, Colt, Sierra or Mac. Reign glances over his shoulder at the thirty-strong army of Knights, all waiting for their orders. They might not have the supernatural firepower, but they have greater numbers. He drops his shoulders and straightens his spine. It's going to be just what they need to win.

It has to be.

"So, what's the plan?" Marlowe looks at Reign in surprise and he shrugs. "Kenna would've been calling the shots if she was here. And I suspect she left you in charge of the Order."

His face tightens. "Yes. She spoke to me about it just the day before. I didn't think it would be...coming into effect so soon."

"All the more reason to kick vampire ass," says Reign.

Marlowe nods, anger flaring in his eyes. "It certainly is."

Rachel frowns, her focus still on the screen. "They're mostly in two parts of the house. The east wing and the west wing."

Shit. They really are going to have split up.

"The majority of the bodies are in the east wing," she continues, her frown deepening. "That's most likely where my mom is."

And where Gluttony is.

"The west wing only has three heat stamps," says Marlowe as he points to the screen. "That's where Jeremy is, with the least number of vamps and demons to protect him,"

Arielle steps forward, holding out the dagger with the ruby hilt to Reign. "You and Rachel should go after Evelyn."

"What?" Reign can't believe he heard her right. "You don't want to help with the Innocent?"

Arielle's the one who has the visions of the obelisks, almost like she's tied to the Innocents somehow. She's the one who recognized Evelyn as the Innocent.

She shakes her head, her gaze not quite meeting his. "I'll focus on Jeremy. His life is also in danger."

"But—"

"I can't, Reign," she says in a low voice. "I can't fight that many at once."

Flashes of what happened with the vamps in the bar rise in his mind, followed by Arielle frantically washing the blood off her hands afterward. Something's not adding up, and yet, there's no time to do the math.

"Good idea," says Dinah. "Reign and Rachel are strong fighters, especially if you have some of the Knights with you. Gluttony won't stand a chance." She glances at Arielle. "I'll go with you. No one will get past my magic."

Reign hesitates, not liking how this is panning out. But when Arielle's gaze finally meets his, it's clear she wants him to agree to this. Her blue gaze is practically pleading with him.

"Okay," he says, even though he's anything but okay. He takes the dagger and tucks it into his belt in the middle of his back. "But you two take some Knights with you, as well."

Arielle nods, looking relieved.

"It's decided then," says Marlowe. He frowns, looking back at the screen. "Some of them are moving throughout the house, mostly on the first floor. They probably know we're here and are trying to ambush us." He looks up. "I'll take some Knights and remove the threat."

Which means they just divided even further.

"We need to get moving," Reign says tensely, wishing there was more time. "The less they can prepare themselves, the better."

Marlowe nods. "You and Rachel take the front door. Arielle and Dinah, you take the back door. We'll move in through the burnt out section."

Reign looks to Arielle, knowing there's so much more than needs to be said. Where does the truth lie? In the kisses that have scorched his heart and soul, or the distance that rests between them? Her flame blue eyes hold his, shifting with currents he doesn't understand, almost darker with the tide of emotion that's drawing him in. A part of her wants him near.

And yet, there's a part of her that wants him far away.

Now, as they're about to enter a fight that he may not walk away from, he's not so sure why he listened to the second part.

Marlowe lifts his arm, indicating with a flick of his hand that it's time to move in. Time's up. They all jolt into action simultaneously. Marlowe takes the bulk of the Knights right, Arielle drags her gaze away and runs off with Dinah and a few others, going left.

Three Knights remain with Reign and Rachel.

She breaks into a run, her face hard with determination, and he quickly joins her. He overtakes her just as she's about to reach the front door, slamming his shoulder into it and smashing straight through. There's no point in being subtle, plus, it's not really his strong suit. Wood splinters and he finds himself in a dusty hallway, an overturned side table on the ground ahead. Reign leaps over it, not stopping.

He plans to save Evelyn, for Rachel as much as the rest of the world.

And then he's getting back to Arielle.

"There are stairs ahead," says Rachel, coming up beside

him, the three Knights right behind her. "We need to get to the second floor. She's in the bedroom at the end of the corridor."

Reign nods, the hallway opening out to a large space, the staircase on the other side. They've only taken a few strides when there's a cry behind them. Reign and Rachel spin around, finding vampires leaping out of shadows and pouring through doorways. One throws aside the limp body of the Knight, blood streaked across his mouth.

With a cry, Reign yanks the wooden stake out of his belt and launches at the nearest one. He ducks the swing that was coming at him, bringing the stake up with everything he has. It powers into the vampire, turning him to ash.

He spins, looking for his next target and finding it leaping at him, teeth bared. He punches it in the face, making the vamp reel back. He follows, impaling the stake through its chest.

Beside him, he sees Rachel's a ball of motion. She jumps, swipes, stabs. The remaining two Knights are also fighting like their lives depend on it after seeing their comrade killed so quickly and brutally.

More vampires stream down the staircase, shouting their lust for blood. Reign, Rachel and the two Knights come together in the center of the room, backs to each other. Evelyn must be on the second floor for so many vamps to be here. They're trying to stop them from saving her.

Reign kicks as one lunges at him, then uppercuts another while driving his stake into another. Ash quickly fills the gloomy space, making him squint. Low visibility isn't what they need right now.

Suddenly, a vampire lets out an ear piercing scream as she leaps high, throwing her arms out wide. And then another joins her. And two more. She lands on one of the Knight's shoulders, gripping his head and twisting it viciously. There's a sickening snap and the man crumples to the ground.

The others aim for Reign, Rachel, and the remaining Knight. Reign and Rachel sidestep a second before the vampires collide with them, watching them crash to the ground. Simultaneously, they drive their stakes into the being's chests. They turn to find the final Knight furiously fighting another vamp. It means she never sees the vampire coming from behind far too fast for Reign to call out.

The vampire grasps the Knight's ponytail and yanks her head back, his exposed fangs slicing into her throat. Reign looks away, not wanting to see any more. He has to make sure that doesn't happen to Rachel.

The thought hasn't finished when she cries out. He spins to find two vampires holding each of her arms, pulling hard. Rachel leaps and executes a backflip, breaking herself free, only to crash into a third. He grabs her, yanking her back against his chest. The vampire glances at Reign, holding his gaze as he flashes his fangs. Saliva glistens on their surface, ready to pierce Rachel's throat.

"No!" roars Reign, breaking into a sprint.

He barrels one vamp as he tries to stop him, then another. Nothing will stop him from getting to Rachel.

The vampire holding her lowers his head, his eyes glowing with excitement. Rachel struggles, her face twisted with desperation, but the vamp is too strong. Too intent on gorging on her blood.

And Reign won't get to her in time.

RACHEL

Rachel is fighting so hard, knowing that the moment the vampire's fangs pierce her throat that it will be her end. that she barely registers the resounding crash to her left. Dust fills the air, making her cough and she wonders fleetingly if she's breathing dead vamp. Has Reign found a way to kill a few at a time?

Is there some chance he might save her?

The blast of light that's so bright it has her seeing spots definitely gets her attention. And that of the vampire holding her.

He screams and releases her. She twists, ready to take advantage and impale him.

Only to find him crumbling to ash.

There's another resounding crash followed by a blast of light just as Reign reaches her.

"What's happening?" she gasps.

"I have no idea," he says, shielding his eyes with his hand.

They both turn to the far wall only to find it gone. Nothing more than rubble.

With Archangel Gabriel standing in the hole he just torpedoed. He scans the space, shooting blast after blast of light from his hands. The vampires run and scream, but they don't get a chance to escape. Gabriel annihilates every one of them.

"Gabriel," booms a voice from beyond the missing wall.

The sound of wings pounding air heralds more angels landing behind him. An angel with silky black hair lands on the lawn beyond. To Rachel's surprise, Gabriel turns to face him, his hands fists at his side.

He doesn't look like he's welcoming backup.

"Get out of here, Raphael," he booms.

Raphael? The other angel faction?

"Let me pass, Gabriel." Raphael steps forward, his white wings extended to their full span. A dozen more angels land behind him. "We will be the ones to end this. The demons cannot come one step closer to raising Lucifer."

"I don't need the likes of you to keep the next Gate of Hell shut," roars Gabriel. His own angels quickly flock around him. "I know what you're trying to do, Raphael, and it won't work. You want nothing more than to gain support so you can free Michael from his prison."

Raphael drops his head, fury rippling across his bare chest. He plants his feet wide apart, his own fists clenching. Gabriel's shoulders drop as his wings expand. Angel faction facing angel faction.

Really? They're doing this now?

A sound behind Rachel has her and Reign spinning around, their stakes raised. Did Gabriel miss a vampire?

But it's not a blood-sucker coming at them. It's not one of anything.

A horde of demons rush into the room, red eyes glowing with the fires of Hell. Like a cloud of evil, they descend, run, flash their deadly claws.

Rachel prepares herself to fight again, ignoring that there are two of them and more demons than she wishes to count. She'll end every one of them if she has to. She will get up those stairs.

But Reign grabs her arm and yanks her to the side. To her surprise, the demons run straight past them and through the huge hole in the wall. Gabriel and his angels have already spun around, ready to meet them. Raphael and his own small army have done the same.

The demons are far more interested in battling the angels than two puny humans.

The angels and demons clash, grunts quickly filling the air along with the thud of fists against flesh and the flash of blades. Suddenly, Gabriel and Raphael are fighting side by side against a common foe.

"Quick, let them fight it out," Reign says urgently. "We have to get to your mom."

Rachel's already running before Reign's finished. He's right. The angels can take care of the demons and then fight among themselves as much as they like. She's going to save her mom.

They run up the stairs and down the hallway, her heart thundering. *I'm coming, Mom. Hold on.*

"That door," she shouts, pointing to the one on the left.

They burst in, ready to fight the next wave of vamps or demons.

But the room is empty apart from one body. A human slumped in the corner of the room, his face bloodied and bruised.

Jeremy.

CHAPTER 34

ARIELLE

The moment Arielle and Dinah step through the back door of the large sunroom at the rear of the mansion, they hear the sound of fighting beyond the walls surrounding them.

Marlowe and his Knights.

Or Reign and Rachel.

Arielle's heart constricts as she thinks of them engaging in hand to hand combat. She'd give anything to be with them.

It hurts to know they're safer without her. That she's as dangerous to them as she is to the vampires or demons.

"Demons are coming," Dinah mutters, her hands tightening into claws.

Yes, the obsidian hisses, its power swelling through her veins. *Blood. Death. Destruction.*

Before Arielle can try and get it under control, the door on the other end of the sunroom flies open. Demons pour through, some leaping into flight, others running over the debris littering the ground. All with red eyes glowing and sharp teeth flashing.

Dinah's hands rise. She grips a handful of air and flings it to the side. The demon flying at the head of the pack suddenly jerks as he's whipped away by an invisible force, slamming into the wall. The same happens to the next and the next.

Arielle's running before she can stop herself. The obsidian propels her toward the swarm of demons, its thirst for death a red haze in her mind. She jumps and kicks, powering her foot into the chest of the closest demon. The sickening crunch as his ribs are crushed jolts euphoria through her. A quick punch to the throat and then a snap of his head, and the demon crumples, black smoke pouring from his nose and mouth.

Arielle tries to slow down as she sets her sights on the next demon, but it's like she's an ant facing a tidal wave. She's helpless to stop what's coming. She withdraws the knife at her belt, striking and slashing. Each one she kills, she refines her deadly technique. She stabs one demon in the chest to the hilt, another through the eye socket. Even when one tries to retreat, fear dulling the glow of her eyes, Arielle chases her. And ends her life with a short, sharp slash across the throat.

With each death, triumph injects through her veins, fluid and exquisite.

More! the obsidian screams. *Yield to me and this will never have to end.*

Arielle only stops when there are no demons left standing. She stands in the center of the room, barely breathing, her heart calmly pulsing in her chest. She blinks.

Holy hell, what has she done?

Bodies are littered around her, black smoke coiling from their mouths. Arteries are severed, bones are crushed. Blood coats her hands. She was the one who killed most of them.

She gasps when she sees the two Knights are also dead, and for a horrified moment, Arielle wonders if she did it. But the jagged gashes across their throats could only have been done by the claws of a demon, no matter how razor sharp they are. She drops her knife and it clatters to the tiled floor.

Dinah approaches her cautiously. "Arielle?"

The way she asks her name, as if she's not entirely sure who's standing in front of her, has bile stinging the back of Arielle's throat. She blinks, discovering the room is progressively becoming lighter, as if someone's lifting a shade.

"Your eyes..." breathes Dinah.

Arielle looks away. That's what the vampire said when she interrogated him. She has no doubt they're the same obsidian black as the stone she can't get rid of. She blinks rapidly, pushing down the bloodlust that overcame her.

"We need to find Evelyn," she says hoarsely.

She's about to turn away when Dinah grips her arms, forcing Arielle to face her. "What's going on?"

"N-nothing. I just know we don't have much time."

"Bullshit," snaps Dinah. "That killing spree was my style, not yours."

Kill her.

She's asking too many questions.

Arielle struggles against Dinah's hold, conscious her control of the obsidian is slipping. "I got the job done. Now let me go."

But Dinah doesn't release her. Her face tightens, a hard glint settling in her dark eyes. "This has to do with what you said in my apartment, when you said it's what's inside of you that's taking its toll. You're hiding something." She leans a little closer. "Carrying something."

Before Arielle can answer, the image of an obelisk rises in her mind. Despite its formidable strength, it cracks, then fractures. The thunderous sound reverberates through her, plumes of red and black pouring out.

"No!" she wails, dropping to her knees as she clamps her hands over her ears. "It can't be too late."

She squeezes her eyes shut as she tries to force the image away. She always sees them *before* it happens. It's nothing more than a warning that they're running out of time.

It's coming. The Innocent will die. Another Sin will be released.
You will be mine.

"Never!" Arielle screams, her hands pressing tightly against her temples. "I will never yield to you."

Warm, firm hands peel away her palms, and Arielle looks up to find Dinah kneeling before her. "Tell me, Arielle."

The truth tumbles out as Arielle no longer has the strength to contain it. She's hurt too many people. Accumulated too many deaths on her conscience. "It's the obsidian," she whispers. "The obsidian's inside of me."

Dinah rocks back on her heels. "A shitload of stuff is making sense right about now."

"And it's winning, Dinah. It wants...me."

"Well, it's not having you," she says sharply. "Anyone else would've given in long before now. You need to hold on, Ari."

"I...I don't know if I can."

"You have to. The obsidian will destroy everything in its path if a host accepts it."

And it will be beautiful.
Everything will break or burn or bleed.
Nothing will be safe.

Nausea is like acid in Arielle's stomach. "It's too strong," she confesses, shame staining her face with heat.

"But you're stronger," Dinah says firmly. "And after all this, I can help you. We can find a way to siphon the obsidian out and return it to the stone."

The words have hope flickering a fragile flame in Arielle's chest. There's a possibility she could be rid of the obsidian!

Unless you yield to me first.

"Okay," she says through gritted teeth. "I'll hold out."

Before Dinah can answer, there's the roar of a car and then footsteps entering the sunroom. Dinah vaults to her feet and spins around, her hands already made into claws.

Klae quickly scans the room, seeing Arielle crouched behind Dinah. "Ari! Are you hurt?"

Arielle stands, ignoring her wobbly legs. "I'm fine, Klae. I just had a vision of the obelisk. We're running out of time." She steps beside Dinah. "This is Klae, a friend of Gabby's. Klae, this is Dinah, a...friend of mine."

Dinah's intake of breath is short and sharp, but Arielle's amplified hearing registers it.

You trust a dark witch? That is how far you've sunk?

Klae nods. "Nice to meet you. Now, what's the plan?"

"Reign and Rachel are in the west wing, rescuing Evelyn." Because Arielle knew the moment she faced too many enemies, she'd be overcome, which is exactly what happened. "Marlowe and his Knights are taking out pockets of vamps. We believe Jeremy is here, in the east wing."

"The angels are here," says Klae. "They're fighting the demons, and winning from what I can tell, so that's one less thing for us to worry about." She waves an arm, her face determined. "Lead the way."

The overwhelmed feeling abates a little more. They have Klae, a golem, and the angels on their side now. The odds are progressively increasing in their favor.

And Arielle now has a reason to fight the obsidian more than ever. A chance she could be free of it.

"This way," she says resolutely, running across the sunroom. "Jeremy's in a room down here."

Dinah and Klae join her as they make their way through the old mansion. They pass the kitchen, then dining room, a library full of moldy books. The occasional cry or thud reaches them, telling Arielle the others are still fighting elsewhere in the house. She just has to hope they're winning. That none of them are hurt. Or worse...

That she'll see Reign again. Have a chance to explain.

The closed door to the room they saw the heat signatures in appears ahead. It looked like an office or a small bedroom, tucked in the back corner of the sprawling house. No doubt the door is locked.

Arielle slows, ready to kick it in, when Dinah pushes past her. "I'll go in first."

Before Arielle can object, Dinah blasts the door and runs in. There are the sounds of her sharp footsteps, then silence.

As if the room just swallowed her whole.

Arielle and Klae glance at each other, then run in after Dinah. They stop the moment they're inside, instantly recognizing the perilous situation they're now in, even though there are only four other people in the room.

Dinah's sprawled on the floor, only a few feet away. For horrified seconds, Arielle thinks she's dead, but then she sees the shallow movement of her chest. She's unconscious, but alive.

Arielle slowly raises her eyes to the three others, her chest painfully constricting.

Gluttony is sitting with one hip hoisted on a large desk, eyes flaring with pleasure to find more intruders. Behind her is a large arch window, the light of the moon piercing the room with a pale glow.

In front of the demon, a man is holding Evelyn against him, a knife to her throat.

The same man who broke into her home months ago and stole the scroll, although his face is now scarred and twisted.

He grins. "Hello, Arielle. You're just in time to see the next Innocent die."

Evelyn's eyes are wide and terrified above the glinting blade. She mouths one word. "Rachel."

Arielle remains where she is, trying to come up with a plan.

Yield to me.

Then we kill him.

"Who are you?" she asks the man.

"My name is Xeven," he says coldly. "That is all you need to know."

"Xeven, let Evelyn go."

He laughs, the sound hollow and hard. "And miss the light show, like when the others died? I don't think so."

Gluttony sashays closer to Xeven. "Enough talk," she purrs. "I want to see my brother."

"You keep Gluttony busy," Arielle says in a low voice. "I'll take care of Xeven."

Klae instantly dissolved into a puddle of mud. She shoots across the floor and reappears in front of Gluttony in her large, golem form. She pushes the Sin back and she crashes into the desk.

Xeven blinks in surprise, giving Arielle the opening she needed.

She runs at him, this time more than ready to draw blood.

This will not end like all the other times.

She will not fail another Innocent.

CHAPTER 35

REIGN

"It's Jeremy. And he's breathing."

Rachel's words are a painful mix of relief and disappointment.

They found Jeremy. Alive.

But that means Evelyn is elsewhere in the mansion.

They rush toward him, kneeling down. "Jeremy," Reign says urgently. "Can you walk?"

Jeremy's lashes flicker as he groans, but there's no other answer. Reign sits back, knowing they won't get much more out of him. He's badly beaten and barely conscious.

They need to get him out of here. The poor guy is close to death, beaten by demons and vampires, purely because he was unlucky enough to know Shell and Paul.

And yet, that means while they're doing that, they're not with Arielle. They're not saving Rachel's mother.

Making a decision, he slips underneath one of Jeremy's arms and hoists him up. "We get him to safety, then we help the others."

Rachel nods sharply. "I like." She slides under Jeremy's other arm and together, they pull him to a standing position.

He groans again, leaning heavily. "No more, please. I told you everything I know."

Reign tightens his grip as the pain in Jeremy's words slice through him. The thought of the torture Jeremy endured so Gluttony could get her information makes him sick. They're doing the right thing in getting him out of here, but that doesn't mean it's easy.

The need to be with Arielle is like a primal drive, drumming through his veins.

Gritting his teeth, Reign angles toward the door. Together with Rachel, they maneuver Jeremy out the door and down the stairs. The sounds of fighting beyond the hole in the wall reach them, but he ignores it. Hopefully the angels can keep the demons busy while they get Jeremy out.

Jeremy groans again and then suddenly goes limp. His body sags as he loses consciousness and Reign hoists his arm a little higher as Rachel does the same. They're now carrying a six foot bag of potatoes between them.

They've just reached the sunroom when they find themselves surrounded by vampires. They morph from the shadows and drop from the ceiling. Reign curses. They'll have to put Jeremy down to fight, leaving him vulnerable. How the hell are they going to protect themselves and an unconscious, battered man?

A vampire leaps, only for her eyes to bulge and her mouth go slack. She disintegrates into ash, revealing Marlowe standing in the opposite doorway. The stake he threw clatters to the floor as gray particles shower down.

The vampire horde spins around, realizing they're no longer facing an easy meal. Hissing and growling, they launch at Marlowe and his men and they pour into the sunroom. A ball of blazing light explodes in Marlowe's hand and he hurls it at two of the closest vampires. They scream as the light pierces them like blades, instantly disintegrating them.

"Marlowe's supernatural?" gasps Rachel.

He releases another ball of light, one similar to Gabriel earlier. "He sure is," says Reign, wondering what the heck the new leader of the Order is.

Marlowe leaps and drives a stake into a vampire that just dodged a ball of light. "Get him out of here!" he shouts.

Not needing to be told twice, Reign and Rachel drag Jeremy between them, staying close to the walls. Shuffling through the ashes of dead vampires, they make their way out the back door.

The night air is warm as they stumble along the back porch. As they make their way down the stairs, the light of the full moon illuminates the vast expanse of what once would've been gardens and lawn.

The glowing scene tells Reign two things.

The moon is up, which means Evelyn's sacrifice will be soon.

And there's nowhere safe to leave Jeremy. Angels and demons are battling in the night sky. Vampires are inside the house with Marlowe and his Knights, fighting them.

They stop where they are, Jeremy sagging between them. There's not even a shrub large enough to consider tucking him under before acknowledging they could never do that.

"Reign," Rachel moans. "We have to get back in there."

She needs to help her mother.

He needs to help Arielle.

And yet, Jeremy can't be left unprotected.

The sound of rumbling engines has them both tensing. That's not the sound of a standard sedan. It sounds like an all terrain truck. Several of them.

Blinding headlights sweep around the side of the mansion. Reign and Rachel quickly duck back against the porch.

"What now?" he mutters.

The lumbering truck stops, three more behind it. As the headlights dim, Reign registers the drab army green painting all the armor-plated vehicles. Kenna said the army was on its way.

"Shit, the army is here?" gasps Rachel.

Just what they need.

By silent agreement, they carefully place Jeremy by the steps of the porch. With hands up, they step away from the shadows of the mansion. There's no way they can talk the military into leaving.

But they have to find a way to stall them.

Enough time for Gluttony to be killed and Evelyn saved.

A tall man wearing camouflage leaps down from the nearest truck. He strides over, his blond hair glinting in the moonlight. "What is the meaning of this?"

"Terrorist attack," Rachel replies quickly. "Haven't you heard of what's been happening in the city?"

To their surprise, the man chuckles. He points to the sky where angels and demons continue to fight. "Russian or Al Qaeda?"

Reign and Rachel stand mute, having no idea how to explain this. If these humans barge into that house, guns blazing, they'll end up dead.

And so will Evelyn.

The man's face softens. "You have nothing to fear, we're here to help. We're not Federal Government. In fact we believe the White House has been infiltrated by demons. It's why they haven't responded to the crisis in Mercy City."

Reign isn't sure if he can trust what he's hearing. If this guy isn't Federal, then what is he?

"I'm nephilim," the man says, his eyes flashing a milky red. "We're securing the perimeter. Humans won't hear about what's going down here."

There's no time to be shocked, let alone ask him what the fuck a nephillim is. Reign points to the porch. "There's a human who's been hurt. He needs medical attention."

The man raises his hand and another man in camouflage appears next to him. "We have wounded. Take care of him."

"Yes, General."

A moment later, two army guys—nephilim—rush past Reign and Rachel carrying a stretcher. Carefully, they load an unconscious Jeremy onto it.

"Rachel," Reign says quietly. "Jeremy's safe."

Her wide eyes turn to him. There's no reason they can't go back into the mansion.

They're about to move when the General speaks. "Is Marlowe in there?"

Rachel stills. "Why do you ask?"

The General narrows his eyes, obviously not used to being questioned. "Because he's my son."

Reign blinks, not having the brain space for this right now. Rachel doesn't reply and he wonders briefly what she's making of all this. There was definitely some chemistry brewing between those two.

She lifts her chin. "He's dusting the interior with vampire ash."

The General grins. "That's my boy." He turns to the convoy of vehicles. "Let's get this place locked down."

His words are the green light for Reign and Rachel. Jeremy's safe. Angels are fighting the demons. Marlowe is taking care of the vampires. And now a supernatural army is here, making sure no humans get caught in the crossfire.

They break into a run simultaneously, clattering up the porch stairs.

Reign's heart batters his ribs, impatient as the rest of him.

Arielle, I'm coming.

CHAPTER 36

ARIELLE

Xeven lifts a hand as Arielle runs at him, loosening his hold on Evelyn. Although his other hand still grips the knife at her throat, Arielle calculates the distance. Notes the exposed part of his chest just below his throat.

Gets ready to do what it takes.

And freezes midstep.

Impossibly, Arielle's body seizes, one leg up, the other still touching the ground. Shocked, she tries to break free, only to find she can't. She's held in suspended animation by bonds of magic.

Her wide eyes focus back on Xeven. He lowers his hand, a cold smile spreading across his twisted features.

No! He's paralyzed her!

A blast of red has her focusing beyond Xeven and registering the web of energy Gluttony just shot from her hands. The sizzling net expands, wraps around Klae in her golem form, and instantly contracts. The massive mud form groans as it struggles against the fiery cords, then screeches as it continues to shrink. Layers fold over themselves again and again as the net constricts until Klae is lying on the floor in her human form, gasping in pain. Everywhere the red rope touches her singes her skin.

Gluttony steps around her, her lip curled. She stops beside Xeven. "Do it," she hisses. "The blade has been magicked to ensure the Grace will be where it is needed. Wrath is waiting."

Xeven's mouth twists as he gazes at Arielle. "There is nothing you can do."

Arielle wants to scream for him to stop. To fight with every cell in her being. The need to break free is a physical pain coursing through her frozen muscles. The thought that she has to watch this, again, is too much.

Evelyn closes her eyes, her face filling with peace. "Tell Rachel I love her," she whispers.

With one sharp movement, Xeven yanks the knife down her breast bone. Evelyn's eyes fly open, her peace shattered by pain. A gurgle escapes her lifeless lips as blood gushes down her chest. Xeven releases her and she slumps to the ground.

Dead.

Another Innocent has been sacrificed.

This time, the effect is instantaneous. It ricochets through Arielle like a nuclear bomb. The sight of the obelisk fills her vision, blazing crimson cracks spearing through it. She wishes she could close her eyes, turn her head away, but her body isn't her own.

And the destruction of the next Gate of Hell would happen, regardless.

The obelisk fractures. Shatters. Disintegrates.

Gluttony throws her head back, ecstasy rippling across her folds. "Yes," she hisses, her gaze returning to Arielle. "Wrath is free."

Dread spreads through Arielle like black ice.

Wrath.

A Sin even more deadly than Gluttony.

And yet you could have stopped this. Stupid bitch.

If you yield now, you can still stop Gluttony.

Mentally and physically, Arielle fights with every fiber of her being. If she gives into the obsidian, then everything is lost in ways no one will be able to fathom.

And yet, Gluttony needs to die. The world doesn't need two Sins wreaking their havoc.

To her shock, Arielle's foot drops to the ground. Her arm punches through the air. She can move!

A movement in the corner of her eye reveals Dinah pushing painfully to her feet. She must've freed her.

Now standing, Dinah focuses on Gluttony. She throws her arms forward, and the demon rockets backward, surprise popping her eyes wide open. Dinah advances, throwing another energy ball, then another. The second hits like the first, but Gluttony quickly recovers, sweeping away the third before it hits her. It slams into the wall, shattering a photo frame and sending shards of plaster everywhere.

It's then that Arielle remembers Reign has the dagger. The only weapon that can kill Gluttony. She hadn't intended on facing the Sin.

Arielle turns her focus away from the fight, refusing to consider that they may not at least have this win. Dinah's a powerful witch, surely she can take care of Gluttony. Arielle can help by taking care of Xeven. The man she has a score to settle with.

He's already running at her, anticipating her assault.

Arielle goes on the offensive, using every skill and tactic Rachel has taught her during their training sessions at the dojo. Her first strike is to the head, the second to the chest, the third to the head again. Xeven ducks and weaves, but the blows are coming at him too fast. Arielle's fist connects with his jaw, her elbow slams into his chest. She batters his thighs with kicks.

Xeven fights with grit and determination. He gets a few blows of his own in, but Arielle barely feels them. Evelyn's gruesome death is still fresh in her mind. The loss of Shell and Paul will never leave her.

This man with the twisted scars and blood stained hands is going to pay.

Except, as the anger rises, so does the obsidian. At first, it fuels her fury, giving her the strength and speed she needs to defeat Xeven. Blood explodes across his face as she powers her fist into his nose, he grunts as a foot plows into his chest.

His death is one she would almost welcome.

She spins around, trying to get more momentum. More power for the kick that will send Xeven flying. She's envisaging his body slamming into the wall, his already twisted face twisting even further in pain.

Except, she moves slower than expected, as if the air just became molasses. When the kick arrives, Xeven blocks it, quickly following through with a punch to her solar plexus. She doubles over as the breath is painfully and forcefully rammed from her lungs.

Quickly recovering, Arielle straightens, raising her fists again only to find they're heavy as lead. They don't come up fast enough to protect her face from Xeven's strike to her cheek. She draws in a sharp breath as her head snaps to the side. The skin splits and warm blood trickles down her face.

You are mine.

Arielle realizes the obsidian is trying to control her body. It's the one making her moves sluggish.

Yield or you die.

The next blow knocks Arielle to the ground. She tries to move her body, even to protect herself from the blows, but the obsidian is wrapping her in invisible rope. Her arms are pinned to her side. She can't even curl up on the floor.

She groans as Xeven's boot plows into her gut. Then her thigh. Then her gut again. She can barely think past the screaming in her mind.

Yield!

Or die!

"No," Arielle whispers.

If she can't beat the obsidian, she sure as hell isn't joining it. "Never."

Then die, the obsidian seethes in disgust.

She sees Xeven's boot coming for her head.

Arielle closes her eyes, wishing she could block out the pain. The obsidian. The knowledge that she brought this on herself.

The knowledge that she let everyone down.

When the next blow doesn't come, she opens her swollen eyes. Xeven is standing above her, frowning. He almost looks... perplexed. His blue eyes almost look human.

But then he shakes his head, any shred of humanity disappearing. He snarls, yanking his boot back again. "I have my orders."

CHAPTER 37

REIGN

R eign's heart stops the second he bursts into the room that Arielle and Dinah headed to. Then stutters.

Then roars with rage.

He runs at the man standing over Arielle, bloodied and sprawled on the ground, his leg poised to kick her. Reign shoves him back, wishing he could tear him apart with his own hands, but returning to Ari.

She's hurt. Badly.

Laying on her back, her face is a canvas of blood, her body is lifeless. Reign drops to his knees beside her, ready to protect her from any further blows.

But he doesn't have to worry about the man. Rachel streaks past them. "You bastard," she screams, landing a punch in the man's face before her feet have touched the ground.

Reign focuses on pulling Arielle away, his gut tightening painfully as he tries to do it gently, but knows he'd be causing pain anyway. More anguish tugs at his insides as he sees Evelyn not far away, her chest sliced open. Dinah's on the other side of the room, still fighting Gluttony, looking like neither are winning. Another girl is by a desk, crumpled and still.

The room is littered with death and destruction.

"Reign?" Arielle whispers.

He looks down to find her looking up at him through puffy, already black eyes. He flicks his tongue across his lips, his mouth suddenly dry. The team's in trouble. "Hey. We'll get you out of here."

Her swollen lips twitch. "I thought you didn't make empty promises."

"I don't," he says, arching a challenging brow.

He's going to get Arielle out of here. Alive.

Her eyes flutter closed. "I wish I was as strong as you," she says, her voice catching.

Reign's frowning so hard it hurts. "You're a thousand time stronger than anyone I know," he says fiercely. "There's nothing you can't do, Ari."

Arielle's hand lifts, the motion slow and painful. Like it's a fight to bring it up. She cups his cheek before it falls away, dropping heavily back down. "I've never understood why you believe in me so...completely."

Reign takes her hand, weaving his fingers through hers. "Some truths can't be denied," he says softly. With conviction.

Like the way he feels for her. Whether she feels it too.

Irrespective of whether he deserves to.

Arielle's gaze traps him. He doesn't see the blood or the bruises. He just sees...her. And it's downright fucking beautiful.

"Reign... I--"

A loud grunt has them both looking at the direction of Rachel and the man. Rachel's just landed after executing a flying kick. Possibly several in a row. The man's body jerks, his arms flying out with the power of the blow. Rachel makes the most of the opening, striking him in his twisted, ugly-ass face over and over.

The man retreats another step with each punch, passing

Dinah and Gluttony as they continue their magical assault on each other.

Rachel pulls her stake out of her belt, lifting it. The man may not be a vampire, but he won't survive the piece of wood impaling his chest. His eyes widen as he registers it, too.

He's a goner.

And Reign isn't going to regret his death. Not after hurting Arielle.

"This is for Arielle," she whispers hoarsely. "And for my mom."

Suddenly, Rachel's entire body is shoved backward, as if by a massive gust of wind. She slams into the wall on the opposite side of the room. Her back arches as her face twists with pain. A second later, she slides to the floor, unconscious.

Shocked, Reign looks up to see what happened. It sure as hell wasn't the man who was about to be dealt the death blow.

Fury slices through his veins when he sees Dinah drop her hands. She lets out a breath, almost looking relieved.

"Bitch!" Reign roars. He pushes to his feet, already running when his foot touches the floor. He launches at her. "Traitor!"

They never should have trusted her.

Dinah flinches. "You don't understand. He's connected to Arielle. He's her—"

Reign's fist powers into her jaw, knocking Dinah to the ground. For a brief moment, she fights the pain and blackness, trying to push herself up, only to collapse again. Out cold.

When a roar fractures the air, he tenses. The man's coming for him. At least Dinah can't sabotage it this time.

Reign's going to finish him.

He straightens to find the man running at him, Gluttony standing behind, smirking."Kill him, Xeven. I've had enough of annoying Grail Keepers."

But before the bastard can reach Reign, a ball of what looks like clay powers past. It bowls straight into the man—Xeven—expands as if it just splatted, and pushes him back. Straight through the window.

Glass explodes as Xeven disappears into the milky blackness beyond, propelled by a cannonball of dirt.

Reign doesn't have time to wonder what the hell just happened. Gluttony's eyes flare with hellfire. "Or I could do it myself." She straightens, moving away from the desk she was casually leaning against. "This is probably more fun, anyway."

Reaching behind him, Reign pulls out the dagger tucked into his belt, enjoying the flash of surprise across her flushed features. "If that's how you want to describe your death."

The smirk twists into a sneer. "Humans. You're the epitome of overconfidence."

Gluttony moves, far faster than a woman of her hefty curves should be able to. Her wings snap out, seeming to swallow the room. Reign sprints forward too, bracing himself for the impact.

They collide, but Gluttony doesn't try to strike his face or torso with her hands. Instead, she twists, the arch of her wing slamming into his face as she grapples for the blade. Reign grips it with everything he has, realizing he may not be a threat.

But the dagger is.

A punch to her fleshy kidneys and she releases her hold enough for him to slip away. Panting, he watches as her gaze flickers to the knife. Slowly, they circle each other and Reign tightens his hold on it, knowing he can't let it go.

Arielle's badly hurt. Rachel's unconscious. Dinah's a traitorous bitch.

It's up to him.

Gluttony makes her move, just like he knew she would. She's hungry for his death. Which is exactly what he's going to let her believe is within her reach.

He makes a show of blocking the strikes she bombards him

with, even dodging a couple, but the majority hit their mark. Pain explodes everywhere, his face, his chest, one narrowly misses his groin.

But with each one, the victory flares a little brighter in Gluttony's glowing eyes. And she moves a little closer to him.

He just has to hold onto consciousness, and the blade, long enough to do this.

The elbow coming at his jaw is the opening he needs. Reign focuses every shred of his attention on what needs to be done. He rises above the haze of pain. The pleading of his body to stop. The part of him that can't believe he's chosen to be beaten.

Gluttony's body angles toward his, her arm lifting.

Exposing her side.

And the layers of excess over her ribs.

Reign grips the dagger, allowing it to become an extension of himself. Gluttony executes the strike, and he waits for the momentum to reach the point of no return. She'll practically impale herself.

Suddenly, the blade becomes a burning length of metal, red and searing. Reign cries out, instinctively dropping it. He cries out again as it clatters to the floor, once again silver and shiny. Like the blast of molten heat never happened. What the fuck!

A movement from the corner of his eye has Reign turning a little. Dinah lowers her hand, her face pale but jaw tight as her gaze connects with him, holding no apology for what she just did.

Saved Gluttony's life.

And ended his own.

The shock he shouldn't be feeling seeing as he never trusted the black witch is the opening Gluttony needed. She grabs him, spins, and slams him so hard into the desk the wood cracks. Or was that his ribs? The breathless pain makes it hard to tell.

She clamps her hand around his throat, her dagger-like fingernails nicking the skin. A warm trickle of blood runs down his neck. "I've never eaten Grail Keeper before."

"We're tough," Reign snarls back between shallow gasps. "And bitter."

"My favorite." Gluttony leans in close. "I'm tired of you and your kind trying to hunt demons when all we want is retribution."

"Screw the humans that get in the way, huh?" he spits back.

"Sometimes war is necessary to pave the way for peace."

"Bull. Shit," says Reign, holding her blazing gaze. He may be about to die, but he's not going to do it listening to a Sin justifying their actions.

Gluttony's hand tightens, sending pinpoints of pain shooting down Reign's spine. "And yet humans have waged hundreds of wars themselves. Your own death toll is far greater than demons will ever be able to lay claim to."

"Is this making you feel better?" he hisses. The pain of his beating is finally registering. The beating he willingly took because it meant the chance of winning. Of killing this sadistic bitch.

Dinah's betrayal sends a fresh flash of fury through him. She's signed Arielle's death warrant. And Rachel's.

For that, he'll never forgive her.

"The seven Sins are nothing but manifestations of human emotions," says Gluttony. "All we do is influence what's already inside of you." She smiles, anticipation lighting her features. "Can you imagine what Wrath will be able to achieve?"

The first frisson of fear trickles down Reign's spine. Wrath's fury and Gluttony's avarice. The world will descend into blood and chaos.

She smiles. "You should thank me. You won't be around to see it."

Reign takes his physical pain, his mental anguish, and the impotent fury that it can't end like this, and channels it into struggling against Gluttony's hold.

His arms flail for short seconds before being pinned to the desk with invisible bonds. A short, sharp strike to his temple and he can barely feel the rest of his body.

Gluttony's fleshy face fills his vision as it starts to darken. Her hands tighten around his neck, cutting off his airway.

Still, he fights, not caring that it's bringing the end sooner.

As blackness envelops him, he clings to the image of Arielle. With every last shred of his dwindling breath, he died trying to protect her.

That's going to have to be enough.

CHAPTER 38

ARIELLE

Arielle's heart is fracturing in her chest, the rupturing pain far greater than any blow she's been dealt.

She watches through tear drenched eyes as Gluttony's face twists with pleasure. Her hands tighten around Reign's throat so hard that Arielle wonders if she's planning on strangling him or just snapping his neck.

And yet Arielle can barely move. The tears coursing down her cheeks blend with the blood, leaving a sickening taste of copper and salt in her mouth. All she can do is watch, tormented by her helplessness.

You can save him.

The obsidian's words a whisper. A promise.

An offer her heart can't resist.

She digs her hand into her pocket, finding the obsidian there. She grips it, feeling the throb of dark energy.

"I yield," she whispers on a broken sob. "I yield."

She can't let Reign die.

She just can't.

The effect of her words are instantaneous. Power far greater than she ever imagined floods her veins with black, cold strength. The pain washes away. In the space of a heart beat, anything is possible.

And yet, there's only one thing she wants.

Arielle scrambles to her feet, wiping away the blood and tears. To her surprise, the blade is only a foot away, and she quickly grabs it.

And so it begins, breathes the obsidian triumphantly.

"Gluttony," Arielle screams with more rage than she thought was possible.

The demon looks up, lip curled. The furious look is quickly wiped away as she registers Arielle standing.

Whatever she sees has terror sweeping across the Sin's face.

She knows.

No one will be safe.

A small part of Arielle hates that whatever Gluttony's seeing can scare her so much. The other part doesn't care. With a flick of her wrist, she releases the blade. As fast as a bullet, it shoots across the room.

With deadly accuracy, it impales the Sin's throat, right to the hilt.

Gluttony staggers backward, mouth working but making no sound. Blood pours down her chest in a steady river. With a sharp, unnatural movement, her head snaps back and her mouth throws open. Black smoke pours out, twisting and writhing as if it's in pain.

It tries to climb upward and escape, but is dragged down, the smoke folding over and over itself as if hundreds of hands are grasping at it. It coils over Gluttony's still-twitching body, a desperately churning mass. Like a giant lung just inhaled, it's sucked down, drawn unwillingly back into the bowels of Hell.

Gluttony's body thuds to the floor. Dead.

For blissful, joyous seconds, Arielle feels relief. Reign's

saved. And it's a small win, but one less Sin on Earth is a victory.

But then the obsidian speaks. And this time, so does she.

"We are now one," she hisses triumphantly.

Arielle arches her back as cold shoots through her veins, starting at her extremities and working its way in. Swiftly, inevitably, her limbs turn to cold, unfeeling ice. Then her shoulders, her hips, her torso. She draws in sharp, panting breaths as if trying to experience something warm and good before her heart freezes.

Before her soul is taken.

"Arielle!" Reign's frantic voice, confirming that he's alive, is the last thing she hears before she's swallowed by deep, dark night.

CHAPTER 39

REIGN

"N o, no, no."

At first, Reign thinks those desperate words are his own, but he quickly realizes that someone else is experiencing the same heartbreaking denial he is.

Rachel crawls across the floor, her hair matted with blood. She reaches her mother, her face crumpling as her hands hover over her lifeless body. A large pool of blood glistens in the moonlight.

"I'm so sorry I failed you," she moans, once more echoing Reign's pain. She folds over Evelyn's body, sobbing.

He stumbles toward Arielle, his knees thudding as they hit the hard floor. She's pale and blood stained, her blonde hair fanned out like a halo. And not moving.

More pain than Reign's ever experienced assaults him. "No," he chokes past the jagged lump in his throat. "Please, no."

He was the one who was supposed to die. His role was to be the one to sacrifice.

With trembling fingers, he caresses her cheek. He doesn't know how, but he knows Arielle did this so he could live. That despite everything, she chose him.

Reign's eyes widen when he sees her chest move. Well, he thinks he does. The movement was so small, he wonders if it was wishful thinking. He stares, holding his own breath, wanting to trade places. Arielle breathes. He doesn't.

"She's not dead," says Dinah behind him. "She's in a coma."

As if Arielle heard her, her chest rises almost imperceptibly. Then it lowers, and rises again. She's alive.

Which means he can now kill Dinah.

Reign pushes to his feet and spins around. Hatred, hot and caustic, explodes through him. "You! You did this!"

Dinah narrows her eyes. "Actually, I saved her life."

He takes a measured step forward, trying to contain the need to hurt this woman. "You're as delusional as Gluttony."

Dinah steps around him, kneeling down beside Arielle and taking something from her curled palm. She holds it up and Reign sees it's a small, black rock. "Arielle has the obsidian inside of her."

"Liar," he roars.

"She told me," Dinah shouts back. "Just before we came in here. She's been carrying the evil of the obsidian. Think about it. She's been fighting it for weeks now."

The disappearing without a word.

The lies.

The ability to kill without conscience.

Reign shakes his head. "It can't be..."

"And she accepted its power so she could save you," says Dinah, her voice now quiet. As if she knows just the words will have enough impact.

And she's right.

Reign almost doubles over with the pain. "Why would she do that?"

"Weren't you about to do the same? Sacrifice everything for

her?" Dinah crosses her arms. "This is a very shitty thank you by the way."

He turns, the banked fury flaring again. "We should never have trusted a black witch. You've just made things worse."

Rachel appears by Reign's side. "You threw me across a room."

"I told you," Dinah snaps. "Xeven is connected to Arielle. I was doing you a favor. And the dagger is cursed. Whoever uses it is put into a deep coma." She shrugs. "That's why I made you drop it, and moved it closer to Arielle when I saw the obsidian was winning. It was her saving grace."

"If you've done all this just to save her, then prove it," he snaps. "Wake her up."

Dinah's shoulders sag. "I can't. If Arielle's not conscious, there's nothing for the obsidian to own and control. We have to make sure the obsidian is removed first."

"How do we do that?" Rachel asks in a small voice. She's just lost her mother. She's an orphan.

And they have no idea whether they can save Arielle.

"I don't know," Dinah says heavily. "But I do know that if Arielle gains consciousness before she's free of the obsidian's hold, that she'll go dark. She'll be nothing but an instrument of evil."

Reign remembers what was written about the obsidian in the Grail Keeper books. Words like world wars and countless deaths were interspersed everywhere.

Arielle would never want that.

The sound of footsteps beyond the room tells him Marlowe and his men, or his father, the General and his army, are about to arrive. Reign kneels down and gently scoops her up, cradling her limp body to his. He glances around the room.

Another Innocent is dead.

Wrath is free.

But the darkness Arielle is carrying is far more evil than all of the Sins combined.

Pressing his lips to her forehead he makes a promise. A vow.

He will do whatever it takes to bring her back, safe and free of the obsidian's hold.

EPILOGUE

Xeven drags his broken body to his car out in the field a mile away from the old mansion. The golem who attacked him is nowhere to be seen. All he can hope is she was as injured by their fall as he was. Maybe that's the reason she didn't finish him off.

Sliding behind the wheel he grimaces. The cuts on his back from where he went through the window aren't healing quickly enough. He can feel the blood sticking his shirt to his skin. He glances in the rear vision mirror, curling his lip at the bloodied, mangled mess staring back at him.

He'll heal. The pain will pass. It's what will come after that he's dreading.

Without some direction, he has no idea where to find the next Innocent. And an idle brain is a tortured brain. He now has the girl's frightened, pain-filled face branded on his mind for some inexplicable reason. If that look hadn't tugged a part of him that he thought was long dead, he wouldn't have hesitated. There wouldn't have been the opportunity for the golem to send him through the window.

He wouldn't be sitting here, blood sticking him to the

leather car seat, wondering what the fuck he's supposed to do next.

The image in the rear vision mirror morphs, turning from bloody and ugly, to pale and perfect. Azazel smiles. "You did well, Xeven," he croons. "Another Innocent is dead. Another Gate of Hell is opened. It won't be long before Lucifer is with us."

Xeven nods. There's no joy at the news. There never is. What he wants and what he does were disconnected long ago.

Azazel's pale blue eyes increase in size, as if he's leaning forward, dominating the small rectangular mirror. "Now, it's time to find Cain."

Relief has Xeven nodding. A task. Something solid to focus on.

He turns the keys in the ignition, calm once more. "It will be done."

CAIN HANGS from the cuffs chaining him to the wall, his body bruised and bleeding. The only thing holding him together is the knowledge that Lydia's torture hasn't broken him. The witch has tried everything, magical and physical, to get into his mind. To find answers for her mystery benefactor.

But she underestimated Cain's strength and determination.

His secrets are his and his alone.

The door opens and Lydia slips through. Her white hair brushes her shoulders as her milky eyes settle on him. She smiles coldly. "I have good news."

"You're dying?" he spits through cracked lips.

Lydia laughs lightly. She's been doing that a lot throughout the beatings of his body and mind. Her light, tinkling laughter has mocked him the whole way through.

She's showing him she's willing to do this for as long as it takes.

She steps closer, her eyes flashing wide, her bleached irises practically blending with the rest of her eyeballs. "The Innocent has been killed."

The words have Cain's knees weakening against his will. The chains clang as his body shudders as he tries to gain control of an emotion he rarely feels anymore.

Fear.

If the Innocent is dead, then Lydia has harvested enough power to break into his mind.

She's about to learn everything.

She reaches up, her white-clawed hands slipping up either side of his face. His skin crawls as he braces himself. He won't let his secrets go easily. It will be painful, but he doesn't care. He will fight this, even if it's useless.

To his surprise, Lydia's hands continue past his head and up his arms. There's a faint *click* and his hands are freed. She steps back, a sly smile playing over her bloodless lips.

Cain rubs at his wrists, the blood rushing back into his arms almost as painful as the torture he's been subjected to. "What are you doing?" he snarls. Does she want to beat him before she steals his mind?

Lydia waves her arm toward the door. "I would make the most of this if I were you."

Confused, but willing to play the game, Cain takes several steps toward the door. Lydia ignores him, waving her hands over the place he was just standing. Another Cain appears, a replica of his battered body, bound to the wall.

"I'll tell them you wanted Lucifer's throne," she says calmly.

Cain doesn't thank the witch. He doesn't like that he already owes her.

But that doesn't stop him from darting out the door.

And running, the scent of freedom already filling his lungs.

SICK OF PACING AND WAITING, Abel spins on his heel and walks to his door. He jerks it open, no longer willing to hear excuses. He's been patient enough.

Revenge is clawing at him, demanding to be sated.

He stops when he finds Virginia on the other side. There's a glint in her gaze he recognizes.

A glint that has the monster in him roaring with anticipation.

"It's time," she says with relish. She steps back, indicating for him to pass. "Are you ready to return the favor?"

Abel smiles, the motion feeling good. No, great. He's been waiting for this moment for millennia.

"I'm ready."

Ready for the next installment in the Keepers of the Grail series?
Check out GATES OF WRATH!
http://mybook.to/GatesofWrath

GATES OF WRATH

Saving those you love comes at a price.

Reign and Arielle know the next Innocent must be found, despite the overwhelming odds. Darkness is rising, threatening the world as they know it.

There's a new enemy—a demon manipulating humans' most basic desires. A mysterious organization with alliances as old as time. And evil is weaving its dark magic among their ranks. Magic powerful enough to rival the Grail itself.

And yet, the battle within is as powerful as those they face. Reign struggles to trust. Arielle's no longer sure what she's fighting for. And love is refusing to be denied.

The price of failure is unimaginable.

Because a plan has been put in motion that goes as far back

as Adam and Eve. And dark forces will do anything to open the next Gate of Hell, bringing Lucifer one step closer to freedom.

GRAB YOUR COPY HERE
mybook.to/GatesofWrath

THE KEEPERS-VERSE IS ALWAYS GROWING!

Exciting news! The Keeper Chronicles will continue to grow, with each new addition adding to its epicness. Each interlinked series will have you falling for unforgettable characters, being swept away by captivating romance and thrilling adventure, and re-visiting old friends (you'll discover all your favorites popping up when you least expect it!).

It's like your very own choose your own adventure! Where will you go next?

Keepers of the Chalice
A vampire. A huntress.
A cure that will change everything.
Check out Book 1, Vampire Unleashed, HERE.

Keepers of Excalibur
A cursed wolf. A fated love.
A supernatural war only they can stop.
Check out Book 1, Wolf Marked HERE.
http://mybook.to/WolfMarked

HAVE YOU READ THE KEEPER CHRONICLES PREQUEL?

As an exclusive for my subscribers,
you can download it for free!!

When Sierra sneaks out, determined to escape her over-protective family, she stumbles across a young man covered in blood. His last words are a plea. *Find the Grail Keepers. Warn them.*

Ryder is the young cop who was last seen with the murdered victim. Sierra doesn't trust him, no matter how drawn she is to him. Except it turns out they're both looking for the same thing—the Holy Grail.

They're quickly drawn into a dangerous hunt involving cryptic clues, a mysterious stone, and a Grail that hasn't been seen for centuries. One that leads to more questions than answers. Can Sierra trust her impulsive emotions? Should she believe Ryder's words or the truth she sees in his eyes? And ultimately, should she follow her heart?

Especially when every decision will decide the fate of countless lives.

CLICK HERE TO DOWNLOAD FOR FREE!

ALSO BY TAMAR SLOAN

PRIME PROPHECY SERIES

He failed to shift like every one of his ancestors.

Until he met her.

KEEPERS OF THE GRAIL

The legendary Holy Grail is real.

Yet everything known about it is a lie.

KEEPERS OF THE CHALICE

A vampire. A huntress.

A cure that will change everything.

KEEPERS OF THE LIGHT

Angels and demons have battled for millennia.

Their inevitable war has begun.

KEEPERS OF EXCALIBUR

A fated love. A cursed wolf.

A supernatural war only they can stop.

DESTINED DEMIGODS

Love that defies the gods.

Powers that define destiny.

ELEMENTAL GAMES

Elemental powers. Deadly Games.

No escape.

THE SOVEREIGN CODE

Humans saved bees from extinction...and created the deadliest threat we've seen yet.

THE THAW CHRONICLES

Only the chosen shall breed.

ZODIAC GUARDIANS

Twelve teens. One task.

Save the Universe.

About the Author

Tamar hasn't decided whether she's primarily a psychologist who loves writing, or a writer with a lifelong drive to make a difference. She must have been someone pretty awesome in a previous life (past life regression indicates a Care Bear), because she gets to do both. She divides her time between helping families and writing emotion driven YA stories set in amazing imaginary worlds that surprise even her.

The driving force for all of Tamar's writing is sharing and connecting. In truth, connecting with others is why she writes. She loves to hear from readers. Find her on all the usual social media channels or her website, www.tamarsloan.com where can download one of her books for free.

(Seriously, I LOVE hearing from you guys!)